The Beacon

Also by Sam Kates

Pond Life and Other Stories

The Village of Lost Souls

That Elusive Something

The Cleansing (Earth Haven: Book One)

The Reckoning (Earth Haven: Book Three)

Strange Shores and Other Stories

Ghosts of Christmas Past & Other Dark Festive Tales

The Elevator: Book One

Jack's Tale (The Elevator: Book 2)

The Lord of the Dance (The Elevator: Book 3)

The Beacon

Earth Haven: Book 2

Sam Kates

This is a work of fiction.
All characters appearing in this work
are products of the author's imagination.
Any resemblance to real persons,
living or dead, is purely coincidental.

First edition published January 2015
by Smithcraft Press
Second edition, May 2018
This paperback edition, June 2018

ISBN 978-1-912718-06-1

www.samkates.co.uk

To Mum and Dad for everything,
including all the good advice
and for not being too disapproving
when I failed to heed it

Contents

Part 1: The Earth is Hushed in Silence

Chapter One

A dog stepped from behind the log-jam of abandoned vehicles. Its fur bristled and its lips drew back to reveal pointed teeth the colour of parchment. A low growl, like an idling two-stroke engine, sounded in its throat. It began to advance.

The boy shuffling down the road noticed the dog and stopped in his tracks. The vague, unfocused expression on the boy's face grew a little sharper. His brow drew into a frown and he closed his mouth. A line of spittle ran down his chin and onto a stinking hooded jacket that might once have been red. The frown deepened as he tried to think past the fog shrouding his mind. He shook his head and a memory or an instinct—little more than a snippet—emerged.

Snarling dog: danger.

The dog wasn't large, but wiry, terrier-like. Short brown fur looked coarse to the touch, like coconut matting. Its stomach brushed the ground as it moved forward in a crouch. Sharp teeth glistened with saliva. Intent eyes. Feral. It was within ten yards of the boy and closing.

Fear caused adrenaline to flood the boy's system, driving away a little more of the fog. He tore his gaze from the dog and glanced to each side. To his left lay pavement, garden walls and terraced houses. To his right a line of cars, bumper to bumper. The cars were closer.

He looked back at the dog. It was on him. When it leapt, he darted to his right.

The dog twisted in mid-air to follow the boy's movement and snagged his jacket. Its teeth clenched in the filthy cloth and it hung on grimly, its body swinging round to thump into the boy's legs.

The boy felt the dog's claws scrabbling at his thighs and shrieked. He clambered onto the bonnet of the nearest car. His jacket tore, sending the dog to the ground. It was immediately onto its feet, shaking its head to dislodge the strip of cloth from its jaws. It leapt again and gained the bonnet, claws scratching the surface as it strove for purchase.

The boy leaned back against the car's windscreen, trying desperately to find a grip for his hands. He lifted his left leg and swung it in an arc, nearly falling off the car in the process. His foot connected with the dog's rump, not with sufficient force to hurt the animal, but enough to ensure its forward momentum carried it off the bonnet and to the ground the other side. Without waiting to see what the dog would do next, the boy turned and scrambled onto the roof of the car. He rose unsteadily to his feet.

The dog jumped at the side of the car, barking in high-pitched yelps. From somewhere behind the boy came an answering bark, gruffer and deeper.

The boy's fear rose a notch or two. At the same time, whatever kept him in this area, this suburb of London—yes, London, he realised, he was in London—whatever kept him working like a chain-ganger each day, carrying and clearing and burning until his arms and legs and back also burned, until he was fit for nothing except to retire to his stinking bed and dream of shifting, terrible shapes wreathed in darkness, whatever enslaved him to this place and bound him to perform this ceaseless work, lifted. Though fog still clouded his mind like a peasouper for which this city had once been notorious, the compulsion that shackled him to remain had been broken.

He took a deep breath, turned and slid back down the windscreen to the bonnet of the car. The dog's yelps grew frantic and a booming bark answered. Louder; closer. Without waiting to see if the dog would leap back onto the bonnet, or for his larger-sounding friend to appear, the boy stepped onto the boot of the next car and clambered to the roof. He ran and scrambled and slithered forward to the next car, and the next, until he reached jumbled wreckage completely blocking this side of the road. The side which the dog was on.

He crawled over the roof of a car that had slewed across the road and imbedded itself in a garden wall, then sat on the roof so he could slide down to the ground. As he pushed off with his hands, the boy's trousers caught on a jagged piece of metal and he ripped them free, tearing a gouge in his right calf. He drew in a sharp breath and the dog's yelps grew more frenzied, as if it could smell blood.

The boy slipped to the ground and heard a thud as the dog threw itself at the other side of the car. The deeper bark sounded again, so close that if he turned around and peered over the wreckage, the boy would be able to see its owner.

He didn't look. Instead, limping slightly, he ran.

The door to the hotel suite opened and two people emerged into the corridor. It was difficult to tell beneath the thick outdoor coat he wore, but the man gave the impression of muscularity and carried himself with an easy grace. His companion came almost to his shoulder. She, too, wore an outdoor coat and was busy tying its belt around her ample waist. As they walked down the corridor towards the staircase, she extracted a woollen hat from her coat pocket and pulled it over her dark curls.

The man nodded approvingly. "You'll need that out there. It's a cold one." He spoke in a cultured, east-coast American accent.

"I think I'll cope, Jason," the woman said. Her accent was also American, with a hint of southern drawl. "After all, you don't get to spend every Christmas in New York City and not know how to stand the cold. Still, I miss the Florida sun." She sighed wistfully.

"Yup, you're not the only one. Will you return to Florida after the Great Coming, Milandra?"

"Most certainly." *Maybe to grow old* she added, but only to herself.

They descended the stairs—the lifts had been disabled to save power—and made their way through the hotel lobby to the exit. The main doors were operational now that the hotel had been wired up to a generator and opened with a *swish*, letting in a gust of icy air. Milandra gasped and her cheeks began to tingle. It felt good.

Jason Grant led the way. Milandra followed in her peculiar rolling gait. They stepped cautiously, for the pavements glistened in the pale sunlight, the temperature not climbing high enough to melt their frosty coating.

Although most of the British Isles, and much of London, lay empty and silent, inhabited only by formerly domesticated animals, and vermin that feasted on rotting corpses, this part of London, centred on the airport and spreading outwards in a radius of three miles, was a relative hive of activity. Buildings had been emptied of the dead and contaminated matter: sopping mattresses, stained carpets and the like. Bodies and bedding were being incinerated in open parkland to the north-west that had become known as the Burning Fields. If the wind was in the right or, more accurately, wrong direction, the acrid smell could be detected faintly in the vicinity of the airport.

The roads here had been cleared of abandoned vehicles, allowing uninterrupted access for delivery of food and drink foraged from houses, hotels and warehouses. Other goods were being collected: diesel and petrol to power the generators and fleet of vehicles, paraffin and lighter fluid for use in the Burning Fields, medical supplies for treating injured drones, and fire extinguishers. If electrical fires did break out when the Grid serving the city was turned back on, they wanted to be prepared.

The occasional car and van passed them, the drivers tooting and waving. Grant ignored them, but Milandra waved back, enjoying being in the fresh air and exercising her legs. She was almost disappointed when Grant turned off the road into a fenced compound.

"This was a park and ride for airport passengers," he said. "Once we cleared the automobiles out, it gave us plenty of room."

They walked through the open gates and past the low building that had served as both security entrance and site office. When the vast space behind the building came into view, Milandra gave a low whistle.

"You *have* been busy," she murmured.

Lined up in ranks, like soldiers awaiting inspection, were more than fifty large vehicles. The red bodywork of double-decker buses glinted softly in the sunlight, lined up alongside an assortment of single-deckers, some white, some blue, others black. Two lumbering yellow bulldozers raised their buckets to the sky in salute, next to two squat municipal vehicles with chutes leading from their tanker-like interiors almost to the ground. A low flatbed truck stood firm under the weight of the caterpillar-tracked crane sitting on its back.

Grant began to list the vehicles, ticking them off on his fingers. "Thirty-two genuine London buses. There's plenty more if we need them, but these are in the best working condition. Almost brand new, some of them. Twenty assorted single-deckers; they call them 'coaches' over here. Again, there's more if we need them. Ditto condition. Two bulldozers to ensure the way is clear. One crane. And two salt trucks. The Brits call them 'gritters'. Hadn't thought about getting some of those, but they were standing about, already full of rock salt." He shrugged. "Might as well put them to use."

"Those bulldozers and the truck with the crane, they'll be slow," said Milandra.

"Yup. That's why we're sending them out first thing in the morning. There are jerry cans of diesel on the truck so they can refuel as needed. The salt trucks will leave the evening before the buses and coaches. If there's a heavy overnight frost or even light snow, the buses shouldn't be held up."

Milandra heard a noise behind her and turned to see the door to the office building open and a man emerge. He walked towards them, a portly fellow with a ruddy complexion.

"Thought I 'eard voices," he said. He nodded at Grant. "Jason." He smiled at Milandra.

"This is Rodney Wilson," said Grant to Milandra.

"Rod will do," said Wilson. "And you're Milandra. Never 'ad the pleasure, so to speak, but I recognise you from the Commune." He spoke in the accent of a Londoner, dropping his aitches with abandon.

"Pleased to meet you, Rod," said Milandra. "So you're the gentleman who knew where to get these splendid double-deckers?"

Wilson nodded, his smile growing wider. Milandra found herself taking an instant liking to the man. "Worked for London Transport for over fifty years, man and… man. Course, 'ad to move about a bit and change identities to stop them getting suspicious. But I've driven these buses for years. Could drive them in me sleep."

"How long?" asked Milandra. "To train other drivers?"

"Well, the 'ow is the easy part, ain't it?" said Wilson. "That'll take seconds. But I can't implant practical experience. That can only be acquired manually. They'll need to get a feel for their handling. Don't want anybody toppling one on an icy bend, do we? Hmm, let's see…" His brow beetled in thought. "Seven days. Five if you're in an 'urry."

Milandra considered for a moment. "Make it five," she said. She turned to Grant. "Let's get the Deputies together. We need to decide how many we're going to send."

The girl raised a hand and gingerly explored her forehead. Her hair, normally silky and fine, felt thick and matted. It crackled under her fingers, reminding her of the crust which kept forming on her eyelids during the fever. The skin beneath her hair was sore to the touch, causing her to wince, and she could make out a ridge and indentation that hadn't been there before.

Before.

Before what? She could remember sitting on the seafront in Looe, huddled against the winter wind, watching the waves and gulls. Then something had happened, something that gave her a purpose, inexplicable though it might have been. Until that moment, she had been adrift, doing nothing but forage, eat and sleep. Her thoughts had been dark; terror her only friend, terror that she was the only one left alive.

It hit her like a slap and she'd cried out, startling a gull that had been regarding her with a yellow, alien eye. A sensation of someone—some *thing*—invading her mind, psychic tentacles encircling, grasping, squeezing…

It did not last long, probably only moments, too quick for her to attempt to resist, though she sensed with a teenager's frank appraisal that resistance would have been futile. The presence withdrew, leaving behind a notion. No, stronger than that: a *compulsion*.

She delayed only to throw together a small backpack with some food and water. She returned home only to fetch her bike from the garage. She did not enter the house. Her parents would still be lying on their bed where she had left them, hands entwined, heads tilted towards each other. Her brother would be beneath his duvet that she had drawn up to cover his rapidly-cooling brow. She had fled the house after her father, the last to go, had taken his final wheezing breath. Coughing and spluttering, she sought refuge in a nearby hotel. Finding an unoccupied room with an en-suite bathroom, she locked the door, retired to bed and rode out her own storm.

Days—weeks?—later, when she returned for her bike, she could not bear to go into the house. She had been in many others that contained corpses, and would never become accustomed to the sweet stench. She did not want to associate it with her own family.

Mounting the bike, she pedalled away, heading north-east out of Cornwall, and didn't once glance back.

It took her five days to reach the outskirts of London. Still weak from what she could only assume was a brush with the Millennium Bug, she tired easily and stopped frequently to rest. If the compulsion to press on hadn't been so strong, she would have holed up for a few days and regained her strength. As it was, after only a few hours' rest each time, it drove her back to the saddle. Any unease she might have felt about the compulsion and where it had come from was itself subsumed into the imperative to reach

London and Hillingdon Hospital.

On the fifth evening, close to exhaustion and her destination, it started to snow. Half-blinded by gritty flakes, she ducked off the main road into what she imagined would be a leafy suburb in summertime, but was now a darkening maze of forbidding brick houses.

The third door she tried was stiff, but opened under her shove to a musty, unlived-in smell, though blessedly free of the saccharine odour of death. Wheeling the bike into the hallway, she forced the door closed behind her.

And that is where her memory of *before* ended.

Fewer than twenty miles from John o'Groats (often regarded, wrongly, as the most northerly tip of mainland Britain), lies the estuary town of Wick. Originally a Viking settlement, the town held a population of around eight thousand people when the Millennium Bug arrived and wiped out most of them. The remaining few headed south to London, summoned in a peremptory fashion they were powerless to ignore.

Now the town played temporary home to four people, and only two of them were human in the generally accepted sense. This bitter January afternoon found these two sitting before a crackling log fire in a waterfront hotel.

Ceri Lewis clenched her hands together and extended her arms until her knuckles cracked. She sighed.

"Warming up nicely," she remarked.

Tom Evans nodded. "That wind outside is biting. If it's this cold here, what does he think it will be like in the middle of the North Sea?"

"Hmm. He does seem set on leaving as soon as he's identified a suitable boat."

"Well, I'm no sailor. And you said you hate the water…"

"I can swim a little, but I hate going out of my depth. The thought of crossing an entire sea in anything smaller than a cruise liner gives me the screaming hab-dabs." She took out a cigarette and lit it, inhaling deeply.

"Whatever he finds, it won't be a cruise liner, that's for sure. It'll have to be small enough to operate on his own, unless *she* knows how to sail. Otherwise, it'll have to be something with a reliable engine and enough fuel to reach Denmark or whatever's the closest."

"He mentioned Norway."

Tom grunted. "I could do with a drink. Fancy one?"

"Vodka, please. Orange or tonic if you can find any."

Tom rose and walked to the bar. Ceri heard glasses clinking and the fizz of bottle tops being removed. She gazed at the flames, momentarily lost in her own dark thoughts.

She blinked and took the glass that Tom handed to her. He resumed his place in the armchair next to hers, clutching a glass of amber liquid.

Ceri took a sip of her drink.

"Hmm," she murmured. "That's found the spot. Thanks."

The spirit's warmth hit her stomach and spread, finishing the job started by the fire. She leaned back in the chair, taking small sips from the glass and deep drags on the cigarette.

It took her a moment to realise that Tom had spoken.

"Sorry?" she said. "I was miles away."

"I said, what are we going to do about *her*?" Tom nodded towards the oak staircase which led from the lounge to the hotel's guest rooms.

"Do? I'm not sure we're going to *do* anything, are we?"

"We can't simply..." Tom sat forward. "Ceri, she tried to kill us."

"Not according to Peter. He says she saved our lives."

"I know that's what he says. But she set out to kill us. With that bloke..."

"Bishop."

"Whatever. I don't see how we can trust her. And Dusty won't go near her."

Ceri glanced at the black dog stretched out on a rug alongside the hearth. He was fast asleep, his paws twitching.

"Dusty won't go near Peter, either," she said. "But you trust him, don't you?"

Tom shrugged.

"Mind you," Ceri continued, "it might help if she would start speaking. Other than thanking us every time we feed her, I've not heard her utter a word."

"Me neither." Tom drained his glass. "'Nother?"

"Why the heck not."

Chapter Two

The boy's limp grew more pronounced. His breath came hot and harsh, scratching his throat. His chest heaved with exertion. Eyes darting from side to side, he moved in a stumbling trot, looking for somewhere to hide. To be safe.

Clarity had pierced the haze enshrouding his thoughts sufficiently for him to know that if he stayed in the open he would die, but not enough to show him that all he needed to do was to hole up in one of the terraced houses he was passing.

A bark sounded from somewhere behind him. Another answered. Then a howl made him increase his pace, despite the pain in his calf.

He stumbled to the end of the street and stopped, leaning against a car, trying to catch his breath. Another bark made him glance back the way he had come. Droplets of blood in a crimson trail led away from him. The right cuff of his trousers felt heavy and damp. At the end of the street, maybe a hundred yards away, an animal appeared. It stood and stared at him. Bigger, considerably bigger, than the dog which had attacked him earlier. A wolf?

Alsatian. The word popped to the front of his mind from behind the misty veil. He didn't wonder what it meant, merely accepted it was what pursued him.

Another dog appeared, black and sleek. Then another: an old friend, wiry-haired and mean.

When the two dogs drew abreast of it, the Alsatian set off in an easy lope towards him, the others close behind. They must have sensed they didn't need to hurry now; he was almost spent.

He pulled himself upright and lurched across the road towards the row of houses which ran at a right angle to the street from which he'd emerged. He almost tripped on the kerb at the other side, but managed to correct himself in time. A hot flare went off in his calf and fresh warmth trickled to his foot.

The notion of entering a house and closing the door had still not occurred to him. It was merely that he was already running towards the house, and his leg hurt more when he turned, that made him continue on through the open garden gate and up the concrete path to the front door.

Instinct made him grab the worn brass knob and twist it. Nothing happened.

He glanced back. The dogs had almost reached the junction; would do so in a few more easy strides.

He half-turned, wincing at the stab of pain in his leg, and stumbled along the front of the house. A waist-high hedge separated the property from next door. He pushed through it, tearing his trousers some more, crying out at the searing heat in his calf.

The steam-train sound of the dogs' panting reached his ears while he fumbled at the door of the next property. It, too, was locked.

Now he could hear the tread of the dogs' paws on the pavement, the soft thuds of their pads, the *clickety-clack* of their nails on concrete.

The next property along was separated by a low wall that he almost fell over in his shambling haste. Insight came to him, clear as mountain air: if the third door was locked, he was a goner.

He shuffled past the window to the front door. His hands were slick with sweat and slipped off the door knob. He tried again and it turned, but the door didn't budge.

A low moan came from his scraped throat and he slid down the door to his knees. When the growls sounded behind him, he brought his arms over his head and fell to his side in the foetal position.

The growls turned to snarls. Grew louder and triumphant.

Milandra and the group of four she liked to call her 'Deputies' met in her hotel suite. As customary, Milandra occupied an armchair at the head of a horseshoe, the Deputies occupying armchairs placed to complete the formation.

"Okay," began Milandra, sitting forward. "Let's talk numbers."

She looked at Grant. Before he had chance to say anything, Simone Furlong spoke.

"Troy Bishop," she said in a flat tone. "We want to know what happened."

Milandra raised her eyebrows at Grant, who shrugged. She looked at each of the other Deputies in turn.

Simone, also known as the Chosen, returned her gaze, as did George Wallace. Only Lavinia Cram did not hold eye contact. Lavinia glanced down at her lap, seeming to suddenly find something interesting about her hands.

"What makes you think something's happened?" asked Milandra.

"Oh, come on!" said Wallace. "We're not stupid. It's been weeks since Bishop and Heidler went after the *traitor*…" He almost spat the last word. "And since then? *Nada*. What ain't you telling us?" He glared in turn at Milandra and Grant.

Before Milandra could reply, Simone once more was quicker.

"We looked, but we couldn't find him," she trilled in the little girl voice she often used. Milandra was beginning to suspect it was a ruse to make others believe Simone was not playing with a full deck.

"You looked? All three of you?"

This time even Lavinia held her gaze.

"Yes," said Wallace. "We looked. And Bishop ain't there. He's dead, isn't he?"

Milandra glanced again at Grant, who nodded slowly. She sighed.

"Okay," she said. "Yes, Bishop is dead."

"Heidler's alive, though," said Simone. Her eyes narrowed and the little girl pitch had gone from her voice. "We found her, but she was vague. Shadowy."

"It was like she was dreaming," said Lavinia. "Not good dreams."

"Injured," said Wallace. "Must be why she's like that. She's injured. Bad."

"I don't know," said Milandra. "Jason and I haven't searched for her, and she hasn't contacted us. But what you say makes sense. If she was badly injured, her thoughts probably would appear shadowy."

"So," said Wallace.

Milandra raised her eyebrows.

"So," he repeated, "who are we going to send after the traitor?"

Milandra shook her head. "We've lost two people already going after Ronstadt. Okay, Heidler might not be dead, but we seem to have lost her all the same. I don't want to risk anyone else. We've more important matters to deal with."

"But we can't let that fucking traitor walk away." Wallace's face was reddening.

Lavinia grunted in agreement. Simone gazed at the wall above Grant's head as though she had lost interest in the conversation.

"Milandra's right," said Grant. "I know there are more than four and a half thousand of us, but we can't afford to lose anyone else. Besides, Ronstadt may be halfway to the continent by now."

"Good riddance!" said Wallace. "Okay. I know the Great Coming is important and all, so the traitor will have to wait. But when it's over, I'm going after him."

"If that's what you must do," said Milandra. "I won't try to stop you. He has an entire planet to hide out in, but it's your choice. However, I don't want any of you trying to look for him, or the drones that are with him, or Heidler, until after the Great Coming. I don't think for one moment that Peter Ronstadt is a traitor or that he intends to try to interfere with the Coming..." She ignored Wallace's abrupt coughing fit. "I don't think there's anything he *could* do to interfere even if he wanted to, but neither do I want to alert him to our plans. And if any of you find him and probe him, you can bet he'll probe you back. Have I made myself clear?"

Wallace and Lavinia nodded.

"Simone?"

The Chosen jumped as if startled. "Huh? Oh, yeah, sure. Whatever."

Milandra leaned back in her chair. It groaned softly under her weight. "Where were we? Yes, numbers. Jason?"

"Okay," said Grant. "Drones. Last count, we have a little over seven and a half thousand here in London. We keep losing the occasional one or two to dogs, but only when they wander away from where we can protect them. Despite precautions, disease keeps claiming more. But not so many as to become a problem. What *is* becoming a problem is the rat population. It seems to have exploded. Either that, or they're coming more into the open without humans around to scare them off. Drones are getting bitten or eating food the rats have contaminated." He shrugged. "Drones can't tell bad food from good."

Simone tittered.

"Why is that such a problem?" asked Wallace. "It's not as if we'll need the drones much longer."

"True," said Grant. "But they'll continue to be useful right up until the Great Coming. Apart from clearing out corpses, we've already started them going around switching off electrical appliances in readiness to turn on the Grid. The healthier they are, the more effective they'll be. And if the rats continue to multiply at their current rate, they'll become a nuisance to *us*."

"Okay," said Milandra. "You have a solution." It was a statement, not a question. Milandra knew Grant well.

He nodded. "Small teams of three. It doesn't take three to control a bunch of rats, but three can watch each other's backs. The teams clear the immediate area of vermin, then spread out in a widening circle. Clear as much of the city as they can. Any feral dogs they encounter can be dealt with at the same time."

"The pied pipers of London," muttered Milandra.

"How will the rats be disposed of?" asked Wallace.

"Well," said Grant, "I thought of the teams taking poison with them and getting the rats to swallow it, but that will merely create another problem: rotting rat corpses. So maybe they could get the rats to go to the Burning Fields and—"

"Jump into the bonfires!" Simone clapped her hands with glee. "I'm gonna go and watch."

"Sounds like a plan," said Milandra. "How many teams d'you think will be needed?"

"At least a hundred," said Grant. "The more, the better."

"Okay. Let's say two hundred teams. That's six hundred people. How many do we have working on the Grid?"

"Around five hundred. Eighty or so engineers in the power plants. The rest supervising the drones switching off appliances. We're ready to switch the Grid back on, but we want to catch as many appliances as we can so there's less risk of overloading or house fires."

"And we have around two thousand scouring the city for food and goods, and supervising the clean-up. That leaves around one and a half thousand of us. How many do we already have transport for?"

"I thought we'd use the double-deckers for the drones," said Grant. "We can carry almost two thousand, two and a half if we get them to stand."

"Pack 'em in," said Simone. "Peas in a pod."

Milandra thought for a moment. "We won't need nearly that many. The crane will do the main lifting. We'll need the drones to dig the pits and to position the stones. Of course, the hundred have to go. I should think another thousand will be more than ample?"

Grant nodded.

"What do you mean by 'the hundred'?" asked Lavinia.

"We've held back a hundred drones from working. We're keeping them well-fed, clean and exercised. Sixty-three of them will be used to power the Beacon. The better the condition they're in, the more effective it'll be."

Lavinia nodded. "Makes sense."

"Okay, then," said Milandra. "What if we send a thousand

drones, plus the one hundred, in the double-deckers, and a thousand of us in the coaches? The remaining drones not involved in clearance can all be put to work switching off appliances. The remaining five hundred of our number can be employed wherever there's a need: clearance, salvage, appliances, vermin. Anyone have any comments?"

"When do we leave?" asked Wallace.

"In five days."

"Yay," said Simone. "If you need me before then, *send* for me. I'm gonna watch the rats burn."

Milandra watched Simone file out with the others through narrowed eyes. The girl didn't seem to have appreciated the full import of Bishop's death or, if she had, she hid it well. For at the moment Bishop's life snuffed out, his memories and experiences passed to Milandra as the Keeper. They had flooded into her consciousness like poison—Bishop had tortured and killed humans for fun—and included his memory of the night before he left to go after Ronstadt; the memory of the Chosen calling to see him, to inform him that Milandra had lied about Ronstadt's location. Milandra had learned something from this memory: that she had underestimated Simone's abilities. She would not make that mistake again. It also showed her that Simone had personal ambitions of advancement, a trait that did not sit easily in a culture which valued the collective over the individual.

Before Bishop's death, Milandra had known the Chosen was unpredictable and she needed to keep an eye on her. Simone's apparent indifference to Milandra learning of her betrayal to Bishop reinforced that knowledge.

Trying to remember what had happened since she entered the house proved fruitless and caused the girl's head to ache, so she stopped trying. Besides, she had more immediate questions to answer, like, where was she now? And why did she feel so cold?

Opening her eyes might be a good start.

She immediately closed them tightly again as a shaft of pain stabbed her forehead. She breathed deeply until it receded, then tried again.

By lifting her eyelids a little at a time and squinting, she created enough of a slit to be able to take in her surroundings. They weren't very prepossessing.

She was lying on her back on a settee in a rundown living room. The ceiling was stippled and cracked. The single overhead bulb dangled inside a paper shade, like a Chinese lantern; a grubby one. Grey daylight entered through a large window, but had to struggle past a drab net curtain that looked as though it had been there since the '80s.

Turning her head slowly, wincing at the pain, she looked around the room. Newspapers and magazines were scattered over a threadbare carpet before two sagging, mismatched armchairs. An ancient-looking gas fire was attached to the peeling wall. A chipped mirror hung above the fire.

Moving gingerly, afraid to make the headache worse, she sat up. It was then she understood why she felt cold. Her top half was naked. Bra, tee-shirt and hooded top lay in a heap on the floor in front of the settee. Disquiet caused her gaze to flit about the room until satisfied she was alone. The bottom half of her body remained dressed in leggings and trainers; that was something, at least.

She leaned forward and gasped as fresh, white-hot pain coursed through her head. She paused, bent forward, waiting for it to subside, wondering whether she would pass out. If anything, she welcomed the sensation; it stopped her from speculating on why she had awoken half-naked.

The pain eased and she collected her clothes from the floor. Straightening slowly, she shrugged into her bra and eased the tee-shirt over her head, being careful to avoid the bump. With her hooded top back on, she felt a lot warmer.

Still moving slowly, she rose to her feet. The world tilted.

While she stood still, waiting for it to stop swaying, she looked inward to see if the compulsion which had brought her to London retained its grip. There was no sign of it. No urge, no *need*, to reach Hillingdon Hospital remained. She had no idea what had caused the compulsion; she didn't spend any time pondering why it had disappeared.

Unsteadily, tottering as though drunk, she moved to the mirror and gazed at her reflection.

Pasty complexion; racoon eyes; bedraggled hair which had lost its golden sheen. A lump above her right eye the size of half a hardboiled egg extended under her hairline. A scabbed cut ran down the middle of the lump. Dried blood stained her forehead like an inkblot.

From the corner of her eye, she saw a figure pass the window and stifled a shriek before it could betray her presence.

Hardly daring to breathe, she turned. The door into the hallway stood open and she only needed to take a few tentative steps towards it to be able to see the main entrance.

The front door comprised white-painted, yellowing wood, with two stained-glass panes set into the upper half. Through the panes, she could make out a dark shape. The faded brass doorknob was turning.

The door had swollen with dampness and didn't open—she recalled the difficulty she'd had opening it—and she let out her breath in a rush. Her tongue felt heavy and wooden; she badly needed a drink.

The figure slumping against the door made her jump. She glimpsed features of a face pressing to the stained glass, until they slid from sight. The figure was male and not very tall. A boy.

She crossed quickly to the door, adrenaline lending her vitality, dulling the ache in her forehead. Using both hands to firmly grasp the doorknob, she twisted it and yanked the door open.

Half-on, half-off the doorstep, a boy lay slumped on his side, arms wrapped around his head. Approaching him, only a few paces away, were three snarling dogs.

The door opening made them pause. The lead dog was larger than the others. A police dog, she used to call them. Otherwise known as a German shepherd or Alsatian. It looked at her and its black lips pulled back further. Saliva glistened on teeth, emphasising their sharpness.

She could have slammed the door closed in the dog's face, but something stopped her. An image bloomed in her mind. Swirling, shifting colours: vivid crimsons and angry purples, muddy-browns and mustard-yellows. She was looking at hunger. Fear and confusion, too, but mainly hunger.

How she did it she didn't know, but she let loose a flood of soft whiteness, covering the colours like a cotton sheet, muting and calming them.

The Alsatian relaxed its stance. Its lips came together and it cocked its head as though puzzled. Its two companions stopped snarling. The smaller dog lay down and placed its muzzle on its paws.

"Away with you, boys," she murmured, though she knew she didn't need to speak at all. "Go and find something else to eat. There's plenty out there if you look hard enough."

The Alsatian uttered a soft whine. The smallest dog stood. Together, the three of them turned and trotted down the garden path, out of the open gate and away.

She watched them until they were gone from sight. Only then did she stagger and would have fallen if she hadn't still been clutching the doorknob.

The movement brought her attention down to the boy. He was dressed in filthy rags, a stench rising off him like steam. A small puddle of blood had formed on the doorstep; judging by the state of his trousers, it was coming from his right leg. He gazed up at her, something akin to awe in his expression. Other than that, his face was blank, as though it only had room to express one emotion, one thought, at a time. There was something incomplete about it; something wrong.

"I suppose you'd better come in," she said.

The main entrance to the hotel swung open and Peter Ronstadt entered in a gust of icy wind. He stamped his feet.

"Brrr," he said. "It's bloody freezing out there. Let me in front of that fire."

He crossed the hotel lobby and stood before the hearth, rubbing his hands. Dusty stirred from slumber, opened an eye to peek at Peter, then went back to sleep.

"Grab yourself a drink and pull up a chair," Ceri said.

"Think I will," said Peter. "It's lovely and cosy by here."

While Peter bustled about, Tom allowed his eyes to close, basking in the fire's glow. He hadn't slept well since their flight from the village outside Hereford. He had hurt his shoulder when Peter's Range Rover smashed into a stone wall and the injury caused restless nights, waking him every time he turned.

He swapped his drink to his left hand and raised his right arm above his head, wincing a little. But the pain had greatly diminished. Maybe it was the alcohol, but Tom thought he might enjoy an uninterrupted sleep that night.

He opened his eyes when Peter pulled up a chair and sat by them, clutching a bottle of lemonade. Tom glanced at Peter's head. It had sported a lump the size of half an orange as a result of the collision with the wall. Although groggy at first, Peter had recovered remarkably. Miraculously. Within hours, the swelling had receded, leaving a purple bruise on the right side of his temple. A few hours later that, too, had gone, leaving no visible evidence of trauma. The man should have been concussed, nauseated, confused. Instead, he had eaten enough for three men and the injury had healed.

Like *hers*. She had been severely injured: broken bones, punctured lung and puncture wounds, cuts, crushed vertebrae. Her internal organs must have been grievously damaged. Not that Tom had any medical training, but he had seen the woman flung from a tree when the helicopter exploded, watched her smash into an adjoining tree and through its branches on a brief but traumatic journey which ended abruptly when she crashed into the frozen ground. He and Ceri had thought she must be dead. Only Peter seemed unsurprised, when they reached her and dragged her out of reach of flaming debris, that she was still breathing.

Tom's reverie was broken by Ceri speaking. She had lit another cigarette and blew the smoke lazily, looking completely relaxed.

"What you been up to, Peter?" she asked.

"Been to the marina," he replied. "Checking out boats."

"And?"

"Mainly small leisure boats. No good for our purposes. But I think I've identified two possible candidates. A fishing trawler, which looks in good nick, and a power launch. I'll need to check the engines over before we decide."

"You a mechanic as well as a sailor?" asked Tom.

"Not really," said Peter. "But I've worked on enough ships to have grasped the basics of how an engine works. I can tell if an engine looks sound. I can carry out basic repairs and maintenance."

"Peter…" said Tom. He hesitated, unsure how to proceed. "Er, we've been talking…"

Ceri sat straighter and flicked the butt of her cigarette into the fire. She looked at Peter.

"I'm not sure I want to go to the continent," she said. "I'm not sure that I *can* go."

Peter sighed. "I've sensed your uncertainty for days, Ceri. Yours too, Tom."

Tom nodded. "I don't want to go either, but not for the same reasons as Ceri. Sure, it won't be much fun crossing the North Sea in winter. It'll be dangerous, but I trust you enough, Peter, that I don't think you'll take unnecessary risks. It's just that… Britain is my home. If we're going to look for survivors, try to rebuild, I want to do it here, not in some foreign land."

Ceri nodded slowly. "That goes for me, too. In fact, I want to go home. To Wales."

Peter looked at them each in turn.

"There won't be any more survivors in Britain. None that haven't been compelled to go to London where they'll have had their brains fried." He shrugged. "We'll talk about it some more when Diane's fully recovered. For now, it's a moot point anyway. There's bad weather closing in. We won't be going anywhere by sea for the next few days."

Chapter Three

Throughout the world, those who had outlasted the Millennium Bug and the black despair which followed went about the business of survival. They dragged corpses outside and burned or buried them. They scavenged houses and shops for food and water. They kept themselves warm and sheltered.

It was survival at its most elemental: satisfy the basic demands that maintain life's spark, but nothing more. They did not seek out others for companionship or support or merely to hear another's voice. They remained where they were, not venturing far. Surviving.

But the human mind is a powerful instrument. Gradually, imperceptibly, the shackles which bound the minds of the survivors were loosening.

Milandra was well aware this would happen.

"The restraint we placed on them during the Commune won't last indefinitely," she said to Grant while they sat in the hotel suite eating lunch. "In fact, it's probably already wearing off."

Grant nodded. "It will have kept them from banding together. Perhaps for a little longer."

"Maybe. But they will start seeking out other survivors soon. And when they start to group, they'll be too strong for us to influence. They could become dangerous."

"Then just as well we're on an island," said Grant.

"And here we'll stay. Until later…"

"Yup. After the Great Coming, they'll no longer be a threat."

Milandra was aware Grant had turned his head and was watching her. Yet again, he appeared to be testing her resolve. She kept her expression closed.

"No," she said. "After the Great Coming, there will have to be a reckoning. *Then* humankind will no longer be a threat. In fact, it will no longer be. Period."

~ ~ ~

In the south-east of Maine, in a secluded section of the foothills of the White Mountains, away from the conservation areas and tourist trails, a rutted track wound through the trees, leading uphill to a chest-high timber gate. Nailed to the top crossbar of the gate was a thickly-lettered wooden sign:

No Trespassers! Visitors NOT Welcome!

The 'NOT' was underlined several times.

A timber fence, also chest-high, the cross posts too close together for anyone larger than a toddler to squeeze through, ran away to either side. A thick chain, secured by a sturdy-looking padlock, attached the gate to a fence post. Beyond the fence, the land had been cleared of trees. Set back in the clearing stood a roughly constructed log cabin and a clutch of small outbuildings.

In case anyone stumbling across this abode might be left in any doubt about the attitude of the owner towards casual callers, rough boards with upturned rows of rusting spikes had been attached to the top of the gate and fence.

Any visitor brave enough to linger in the face of such antagonism might have looked closer at the log cabin and wondered if their first impression of a crude dwelling was correct. The gable end of the roof confirmed that it, like the walls, had been constructed of rudely-hewn, split trunks of pine, complete with peeling bark. But a closer examination of the gables would reveal the roof had been overlain with felt and tight-fitting roof tiles that would ensure a leak-free interior. The tiles were now covered in snow, except for a six-inch radius around the galvanised steel flue which protruded from the roof, emitting a gentle stream of billowy smoke.

One or two of the trunks forming the walls of the cabin had warped under the extremity of the elements; a casual glance might lead an onlooker to believe the interior must be cold and draughty. But if the onlooker was intrepid enough to risk impalement by scaling the fence and approaching the cabin for an up-close look, he would glimpse in the gaps between the warped trunks a high-quality wind- and waterproof membrane. Poking the membrane with a finger would yield the impression of a thick layer of insulating material behind it, making the notion of wind howling through the gaps a foolish one.

A stroll around the cabin would show the increasingly foolhardy observer a double-glazed window set snugly into the wall facing away from the gate, alongside a thickset, well-fitting door. Peering in at the window would not yield any clues about the interior for the glass was tinted and the onlooker would see only a snow- and tree-framed reflection of himself.

This was a log cabin that gave only the pretence of being a humble abode. It was the home of Zacharias Trent, a survivor of Vietnam, of alcoholism and, more recently, of the Millennium Bug.

She made the boy lie on the sagging settee she had recently vacated. He obeyed her willingly, staring up at her with wide eyes that conveyed trust but little else.

"Phooey!" she exclaimed. "You don't half stink."

The boy smiled at her. It made his expression appear a little less vague.

"Phooey!" he said, mimicking her.

She grunted. "Well, at least you can speak." She eyed his trousers. They were so encrusted in filth she couldn't tell what colour they had been. The lower half of the right leg was deeply stained with blood. "We need to fix you up." She grimaced as she tried to swallow. "First, though, I need to drink."

Moving deliberately—the pain behind her eyes was threatening to overcome her—she went out to the narrow hallway. Her last memory of *before* was of wheeling her bicycle into the hallway. It had gone. Her backpack lay on the floor. It did not look as though it had been tampered with.

She knelt and undid it. An unopened plastic bottle of water lay within, together with an opened one around a third full and a few bars of chocolate. She removed the top of the opened bottle and raised the bottle to her lips. The water tasted unbelievably sweet, like nectar, and she had to force herself not to gulp it. Nevertheless, in what seemed no time at all, the bottle was empty.

Her stomach grumbled, low and insistent, like the growling of the dogs chasing the boy. She fished a bar of chocolate out of the knapsack and tore off the wrapping. Unable to help herself, she chewed the first bite as if it was toffee and almost swooned when the sugar rush enveloped her. Within moments, the bar had gone. She glanced at the full bottle of water, but resisted the urge to open it. Instead, she took it back into the living room with another bar of chocolate. Already the intensity of her headache was fading and she was able to think more clearly. She placed the bottle on the floor next to the settee.

Something caught her eye—a round object made of glass lay in the dust which thickly coated the carpet beneath the settee. A paperweight. Without knowing why, the sight of it made her shudder.

"Here," she said, handing the boy the chocolate. "Eat this while I find something to sort out that leg. And some clean clothes."

The boy took the bar and held it, staring at it as though he hadn't seen chocolate before.

"Oh, for goodness' sake," she muttered, snatching the bar back and tearing off the wrapper. "Here. Don't look at it. Eat it." She mimed raising her hand to her lips and biting.

After a pause, the boy followed her lead. Such a look of delight lit up his face while he slowly chewed that she regretted her impatience.

She smiled. "Good, isn't it? Well, you lie there and enjoy it. I won't be long."

Feeling a little stronger, she moved more naturally, in less stilted fashion. The door at the rear of the living room led to a small kitchen which smelled dank and musty, like an old root cellar. An open tin of baked beans stood on a cluttered worktop.

She glanced inside. The contents had blackened and dried. She looked around, taking in the jumble of scrap-encrusted crockery, dirty appliances, bundles of creased clothes, a pile of unopened official-looking mail. Whoever had occupied this property before the Millennium Bug came calling had surely not been house-proud.

A fridge stood next to the worktop. She opened the door, expecting and receiving a rush of foul air. Breathing through her mouth, she explored the interior. The fridge was sparsely stocked and most of the contents had spoiled, but she pulled out three unopened tins of food, a can of cola and a litre bottle of water with the seal intact.

She carried her prizes back into the living room and placed them on the coffee table. The boy had nearly finished the chocolate bar and favoured her with a brown-toothed smile.

Returning to the kitchen, she made for the sink and turned the taps. The cold tap shuddered and spat out a cupful of brown, brackish water before falling still. The hot tap did not issue so much as a thimbleful. She turned to the kettle standing beside the sink and hefted it, judging its weight and hearing the slosh of water. She lifted the lid and sniffed. The water smelled stale, but not stagnant, and would serve her purpose.

Her attention was diverted by a green, thick glass bottle. Gin, according to its label. She unscrewed the top and sniffed. Wrinkling her nose, she wondered whether it tasted better than it smelled. She brought the bottle to her lips and raised it.

With a small cry of revulsion, she turned and spat the fiery, perfumed liquid into the sink.

"People *choose* to drink this stuff?" she wondered aloud.

She took the bottle and the kettle into the living room. The boy had finished the chocolate and was gazing at the can of cola.

"Go on then," she said.

She handed him the can. He took it from her and stared at it for a moment as though uncertain what to do next. She was about to take it from him to pop the ring pull, when comprehension seemed to dawn and he performed the task himself. He took a deep slug of cola and issued a loud belch. He grinned. For a moment, his face went blank and then he held out the can to her.

"No thanks," she said, smiling. "You enjoy it. We'll eat some proper food soon, but after I've cleaned you up. You smell like a rubbish dump. Now, what else do we need?"

Back in the kitchen, she rummaged through the piles of wrinkled clothes. They had taken on the musty odour which pervaded the house, but at least appeared to have been washed. She pulled out a dark-blue football shirt that looked as if it might fit the boy, but the rest of the clothes were too big.

The boy's eyes widened when he saw the shirt she was carrying. He shook his head.

"No," he said. "Millwall."

"Huh?"

He shook his head again. "Not Chelsea."

"Ah… this is a Chelsea shirt and you support Millwall, right?"

The boy smiled, again making him look more with it, less simple. "Millwall."

"Okay. I get it. Doesn't much matter now, though. I'll see if I can find more clothes upstairs."

She went into the hallway and up the creaking stairs. Her headache had faded to a dull background throb, one that enabled her to function in spite of it, like having a mild period pain. And *that* was due soon, judging from the occasional twinge she was experiencing in her lower abdomen.

Four doorways led off the landing. A double bed stood in what looked like the main bedroom. The bedclothes were rumpled, the duvet thrown back as if the bed had been vacated in a hurry. She stared at it for a moment, feeling troubled but not knowing why, a similar reaction to that provoked by the paperweight. She suspected it had to do with *before*, but she still had no memory of what had happened between entering this house and awaking half-clothed on the settee.

The other bedroom was smaller and contained a single bed. A

poster of Chelsea Football Club's squad was pinned to a wall. A quick rummage through an old chest of drawers produced a tee-shirt with the imprint of some heavy metal band on the front, a thin jumper and a pair of jogging bottoms, which looked a little big for the boy but would be a vast improvement on his current attire. The bottoms had a drawstring waist which would keep them from falling down.

"And if you don't like this band, tough shit, mate," she muttered.

She also found some underpants and socks. The trainers she dug out of the bottom of the rickety wardrobe were cheap but fairly new; they might also be too big, but should serve until they could find a pair of shoes to fit him. He couldn't carry on wearing the shoes he had on. They were falling apart and one was soaked in blood. The wardrobe also contained a navy, padded jacket which would keep him warm. She carried the clothes and trainers to the landing and dumped them at the top of the stairs.

She entered the bathroom and opened the cabinet, hoping to find antiseptic cream and bandages. No such luck, but she grabbed a packet of painkillers, a bar of soap and half a bag of sanitary towels. Not what she normally used, but they would do the job when the time came. Standing on top of the cabinet was a can of roll-on deodorant for women and a plastic container of talcum powder. She grabbed these, too.

The final door opened to a small airing cupboard. She had become so accustomed to the musty odour that she barely noticed it. She grabbed a few folded towels and added them to the pile by the stairs. Pushing past more towels on the airing cupboard shelf, she found the last item she needed: a white cotton sheet.

Bundling everything into her arms, she struggled back downstairs.

The boy had lain back on the settee, eyes closed. The empty cola can stood on the floor. She kicked it aside and dumped everything onto the carpet.

"Right," she said briskly. "Clothes off."

~ ~ ~

The woman stirred and came to full awareness for the first time in weeks. She turned onto her back and stretched. Joints popped and crackled like logs on a fire, sinews tightened and muscles clenched. No pain. It felt good.

Diane Heidler opened her eyes and waited for her vision to adjust to the gloom of her surroundings. She was lying in a double bed in a room cast in shadow by closed, heavy drapes. The darkness was too familiar. It was all she could remember since standing at the door of the Sea King helicopter in the instant before the fuel tanks exploded. Darkness interspersed by agony-filled moments of wakefulness, during which she had eaten every morsel of food brought to her lips before slipping back into the pit.

She craved light.

Wincing in anticipation of fresh bolts of pain, Diane tugged back the duvet and swung her legs to the floor. The pain did not come. Stiffly, accompanied by more brittle noises from her joints, she stood and tottered to the window. Drawing the drapes aside, she blinked at the weak daylight entering the room.

She looked out onto a grey coastal town. The window was double- or triple-glazed and no draughts or sound intruded, but she didn't need to feel or hear the wind. Trash and dead leaves swirled in flurries and accumulated in doorways. A few strands of Christmas lights strung across the street had blown loose. The masts of boats in the harbour rocked and swayed. Gulls swooped and circled, barely needing to flap their wings. The sky glowered, low and rain-heavy, the colour of smudged print.

She turned and surveyed the room. A trouser-press attached to a wall; a notice outlining fire escapes; sachets of coffee next to a small kettle and long-life milk in plastic containers, the type that spray the contents in all directions when opened carelessly. A hotel room.

Diane glanced down to see she was wearing some sort of oversized pyjamas. They hung from her emaciated frame like a dust sheet on a hat stand. She felt depleted, like an overused tea bag, and what she was about to do would weaken her further—she couldn't do it standing up. She crossed back to the bed and sat.

Closing her eyes, Diane set her mind free. She didn't need to send it far. He was in the same building, a little way below her. He noted her presence immediately.

Feeling better? Peter sent.

Yes she sent back. *But weak. Hungry.*

I'll fix you some food. There are clothes in the wardrobe. Ceri picked them out. Hope they fit. Go now, before you overdo it.

Diane reeled her mind in and leaned back on the bed, breathing shallowly. Panting. It took a few minutes before she felt sufficiently recovered to sit up. Minutes more to be able to stand. The room darkened and she swayed. She waited until the light had returned and the room had stopped spinning before making her way unsteadily to the wardrobe.

Without paying too much attention to the clothes she found hanging there, she began to dress.

The hotel was fitted with a modern kitchen, all stainless steel and gleaming in the thin light entering through the windows. It did not have its own generator so they prepared food on Peter's camping stove. They preferred to do this in the bar and lounge area, where they could enjoy the warmth of the fire.

Ceri was roused from her light slumber by the clatter of crockery and the fizz of the stove's gas flame. She glanced at Tom. His empty glass was on the floor by the side of his chair and his head lolled to one side. He snored softly. Dusty lay at his feet, sleeping soundly, too.

The fire gave off a rich orange glow. Ceri stood and placed a fresh log onto the embers, then walked to the bar and took a stool in front of the long oak counter.

Peter was behind the bar, frying slices of pink, processed meat in a black skillet. An opened tin of potatoes stood next to a saucepan ready to be heated. He smiled at her.

"You hungry?"

Ceri shook her head. "Only been a couple of hours since lunch." She nodded towards the skillet. Judging from the number of thick, sizzling slices of meat filling it, a whole tin had gone in there. "You must be."

Peter's smile narrowed a little. "This isn't for me. Diane's woken up. She'll be down presently."

"You've been upstairs…?"

"No." Peter's smile faded entirely, as though he didn't like to be reminded of how different he was from her.

"Ah," said Ceri. "Tell me, Peter…" She leaned forward, resting her arms on the rich wood. "… if you can communicate by telepathy, why bother speaking at all?"

"Well, to communicate with you and Tom without speaking, you'd have to open your minds to let me in. Like you did when I showed you our arrival on this planet, remember?"

Ceri nodded, recalling sitting cross-legged in the middle of a road in mid Wales, holding hands with Peter and Tom, the fluttering sensation in her mind that she could have kept out but allowed in, the stream of images…

"But it would be a little pointless," continued Peter, "since you'd have to speak to reply."

"Yes, okay," said Ceri. "But you and Diane could hold entire conversations without talking?"

"We could. But we won't." Peter lifted the skillet and set it to one side. He emptied the tin of potatoes into the saucepan and placed it on the stove. "For a start, it would be like you and Tom conversing in front of me in Welsh. It would be a little rude, considering I can't speak the language."

"Crap analogy. I can't speak it either. And I don't think Tom can." Ceri shrugged. "Learning it was on my to-do list. I'll have to rename it the no-point-doing-now list."

"You're right: crap analogy. There's a much more compelling reason Diane and I won't hold conversations that way. You see, having the ability to communicate with our minds can be useful, particularly over large distances. But there's a downside."

Ceri grunted. "Isn't there always?"

"I guess it's all about balance," said Peter. "Setting our minds free employs a great deal of energy. Even when we combine our psyches, like during a Commune, it drains our energy reserves so much we have to eat like pubescent teenagers to replenish them. Or soak up sunlight, though there's not much of that in Britain during the winter months."

"Ha! Nor the summer months."

"True enough. Someone like Milandra, who leads the Commune and who holds the sum total of my people's knowledge within her psyche, has to eat a prodigious amount of food. It's why she's rather, er, rotund. It's essential she has physical energy reserves to be able to constantly replenish her mental energies. And it's why she normally lives in a sunny place like Florida." He took a spoon and stirred the potatoes. "The gas in this cooker has almost gone. I noticed a camping shop when I was out. We'll have to pay a visit and replenish our supplies."

Ceri turned at the sound of Tom approaching. He took a stool next to her and yawned.

"I must have dropped off for a minute or two," he said.

"More like an hour," said Peter with a grin.

"Tom," said Ceri, trying not to sound anxious. "Diane has woken up. She's coming down now."

"Well, perhaps in a few minutes," said Peter.

"That's what I meant," said Ceri. "Now. In a few minutes."

"This food's for her," said Peter. "I was explaining to Ceri how communicating with our minds saps our energy. Diane contacted me from upstairs. Since she's weak anyway from all the healing she's had to do, that few moments of mental communication will have pushed her back to the point of exhaustion. She'll need this food. And more."

Ceri was watching Tom's expression. All traces of sleepiness had disappeared. His brow furrowed in a deep frown.

"Are you sure about her, Peter?" he said. "*Really* sure?"

Peter nodded. "We've been through this. I probed her while she was unconscious. Not the most gentlemanly of actions, but…" He shrugged. "Needs must. I saw everything that happened in the cabin of the helicopter. Bishop was the one who wanted to kill us, not her."

"But she was with him!"

"And if she hadn't been, we'd likely be dead now. Tom, I've told you before and I'll tell you again. Diane Heidler saved our lives."

"But for what?" The voice, thin and reedy, came from behind Tom and Ceri. They spun around on their stools. The woman stood at the foot of the staircase, clutching the banister as though without it she would not have the strength to stand. "I might as well have let him kill you," she said. "I've only postponed the inevitable. Mankind's time is up."

Chapter Four

By splashing water onto towels to dampen them, and wrapping the bar of soap inside the towels, she eked out the contents of the kettle sufficiently to get the boy cleaned up. When she had finished, the soap was worn to a grubby blob and three hand towels, looking as though they had been trodden into a patch of mud, lay on the floor next to a pile of stinking clothing.

With the grime removed, the boy looked thin, pale and prepubescent. Maybe aged nine or ten. She rolled the deodorant under his arms and liberally powdered his torso with talc, making him look even paler. Wraithlike. He shivered and didn't demur when she pulled the heavy metal tee-shirt over his head. Being careful to avoid the cut on his right calf, she eased on underpants to cover his modesty, then turned him onto his stomach.

She poured the last of the water from the kettle onto his calf and wiped away the dried blood with a fresh towel. To her inexperienced eye, the cut looked clean, the edges not ragged or inflamed. It was about three inches long, across the meatiest part of the calf, and stood proud of the white skin around it. Watery blood started to pool at the surface. She picked up the bottle of gin and unscrewed the top.

"This might sting," she said.

Using one hand to spread the edges of the cut apart, she sloshed the spirit generously into the narrow opening. The boy drew in a sharp breath and stiffened, but didn't kick out or try to draw away.

Putting the bottle to one side, she went back into the kitchen and returned with a vegetable knife and tin opener. She had brought a tin opener with her from Cornwall, but figured that having another wouldn't hurt. Losing her parents and brother, her friends, and everyone else she knew, *that* hurt. The pain nestled like a boulder in her stomach, too big to expel. She hurriedly pushed the thought away. In the long, lonely days in Looe after pulling out of her illness, before the compulsion to come to London had overpowered her, she had grown used to carrying the boulder. It didn't diminish the hurt, but made it a little easier to bear. Giving in to grief might lessen the pain, but until she could find somewhere she felt safe, grieving would have to wait.

She used the knife to cut a strip from the cotton sheet and bound the boy's calf as tightly as she dared. He lay still, hissing through his teeth when she pulled the sheet tight, but allowing her to work on his leg without interference. She stared at the impromptu bandage for a few tense moments, expecting it to bloom pink then red as fresh blood seeped from the cut. To her relief, it remained white.

Once the boy was dressed, his shivering subsided. The trainers were a little big, but laced tightly they would stay on and would do for now. She took a painkiller from the packet she'd found in the bathroom cabinet and placed it on the boy's tongue.

"Swallow," she said.

He grimaced, but obeyed.

She opened the tins of food from the kitchen, drooling while she did so. The boy watched her attentively, his tongue coming out to lick his lips. In clean clothes and without a coating of grime, he looked less like an extra from the cast of *Oliver*. She turned the food into bowls and they ate it cold. Vegetable soup, tuna, red kidney beans in chilli sauce; not the best of combinations, but they emptied their bowls in minutes. They washed it down with the bottle of water from her backpack.

Once they had finished, she sat back and regarded the boy solemnly.

"So," she said, "what's your name?"

The boy stared at her, expressionless.

"Name?" She sighed. "My name's Brianne, but everyone calls me Bri. Like brie the cheese, only without the e."

No clue showed on the boy's face of his thought processes, or whether he had them.

She tapped her chest impatiently. "Bri. My name. Like the

cheese but without the e. Call me Bri."

She was about to give up, when a light seemed to come on behind the boy's eyes.

"Bri." He said it slowly, like something new to be savoured. "Bri… Bri… Bri..."

"Yeah, okay, okay. Don't wear it out. So what's your name?" She tapped herself on the chest again. "Bri." She leaned forward and lightly tapped his chest. "And you are…?"

She watched his face, looking in vain for signs that something was going on in there. Then it came. "Will," he said. "William Harry Clarkson."

"William Harry? Really? I'll bet someone's parents were into the royal family. Never mind. We can't all be perfect. Anyway, it's nice to meet you, Will."

Bri held out her hand and took his, shaking it up and down. The boy seemed a little bemused at first, but then gripped her hand back and started to pump it—faster and faster, until it felt her arm must work loose from its socket. The boy began to chuckle and, before she knew it, they were both hooting with laughter.

It was only the fresh twinges of pain in her head that brought her out of the laughing fit. As her giggles receded, she rescued her hand from his.

"Well," she said, "that was unexpected. I didn't think I'd ever laugh again, even if it was a little on the hysterical side." She glanced at the boy. All trace of humour had left his face. He was looking at her intently. "What?"

"Dogs," said Will. "Nasty dogs. Bri made them go away."

"Yes, I did, didn't I? But don't ask me how 'cause I have no idea. And it makes my head hurt to think about it." She stood carefully, afraid the world would start to tilt again, but it held steady. "Come on. We need to get out of here. I don't feel safe. Whoever took my bike might be coming back. Put your jacket on while I get ready."

Bri retrieved her backpack from the hallway. She added the tin opener she'd found to the one she already carried, and the litre-bottle of water from the kitchen. The bottle made the material bulge and would cause the straps to dig into her shoulders, but she felt relieved to have it. She cut strips from the cotton sheet and folded them away into a side pocket to keep them clean.

Will had managed to don the jacket and zip it up without her help. He stood waiting, favouring his right leg, leaning a little to one side.

"Yeah," she said, "that's going to be sore. It can't be helped. We can't stay here. Right, let's get going. Oh, wait. Better have a pee first. Do you need to go?"

So close to leaving, Bri didn't have the patience to wait for Will's penny to drop. She grabbed his hand.

"Come on. I'm sure you can squeeze one out."

She made him wait on the landing while she did her business. She didn't expect the flush to work, but tried it anyway. To her surprise, water swooshed into the bowl, but the sound of the cistern refilling was conspicuous by its absence. She lifted the toilet seat and ushered Will in. She unzipped his jacket and untied the drawstring waist of the jogging bottoms.

"There," she said. "Pee. Then wait on the landing for me to tie you back up. They'll fall down otherwise. I'm going to find a coat."

Bri had been warm enough on her journey from Cornwall, at least until it had begun to snow, in tee-shirt and hoodie, the exertion of pedalling performing the job of extra layers. Now she would be travelling by foot, she needed something warmer.

She returned to the main bedroom. Again her eyes were drawn to the bed and the thrown-back bedclothes, and she once more felt troubled without knowing why.

Inside a large wardrobe, she found a tangle of empty hangers, as though the owner had packed in a hurry. On the floor of the wardrobe, crumpled into a heap with other old clothes, she discovered an olive-green padded anorak. It was grubby and smelled like old shoes. The sleeves were torn in a couple of places and stuffing bulged out like loft-lagging.

"This is no time to be fashion-conscious," she muttered, shrugging the anorak on. It was too big for her and the zip was broken, but it also had popper fastenings, most of which still worked. They would help keep the worst of the wind and rain out.

She gave one last, disturbed glance towards the bed, and went back onto the landing where Will was waiting, jogging bottoms puddled around his shins. She took the opportunity to examine the dressing on his calf. A faint line had appeared in the centre of the makeshift bandage, as though inscribed by a red biro running out of ink, but the dressing still covered the cut and should keep it clean.

Bri nodded and allowed a small flush of self-satisfaction to bloom in her chest.

"Good job!" she said.

"Good job!" echoed Will, grinning in the goofy way she was beginning to find endearing.

A few moments later, they stepped out into the street.

Zach Trent went to Vietnam a fresh-faced eighteen-year-old, bursting with vigour and ideals. He returned three years later, his body whole but his spirit in shreds. Mumbling and aloof to strangers, a stranger to his family and friends, he shunned society and was shunned by it. For five years, he trod the back roads and railway sidings, doing odd-jobs for farmers and ranchers, enough to keep him fed and in liquor, moving on before they asked him to leave. Always moving.

He learned of his parents' deaths through a discarded newspaper he found in the gutter. While he glanced through it by the flickering light of the fire, numbed by cheap bourbon and almost ready to pass out, his gaze snagged on his name.

Zacharias Abraham Trent read the advert. *Contact the below-mentioned attorneys-at-law to learn something to your advantage.*

A grainy reproduction of his high school graduation photograph appeared below the address and telephone number of a firm of lawyers in Michigan. He no longer recognised the youthful figure in the photograph.

When he awoke from a fitful, alcohol-fuelled slumber hours later, he was still clutching the newspaper. Later that day, he used the last few coins in his pocket to call the number in the advert from a payphone in a gas station at the edge of some town.

The efficient woman who answered the call informed him he needed to speak to Mr Benton. Zach waited patiently to be put through. He had nothing better to do. A man's voice came on the line, sounding brusque and a little wary.

"Yes, hello? Who am I speaking to, please?"

"Um," said Zach. He was suddenly uncertain whether he wanted to know whatever it was these people wanted to tell him badly enough to take out a newspaper ad. "I saw my name. In a newspaper. It said to call this number."

"And your name is?"

"Zach… er, Zacharias Trent. Zacharias Abraham Trent."

"You're about the tenth caller I've had claiming the same thing," said Mr Benton. "What's your date of birth, please?"

Zach told him.

"And your social security number?"

"Um… I don't know. No, wait…" Zach thrust his hand into a chest pocket of his faded denim jacket. The paystub remained where he had shoved it in disgust after remonstrating with the workshop owner about why tax had been deducted from his few hours' earnings. The owner had muttered something about the IRS and refused to budge. Zach had moved on and the paystub was still there, crumpled but legible. He read out the number printed at the bottom next to 'Employee ID'.

There was a short silence. When the lawyer spoke again, the note of wariness had gone from his voice. It had been replaced by something else. Pity?

"Mr Trent. One last question, if you don't mind. What were your parents' names?"

Zach told him. He added, almost as an afterthought, "What do you mean *were*?"

Mr Benton let out a long breath before replying. "I'm afraid I have some bad news, Mr Trent."

It turned out that his parents, whom he had not seen or been in contact with for over four years, had been travelling home in their car from a fund-raising function for Vietnam vets, when a truck skidded on black ice, shedding its load. The load—pine and spruce and cedar trunks headed for the sawmill—bounced across the two-lane blacktop and squashed his parents' car, and his parents, as flat as roadkill.

Zach took the news with detachment, as though watching a movie where some down-and-out, some dirty hobo, is given bad news during a phone call. He watched the hobo make arrangements with the fancy-pants lawyer on the other end of the line to collect a ticket in town—the hobo had to holler to the gas station owner to find out the town's name—to catch a Greyhound to Indianapolis and from there to Lansing in Michigan. The lawyer also arranged at the hobo's request—his *wheedling* request, thought Zach, while he watched with disgust—for the hobo to collect fifty dollars in cash from the town's bank. Before the call ended, the hobo asked one last question.

"The funeral. When's their funeral?"

Mr Benton let out another long breath. "I'm sorry, Mr Trent, it took place yesterday."

Zach used some of the lawyer's money to buy himself a meal and a pint of cheap bourbon. He could have afforded the expensive stuff—fifty dollars went a long way in the mid-seventies—but old habits die hard. Besides, he liked the way cheap liquor seared his throat; it was how he imagined napalm would taste.

He sipped the bourbon while he sat on the Greyhound and stared out of the window, trying unsuccessfully to picture his parents' faces. The next day, in Indianapolis, he bought another pint. It was almost gone by the time the bus pulled into Lansing.

Mr Benton was tall and gaunt. He looked down his long, bony nose at Zach and wrinkled it.

"I was your parents' attorney for many years," he said. "You might not believe it or even care, but they loved you dearly. Their only child." He wrinkled his nose again. "Cheap whisky. Dirty clothes. Unshaven. Unwashed. You're what, twenty-six? You look forty-six." He sighed. "Knowing what you've been through, don't suppose I can blame you for what you've become." He lowered his head a little to peer at Zach over his wire-framed spectacles. "Hard liquor's not the answer, you know."

Zach reached into his pocket and withdrew the bottle of bourbon in its brown paper wrapping. He lifted the bottle to his lips and took a deliberate swig. "'ll do me," he muttered. "Besides, how can you know what I've been through, sitting here in your swanky office and hundred-dollar suit." Zach sniffed and took another sip, savouring the burn as the liquor traced a fiery path to his gullet.

"Oh, believe me, I know," said Mr Benton. "Did two tours of duty myself. In Korea. Volunteered." He snorted as though the notion now amused or disgusted him. "Hit the bottle, too, for a while."

Zach sat straighter, sudden curiosity driving away a little of the alcoholic stupor. For a moment, he forgot to be angry at the world. "Why? Why'd you stop drinking?"

Mr Benton continued to regard Zach over his spectacles, his gaze as intent as a hawk's. "We drink to banish the demons, right? The demons with their reminders of the jungles and the stench of death and the screaming of children. Spreading those memories around like rat poison, under our noses, in our ears, burrowing into our brains until it seems they must burst. So we drink, and the demons recede for a while. But they come back."

Zach nodded slowly.

"I realised," continued Mr Benton, "that alcohol wasn't banishing the demons, but making them stronger. They were feeding on it. It was getting to the point I would have to drink myself to insanity or death. Lucky for me, I retained sufficient clarity to see the truth. I stopped drinking. Threw myself into the law. Passed the state bar exams. Got myself into private practice. Eventually started my own firm."

"And the demons?" Zach's voice was little more than a whisper.

"Oh, they never go away entirely. But each time they return now, they're a little weaker. Less strident. Less insistent. I have no trouble keeping them at arm's length. Course, you'll have your own way of keeping them at bay. The law was my answer. You'll need to find your own. But believe me when I tell you that you won't find it in no bottle."

Thirty minutes later, Zach walked out of Mr Benton's office a wealthy man. He had known his parents were comfortable financially, but hadn't realised the full extent of their riches. After state and federal taxes, probate and administration costs, and Mr Benton's fees, Zach as the sole heir would receive more money than he could imagine ever spending.

A block from the lawyer's office, Zach upended the bottle, ignoring the disapproving glances of passers-by, and poured the last dregs of fiery bourbon down his throat. He dropped the bottle into the next trash can he passed.

He never bought another.

Tom watched the woman wolfing down food. Her fair hair was tied back in a ponytail, emphasising the gauntness of her features. Her cheekbones poked against her skin like his had done when he had awoken from his bout of the Millennium Bug. But no outward signs of her injuries remained. No scabs; no yellowing bruises; no wheezing. When she crossed the hotel lobby to the bar, she had done so gingerly but with no hint of a limp. Tom found it difficult to believe. She had been battered and broken only weeks before, surely on the brink of death. Now she sat before them, pale and weak but otherwise healthy-looking. It should have taken her months to recover fully from the injuries she had suffered. Years, even.

If she was discomfited by his frank regard, she didn't show it.

When she glanced in his direction, her expression gave no hint of what she was feeling. Tom suspected she would make a good poker player.

He shifted a little on his stool and glanced at Ceri. She, too, was watching the woman eat, but her expression was also neutral, giving Tom no clue as to whether she felt as uncomfortable as he to be in this woman's presence.

Peter busied himself preparing more food. He had asked Tom and Ceri to allow her to eat in peace, to build up some strength, before subjecting her to the barrage of questions they no doubt wished to ask following her doom-laden pronouncement. Ceri had readily acquiesced; Tom more reluctantly.

The woman—Tom could not yet bring himself to think of her by name—cleared the plate of fried meat and potatoes. By the flickering light of the paraffin lamps, Tom could see some colour had already returned to her cheeks.

"Thank you," she said to Peter. "I feel a little stronger." Her accent was mild, but unmistakably American.

"There's another plateful to come," said Peter. "It'll help some more."

"It might just." She half-turned on her stool to face Tom and Ceri. "I guess you folks have a few things you want to get off of your chests."

"You could say that," said Tom. He sat straighter and folded his arms. "Like why you tried to kill us."

The woman's expression didn't change, as if guardedly neutral was its permanent state. "You mean, the virus…?"

"No. Peter's told us about that, though I'd like to hear your version. Peter's sounded like a fairy tale." Tom paused to take a deep breath. He was determined to remain calm, to hear what the woman had to say. "I mean, when you were in the helicopter."

The woman blinked. "I didn't try to kill you."

"Excuse me." Ceri spoke for the first time. "The bullet you fired hit the wall of the cottage above my head."

"Oh, that." The woman spoke in the same tone she might use

to discuss the weather. "I only took the shot to make Bishop quit his whining. I didn't even aim at you."

"Oh, that's all right, then," said Ceri. "So long as you weren't *aiming* at us." Her voice dripped with sarcasm and Tom was surprised to note the high spots of colour in her cheeks, like blusher applied by a three-year-old.

The woman shrugged and Tom sensed Ceri stiffen. He brought one hand across and gave her forearm a squeeze.

"Easy, Cer," he said. "You're the one who said we weren't going to do anything, remember? That she'd saved our lives."

"I know," said Ceri. "But now she's sitting in front of us, acting so bloody indifferent, I want to scratch her eyes out."

"You're right," said the woman. "I am indifferent. Or *was…*" She frowned as though unsure quite what she meant.

Peter placed another dinner plate piled high with food in front of the woman. "Diane, eat this." He looked at Tom and Ceri. "She *did* save our lives. Try to remember that."

The woman offered Peter a thin smile and started to eat.

"Er… *Diane*," said Tom. "Can we carry on talking while you eat?"

Diane did not look up, but nodded.

"Okay," said Tom. "Maybe you can explain why you came after us with that man—Bishop, was it?—but ended up saving us."

Diane seemed deep in thought. She finished her mouthful and took a drink from the glass of cola Peter had also given her. Only then did she look at Tom.

"Honest answer? I'm not sure. I saw a glimpse of both of you during the Commune. I saw Peter protect you. That bugged me a little. Any drones that survived the virus in England were to come to London to help clear up."

"We weren't in England," said Ceri, her voice still containing an edge. "We were in Wales. And we're in Scotland now. It's Britain, but it's not England."

Diane shrugged again. "England. Britain. Same thing." She turned her attention back to the food.

"No, it's bloody well not!" Ceri spoke through gritted teeth and it came out in a hiss.

Tom placed his hand once more on Ceri's forearm. "Steady, Tiger. She's American. Many of them say England when they mean Britain. It doesn't really matter, not any more, does it?"

Ceri turned to look at him and he was surprised to see her eyes glinting with moisture. "Well, what *does* matter now, Tom?" Her voice rose and she shrugged off his hand. "Art? Politics? Religion? Sport? All gone. The most important thing to me was my family and they've gone, too. To see *her* sitting there stuffing her face, when she's one of the ones who killed them…" Ceri took a deep breath and Tom could see she was struggling to keep herself under control. "So tell me, Tom, what matters? Because if the answer's that nothing matters, we might as well step off the harbour wall and let the sea finish what she and her kind started."

Ceri stared at him, eyes glistening.

"You're right," he said slowly. "None of that stuff matters any more. But maybe… maybe *we* matter. We survived. Others might have, too. Maybe what's really important is that we carry on surviving."

Ceri snorted. "After what *she* said earlier?" She turned towards Peter, who stood behind the bar watching them, a concerned frown wrinkling his brow. "Please will you pour me a vodka and orange. A large one."

She lit a cigarette and faced forward.

Diane hadn't looked up. She continued to work at the food on the plate, which was almost empty.

Tom cleared his throat.

"I'd still like to know why you saved us from Bishop," he said. "Diane?"

She chewed and swallowed.

"Bishop was a prize jerk," she said. "An arrogant, overbearing jerk."

"He was more than that," said Peter. He handed Ceri her drink and she sipped at it while she smoked, staring fixedly ahead. "He probed me when you were chasing us. Before I expelled him, I caught a glimpse of the real person. Twisted, cruel, ruthless. I think he used to torture and kill humans for pleasure."

Diane nodded. "It wouldn't surprise me. He was passionate about killing you, Peter. And these two." She nodded towards Tom and Ceri.

"Okay," said Tom. "I get that he wasn't nice. But it wasn't only him who set out to kill us, Diane. You still haven't explained why you changed your mind."

"I had never decided to help him kill you," said Diane. "I'm not sure why, but even before we left London I took steps to make his task difficult."

"How?" asked Tom.

"I made it so that his Uzi wouldn't fire." She frowned. "He was also carrying a handgun. He always kept it on him so I had no opportunity to interfere with it. I don't know why he didn't use that on you. Or on me." Her expression cleared. "Oh, wait. I remember. He *did* try to reach it, but it was behind him and he was strapped in too tightly."

"Okay, but *why* did you help us?" insisted Tom. The answer seemed important.

Diane shrugged again. The gesture was starting to irritate Tom. It was as well Ceri wasn't watching, though no doubt she was listening. Diane looked at Peter.

"Do *you* know why?" she asked. "You must have taken a peek when I was unconscious."

"Yes," said Peter, "I did. Your memories were intact, but shrouded. I think because your injuries were so severe. Your motives for behaving as you did were cloudy, though I don't believe that had anything to do with your injuries." He glanced at Tom. "She's not lying when she says she doesn't know why she saved us."

Tom fell silent for a moment. Diane turned back to her plate to finish the last of the food. She no longer looked pale or frail. Tom glanced at Ceri. She had almost finished her drink and had lit another cigarette.

"Cer? You okay?"

She nodded. "Tickety boo," she said. "Though I doubt I will be when she answers the next question."

Tom suspected she was correct, but asked the question anyway.

"Diane, what did you mean when you said mankind's time is up?"

Diane had cleared the plate for the second time; she pushed it away.

"Thank you, Peter," she said. "I feel a lot stronger already." She indicated Tom and Ceri. "You haven't told them, then?"

Peter shook his head.

"Um, Peter?" said Tom. "Haven't told us what?"

Peter raised his eyebrows at Diane. She gave a curt nod.

"Okay," said Peter.

Ceri turned on her stool to stare at Peter, her jaw set firmly as though expecting the worst. Tom felt his stomach lurch and swallowed hard.

"I have told you," said Peter, "about the plan to eradicate the vast majority of the human race. Not the *entire* human race, though we could have if we had wanted to. The virus, so quaintly nicknamed the Millennium Bug—"

"Hate to interrupt you, Peter," said Ceri, "but there was nothing *quaint* about it."

Tom thought back to the condition of his mother when he had found her lying in her own waste, unable to open her eyes through the crust which had formed over both lids, each tortured breath seemingly her last, until it was. He grunted his agreement with Ceri.

"You're right," said Peter. "And I apologise. It wasn't my intention to make light of what has happened. Anyway, the virus was specifically designed to kill *almost* everybody, but not quite."

Tom could feel his hackles rising. "So you could have killed us all, but chose not to," he said. "Fucking big of you."

"Why, Peter?" asked Ceri. "Why leave any of us alive?"

"We needed a workforce to prepare for the Great Coming," he said. "A survival rate of around 0.02 percent gave us enough humans to do what is needed, but not so great a number that we are unable to control them."

"Once they've had half their brains fried, you mean," said Tom.

"Yes," said Peter. "I suspect it is what happened to the survivors when they arrived in London." He glanced at Diane, who nodded but didn't look up.

"Okay," said Tom, "so once this Great Coming has happened. What then?"

Peter shifted on his feet, but didn't drop his gaze from Tom's.

"Once the remainder of our civilisation arrives on Earth, they will bring with them the knowledge of how to create new drones. This time drones will be created without the urge to procreate or survive. Simple creatures to serve our wills, but without the capacity to evolve. We won't make the same mistake again."

"You don't already possess such knowledge?" asked Ceri.

"Our geneticists do, but they remained on our home planet. It was considered too risky to send such expertise so vast a distance. Don't forget, we don't keep written records. If some disaster had befallen us who travelled here five millennia ago, the knowledge would have been lost for all time."

"So when the rest of you arrive, you'll create a new version of us," said Tom. "A weak, unambitious, subservient version."

"That's about the size of it," said Peter.

"And us?" said Tom. He glanced at Ceri. She was staring at Peter, her eyes wide and fearful. "What will happen to the surviving humans? There could be hundreds of thousands of us spread throughout the world."

"A million and a half," said Peter.

"Huh. That many. What will happen to us?"

"After the Great Coming, the will of seventy thousand people will join with the five thousand already here. The combined strength will far exceed the force you felt during the recent

Commune. I won't be able to protect you from it."

"They'll hold another Commune?" said Ceri.

Peter nodded. "Once they've gathered together somewhere large enough to take them all so their psyches can be combined and concentrated. Probably some wide, open space, like Hyde Park, or somewhere more contained, like a sports stadium. The surviving humans worldwide will be powerless to resist the compulsion that will be thrust upon them. They will have no choice but to act upon it."

"And this compulsion?" asked Tom, though the churning sickness in his stomach was already suggesting the answer.

Ceri had guessed it, too.

"Mass suicide," she said in a small voice. "They'll tell us to kill ourselves."

"Yes," said Peter. "I am very much afraid that is precisely what will happen."

Chapter Five

The only living thing Brianne and Will encountered while they looked for a safe place to spend the night was a rat. Large and brown, it had its nose buried in a ragged corpse lying in the gutter, too torn apart for Bri to be able to tell whether male or female. The rat must have heard or sensed their approach, for it withdrew from its meal and rose onto its hind legs, nose aquiver.

"Scat, rat!" said Bri, as they drew nearer.

"Scat, rat!" the boy echoed.

Will hadn't displayed any ill effects from his encounter with the dogs, except he stayed close to Bri while they walked and glanced around from time to time as though checking they weren't being stalked. When they approached the rodent, he tucked in by her side, so close her hip almost bumped his elbow.

The rat watched them, showing no sign of fear. Just when Bri was thinking of changing direction to avoid the creature, it dropped to its haunches, turned and scurried away along the gutter. The sky was darkening as evening drew in and the rat was soon lost to sight in the gloom.

Bri shuddered.

"I hate rats," she said.

When they had walked three or four streets from the house where she'd woken up, Bri felt a little safer. If the person who had taken her bike returned to look for her, he or she would not have any clue of her whereabouts. This housing estate must contain hundreds of terraced houses. Trying to find the one she was in, without being certain she was in one and with many of them locked by their former occupants, would be an almost impossible task.

Bri tested her own theory when she started approaching properties and trying the front doors. Most of them were locked. The few that did open let loose a waft of corrupted air, stale but as recognisable to her now as the smell which used to come from the fishery at the harbourside in Looe.

Darkness had fallen fully by the time they found a house with an unlocked door that did not emit the odour of old, rotted flesh.

Bri entered the hallway, Will close behind. She shut the door and inspected it from the inside. Made of hardwood, the door contained not only a keyhole, from which protruded a brass key, but two sturdy-looking bolts. Bri tried to turn the key, but it wouldn't budge.

"Damn!" she muttered.

She drew the bolts across.

"They'll have to do," she said, although she wondered quite how secure the door would prove against a determined intruder.

Will stepped forward. He took hold of the door handle and yanked it upwards. Bri heard a smooth sliding sound as some mechanism engaged. Will gripped the key and twisted it easily. He grinned his goofy grin.

Bri took hold of the handle and tried pressing it down. When it didn't move, she shook it. The door did not so much as rattle.

"Good boy, Will!" she said and punched him lightly to the shoulder.

The boy's grin grew wider.

Bri dropped her backpack in the hall and blundered about until she found an understairs cupboard. A little blind rummaging produced a torch. The batteries were weak, but generated sufficient light for her to explore downstairs.

The windows were all hardwood, double-glazed and securely fastened. The rear door was of the same material, securely locked and bolted. It didn't budge when Bri shook it.

The kitchen cupboards produced a variety of tinned food and, to her delight, boxes of candles and matches. She lit a candle and dripped molten wax into the bottom of two mugs. Before the wax could set, she stood a fresh candle into each puddle. She and Will could now explore the rest of the house without being splashed by hot wax.

The living room contained comfortable-looking furniture, a

huge and defunct television, and a bookcase bursting with a variety of modern paperbacks and older-looking hardbacks.

Bri led the way upstairs, their shadows dancing ahead of them along the walls and ceilings like agitated elastic figures. Three bedrooms, beds all made, and a family bathroom led off the wide landing.

The house gave up no clues as to what had become of its owners. Although overlain by a thin coating of dust, everywhere they looked was well-maintained and tidy. A stale, unlived-in odour permeated every room, but the stink of decay was wholly absent. Quite why such a prosperous, clean household had upped and left without bothering to lock the front door Bri had no idea.

They sat side by side on the living room's leather couch, which was indeed as comfortable as it looked, and ate a supper of tinned meat, baked beans and pineapples.

Appetites sated, they drank the pineapple juice from the tins.

Bri sighed. This was the safest she'd felt since waking up in London. But tiredness was creeping up on her. The headache, which had been like a faint background noise for the last few hours, was beginning to gain intensity.

Will's eyelids looked heavy and dark smudges bruised the flesh beneath his eyes. He yawned.

"You look like I feel," said Bri.

The boy said nothing.

"Hmm," she mused, "what's the deal with you, anyway? Do you have learning diffs or something?"

Without thinking about what she was doing, Bri stretched out her hand and touched Will's brow. He blinked, but did not shy away.

Leaving her fingers in contact with his forehead, she narrowed her focus until she was no longer aware of the flickering living room, only Will's expressionless features.

They began to waver and soften until she was seeing an abstract version of the boy, an artist's impression. Then that, too, was gone as her gaze shifted inwards. She became incorporeal, a mind only, an untethered intellect which could extend itself. Reach out…

If the boy gasped, she didn't hear him. She was inside his head, examining his psyche, viewing it as a swathe of shifting colours. Greens, blues, indigos, violets. Muted, pastel shades.

With anomalies: two dark marks, as incongruous amidst the soft swirls as fresh bruises on a bride's cheeks. She looked closer, probing a little deeper.

Like furrows in a virgin hillside, two wide gashes cut through the boy's mind. Black at the edges, they tinged to muddy green, to khaki, before becoming a vivid, violent orange at their centres. Beyond the gashes, or behind them, lay a limpid pool of pastels. The colours of the pool had lost definition, had perhaps once been vibrant before fading almost to grey.

She sensed that within the colours more could be revealed: images and movie reels of events and emotions, of people and places. All shrouded in a mist, greying like the stagnant colours in the pool. To see more she would need to delve deeper, but something was yanking her back—

"Yeow!"

Pain coursed through her head, originating behind the cut on her forehead and spreading outwards to engulf her. She squinted at Will. He gazed placidly at her, apparently unaffected by her invasion of his mind.

She scrabbled at the pocket of her hoodie and extracted two painkillers. With a grimace, she dry-swallowed them.

"Come on," she said to Will. "I need sleep. We both do. Whatever's been done to you to make you this way, I can't think about it now. My head hurts too much."

She stumbled up the stairs, Will putting out a hand to steady her. The pain had begun to recede a little by the time she had seen the boy into one of the beds and had climbed into bed in the room next door. The duvet felt a little damp and smelled musty. She barely noticed.

~ ~ ~

It took Zach Trent a further three years to discover what Mr Benton had described as his 'own way' of keeping the demons at bay. Although wealthy beyond any measure he might previously have employed, contentment eluded Zach. The concept of using some of that wealth to put down roots, to become part of a community, repulsed him. He continued wandering, though now in luxurious train compartments or swish rental cars rather than by weary foot, alighting at towns and cities on whims, taking off again when the fever took him, and take him it always did.

Except for the occasional chilled beer, though never more than two at one sitting, he remained dry. When the fever came on him—the aching, shaking fever—he moved on, always moving, trying to stay one step ahead of the demons.

He dabbled in blackjack and roulette, lured by the glitzy façade, awed and at the same time appalled. When he began to lose big and felt the pull to keep placing the chips—he'd win them back and more, and if not this time then on the next spin of the wheel or turn of a card—he had regained sufficient self-awareness to recognise he was replacing one bleak addiction with another.

He moved on.

On and on. Always moving. Never outrunning.

And everywhere he went, people.

Three years it took him to come to a realisation: that where people were, he oughtn't to be. The demons found it easier to reach him in a crowd.

Mr Benton's way was to immerse himself in the study and practice of law. Zach Trent's would be immersing himself in solitude.

He moved again, but this time with purpose. He bought a pick-up truck, a mule of a vehicle, sturdy and steadfast, capable of traversing all but the most churned terrain.

Passing through backwaters and one-horse burghs, he stopped and forced himself to approach gas station proprietors and grocery store owners, tapping into local knowledge. He knew what he was looking for wouldn't be found in the display window of any realtor.

After meandering through half a dozen or more states, he pulled in to a roadside diner in Maine. Tree-clad slopes rose in the background to white-tipped peaks. Summer had not yet given in to fall, yet the air contained a nip that made him pull his jacket tighter. Only a few battered pick-ups and flat beds occupied the diner's parking area, suggesting the interior wouldn't be crowded.

So it proved. Plaid-shirted, grizzled men sat alone in booths, paying attention to nothing but their food and mugs of steaming coffee.

Zach took a stool at the empty counter.

"What can I get ya?" The waitress looked late middle-aged and tired.

"Coffee," said Zach. "What's the special?"

"Corn chowder. Fresh baked bread." She spoke with a way of broadening certain vowels—'chowdah'—that marked out a local.

Zach nodded. "Please," he added.

The waitress seemed disinclined to try to engage Zach in small talk, which suited him just fine. He ate the chowder and the bread—both tasty—and drank coffee strong enough to clean ovens, in silence.

"Refill?"

He nodded and the waitress filled his mug. When she turned to leave, Zach cleared his throat.

She turned back to him, eyebrows raised.

"Them mountains," he said. "Good hunting?"

"Bear. Elk. Deer."

"Wolves?"

The woman shook her head. "No wolves in these parts since long before I was in pigtails. And that's too long, mister."

"Anyone live in them foothills?"

"Some. But most of the habitable land is being partitioned by the gov'ment for nature reserves and tourists." She shrugged.

"Ain't much pioneering spirit left around here."

"D'you know of any homesteads for sale?"

She narrowed her eyes. "Why you fixin' to live out there? Ain't nothing but trees. And snow for five months each year."

"Splendid isolation," Zach murmured. "D'you know of any for sale?"

The waitress hesitated, then sighed. "I guess the wilderness suits some folks and Old Ben's place is as close to wilderness as you can buy. It ain't much, mind. Just some ole log cabin and trees."

"And Old Ben, he's looking to sell?"

"Ayuh. That's what I hear."

"How do I get there?"

Will lay awake in silent darkness, straining to sort his thoughts into a coherent pattern. Knowledge, experiences, memories, all lay shrouded in a dark, impenetrable fog. Occasionally, a snippet might rise from the cloud, bobbing to the surface like a bottle in an ocean. An image of a young girl, pony-tailed and freckled: his sister, though her name remained hidden. A spotted, yapping puppy, jumping up, trying to lick his face while he laughed...

"Pongo," he murmured.

The memory of his puppy—at least, he *felt* it had been his puppy—brought a more unpleasant, more recent memory: snarling dogs chasing him through deserted streets. He tried to push it away by thinking about the girl who had saved him.

"Bri," he muttered. "Like the cheese but without the e."

He didn't even know what that meant, but he liked the sound of it.

"Bri. Like the cheese but without the e..."

The image of Bri comforted him. The sound of her name lulled him. Whispering it softly under his breath, Will drifted into sleep.

A mile or two across West London, Milandra and Grant sat in the hotel suite, discussing the Great Coming and the tasks which awaited once it had been accomplished.

"… in places like India," Grant was saying. "That's where we'll need to concentrate our initial efforts. The reactor cores should remain stable for months yet, but we don't want to take chances."

"Have you spoken to our people who were in high positions of trust?" asked Milandra. "I've not had chance to. I doubt you have, either."

"No. I haven't," admitted Grant. He had been too busy overseeing arrangements for ridding the surrounding area of decomposing corpses and for the forthcoming trip to Salisbury. "But I've had others talk to them and report back. It seems as if every government with nuclear facilities took every precaution to make them safe while they still could."

"Hmm. Unusually noble, don't you think? The entire human race is dying around you and you spend your last days trying to ensure the world is as safe as possible for any survivors. Maybe those who say humanity is weak and self-serving have it wrong?"

"I never thought…" Grant tailed off when he caught the sharp glint in Milandra's eye. He cleared his throat. "No matter in how safe a condition they've been left, nuclear reactors by their very nature continue to degrade and each installation will need attention before the year's out. That, in my view, will be the first task once this planet has truly become ours."

"Earth Haven," murmured Milandra. "I guess we can drop the Haven then. It will become our home." The dreamy look which had briefly appeared in her broad face abruptly faded and she became businesslike once more. "What else?"

Grant had already been giving this a lot of thought. "Communication systems—satellites, servers and the like—will require attention if we want to maintain networks. Of course, we won't *need* radio and the internet, but they are useful tools. With seventy-five thousand of us spread about an entire planet, they might be worth keeping.

"Energy and water supplies can be turned back on as and where required. The London Grid will be switched back on in the

next few days since we require it at the moment. But later—"
Grant shrugged "—it can be turned off again if nobody intends
settling here. I suggest we share knowledge of these systems so we
all can utilise energy resources if we wish wherever we decide to
roam. They are basic systems, backward even, but they are here
and those who want may as well make use of them."

"But you don't envisage having to mine for coal or drill for oil
to keep power sources available?"

Grant shook his head. "We won't need to. There are
hydroelectric stations around the world that will require regular
maintenance, but they will produce electricity for as long as the
rivers flow. Those who don't wish to settle near such stations may
be happy to exist without electricity. After all, it is what they are
accustomed to on Earth Home. And the boon they will receive
from the sun will make notions of wanting artificial energy
redundant. I can still remember the first time I stood in sunlight
on Earth Haven. It was like being born anew."

"Yes," agreed Milandra, a wistful tone in her voice. "So
humankind's means of producing energy can be allowed to decay
into the soil."

"I think so, along with military installations and buildings like
hospitals. We will have no use for them. Entire towns and cities
will go the same way. I'm not sure what the optimum size of our
civilisation will be on Earth Haven—many tens of thousands
more than seventy-five thousand, I suspect—but we shall still be
too sparse to need them all."

"What about food and transport?"

"Global food production won't be necessary. Those who want
to farm can take their pick of the best arable land. Cows, pigs,
sheep, poultry, many will have died without man to feed them, or
have been killed by predators without man to protect them, but
many more will be wandering around waiting to be herded by
anyone who takes the fancy. Fish stocks will rise dramatically. Fruit
in season will be hanging off the branch waiting to be plucked.
And there will be warehouses in every town and city piled high

with tinned and dry goods. There will be enough food to go around for many years to come without us having to do anything.

"As for transport, there will be no need to maintain networks and produce more oil to power automobiles and airplanes and ships. Why should any of us *need* to travel anywhere at speed? We shall have no use for global commerce or tourism or sporting events or any of the other things for which mankind developed high speed travel in order to accomplish. If someone takes the fancy to travel to Australia, what will it matter if it takes six months under sail? Earth Haven's sun is young and life-giving. We don't labour under the limited lifespan that shackled man and made him rush to achieve things as if there were no tomorrow. Which, I suppose, for them, there wasn't. But there will always be tomorrow for us… next week, next year. For so long as each of us wants it."

Grant peered closely at Milandra while he said this. He hadn't noticed any fresh wrinkles under her eyes or grey tinges to her hair, but he knew she had thought about allowing herself to grow old. And once the process began, it became extremely difficult to halt, even under a sun as powerful as this one.

Milandra returned his gaze and smiled. "Don't worry, old friend, I intend sticking around for now."

Deciding not to press the issue, Grant shrugged. "All this will be subject to consensus, of course."

"What about decaying bodies," said Milandra, "in places where there are no survivors? I know there are no diseases they can harbour that could affect us, but they'll attract vermin. In sufficient numbers, they can cause us a problem."

"And large gatherings of vermin might attract larger predators," said Grant. "I think it would be a foolish person who opts to live alone. A single person can be overcome even by something as small and inferior as a rat if they come at him in sufficient numbers. Packs of dogs or coyotes or wolves *will* be able to get the better of a person on their own. Controlling more than five or six larger animals simultaneously takes some doing. It will be wiser to travel in twos or threes, at least until a new status quo is reached.

"As for decaying corpses, by the time the Great Coming has taken place and people start heading out into the world, most will already have rotted away, especially in warmer climes. Bones, hair, teeth, kidney and gall stones are likely to remain. Maybe finger- and toe-nails. And rotting clothes. But the remains will be easier to dispose of than those we are dealing with now. Less messy. Except, of course…"

"Except for the million and a half fresh corpses," finished Milandra, her expression neutral. *Cautiously* neutral, Grant thought.

He chose his next words carefully, opening a door to see if she would step through. "That's if we decide to press ahead with the complete eradication of the human race," he said.

"We will," said Milandra, slamming the door shut. "We have no choice."

Ceri sat alone before the dying fire, nursing another vodka and orange. The alcohol was quelling the black depression threatening to bubble to the surface and spill over. Quelling it for now.

Clangs and bangs came from behind the bar where Peter was tidying up. He had cooked food for himself, but neither Ceri nor Tom had felt much like eating. Ceri rather believed she would stick to a liquid diet this evening. Maybe for lots of evenings, or for as many evenings that remained. She lit another cigarette and inhaled without much pleasure. Sometimes cigarettes tasted nasty, but that wouldn't make her give up now. If anything was pointless in this new world, worrying about her health was high on the list.

The other woman—it was Ceri's turn to struggle to think of her by name—had disappeared upstairs, muttering something about needing more rest to complete her recovery. Ceri found she didn't much care whether the woman recovered or not.

Tom had wrapped himself up warm and taken Dusty out for a walk. Like her, he hadn't said much since Peter's revelation of what their future held. He seemed preoccupied, lost in his own thoughts. Ceri hoped for his sake they weren't as dark as hers.

The pain of losing her son, her husband, her parents and everyone else she held dear within the space of a week had left her broken. Terror that she was the only person left alive had completed her desolation. Tom and Peter had stumbled across her when she was on the verge of allowing grief to overcome her. The bottle of sleeping pills still stood on the coffee table back in her terraced house in Wales. When she had taken the decision to leave the house behind and go with the men, she also decided to leave the pills behind.

Although she hadn't overcome her loss, had not grown accustomed to its weight, she had resigned herself to the fact of it. That grief was now a part of her, a part she didn't want to lose since it meant her loved ones would also be part of her until the day she died.

Until recently, she hadn't given much thought to how long she might have left. The attempted invasion of her mind by a powerful alien intelligence, the flight from Wales and the ensuing helicopter pursuit had not allowed much time for introspection. But since arriving in Wick and settling into the hotel, long hours by the fireside and long nights in bed had granted her thoughts free rein. Those thoughts remained dark, but she had reached an agreement with herself, a sort of accommodation. No matter how bleak the future looked, she would strive to go on for as long as she could; to survive. It is what her family would have wanted her to do.

"Mam," said Rhys in his soft, lilting voice which had yet to break. In the black small hours she could conjure his image at will. "When your time comes, we'll still be here waiting for you. Me and Dad and Gran and Grandpa. We're not going anywhere. Take your time."

The thought of her loved ones waiting to greet her comforted her and gave her the strength to carry on.

Now it appeared her time was indeed measured. Tom's too, and that of anyone else who had survived. Measured in mere months.

The sound of a throat clearing made her glance up. Peter stood there, clutching a book and a paraffin lamp.

"You all right?" he said.

"I'll survive," said Ceri. "Ha! Okay, perhaps I won't."

"Well, don't give up yet. The Great Coming may not succeed."

"Peter, no offence, but I really don't want to talk about it now. I just want to sit in front of this fire and get shitfaced."

"Fair enough. I'm retiring for the night." He held up the book: *The Stand.* "There's a tiny library off the corridor leading to the dining room. Do you know, I used to read a lot but haven't picked up a book for probably sixty years or more. Ever since television became popular. Anyway, I'll bid you goodnight."

Ceri watched him go, idly wondering whether she should have warned him what the book he intended to read was about—with all that had happened these past few weeks, it would hardly provide escapism, if that's what he wanted.

No sooner had Peter disappeared up the staircase than the embers in the fire glowed a bright orange when a gust of cold air swept into the room. Dusty bounded to Ceri's side, a wide doggy grin on his face, attempting to lick her.

"Gerroff, you daft mutt!" she said, but there was no malice in her tone. "You're perishing. Sit in front of the fire and warm up."

Dusty needed no second invitation. Giving her hand a last lick for luck, he curled up on the thick rug covering the flagstones before the hearth.

Ceri glanced behind her, but there was no sign of Tom. She stood, placed a log on the fire and went behind the bar to make herself a fresh drink. By the time she returned to her seat, Tom had entered the lounge, still wearing his coat and thermal beanie, clutching a leaflet.

He crouched by the side of her chair, an excited look on his face.

"Look," he said. "I found it among the leaflets at Reception."

Ceri took the leaflet in her free hand and squinted at it in the faint light.

"A gun club," she said. "So what?"

"Isn't it obvious? A gun club. It'll have guns."

"Ye-es. I grant you that's likely. But, again, so what?"

"Well," said Tom, a sober expression settling over his features. "I think it's high time we armed ourselves."

Chapter Six

The idea came to her during those soft moments that occur when, after an unbroken ten hours of sleep, a mind is drifting gently up towards full awareness.

Bri opened her eyes. Daylight entered the room around the edges of the closed curtains, but did not make her scrunch her eyes closed again. Last night's headache had receded, for now.

She nodded to herself. "Why not?" she muttered.

She clambered out of bed and quickly dressed, shivering in the frigid air. She opened the curtains and glanced outside. The bedroom was at the front of the house and looked down onto the road. The edges of the road and the pavement held a thin covering of frost. The sun peeked above the roofs of the houses opposite from a sky so pale it might have been washed in bleach.

A tiny bathroom led off the bedroom. Bri went in and shut the door. She needed to empty more than her bladder. The toilet paper felt a little damp, but was adequate for her purposes. When she had finished her business, she closed the toilet lid and tried the flush. Nothing. She shrugged. She had no intention of remaining in this house so didn't suppose it mattered if she left a calling card. Neither would it matter to Will; he could use the main bathroom.

She doubted he would even notice, anyway. Whatever damage had been done to his mind—and she had clearly understood those dark greens and vivid oranges to represent damage inflicted from an external source—made him unconcerned about pretty much everything.

Bri glanced longingly at the shower cubicle which occupied most of the tiny bathroom. She had last taken a shower in the hotel in Looe after pulling out of the fever. Weak as a kitten, she had stood trembling under the spitting cold water until, with a clanking of pipes, it sputtered to a halt.

She turned to the sink and tried the cold water tap. Nothing. A plastic bottle of liquid soap stood on the sink; maybe she could use it to feel a little cleaner. She looked for a towel and found a pile of them, slightly damp but clean, in the wardrobe in the bedroom. She also found a thickly padded ski jacket, which meant she could dump the tattered anorak.

Returning to the en suite clutching a couple of bath towels, she closed the door and undressed, the cold air making her skin dimple like orange peel. The dispenser on the soap bottle was clogged, so she unscrewed it and poured a few drops from the bottle onto one palm. She lifted her other arm and rubbed at the armpit with the soap. Greasy, not particularly effective, but better than nothing.

On impulse, Bri tried the hot water tap on the sink. To her astonishment, a thin stream of brown water came out. She turned the tap off. Sliding open the door to the shower cubicle, she examined the shower controls: an 'on/off' dial and a temperature dial. She twisted the temperature dial fully to hot and the other to 'on'.

With a cough, a splutter and a groan, water spat out of the shower head. Like the water that had come from the tap it, too, was brown but as she watched, it began to run steadily and clear. Uttering a small squeal of delight, Bri grabbed the soap bottle and stepped under the water.

It was how she imagined it must feel to be flayed with whips of ice. Her breath left her in a gasp and her instincts cried at her to step back out. She ignored them and began to slather herself in liquid soap, rubbing vigorously at her skin in as much an effort to get warm as clean. Her scalp turned numb while she worked water and soap through her hair. Her fingers brushed the lump on her forehead, making her wince.

She managed to soap and rinse her entire body before the water gave out. She stepped out of the cubicle, shivering uncontrollably, but feeling alive and vital. Her skin tingled as she wiped it dry in a towel, using exaggerated movements to warm up.

Glancing at her clothes on the floor, she wrapped herself in a clean towel and stepped back into the bedroom. She returned with clean underwear and a selection of toiletries. The underwear was too big, and definitely not her style, but she shrugged it on anyway.

A few minutes later, feeling fresh and smelling fragrant, Bri went to find Will. He was sitting on his bed, half-dressed, playing with a toy. A baby's toy.

That's just what you are, she thought. *Or what you've become after what they did to you.*

Quite who 'they' might be, Bri had no idea.

Since Will did not have the jogging bottoms on, she took the opportunity to change the dressing on his leg. She was pleased to see the cut had scabbed over. The skin beneath the scab looked pink and healthy, and she breathed a sigh of relief.

"Come on then, mister," she said. "Go use the bathroom, then get dressed. I'm going to make breakfast. I don't know what it will be, but I can tell you this: it'll come from a tin."

She giggled and Will gazed at her, wide-eyed and uncomprehending.

When they had eaten, Bri took a couple more painkillers. She suspected she would need them if she was going to put her idea into action.

Leaving the breakfast dishes where they were, she led Will into the living room and sat next to him on the settee.

She reached out and touched her fingers to his forehead.

"Okay," she said. "I'm going to try something. It shouldn't hurt. You, at any rate."

She stared at his face and narrowed her focus. It happened quickly and easily, as though having already done it once, it had become second nature.

The swirling pastels, the grey pool, the dark gashes… all as she had seen them the previous evening. She headed straight for the gashes and into them, surrounding herself with muddy greens and bright orange. Concentrating fiercely, aware she may not have long to try this, she focused on the orange.

Gradually, like a developing photograph, it changed. Became terracotta. Then burnt umber. Brown. Muddy green, melding with the surrounding colours.

She turned her attention to the greens. They became less muddy. Lightened, spreading to the black edges of the gashes, which absorbed them.

The gashes faded, had all but disappeared. Beyond them she could sense the limpid pool, except it wasn't so limpid now. Colour was returning, pastel shades of green and blue, as though a couple of dye bombs had been dropped into it.

Bri gasped as she lurched back into herself and clutched at her nose. Blood was gushing from it in a hot stream. She stood and stumbled to the kitchen, where she grabbed a cloth to try to stem the flow. Her headache had returned, but to nowhere near the intensity of the previous evening. Whether because of the pain killers or the nosebleed acting as a pressure release valve, she didn't care.

Holding the cloth to her nose, she returned to the living room and resumed her seat next to Will.

"Bri? Are you okay?"

She looked at the boy. The blank, vapid expression had gone. In its place he wore a frown of concern.

"Are you okay?" he repeated.

"Yes, I'm fine… I'm hungry. How can that be? We've only just eaten. But never mind me. How do you feel?"

The boy's frown grew deeper. He looked down at his hands on his lap.

"Nasty people with guns." He brought a hand up and rubbed his temples. "They put something—" he pronounced it 'sumfing' "—on my head. Then…"

"Yes?"

Will looked up, his eyes wide, perplexed. "Have I been dreaming?"

"Maybe. In a way. What do you remember?" Bri brought the cloth away from her face. The flow of blood seemed to have stopped. She dabbed at her nose while they talked.

"My mum," said Will, "and my sister. Poppy. She was six. They died."

"How old are you, Will?"

"Nearly eleven. All my friends died, too."

"I know. So did mine. Where are you from?"

"Lambeth. South London."

"'Sarf Lundarn'," Bri mimicked with a smile. "You sound as if you're in *EastEnders*." Will returned the smile, but it seemed forced and quickly faded. "So what are you doing in this part of London?"

"The hospital," said Will. "I had to go to the hospital."

"Hillingdon Hospital?"

Will nodded.

"What else do you remember?"

The boy's brow furrowed in thought. He shuddered and clutched his arms to his thin chest.

"Bodies," he whispered. "Dead bodies. Smelly. I had to help carry them. We burned them. And dogs. Snarling dogs. Sharp teeth." His eyes opened wide again. "How could it be a dream, Bri? You were in it. Like the cheese but without the e."

Bri leaned forward, dropping the cloth to the floor, and grasped his hands.

"It wasn't a dream, Will. I don't know why and I don't know who, but they did something to you at the hospital. They hurt you. In your mind. Somehow I fixed it."

"And you saved me from the dogs." He looked at her with something approaching awe.

"Yeah, well…" She was suddenly self-conscious under the weight of his regard. "Forget it." She let go of his hands. "I'm incredibly hungry again. There are plenty more tins in the kitchen. Since we won't be able to carry them all when we go, we might as well eat as much as we can now. Then I think we should split this joint."

"Where will we go?"

"I don't know, but I really feel we need to get away from London. Have you ever been to Cornwall?"

The boy shook his head.

"Then it's about time you did."

Had Old Ben been nicknamed Grizzled Ben or Ornery Ben or Gummy Ben, they would have been equally apt epithets as 'Old'.

After a few false turns, Zach found the rough track leading to the ramshackle log cabin and, ten minutes later, pulled the pick-up to a halt in the narrow space before it. The fence and gate had not yet been erected; they would be added later, a couple of Zach's personal touches. All that marked out the plot was a thin strand of wire strung between stakes hammered into the ground. The wire twisted between trees crowding the plot like jostling children.

When Zach stepped out of the truck, the door to the cabin creaked open and an old man emerged. He stooped slightly and walked with a limp. The barrel of the shotgun cradled under his arm was broken, but ready to be snapped into position and poised to fire in one motion.

Zach waited by the side of his truck. When the old man had approached within five yards, he stopped.

He nodded at Zach. "Help ya?"

"You called Old Ben?"

"That depends." The old man leant to one side, hawked and spat a brown string of spittle. He moved his tongue and Zach saw a wad of something pass in front of what remained of his teeth. Chewing baccy. "Who's asking?"

"I'm Zach Trent."

The old man's eyes narrowed a fraction. "Ain't never heard of you."

Zach shrugged. "No reason why you should have. I hear you're looking to sell up."

"Oh, you do, do ya?" His eyes narrowed further. "Don't look as tho' you amount to a hill of beans."

"Nope. But if your price is fair, I can meet it."

The old man continued to regard Zach, who gazed steadily back.

At last, Old Ben seemed to come to a decision. He grunted. "Best come in, s'pose. Mind, I don't hold with no dickering. The price is the price. Take it or get the hell off of my land."

A couple of hours later, Zach placed a call to Lansing from a motel.

"Mr Benton? It's Zacharias Trent."

"Zach! To what do I owe this pleasure?"

"Um, do you handle property transactions? Land purchases?"

"Sure do. You settling down?"

"I guess so." Zach discovered the idea of living in only one place, a notion he would have scoffed at through a bourbon haze a few years ago, suddenly held huge appeal. "Yep, that's precisely what I'm doing. Settling down."

The bulldozers' engines clattered to life, shattering the dawn silence. Birds in nearby trees, no longer accustomed to the sound of heavy machinery, took to the air in alarm. With a clunk and a roar, the engine of the flatbed truck started and added its bass notes to the mechanical cacophony.

"They're loud," Milandra said, raising her voice.

"What?" said Grant, cupping his ear.

"I said… oh, never mind."

She and Jason Grant watched the two yellow bulldozers lurch into motion, their caterpillar tracks easily gripping the surface of the parking lot through its thin covering of frost. One took the lead and they proceeded from the lot in single file, at a little above walking pace. The flatbed truck, with its weighty cargo of crane and sloshing twenty-gallon drums of diesel, lumbered behind them, the low speed suiting it. Milandra waved to the drivers when they went past and they returned her wave with grins.

The 'dozers and truck turned to the west, making for the M25, the motorway which described a rough circle around Greater London. They would follow it south until it intersected the M3. That motorway would take them south-west to beyond Basingstoke, where they would turn off and strike across country on A roads for Andover and Salisbury. Every abandoned vehicle they encountered on the left-hand lanes of each road was to be shunted aside by the bulldozers, ensuring an unimpeded passage for the buses and coaches that would be following in five days' time.

Rodney Wilson, his complexion more ruddy than normal in the cold morning air, joined them as the vehicles began to fade from earshot.

"Morning," he greeted them cheerfully. He nodded towards the double-decker buses. "The drivers'll be taking their first practical lessons today. They'll start to get a feel for 'andling those beauties."

"They've received their, er, theoretical training?" asked Grant.

Wilson nodded. "They know everything I do about driving a Red Lady. Give me five days to put 'em through their paces and they'll be able to drive them as well as I can." Milandra could almost see his chest swell with pride. "And that's bleeding well, begging your pardon an' all, miss."

Milandra smiled. "What about those trucks with the chutes?"

"The gritters? Got two volunteers lined up. We'll get them started the day before they're due to go. Much easier to learn to drive a gritter than a Lady. The 'ardest part is learning the controls for the salt, and that's about as 'ard as a nun's tit. Oops, begging your pardon again."

"And those one-deck buses…" said Milandra. "What do y'all call them?"

"Coaches, miss. We've got a dozen drivers who already 'ave experience driving them. The other eight will start getting a feel for it tomorrow. Again, they're easier to learn than the Ladies."

"Excellent," said Milandra. "Well, Rod, you certainly seem to have everything under control here. Good man."

"Thank you, Miss Milandra."

"Tell me, Rod, what will you do later? After the Great Coming?"

The man's face crinkled in thought. "Don't rightly know. I haven't been off this island for almost four centuries. Lived most of that time in London. Saw the Great Fire. Helped to rebuild St Paul's. Saw revolt and wars. Fought in a couple. Watched people die of the plagues—the sweating fevers and the Black Death. Saw people blown to bits by Hitler's bombs. Seen the city double and triple in size. It used to be a right cesspit. But I love it. Or used to…"

"Not now?"

"No…" Wilson shifted from foot to foot as though wanting to say something, but uncertain how it would be received.

"It's okay," said Milandra. *You can tell me* she sent.

"It's the people," said Wilson. "They made the city what it was. Without them—" he shrugged "—it's just a lot of buildings."

"So you're not going to stay… later?"

He shook his head. "Got me a fancy for warmer climes. Somewhere I can feel the sun on me back all year round. Egypt, maybe. See how the Great Pyramid is holding up. I was involved in building it, you know."

"Ramps and rollers?" asked Grant.

"Pulleys and counterweights."

"Ah." Grant nodded. "It must have been quite a sight when it was new. I only saw it after it had fallen into decay."

"Oh, yes." His eyes glinted with fond memory. "When the sun caught the marble cladding, it sparkled like jewels. Could be seen for miles. The architecture on Earth Home never did that. Sun too weak, I s'pose." He shook himself. "Anyway. Can't stand round nattering all morning. The drivers will be here any mo'. Maybe see you later."

Milandra watched him walk towards the row of red buses, feeling as melancholic as Wilson had sounded while he recounted his memories.

In marked contrast to the dry, cold weather holding sway in the south of the British Isles, the north was buffeted by strong winds and rain sweeping in from the North Sea. The hotel entrance door rattled in its hinges and rain dashed against the windows like hurled gravel.

Ceri and Tom sat on stools by the bar, shooting uncertain glances at each other. Peter sat next to them, tucking into a plate of fried meat and beans. Diane Heidler stood the other side of the bar, cooking more food.

When Ceri had come downstairs after a deep, alcohol-fuelled sleep, Tom was already down, sitting next to Peter at the bar. Diane had been cooking Peter's food and was now preparing theirs.

Apart from Peter wishing her good morning and informing her breakfast would not be long—"Diane's a dab hand with the frying pan"—nobody had spoken.

She watched the woman divide the meat and beans between two plates, and wordlessly slide them across the bar to her and Tom. Ceri cleared her throat.

"Er, thank you," she said.

"Yes," said Tom. "Thank you… um…"

He shot Ceri another glance. Neither of them picked up their forks.

Diane raised one eyebrow. "Would you like me to taste it first?"

Ceri felt herself colour. "Don't be silly." She picked up her fork and dug it into the beans. With only the slightest hesitation, she brought the fork to her mouth and began to eat. "Mmm, it's good."

Diane looked at Tom, who still hadn't touched his food.

"Can I ask you one more question?" he said.

Diane sighed. "If you must."

"Now you're better, do you intend staying with us?"

She didn't drop her gaze from Tom's. "If you're willing for me to stay." She shrugged. The gesture didn't seem quite as irritating to Ceri this morning. "After what happened with Bishop, I can't go back to London."

Tom seemed to consider her for a long moment. Then he pointed. "Would you do me a favour, please? Pass the tomato sauce."

When they had cleared their plates and sipped at scalding mugs of black tea, Ceri lit a cigarette and sighed.

"That's better," she said. "I needed that food to soak up all the vodka I put away last night. You're not eating, Diane?"

Diane had come around the bar to sit next to Peter.

"I ate before you came down," she said. "Now I'm almost fully recovered, I don't need much sleep. After a few more days, I won't need to sleep at all."

She did indeed look to be fully healed of her wounds. All traces of frailty had gone and her face had lost its gauntness.

Ceri waited until both Peter and Diane were looking away, before mouthing to Tom, "Shall we tell them?"

Tom frowned. "Tell them what?" he mouthed back.

"The guns."

His frown grew deeper in what Ceri had started to recognise as his deep thought expression. Then he shrugged as if to say, 'Why not?'

He turned on his stool to face Peter and Diane, and cleared his throat.

"I was thinking," he began. "There's a shooting club not far away. It might be a good idea to arm ourselves."

Diane spoke first. "Who you gonna shoot?"

Tom gave a nervous laugh. "Well, no one I hope. Although if more like Bishop come after us, I'd like to be able to shoot back."

"I don't think they'll bother sending anyone else after us," said Peter. "They'll have other things on their minds."

"I hope you're right," said Tom. "But I think I'd feel a little less vulnerable with a gun by my side."

Peter nodded. "Actually, I don't think that's a bad idea. I don't want to carry a gun..." He glanced at Diane, who shook her head emphatically. "Diane and I can defend ourselves against dogs and other local wildlife without firearms."

"Other local wildlife?" said Ceri.

"Without any people around, who knows how animals like deer, horses and cows might behave. They might take a fancy to trampling over any humans they do encounter. Revenge for centuries of oppression." Peter grunted. "You don't want to be facing a pissed-off stag without any form of defence. Diane and I can protect you if we're with you, but when we're not you need something in case."

Ceri had started to smile at the thought of being savaged by a sheep, but it quickly faded when she imagined a bull charging at her or a stallion rearing over her, clipping her head with its hooves. She shuddered. "Maybe it is a good idea, after all." She glanced at Tom. "I wasn't enthusiastic when you mentioned it. Think I was wrong."

"Where is this shooting club?" asked Peter.

Tom pulled the leaflet he'd shown Ceri from his pocket and handed it to Peter. "It's actually a hotel. Used to be a castle by the looks of it. But they do, or *did*, clay pigeon shooting and target rifle shooting."

"Doesn't look far," said Peter, skimming the leaflet. "Maybe fifteen minutes' drive. Have either of you ever shot a gun before?"

"No," said Ceri. "Unless you count an air rifle at Porthcawl fairground."

"I've tried clay pigeon shooting," said Tom. "I wasn't very good. The bruise on my shoulder from the recoil took a week to fade."

"Hmm." Peter handed the leaflet back. "It looks as though there'll be small-bore rifles, probably .22 calibre, and shotguns at this hotel. I'd recommend you each get shotguns. Accuracy will be slightly less important and shells will be easier to come by."

"Okay," said Tom. "Will you come with us, Peter? Be on hand to advise?"

"Of course. Nothing much else to do in this weather. We'll need to find a hardware shop first to get some bolt cutters and maybe a crowbar or some sort of jimmy. The guns should be securely locked away. You coming for a ride, Diane?"

"Why not? One thing, though…" She glanced at Tom and Ceri. "You do realise guns won't do you any good in the long run?"

Tom grimaced and Ceri felt her stomach give a small lurch.

"Yes," she said. "We do realise that." She smiled sweetly at Diane. "But, please, don't ever hesitate to remind us we've only got five months left to live."

Chapter Seven

Although the sun rode high in a pale, clear sky, the temperature did not rise above freezing. Frost still dusted the pavements and roads, and their breath steamed in the frigid air. Bri tucked her hands into the pockets of the ski jacket, glad of its warmth.

"You okay?" she asked Will.

"Yeah," he said. "This jacket don't 'alf stink, but it's warm. As warm as toast." His brow crinkled into a frown.

"What's wrong?"

"Nothing. It's just… Warm as toast. It's what me mum used to say."

"My mum used to say, 'as snug as a bug in a rug'." She reached out and squeezed his arm before thrusting her hand back into her jacket pocket.

They were standing on the pavement outside the house where they had spent the night. All Bri could see from here was row upon row of houses. She nodded at the street in front of them.

"The sun rose from behind those houses this morning," she said, "so that must be east." She turned around and held out her left arm. "That's south-west, the direction we need to take. Can you ride a bike?"

"Course I can," said Will. "I'm not a kid."

"Then we'll have to look out for a couple. I don't fancy walking all the way to Cornwall." She sighed. "It'll take too long to look in every house or garage or shed we pass. Most of them'll be locked anyway. A cycle shop is what we need. Get ourselves some brand-new wheels. Some fancy ones."

Will smiled and the last trace of his frown disappeared.

"For now, though," said Bri, "walking it'll have to be."

Bri felt, although didn't voice it, they would have to walk for quite some way before they found a shopping centre that might have a cycle shop. She had been blinded by driving flakes of snow when she turned off the main road she had been following into

London, and could not recall passing anything other than houses. She assumed any shops servicing this residential district lay behind them, to the east. The last direction she wanted to go.

The longer they remained here, on the edge of London, the more uneasy she became. Nothing she could put her finger on precisely, but it had to do with whatever had happened to her after her memories of *before* ended and with whatever had been done to Will to make him almost catatonic. Not to mention the sense of invasion of her mind in Looe, which had implanted the compulsion to come to London in the first place. On top of all that, her newfound abilities to calm angry dogs and apparently heal brain-damaged young boys gave her the jitters. She tried not to think about them. Doing so would likely only bring back her headache; it lay just below the surface of her consciousness like a circling shark.

They walked side by side, sticking to the pavement from instinct. Bri noted with satisfaction that Will showed no trace of a limp. Judging from the height of the sun, it was around noon and at least five daylight hours remained to put some distance between themselves and London. The cut to Will's calf did not look as though it would delay them in any way. She didn't know this area, but figured they would easily find a town or village within ten or twelve miles where they could find somewhere to spend the night. And tomorrow they would find a larger town, where they could sort out transport.

A little preoccupied with her thoughts, Bri didn't notice the rats until Will stopped dead in his tracks and gasped.

"What…?" she began, but tailed off when she saw what Will was looking at.

They had almost reached the end of the road. About twenty yards ahead it entered another street running across it at right angles. From around the corner, on the same side of the pavement where they stood, came a pack of brown rats. Three or four abreast, around thirty strong, the rats ran in close formation. The first thought which popped into Bri's mind was that they moved together as though trained to do so, like circus rats, if there was such a thing.

She stepped into the road to get out of their path. Will did the same a moment before the lead rats reached them. His groping hand grabbed Bri's and clutched it fiercely. Completely ignoring the humans, the rats continued along the pavement, neither swerving nor paying the least bit of attention to anything they passed.

"Where are they going?" Will whispered, as if afraid to speak too loudly in case the rats heard him and turned around. Bri suspected he could hail the rats with a megaphone and they wouldn't twitch a whisker, so intent had they been on whatever purpose drove them.

"I have no idea." She, too, kept her voice low. "But I don't like it. Stick close."

Will did not release his grip on her hand. They stepped back onto the pavement and continued to the junction, keeping tight to the walls and hedges on their right.

They reached the garden wall of the last house and stopped. Bri let go of Will's hand and raised her finger to her lips. She pointed to the adjacent street and motioned she would take a peek. Will nodded.

Knees bent to bring her head above the level of the wall, Bri edged forward. Gradually, the next street came into view. Walking down the centre of the road were three people: two men and a woman. One of the men was looking directly at her.

As she darted back out of sight, she heard a shout.

"Hey! You! Do not move!"

"Come on," she said, grabbing Will's hand. "Run!"

Gripping the strap of her backpack with her free hand to stop it bouncing around, Bri ran back the way they had come. If Will wondered what the hell was happening, he didn't waste breath asking her.

In any event, she would have struggled to explain why she felt such an overwhelming need to run. She had no idea who the approaching people were, but all her instincts clamoured not to go anywhere near them, and she was a girl who obeyed her instincts.

They had almost reached the point from which they'd started, the house where they had spent the night, when Bri felt a fluttering sensation inside her head and Will skidded to a halt. Her hand tugged briefly at his, but he relaxed his grip and her momentum carried her free.

She stopped running and turned. Will was standing statue-still, his face contorted into a grimace. Behind him, Bri could see the three people. They had turned the corner and were standing together, staring intently in their direction.

The fluttering sensation in her mind grew in intensity, became more insistent. Without thinking about it, Bri resisted, blocked it, and the fluttering disappeared like fingers snatched back on encountering a painful barrier.

While the three people conferred urgently with each other, Bri ran back to Will's side.

"What's wrong?" she hissed. "Is it your leg?"

"Ngh!"

She grabbed his shoulder. He felt stiff, like wood. Instantly, she was in his head, noticing the new change: a heavy, purple fog overlaid everything like a velvet drape. Paralysing him.

At the same time as she saw and understood the impediment, Bri knew how to remove it. The blanket she cast over Will's psyche was not white like the one she had used to calm the dogs, but the warm, clean yellow of a newly-bloomed daffodil on a bright spring day. It swirled onto and into the purple pall, dissipating, dissolving…

She left the yellow blanket there as she withdrew; it would protect him. Ignoring the fresh stabs of pain in her head, Bri glanced up the road. The three people were gazing at her, brows drawn, one of the men's mouth forming an O of surprise. Without waiting for them to recover their poise, Bri grabbed Will's hand. He gripped it back.

"Are you okay?" she asked, the words tumbling over one

another in her haste.

"Yes."

"Let's move."

They broke into a run. Nearing the gate of the house they'd left only a few minutes ago, Bri had an idea. She swerved into the garden and up the path. Before flinging open the door, she risked another glance.

The people were on the move, sprinting down the road towards them. The woman and one of the men each clutched a dark object. With a start, Bri recognised the objects as handguns.

"Oh shit!" she muttered. "Inside. Quick!"

Within moments, they stood inside the familiar hallway. While Bri drew the bolts across, Will thrust the handle upwards and locked the door. He yanked out the key and threw it towards the stairs. As they ran through the living room to the kitchen, Bri glanced outside. The people had reached the house. The woman was peering at the window and levelling her gun.

"Shit shit shit…" muttered Bri, but they were already in the kitchen.

A report like a firecracker sounded behind them, followed closely by a crunch and a thud like a fist hitting a punchbag.

Will unlocked the back door, using the key protruding from the lock, and stooped to undo the bottom bolt.

"Bri," he said, "the top bolt. I can't reach."

Another report came from the direction of the living room. It was followed by the tinkle of breaking glass.

"Bri! The top bolt!"

She darted forward and slid back the bolt. Will fumbled at the key, trying to remove it from the lock.

"What are you doing?" she yelled. "There's no time!"

The key came free. Clutching it tightly in his hand, Will yanked the door open and they were outside. Will turned and pulled the door closed. He inserted the key, thrust up the handle and locked the door.

"Leave the key in the lock," said Bri, pulling him away. "In case they find a spare inside."

They ran down a path leading between two lawns to a close-panelled rear fence. The gate in the fence was bolted, but only once. It didn't look like the gate was much in use: the bolt was rusty. Bri had difficulty lifting it into a position where it could be slid open. She hissed in pain when one of her nails broke.

"Hurry, Bri." Will spoke quietly, but she couldn't mistake the note of panic in his voice. "They're in the kitchen."

At last the bolt moved upwards and Bri gripped it between her fingers. It slid back reluctantly with a metallic screech. Something sharp hit her cheek, making her cry out. She stared uncomprehendingly at the jagged hole which had appeared in the gatepost an inch to the side of her head.

The gate swung open and Will shoved her through the gap.

Another firecracker sounded and the gravel of the path beyond the gate kicked up in a puff of dust by their feet. Then they were running again, to their right, shielded from view by the fence.

They were in a narrow alleyway passing between the rear gardens of two rows of houses. At the same time Bri realised they were running east, she also understood that to have run to their left would have meant heading towards the street from which the people had emerged. Not knowing whether more people were making their way up that street, for now east was preferable.

They reached the end of the alley and skidded to a halt. Bri poked her head out and looked to the right so she could see the end of the street from which they had escaped. There was no sign of their pursuers, but they must surely have already left the house by the front window and be sprinting towards them.

"Left," she said, giving Will a push in that direction and taking to her heels after him.

Bri could see another side street ahead on the other side of the road.

"Cross over," she gasped to Will. "Down that street."

Without daring to look behind to see whether the three people had come into sight, Bri and Will darted between parked cars and into the side road. They raced to its end and into the next street. Halfway along was the opening to another alley which passed between the backs of two rows of terraced houses. Into it they ran.

They stopped midway down the alley, sheltered from view by high fences and skeletal trees. Bri shrugged off her backpack and sank to the ground, her back to a fence. Will joined her. Together they sat there panting, catching their breath. Bri could feel sweat cooling on her back and running down between her breasts. *So much for my shower* she thought ruefully.

Gradually their breathing became less laboured. Apart from the occasional snatch of bird song and the distant bark of a dog—she felt Will stiffen beside her at the sound—Bri could hear nothing. No shouts, no footsteps, no gunfire.

"Who were those people, Bri? Why were they trying to kill us?"

"I don't know. But they must have something to do with the damage to your mind. They did something to you just now so that you couldn't move. They tried the same on me, but it didn't work."

Bri felt a shy tugging on the sleeve on her jacket. Will was gazing up at her with a look of frank adoration.

"You saved me again," he said.

"Yeah, well," she said gruffly, "I guess I'm your guardian angel." She stood and yanked the backpack over her shoulder. "Right, back on your feet. We need to keep moving. I think we've lost those three, but there could be more like them. And if they can mess with our minds, maybe they can communicate with each other like in science fiction films. Telephony, or whatever it's called."

Will's eyes widened. He jumped to his feet.

"I'm ready," he said in a low voice.

"Okay. The direction I want us to go is back where we've come from. Don't look so scared; we *can't* go that way. Too risky. We could try to circle around, but we don't know how many of them there are. So, instead, we'll have to keep moving east. Maybe a little to the south, too. Put as much distance between us and them as we can. Then tomorrow we can head due south, get out of London that way. Perhaps make for the coast." She shrugged. "We can worry about tomorrow in the morning. For now, let's get our arses away from here."

And so they weaved their way through West London, ducking down alleys and lanes and side streets, scaling fences and walls, crossing gardens and allotments and back yards, slowing to walking pace when they had little energy remaining, jogging when they could, but always moving.

Within the first couple of hours, they spotted three or four groups of rats moving in that organised, purposeful way. Whichever direction the rats had come from, Bri took Will in another.

Once they ducked out of sight when a sound reached their ears that had not long ago been familiar, but which now seemed incongruous: the grumble of an idling engine. They crept forward, oh so cautiously, until they could peer over a wall to see. In the distance, outside a block of flats, a flatbed lorry stood by the side of the road. Milling around the lorry, moving in and out of the building, were around a dozen people. They were bringing items from the building and depositing them onto the back of the lorry. Bri and Will were too far away to make out clearly what most of the items were, but one was obviously, from the awkward way it was handled, a mattress. Some of the items, Bri realised with a gulp, might have been sheet-wrapped bodies. The people were dressed in drab-looking clothes and moved in the shambling, detached manner that had characterised Will's movements when Bri first met him.

Standing a little to one side, watching the people work but offering no assistance, were a man and a woman. Even from this distance, Bri could tell they were cleanly clothed. By each of their sides hung a dark object. Bri could not be sure, but thought the objects might be some sort of machine guns. She swallowed hard. They moved on, giving the building a wide berth.

They made their way through housing and industrial estates,

down tree-lined avenues, through deserted parkland. They passed shops, but none that appeared to sell bicycles. Later, they saw Underground stations with names Bri had never heard of: South Ealing, Hammersmith, High Street Kensington. She toyed briefly with the notion of descending beneath the streets of London, of working their way south, or even heading back west, below ground, safe from prying eyes. Then she thought of rats. If they had become so brazen above ground, what must it be like in the tunnels of the Underground, with no trains or lighting or people to confine the creatures to the margins? The platforms and concourses and escalator shafts, once brightly lit and alive with the constant bustle of mass human movement, ventilated by fans and the passage of trains, must now be dark and stifling, seething with the scurry and scrabble and squeak of thousand upon thousand of furry rodents, claws clicking on tiled floors, tails entwining like serpent lovers. Bri shuddered and dismissed the notion of going underground firmly from her mind.

After six hours or more, long after darkness had fallen, they felt safe enough from the risk of pursuit, or too tired to care any more, to find somewhere to hole up for the night.

By flickering candlelight, Will removed a splinter of wood from Bri's cheek. She dry-swallowed the last of the painkillers; they had drunk the last of their water an hour before.

Physically exhausted and mentally drained, they fell asleep side by side on a cold, hard floor. They had travelled miles as Bri had intended, but in the opposite direction from the one she had wanted them to go. When they awoke the next day, they would find that far from leaving London behind, they had travelled deep into its heart.

Old Ben's log cabin was cold and draughty. The tin stove standing in the centre of the pressed dirt floor gave off fierce heat that was immediately lost through gaps in the walls and roof. Rain and meltwater entered through the same gaps, giving the interior a smell like old cellars. In one corner, a pale grey fungus pointed to the ceiling like a dead finger.

Zach sought isolation, not squalor and deprivation. He possessed the means to make improvements and he didn't hold back.

Although warped and weathered, the timbers forming the walls of the cabin were sound so he left them alone. He insulated the cabin with materials fitted with a wind- and water-proofed outer membrane, and set ventilation ducts high in the walls, under the eaves and out of the wind. He replaced the timber roof with felt and tile, lagged and boarded from within.

He used timber from trees he cleared around the cabin to erect more outbuildings to house a modern privy (after years of squatting behind trees while on the road, Zach valued the relative comfort and privacy so provided), his pick-up truck, an oil-powered generator, and supplies of gasoline and oil.

He constructed a timber-framed greenhouse in which he cultivated fruit and vegetables during the long winter months, before transplanting the hardier species to a vegetable patch enjoying full sunshine during the summer.

He replaced the ill-fitting doors and windows with custom-made security units, the glass double-glazed and tinted, the door capable of withstanding attack from a sledge hammer.

Cold water was pumped via a filter to a faucet housed over a Belfast sink inside the cabin. Hot water was heated by the log-burning range with which Zach replaced the tin stove. The range catered for all his cooking requirements, simple as they were.

He paid skilled tradesmen to carry out much of the installation work and studied what they were doing with such grim concentration that one or two of the workmen seemed a little put out, though none dared mention anything to his face. If Zach noticed their discomfort, he ignored it. He watched and noted and learned so if anything went wrong with any of the installations, he would be able to fix it himself. And so he became largely self-sufficient. He still needed to take a monthly trip to town to stock up on supplies of grain and fuel and beer (though never bourbon or other hard liquor), ammunition for his rifle and reading materials for long winter evenings. He needed to buy batteries for his radio, at least until he replaced it with a clockwork model. Occasionally, he needed to replace worn clothes or boots, or broken tools, or light bulbs. He sometimes needed spare parts for the generator or pump. But everything needing to be replaced or repaired he did himself. Once the initial work on the land and cabin had been completed, he never again summoned a workman to his property.

Zach learned to bake his own bread. He laid traps for rabbits. He hunted deer and elk and bear. He supplemented his dwindling savings by selling furs and surplus fresh produce in town.

Dwindling they might have been, but his savings sustained his meagre needs for over forty years. He erected a fence around his land and a sturdy gate. He did nothing to improve the condition of the access track or to discourage undergrowth to encroach upon it in spring and summer, partly concealing it.

Aside from his monthly trips to town, when he interacted with local people only in as much as was necessary to conduct his business, and less frequent visits to Augusta to satisfy another need, Zach Trent cut himself off from the world. He did not contact the closest thing he had to a friend, the lawyer Mr Benton. For all Zach knew, Mr Benton had died many years ago. If not, he must now be dead from the Millennium Bug that had seen fit, for reasons at which he could not even begin to guess, to spare Zach.

Although he did not often listen to news reports on his radio, preferring light music or comedy shows, Zach could not avoid hearing about the spread of the virus that was killing indiscriminately and by the thousand at first, then by the million, and finally by the billion. He had fallen ill, laid low by a sweating, shaking fever that he thought must spell his end. He retired to bed, ready to look his maker in the eye, and perhaps to spit in it. It was more to a feeling of great surprise than relief that he awoke, weak and stinking and thirsty, but alive.

While he recovered his strength, an incident that had struck him as a little peculiar at the time, but had almost passed from his mind, played on his thoughts.

It had been a week or two before Christmas and Zach had gone into town to stock up for the festive season. Not that he celebrated the religious aspects of the holiday, but used the occasion as an excuse to spoil himself a little with chocolate and a fat cigar. And maybe an extra crate of beer.

As usual, he had pulled up in front of the hardware store where he would transact most of his business. It was as he climbed out of the pick-up that he noticed the woman. Ordinarily, he kept his gaze cast down so as not to make eye contact with anyone and prompt an attempt at conversation. But that morning he paused beside his vehicle, head raised, watching her.

It wasn't the woman's looks which caught his eye. She was of unremarkable height and build, middle-aged, hair shoulder-length and mousey. It was the way she was behaving. An open shoulder bag hung by her hip and she dipped her hand inside frequently while she made her way past the row of storefronts. She approached each store and grabbed the handle of each door as though about to enter, but then walked on as if she had changed her mind at the last moment. At the bank, she stopped in front of the ATM and dipped her hand into her bag. Zach did not notice her insert her bank card into the machine or withdraw any bills or statements, but she nevertheless pressed every button of the pad before moving to the door of the bank and briefly clutching the handle.

Now and again, she would wander away to the wooden rail bounding the boardwalk in front of the stores. There she would pause, lightly gripping the rail, running her fingers along it almost playfully. Her features were plain, nondescript, but she gazed off into some unseen distance, a hint of a smile playing at the corners of her mouth. In those moments, in the pale December morning, she looked angelic.

Then she turned back to the stores and was in front of him, grasping the handle of the door to the hardware store. This time she did not change her mind, but pulled the door open and entered. Zach hurried up the steps to the boardwalk and followed her in.

The familiar smells of paint and creosote and wood shavings assailed his nostrils. The interior, as usual, was not well lit and he stood for a moment inside the doorway, allowing his vision to adjust to the gloom.

He noticed her immediately. She was wandering among the shelves, picking up items apparently at random then replacing them. Tools, cans, packaging, she seemed intent on touching objects for the sake of touching them.

As she approached the door to leave, Zach found he couldn't bring himself to lower his gaze in his customary fashion, but continued to watch her. The woman halted before him and stared up into his face.

Zach was distantly aware of a faint scratching somewhere. It sounded crazy, but he had been sure at the time and he was sure now with hindsight: the 'somewhere' was inside his head. The woman's eyes widened; then her features softened. She regarded him with something akin to pity.

"Never mind, honey," she said gently. "All the pain will soon disappear."

The woman raised her hand to Zach's cheek and caressed it. Befuddled by the sensation in his head, Zach did not obey his instinct to shy away from her touch. By the time he thought to do so, she had dropped her hand, stepped past him and disappeared out of the door. When he emerged a few minutes later, clutching his purchases, she had gone from sight.

Once or twice on the drive home, Zach raised a hand to his cheek where she had touched him.

That night, he heard on the radio the first reports of a strange virus which had killed some people in Los Angeles and Sydney, Australia. A day or two later, he was coughing and shivering, and the weak December light had become too bright.

In the hours before he retired to what he assumed would be his death bed, Zach listened to the radio when it became apparent that what they had taken to calling the Millennium Bug was a full-blown pandemic of epic proportions. While civilisation teetered on the brink and slowly toppled, airtime was given over to an increasingly zealous-sounding string of people propounding weird and wonderful theories of why the Millennium Bug had been visited upon humankind. Most of these theories were so outlandish as to make him laugh, despite his growing sense of doom, but there was one that struck a chord and made him think again of the woman in the hardware store.

"… cannot prove it, but I believe the Millennium Bug was started deliberately," said the earnest voice of the theorist, a young-sounding male.

"*Deliberately*?" said the incredulous voice of the talk-show host. "But how? By whom? And why?"

"How is probably the easiest of your questions to answer," said the theorist. "There are many possible methods, from infecting water supplies to releasing spores into the air on a windy day. But the most likely to my mind is to manufacture the virus in the form of an organic powder, one that can be spread by contact. Of course, that only works if you have sufficient disciples to be able to spread the powder globally. Which brings us on to your next question—by whom? Extreme right-wing cults are the most likely suspects, though I have heard speculation it might be aliens…"

Zach had stopped listening at that point. His mind was replaying the scene: the woman dipping her hand into her bag and touching things. Touching him…

When Zach pulled out of his brush with the Millennium Bug, he was probably more fortunate than many other survivors, if there were any. His electricity and water supplies still worked. He had fresh food in his greenhouse and a stock of preserved foods in his pantry.

He had fully recovered, been out and shot a deer, when it happened. He was sitting on a log behind the cabin, skinning the buck and musing on whether to take a trip into town to see what supplies he could salvage, and whether indeed there were any other survivors around—the answer to this question wasn't a burning issue as far as Zach was concerned, but he was curious nonetheless—when he felt the same scratching sensation inside his head he had experienced in the hardware store when the woman stopped and stared at him. This time, the sensation was stronger; he could *hear* the scratching, like fingernails scraping the inside of his skull. With a low moan, he dropped the knife and raised bloody hands to his temples.

Do not seek out others said the voice. Zach glanced wildly around, but there was nobody to be seen. *Remain where you are. Burn bodies. Do not seek out others.*

The only time Zach had obeyed orders was when he had been a grunt in 'Nam and even then he had privately resented being told what to do. This voice, wherever it had come from—he knew it had come from somewhere; he didn't believe he was mad despite evidence to the contrary—this voice was *compelling*.

Zach obeyed.

Chapter Eight

All five of them braved the wind and rain. Only Dusty seemed to enjoy it, scooting away to investigate a curious scent, reappearing with his tail wagging and tongue licking at raindrops on his muzzle. Nothing else moved on the streets, except blown litter and forlorn fairy lights swaying overhead in the gusts.

Peter pointed at a plaque attached to the wall of a building.

"Look. They have a small-bore rifle club here in town." They crossed the road and Peter tried the wooden door to the building. "Hmm. This door's sturdy and very firmly locked. Not sure how we'd break in. Probably have to ram it with something." He let go of the handle. "Doubt there's any shotguns in there. You don't want to be messing around with rifles, not with your lack of experience. You'll be better off with shotguns."

They moved on through the streets. The raucous cries of gulls sounded overhead and, in the distance, they could hear the rattle of spinnakers from the boats in the harbour.

The shops were all locked, many shuttered. If there had been any civil unrest in Wick during the last days of the plague, they saw no evidence.

After twenty minutes of trudging through the rain, Tom was beginning to feel damp in both body and spirit. He stopped. Ceri and Peter stopped, too, but Diane carried on walking.

"I don't think we're going to find a hardware shop," Tom said. "Is there even such a thing any more?"

"Not likely," said Ceri. "It's all charity shops and fast food bars these days."

"I think you may be right," said Peter. "Let's walk to the end of this street. If there's nothing, we'll try to find an out-of-town store."

"Hey, guys!" Diane had halted twenty yards ahead in front of a plate-glass window. "This place has tools."

Tom stayed outside with Dusty to keep him from cutting his

paws on broken glass, while the others entered the shop through one of the doors. Tom and Peter used a cast iron litter bin as a battering ram and it made short work of the plate glass of the door.

They emerged after ten minutes, carrying canvas tool bags.

"Got hammers, pincers, screwdrivers, chisels, rasps, hacksaws," Peter informed Tom.

"Bolt cutters?"

"Nope. Some powerful pliers, though, and a huge screwdriver we'll be able to exert a lot of leverage with. And I've got a cordless drill with some charge in the battery. Brought a load of spare batteries as well. If all else fails, we might be able to drill through any locks we encounter."

Peter handed him a bag. "We won't need to break into the camping shop. We found oil lamps and camping stoves that burn lumps of paraffin. There are enough in there to keep us going for weeks. They'll be useful if we decide to cross to Norway."

During the ensuing awkward pause, Ceri and Tom glanced at each other, while Diane looked on, bemused.

"That's a big 'if'," said Ceri.

"Norway?" said Diane with a frown of puzzlement. "You folks are thinking of going to Norway?"

"No," said Tom. "*Peter* is. *We're* not."

"Maybe now isn't the best time," said Peter.

"No," agreed Tom. "Let's get going. I want to call in that shop we passed which sells pet food."

Ceri stifled a giggle. "Except we'll have to bash the door in and our 'purchases' won't cost us a penny."

They also broke into a small supermarket and a clothes shop, and were heavily laden by the time they made it back to the hotel. They left the food—for person and dog—and the cooking equipment in the hotel kitchen. They each exchanged wet outer garments for dry ones they had brought back with them. The tools they loaded into the back of the Range Rover. The body of the vehicle was dented and scraped as a result of its encounter with a drystone wall in Herefordshire, but the engine and tyres were undamaged, and it still handled well according to Peter.

Tom took the passenger seat. Dusty sat in the middle of the rear seat, between the two women, but curled up tightly against Ceri with his head on her lap. While he did not display open antagonism towards Diane, he seemed more wary of her than he was of Peter, and avoided her whenever he could.

Although unused for a few days, the engine started first time. Peter pulled away from the kerb and headed out of town.

"So," said Tom, addressing Peter. "This beacon thing, er, Stonehenge…?"

"What about it?"

"What is it?"

"It's a beacon."

"O-kay. Can you elaborate?"

Peter sighed. "It won't do you much good, but all right. When configured correctly, it will send out an electromagnetic pulse. A powerful one. It will be picked up by our people, who are making their way through the outer reaches of Earth Home's solar system as we speak. When they are free of that system's gravitational fields, they will hitch a ride on a, well, for want of a better word, a current. The pulse will ensure they leave the current in the correct solar system. It will also ensure they land on the correct planet. We almost chose the wrong one when we arrived." He uttered a short, humourless laugh.

"What will they have to do to configure it correctly?"

"Well, Stonehenge—the original one I saw constructed almost five thousand years ago—consisted of sixty-three stones, each with a strong electromagnetic potential. Bluestones they're known as."

"Are they the ones that came from the Preseli Mountains in West Wales?" asked Ceri from the back.

"The very same. When our craft landed in the Atlantic and we made our way to land, some of our people came ashore in West Wales. They discovered the stone on their way to Salisbury Plain.

After we had called the drones to us, we set them to quarrying and transporting the stones. It took many months."

"And we still speculate as to how they were transported," mused Tom. "Or at least we did. So how was it done? Wooden rollers? Rafts?"

"A combination of both," said Peter. "And a *lot* of manpower. There were many drones and our control over them was absolute."

"You could work them until they dropped?" asked Ceri, an edge to her voice.

"Yes," said Peter. "Be angry at me if you like, Ceri, but I'm not going to apologise for cruelty that took place five millennia ago to creatures you and Tom would barely recognise as human if you were to meet them today."

"Oh, that's all right then," said Ceri. "If they were only *creatures*…"

"Look," said Peter, "if you want to start debating the rights and wrongs of the way drones—"

Ceri pointedly cleared her throat.

"Okay," said Peter, "the way *humans* were treated back then, you'd better be ready to defend the way humans have treated animals and each other during the intervening years. Battery farming, slavery, genocide… Need I continue?"

"Back to this beacon," said Tom, before Ceri could respond. "The bluestones were brought to Salisbury from West Wales…"

"Yes," said Peter. "They were each upended into pits to form a circle."

"Why sixty-three? Is that some magical number?"

"There were sixty-three stones because sixty-three was sufficient to do the job."

"But I've been to Stonehenge," said Ceri. "The bluestones don't form a circle. They're dotted about between the other stones, you know, the huge ones placed on top of each other like goalposts. They've got a name. Begins with 's'."

"Sarsen stones," said Tom. He glanced back at Ceri and shrugged. "My class did a project on Stonehenge."

"What you say is true, Ceri," said Peter. "But the sarsen stones weren't brought to the site, from a quarry much nearer incidentally, until a few hundred years later. The bluestones were moved from their original positions at around the same time. It had nothing to do with us. The Beacon had served its purpose by then. Since we can't be certain the source of the pulse that was transmitted five millennia ago hasn't been lost or forgotten, we will need to send another to be sure."

"So how can we stop it?" asked Tom.

Peter took his eyes off the road for a moment to favour him with a look of incredulity. "We can't," he said. "We are four. They are almost five thousand. And they probably have control of at least that many humans."

"Not humans any longer," said Diane. Tom had almost forgotten she was with them. "All survivors who arrived in London have been treated so our control over them is once more complete. Whether Ceri and Tom like the expression or not, they are nothing now but drones."

"Yes," said Peter. "And there is nothing we can do against so many."

"But surely," said Tom, "they won't all need to go to Stonehenge to do whatever they have to do to get it working again."

"Maybe. I don't know."

"Actually," said Diane, "Tom's probably right. They only need take sufficient drones to reposition the stones and to reactivate the Beacon. And only sufficient of our people to control the drones."

"That'll still be too many for us to be able to interfere," said Peter. "Way too many."

"We could get a tank," said Tom. "Machine guns. Hand grenades. Missile launchers. There must be tons of this stuff lying around waiting for us to pick it up. Wait! We could probably get hold of a nuclear warhead. Blow them all to hell while they're gathered in one place."

The vehicle slowed to an abrupt halt. Ceri gasped from the

back and Dusty uttered a soft whine.

"Sorry," muttered Peter. He turned to face Tom. "Can you hear yourself? Tanks? Missile launchers? Nuclear bombs? Even if they were simply lying around, which they most certainly won't be, do you seriously think we'd know how to use them? I was in the merchant navy, Tom, the *merchant* navy. I've not fired a gun since 1945 and that was a bolt-action Enfield. And you're a schoolteacher, Tom. A schoolteacher. Not bloody Rambo!"

Tom felt his face reddening under Peter's onslaught. He opened his mouth to say something, though he was not sure what, but Peter hadn't finished.

"And Ceri," Peter said, turning to gesture towards her. "Ceri's a school dinner lady. You want to stick a rocket launcher in her hands and send her up against a couple of thousand people? Armed people, at that. Diane and I can protect you to a point against their mind control, but we can't stop their bullets from cutting you in half. Which only leaves Diane. Unless she's trained in modern guerrilla warfare…?" Peter glanced at her.

Diane shook her head. "Can't stand guns," she said. "They frighten me."

"With good reason," Peter said. "Tom, I said it was a good idea for you and Ceri to arm yourselves—and it is—but for protection against animals. Not so you can take it into your head to launch some sort of charge of the light brigade. Seriously, you need to dismiss such thoughts right now. Or I'm going to have second thoughts about helping you to find weapons."

Tom chewed on his bottom lip, the gesture a throwback to when he was a child being scolded. His mind churned with possible retorts, but ultimately he knew Peter was right. He let out a deep breath.

"I don't know what I was thinking." His shoulders sagged. "I feel so helpless. I want to be able to *do* something. I don't want to sit around for the next five months waiting to die."

He felt a hand squeeze his shoulder. Ceri had leaned forward, tears glistening in her eyes. He laid his hand on top of hers and squeezed back.

"Okay," said Peter, the anger gone from his voice. He gestured through the windscreen. "There's your castle. Let's go find your guns."

The man, whose name was Luke, had washed and changed out of his blood-stained clothes. He stood before Milandra and the Deputies, scrubbed and shiny, rocking a little from foot to foot as though uncomfortable under their scrutiny.

"Please, sit," said Milandra, nodding to a nearby chair.

Luke sat and folded his hands in his lap.

"Tell us what happened," said Milandra.

He cleared his throat. "I was out on patrol this morning." He spoke with a hint of eastern European accent: 'was' sounded like 'voz'. "Three of us in a team. Looking for rats. And, wow, we didn't have to look too hard. They are everywhere!"

Simone giggled. "They're pouring into the Burning Fields and running into the bonfire." She clapped her hands like an excited schoolgirl. "The smell is like, phooey, but you can hear them exploding. They sound like popcorn. Can I go back soon?"

Milandra glanced at the Chosen and tried to mask her irritation. "It is important we all hear this, Simone. Once we've digested what Luke has to tell us, then maybe." She turned back to Luke and nodded. "Please, continue."

"We started not far from here, in West... pardon me, I forget the name."

"West Drayton," said Grant.

"Ah, yes," said Luke. "West Drayton. Thank you. We had only been out for a few hours and had already encountered two, maybe three hundred rats. They are easy to control with three of us working together. Even the largest group—you say 'pack', like 'rat pack', yes?—of fifty or sixty creatures presented no difficulty. We took over their minds, such basic organs, yet filled with greed and cunning, and sent them to the Burning Fields."

"Yes?" prompted Milandra.

"We had sent a pack of thirty away when I saw the girl. She was watching me from behind a garden wall in the road to our left. The same road we had sent the rats into. When she saw I had noticed her, she ducked out of sight.

"I told my companions what I had seen and I think I shouted to the girl to stay where she was. We hurried to the corner so we could look down the road. There were two, the girl and a boy, running away from us."

"How old were they?" asked Wallace.

"Not easy to say," said Luke. "We did not get close enough to see them clearly, but I estimate the girl was between fourteen and sixteen. The boy, twelve. Maybe younger."

"Why didn't you get close enough?" asked Lavinia. "Why not combine psyches and force them to stop?"

"That is precisely what we did," answered Luke. "Or tried to. It worked on the boy. He stopped running. But the girl…" He frowned.

Milandra had been filled in on the gist of what Luke would be telling them, but was hearing it from Luke himself for the first time. She felt a sensation deep in her stomach, like something alive waking up, and it took a moment to recognise it. Excitement. Not dread or sorrow as she had experienced, although was still reluctant to admit even to herself, when sending the signal to release the virus. Pure excitement, that maybe something good was about to happen.

"What about the girl?" she asked, keeping her tone soft and neutral.

"The girl resisted. Completely."

"So?" That was Lavinia. "There were only three of you and you were already controlling the boy." She shrugged. "Humans are still strong enough to keep us out unless we heavily outnumber them."

"There is more to tell," said Luke. "Then it may not be so clear." He looked at Milandra, who nodded for him to continue. "When she realised the boy could not move, the girl ran back to him and…" He paused and took a deep breath. "She did something. I don't know what. But in the next instant, we had been expelled from the boy. We tried to go back, but could not. His mind was no longer open to us. The girl had blocked it."

There was a moment's silence.

Wallace broke it. "No way. That's impossible, man. Freaking impossible."

Luke held out his hands, palms upwards. "When the impossible happens, it is no longer the impossible." His gaze locked with Milandra's once more. "There is something else…"

Milandra nodded. The feeling of excitement was growing. She sensed the others were experiencing it, too, though perhaps not in quite the same way as she.

"For the few moments we were in the boy's psyche," said Luke, "I could see he had been subjected to the electrical process that makes drones easier to manage. But the evidence was faint, like a scar that marks human skin after an old surgical procedure." He took another deep breath. "The electrical process had been reversed. Not entirely, as shown by the scars, but there is no doubt what has happened. The other two members of my team are in full accord. The boy's mind has been healed."

"Holy shit," muttered Grant.

"Humans can't do that, can they?" That was Simone in her best silly little girl's voice. "Are you sure she's not one of us?"

Wallace turned on her. "You know as well as anyone we don't emerge as young-looking as fifteen or sixteen or anything-else-teen. For fuck's sake, Simone, if you're going to ask a question, try to make it half-intelligent."

Simone opened her mouth to retort, but Milandra could not face that high-pitched warble again.

"Leave it, Simone. I don't agree with George's choice of words—he has never been the diplomat. I do, however, agree with his sentiment. Now, let's hear the rest of Luke's tale without interruption."

It didn't take long. Luke recounted how the two humans had

taken to their heels again and disappeared into a nearby house, locking the door behind them. The female member of his team, Olga, had shot in the double-glazed front window with her pistol, but had badly cut herself in gaining entry to the property.

"As she was stepping through the opening, she slipped." Luke grimaced. "The glass that remained in the window frame was jagged and sharp. It cut deep."

Luke and the other man had squeezed past their stricken team-mate and arrived at the back exit in time to let off a couple of shots at the fleeing humans through the thickly paned glass of the kitchen window, but the girl and boy scurried down an alley that ran behind the back garden. By the time Luke and his colleague had staunched the worst of Olga's bleeding and returned to the street, the humans had disappeared.

"Olga had weakened considerably through loss of blood," said Luke, "but we nevertheless managed to *send* a message to every other team in the vicinity, warning them to be alert for the humans and to shoot them on sight. Nobody else saw them." He shrugged. "There are many places to hide in London."

"And Olga?" asked Milandra. "Is she okay?"

"She will be," said Luke. "We had to sacrifice a drone from a clean-up crew. She was losing blood faster than she could replace it. She needed fresh blood, and energy, before her heart and brain started to shut down."

"Slurp, slurp, slurp," said Simone, and tittered.

Luke regarded the Chosen with a carefully guarded expression. Milandra suspected he found her a little distasteful, but was unsure about revealing his true feelings. Quickly, she cleared her throat.

"So we lost a drone, but saved Olga?"

Luke nodded. He looked relieved to be distracted from Simone. "She is undergoing intensive solar treatment, but will fully recover."

Milandra recalled the Commune, when she had joined with almost five thousand other minds and called the survivors of mainland Britain to London, before spreading the net worldwide to persuade survivors outside Britain to remain where they were and not seek out other survivors. It had left her so drained not even copious amounts of food could fully replenish her energy reserves. Jason Grant had done the trick by rigging up a sunlamp to a series of car batteries and she had bathed in the warm, white glow until the batteries ran out. The lamp still stood in a corner of the hotel suite. Jason had reattached the plug and now the hotel's electrical systems were running from a diesel-powered generator, the lamp was ready to use in need. She suspected the need might soon arise.

"Okay," she said. "Thank you." She glanced around at the Deputies. "Does anyone have any questions to ask Luke?"

"I have plenty of questions," said Wallace. "Like how in the heck did this girl, a *drone*, shield the boy from the team's probing? And did *she* heal the mind of the boy? How can this be?"

Lavinia murmured in agreement. Grant nodded thoughtfully. Only Simone didn't react; she was staring off into space as though her part in the proceedings was done.

"Well, those are questions we'd all like answers to," said Milandra, "but I doubt Luke knows them."

Luke shook his head.

"I'd like each of us to give some thought to what we've heard here this afternoon," continued Milandra. "We'll meet again this evening when we can bounce ideas off of each other. Luke, if you think of anything that might explain this, come straight to me or to one of the Deputies."

He nodded and shifted in his seat as if to stand.

Milandra held up her hand to indicate he should remain seated. "I want to ask you a favour," she said. "With your permission, I'd like to see for myself the encounter with the two humans."

Luke shrugged. "No problem."

"Good." She turned to the Deputies. "There's no need for any of you to remain. Let's meet back here at, say, eight o'clock."

Three heads nodded in assent.

"Simone?"

"Huh? Oh, yeah, sure. Eight o'clock. I'm gonna watch rats pop till then." Milandra frowned and Simone rolled her eyes. "I can think just as well about the drones in the Burning Fields."

Milandra sighed. "Okay. But I'll expect you to come up with at least one idea as to how the girl might have healed the boy."

"Jeez. It's like being in school."

Lavinia snorted. "How would you know what being in school's like?"

Simone grinned. "True. Till later."

She stood and trotted from the room. The three other Deputies filed out after her.

Milandra turned back to Luke.

"That Simone…" she said.

"Yes," said Luke. "Is she always so infantile?"

Milandra smiled. *So you can't see it's an act?* she thought. "Back to what happened," she said. "Are you sure…?"

"Of course."

"Thank you."

Milandra *reached*. As the Keeper, she didn't need Luke's permission to probe his mind, but saw no need to be invasive without the subject's consent. Besides, having a willing subject made the process easier and quicker.

With a skill honed over many centuries, Milandra located the memory and ran it, watching closely as though she were viewing a reel playing on a cinema screen.

A girl's head ducking behind a wall; a longer view down a house-lined street with two small figures running into the distance, holding hands; both wearing bulky jackets that hid their builds; a knapsack bouncing up and down on the taller figure's back; the smaller of the two coming to a halt and the girl turning to face Milandra's viewpoint. The perplexed faces of Luke's companions came into view while they hurriedly conferred.

Milandra studied the girl's face as she returned to the boy's side. Too far away to make out her features clearly, but Milandra thought Luke's estimate of the girl's age was about right. Some sort of mark spoiled the clear lines of the girl's brow: a wound of some sort, maybe a lump? The girl gripped the boy's shoulder and seemed to be studying him intently. Then she glanced towards Luke and his companions. Now Milandra was certain the girl had suffered an injury to her forehead. Even at this distance, it stood out like a molehill on a bowling green.

The girl grabbed the boy by the hand and they spoke briefly. She turned and together they ran. At this level of probing, Milandra could only view the memory; to experience what Luke was feeling, she would have to delve deeper into his mind. That would not be necessary. She could imagine how dumbfounded Luke and his companions would have felt at how easily the girl had shaken off the mental shackles with which they had bound the boy.

The memory wound on and Milandra watched until the young pair had run into a house and slammed the door behind them.

She withdrew.

Luke was watching her closely. "What does it mean, Milandra?"

She shook her head slowly. "Quite honestly, I don't know." She stood. "Thank you for your help, Luke. Please, if you see Olga, pass on my best wishes for a full recovery."

After he had gone, Milandra considered what she had heard and seen. The sensation of excitement had faded, to be replaced by something else. An idea. It nagged at her, demanding her full attention, but she did not dare confront it head on. To do so would be to concede her feelings towards the surviving humans ran far deeper than mere sympathy. She wasn't yet ready to take that plunge.

Chapter Nine

The throngs of people that used to clog the centre of London had been replaced by pigeons. Gulls and crows and ravens, too, had taken over the tourist and shopping thoroughfares, feasting on waste and corpses. Rats and dogs, alone and in small packs, roved among the birds, fighting them for the choicest morsels. Cats stalked pigeons—quite successfully, judging by the number of headless, partly-chewed pigeon carcasses Brianne and Will passed—and spat at dogs.

Will stuck close to Bri's side, grasping tightly at her hand when any dogs came near. They were approached frequently, occasionally by an animal that seemed nothing more than inquisitive, sniffing in their direction, ears cocked, before moving on, but more often by dogs with bared teeth and bristling fur.

Acting almost subconsciously, unable to explain to Will when he asked how she did it, Bri enveloped herself in an aura extending perhaps two yards in all directions, one which told any encroaching creature, whether bird, rat, cat or dog, she was not to be messed with. Even the meanest looking dogs, those with wild eyes and slavering jaws, understood the message and slunk away with a whine.

Bri's head twanged when she first cast out this aura, but maintaining it seemed second nature and cost little in terms of mental effort. Thus her headache remained at bay, although she kept an eye open for a chemist where she could obtain a fresh supply of painkillers.

The number of corpses increased the closer they drew to the centre of the city. Some had already been torn apart by bird or beast. A few had decomposed to only skin and bone, held together by ragged clothes. Most were still in the process of decomposition, the cold weather delaying nature's relentless march. Bri and Will became, if not accustomed to the sight and stench of decay, inured to them. Although neither was keen to step too closely to a body, they stopped staring in stomach-churning fascination or averting their eyes in horror. They stopped clenching their nostrils in disgust.

Bri remained wary, but they had not seen any more packs of rats running in formation—what she thought of as 'trained rats'—and gradually she began to relax.

"I'm hungry," said Will, after they had been walking for an hour.

"Me, too." Bri shrugged her right shoulder to indicate the backpack. "I want to keep all the food we've got in case we need it later. We'll find a place soon. There seem to be plenty of shops ahead."

They were walking down a silent street, lined each side by tall buildings, some as high as six storeys. The road was empty except for the occasional abandoned vehicle. Ahead of them, strung across the road between buildings, they could make out rows of giant Christmas baubles and snowflakes, expensive-looking, not gaudy.

"Wow," breathed Bri. "They must look quite a sight lit up. Where are we anyway? It's a bit posh around here."

Will stopped. He glanced around and a slow smile stole over his features. "I know where we are. This is Knightsbridge." He pointed ahead. "Harrods is just up the road. Mum used to bring me and Poppy." His smile faded. "We could never afford to buy anything. She used to like looking. 'Seeing 'ow the other 'alf live,' she used to say."

"Harrods…" Unlike many of her friends, Bri hadn't been one for make-up and jewellery. She had always preferred surfing on the ocean to surfing online for clothes, but nevertheless an image popped into her mind with the clarity of a memory: her posing in a designer ballgown, a diamond tiara twinkling on her head, rubies dripping from her neck. *You might be sixteen*, she told herself, *but you're never too old to dress up*.

She glanced at Will. He was gazing up at her, his smile returning. She grinned back.

"Shall we?" she said.

They didn't need to break in. Someone had beaten them to it. The glass in one of the entrance doors had been smashed and most of the jagged pieces removed. Trickles of black, long-dried blood smeared the remaining shards of glass and the doorframe. Inside, all was silent with no rotting corpse smell, but whoever had been in here had gone on a mini rampage. Their feet crunched broken perfume bottles which littered the ground floor and the faint scent of expensive perfume still hung in the air. Elsewhere, cases of jewellery designed by people most of Bri's friends would have heard of had been smashed, clothes seen on catwalks in New York and Milan torn from racks and thrown to the floor, gigantic pottery urns with two thousand pounds price tags hurled against the wall.

It didn't spoil their fun. For the rest of the morning, they forgot their peril and became as children again. The floors of Harrods echoed to their gleeful laughter.

Three hours later, stomachs full of tinned caviar, potted hare and luxurious sweets, they reluctantly left the store. Each was clad head-to-toe in new outfits, including water- and wind-proof jackets, and training shoes that alone would have cost more than Bri's dad used to earn in a week.

Will had acquired a backpack of his own. It bulged with gadgets and sweets. They included three new mobile phones, even though they had tried a few inside the store and not found a single network that was working. They each carried tins of fancy meats and fish, packets of biscuits and crackers, and bottles of mineral waters with French names.

Bri had dropped the bracelets and necklaces of pearls and emeralds and diamonds onto the counter with only a twinge of regret. She had kept only one item: a ridiculously expensive watch which ran off a battery guaranteed for ten years. All the battery-powered watches had told the same time, so she assumed it was correct.

They left Harrods at 12:34pm. If the date setting on the watch was also correct, it was the 16th of January. Bri had no idea what day of the week it was. She didn't suppose it mattered one jot.

"Which way shall we go?" she asked, when they stood once more in the open air. The wind had freshened and she felt glad of the jacket. She pulled her new hat down a little tighter around her ears, wincing when the material moved across the lump on her forehead.

"Have you ever seen Buckingham Palace?"

She shook her head. "Never been to London before so never seen the Houses of Parliament or Nelson's Column or Big Ben."

Will grinned. "You can see them all if you want. I know the way from here. Past Hyde Park and down to the Palace. Then we can go to Trafalgar Square, down Whitehall and cross the river at Westminster Bridge. You can see the Eye, too." His face fell a little. "It won't be working though, I s'pose."

"Will we be heading south?"

"I think so. More or less. We'll end up in Lambeth."

"Oh, Will, we could spend the night in your flat..." She tailed off when she noticed his expression. "What's wrong?"

Sorrow and fear in equal measure clouded Will's face. He shook his head firmly and looked away when tears squeezed from the corners of his eyes.

"Will? It was only an idea. We don't have to go anywhere near... Oh." Bri raised her hand to her mouth as realisation hit home. "Is it your mum and sister? Are they still there, in the flat?"

Will nodded. Bri stepped forward and threw her arms around his thin shoulders. She held him tightly until he stopped quivering.

He pulled away, wiping his eyes on the sleeve of his jacket.

"Don't worry, Bri," he said. His breath hitched as he choked back a last sob. "I know other places we can sleep where the dogs and rats can't get us. But I know of somewhere in Lambeth even better."

"What?"

"A cycle shop."

~ ~ ~

For three weeks, Zach Trent obeyed the voice that had spoken in his head without passing through his ears. Although his strength had returned as if he'd never been ill, he did not venture into town in search of fresh supplies or survivors. He only left his land to go into the hills, and then only far enough to bag fresh meat.

He was running low on oil for the generator and cartridges for his hunting rifle. He had read his supply of books and needed more. Without any radio channels to listen to—he tried tuning the radio every evening, but if somebody somewhere was broadcasting, he wasn't able to pick it up—books were his only source of entertainment. A few more cases of beer would also be welcome.

He wondered about the radio. If there were other survivors, he felt sure someone would be transmitting a message. Maybe he would pick up something if he had a CB receiver. Not that he would necessarily respond or go off in search of the broadcaster. Zach had found his version of Utopia here in the foothills. The fact that most, maybe all, of mankind had disappeared from the face of the Earth did not alter his needs or desires.

As the days passed, the compulsion not to stray lessened. Imperceptibly, happening unnoticed like the growth of a shoot, the bond forcing him to remain where he was loosened.

By the end of the third week, his rifle cartridges were all but gone. That was okay—he had his traps and his hunting knife, a nine-inch blade serrated on one edge and wickedly sharp on the other—except for one thing. Wolves had returned to Maine.

At least, one wolf.

For the past three nights he had awoken to howling. A lone voice, a scout maybe, calling to the pack. Signalling that the scent of man had gone from these mountains. Or nearly gone.

This night was no different. He awoke to pitch blackness, but did not switch on the lamp. He reached instead for the hunting knife that he kept within easy grasp. The howl rose and undulated like the wind of a storm. It was louder than the sound he had heard the previous three nights. Closer. The wolf was immediately outside the cabin.

Zach slipped out of bed and into clothes. Pants and sweater over his long johns. Enough to keep out the worst of the night cold, while not hampering his ability to move. Now in his mid-sixties, his frugal lifestyle had allowed him to regain the wiriness that had begun to turn to flabbiness during the dark days of liquor and gambling.

He gripped the worn leather handle of the knife and noiselessly unlocked the door. The rush of adrenaline flooded his system like an old friend not seen for many years, yet as familiar as his own face in the mirror. He could be twenty again, standing beneath the dripping jungle canopy, willing his heart to stop beating so loudly it must bring every Charlie within five hundred yards to his position. As he had been forced to learn in times of combat back then—learn it or die—he waited stock-still until a sense of calm settled in, not overriding the adrenaline, but taking it and using it to his advantage.

At the same time, less welcome memories tried to intrude: the stink of fear and burning flesh, the screams of dying soldiers and dismembered children, the pleas of fading eyes and grieving mothers, the tastes of napalm fumes and terror. He shoved them away. They would return, as they always did, in his dreams.

Zach opened the door. He kept the hinges well-oiled and they made no sound. A few inches of snow covered the ground, but the overhang of the eaves maintained a clear border around the cabin. He hugged the wall, stepping softly on the clear strip of ground, heading towards the howling. In the still night air, the sound seemed as strident as an air-raid siren. It would soon stop when its maker caught his scent.

The howling turned off as though someone had flicked a switch. Zach stood still, his right shoulder touching the rough wall of the cabin. His senses heightened while his breathing slowed. The next few moments passed as if he was experiencing them in slow motion:

Exhale. Listen.

The gentle crackle of frosted grass bending.

Inhale. Listen.

The whisper of stiff fur brushing against bark.

Listen.

The soft snuffle of a snout tasting the air.

Look.

The faintest glint of orange eyes. Unblinking.

Lower chin to protect throat.

Raise knife...

When Zach stepped outside again in the daylight of morning, the carcass of the wolf had disappeared. A scuffed line of blood led across the snow into the trees. He hunkered down and examined the tracks. The snow was stiff with an icy crust so it was difficult to be certain, but he was as sure as he could be. The pack had caught up with the scout.

A lone wolf he could handle. A pack was another thing altogether. If he stayed put without replenishing his rifle ammunition, he would be making himself a prisoner in his cabin.

He thought about leaving and found that the voice which had compelled him to stay had faded. It was still there, but he knew it was no longer strong enough to restrain him.

It was time to leave in search of fresh supplies.

Zach secured the cabin. He had doused the cooking range and switched off the generator before realising he had done so. They only needed to be turned off if he was intending taking a long absence. He stopped and examined his feelings.

He had sought and found a place to escape company. Somewhere he could avoid contact with other people. Somewhere that provided the solitude he craved.

That craving, the need to be alone, had not gone away. Yet something had changed. A fresh yearning was making itself felt deep inside.

He had lived for many years in these mountains among the

trees. He had grown grizzled and hardy, adapted to survive in the harsh winter conditions. He could not remember the last time he had smelled the salty tang of the ocean.

Realisation slowly stole over him. What had driven him here—the crush and clamour of people, everywhere people—had ceased to exist. Maybe entirely. If he wasn't the last person alive, then surely other survivors would be few and far between. Easily avoided.

His feelings resolved into simple desires: he wanted to see the ocean, walk barefooted on sand, feel the sun on his back in winter, eat fish cooked over a driftwood fire.

Zach topped up the fuel tank of his pick-up and stowed the spare gasoline in the back. He placed his rifle and few remaining cartridges, together with his hunting knife, in the cab of the truck.

He pulled onto the track leading down the hill; got out of the truck to close and lock the gate behind him. He paused and stared at his cabin. He did not know if he would be back.

Zach headed east.

The hotel did indeed resemble a castle, complete with crenulated roofline and towers. But it didn't take a close inspection to realise the archery holes were for show and the battlements fake. The stone from which the building was constructed was a smooth, light grey, not the rough, dark granite of mediaeval vintage, and was not held together with flaking daub through which keen draughts could find a way, but with tightly-pointed builder's mortar. This was probably a manor house built rather pretentiously in the style of a castle, maybe sixty or so years ago, and since converted to a luxurious and splendidly appointed hotel, set in its own extensive grounds.

The building was the only one on this stretch of coast and it dominated a wide, unsheltered bay. A gravelled parking area in front of the hotel gave way to a sloping lawn leading to the beach. To reach the long strip of sand it would be necessary to clamber over a storm bank of smooth pebbles. Deep, foaming waves rolled in from the North Sea, their tips whipped into froth by the strong wind, breaking fiercely onto the sand and almost reaching the line of pebbles before petering out.

Only Dusty seemed pleased to step out into the wind that drove stinging rain into their faces. While he ran down the lawn to the pebbles and back, barking excitedly, Tom and Ceri helped Peter to unload the tools from the boot. Diane stood and stared out to sea, bringing a dark muttering from Ceri about people pulling their weight.

As they lugged the heavy bags to the hotel entrance, Diane joined them. Her hair had wrapped itself around her cheeks and she was smiling. It was so unusual an expression to see on her face that Ceri forgot to be mad at her.

"It's so bleak here," said Diane breathlessly. "And wild. I love it."

Ceri grunted. The woman was right. It was a beautiful, unspoiled place.

They dropped the bags to the gravel in front of the door. Peter took hold of the brass door knob. He twisted and shook it. The door rattled a little in its frame, but didn't open.

"Hmm," he said. "We could smash the glass, but I'd rather not. If the inside isn't ruined by… well, you know, and there's food in the kitchens, it might be nice to spend the night here."

"Yes!" said Diane immediately. Ceri had never seen her so animated.

"Why not?" said Ceri. "No reason to rush back to Wick as long as there's food here and some way of keeping warm."

"I'm game," said Tom. "So, yeah, let's not break the glass. The wind will come howling through if we do."

"By the same token," said Peter, "I want to avoid breaking the lock if we can. No good keeping the glass intact if the door's going to be flapping open in every gust of wind."

"Why don't you and Tom see what you can do with the door," said Diane. "Ceri and I can walk around the building to check for any open windows or other doors that might be easier to break into." She looked at Ceri, eyebrows raised.

Ceri nodded. "Good idea. I'd rather be doing something than just standing around in this wind. You go left, I'll go right?"

"Cool," said Diane with a grin. It made her look a little more attractive, less nondescript. Ceri wasn't sure what to make of this new, animated Diane. She had at least known where she stood with the old, dour one: firmly in the 'I can't stand her' corner.

Ceri walked along the front of the building, checking windows. They were all firmly closed. The gravelled area continued around the side of the building and to the back, where there was space for more parking. A tall, stone wall beyond the gravel driveway ran parallel to the side of the hotel. A wooden door was set into the wall. On it was attached a sign: *Proceed with caution. Shooting range.*

The windows at the side were also tightly shut. As Ceri neared the back of the building, she could see metallic structures protruding from the wall. They looked like outlets for extractor fans and coolers. The kitchen must be on the other side of the wall, she surmised.

She turned the corner to the back of the hotel and the wind dropped. Diane was approaching from the opposite corner. Set into the back wall was a white, wooden fire door, the type that normally has a push-bar to open from the inside. On the outside, the door contained a grey, metal knob. Ceri took hold of it and twisted. The lock did not disengage, but the door rattled when Ceri shook it. She could see the locking mechanism in the space between door and frame. The gap looked wide enough to be able to force the end of a screwdriver into.

"Nothing doing my side," said Diane.

"I think we should be able to break in through here," said Ceri. "The lock looks a little flimsy. I'll bet this door was alarmed so the owners never bothered replacing it with something more sturdy."

"Think you're right," said Diane. "Good work. I'll go get the others."

By chiselling away part of the wooden frame, Peter was able to widen the gap between it and the door sufficiently to slip the blade of a screwdriver in past the locking mechanism. He wiggled the screwdriver, grunted a few times, swore once or twice, then grinned when the lock clicked open. He pulled the door outwards.

"Beautiful," he said. "Didn't even need to break the lock."

The door was indeed operated from the inside by pressing down on a wide, metal push-bar. Peter pressed it a few times to check it worked. They all filed into the kitchen, Dusty trotting ahead, nose to the floor. Enough light entered through windows set high in the walls for them to see, so Peter pulled the fire door firmly closed behind them.

Ceri inhaled deeply while she walked down aisles formed from gleaming stainless-steel work surfaces and storage areas. The kitchen was clean, but smelled stale and musty, and there was a whiff of rotting vegetables or fruit. She could not detect any death smells, but she had less experience of that odour than the others.

"Tom?" she said. "Can you smell any dead bodies?"

"Not in here," he said. "But somewhere… I'm not sure."

They moved from the kitchen through swing doors into a spacious dining room. Although overlaid with a fine layer of dust, everything was orderly: tables laid with clean cloths and cutlery, chairs tucked neatly beneath tables, serving areas clean and uncluttered.

Ceri inhaled again. She detected an odour, something that wasn't quite mustiness.

"Tom?"

He nodded. "It's a little stronger here."

Ceri swallowed. Apart from passing the occasional corpse lying by the side of the road or slumped in a vehicle during their drive to Scotland, Ceri had not seen many rotting bodies, and none close up. She had found it a little unsettling spending the night beneath a couple of corpses in a village pub in Herefordshire, but she had not been able to smell them and hadn't the faintest inclination to go upstairs to the pub's living quarters to view them. She suspected she might have to endure her first close encounter within the next few minutes and steeled herself.

Dusty had gone ahead and Ceri heard him utter a low bark. She followed the others out of the dining room into the hotel foyer. The odour of decay, sweet and off-key, was stronger now and Ceri had no trouble recognising it. Dusty was standing at the foot of a mahogany staircase, staring up the stairs.

Tom walked over to him and bent to ruffle the fur on his sides.

"It's okay, boy." He glanced up the stairs. "I think you're right. That's where we'll find them."

Ceri walked over to the front door. It was bolted top and bottom, and she slid the bolts free. She tried the handle, but the door remained locked.

"There's a keyhole," she called over her shoulder, "but no key."

"Here," said Peter. He was rummaging behind the reception area. He tossed a bunch of keys to Ceri. They landed on the carpet by her feet. "Try these."

Of the dozen or so keys on the ring, only two looked large enough to be likely candidates to fit the lock. The first one slid in, but she couldn't turn it. The second turned with a well-oiled *click*.

"*Voilà*," said Ceri, turning the knob and opening the door. Immediately, a gust of wind hit her face, making her eyes sting. She yanked the door shut and tugged at it experimentally. The latch seemed sound and held the door firmly closed. Ceri removed the key from the lock and walked over to the reception desk. "Don't think we'll need to lock it again," she said, handing the keys to Peter. "We can use the bolts if we need to secure it, though I can't imagine why we would. If you're right that no one else is coming after us, who is there to lock the door against?"

"Quite," said Peter. "I'm hoping one of these keys will open that." He nodded to a sturdy-looking door behind the reception area. It bore a stern sign: *Private—Staff Only. Guest entry strictly prohibited.* "I suspect the guns are stored in there."

While Peter fiddled with the door and keys, Ceri glanced around the foyer. The reception counter was carved of the same mahogany as the staircase. While it lent the space an air of superiority, it also made it darker and feel smaller, a little cloying, a sensation not helped by the odour that was stronger near the foot of the stairs.

"Nope," said Peter, straightening. "None of these." He returned to the counter and placed the bunch of keys on the surface. "We'll keep these handy, though. They'll open something."

"Can we break through that door?" asked Tom.

"Probably, though it's tight-fitting and will take a considerable amount of time and energy. Much quicker to locate the key." He nodded towards the stairs. "I think we'll find it up there. Near the source of the smell."

Ceri swallowed hard again and glanced at the stairs. A simple staircase, though elegantly carved and sumptuously carpeted. It swept up to a landing illuminated by a large picture window looking out to the back of the hotel, before bending back on itself and curving out of sight. From her vantage point, Ceri could make out a door on the left of the landing. If she had been in a horror film, she thought, at this point the camera would fast-zoom in on that door before switching to a close-up of her terrified face.

"Come on, then," she said, trying to sound braver than she felt. "Let's find this key."

She strode to the stairs and started up them. She did not glance back until she had gained the landing. The others were following, Dusty in the lead, bounding up in easy lopes. He reached the landing and favoured her hand with a brief lick before sitting in front of the door. A sign similar to the one downstairs was attached to the door, but only one word: *Private*. Now the smell of decay was strong enough to qualify as a stench. Ceri felt her stomach lurch. She tugged at the neckline of her jumper and drew it up to cover the lower half of her face. She did not smell particularly pleasant—how she yearned for a long soak in a hot bath—but her own odour was far preferable to the stink emanating from the cracks around the door.

Tom offered her a half-hearted smile and took hold of the door knob. It seemed to twist easily and, with a creak, the door swung open. Tom grimaced and pinched his nostrils between thumb and finger.

Even through the thick material of her jumper, Ceri smelled the waft of corruption and gagged on the foulness. Only through a monumental act of will did she manage to keep her breakfast down.

The interior of the room was dark. By the daylight entering through the doorway, Ceri could make out a double bed to the left, behind the door. On the wall opposite, the window was covered in thick velvet curtains.

Clutching one hand to his nose, Tom took a few steps into the room and tugged back the curtains with his free hand. Around a dozen flies took to the air, buzzing angrily. The room remained cast in darkness. Tom tore down the black plastic sheeting that had been taped to the glass and daylight flooded in, banishing the shadows.

Ceri barely noticed Peter brushing past her. Her gaze was transfixed by the bed. Two corpses occupied it, the coverlet concealing them to their chests. The one nearest Ceri had dark, thick hair. Facial skin had sunk to the bone, revealing the shape of the skull. The corpse furthest away had much longer, fair hair, the face rounder and fuller. The eye sockets writhed with maggots.

With an effort, Ceri tore her gaze away. Tom was reading something taped to the end of the bed. A note. Trying to breathe through her mouth, Ceri stepped to his side.

"Ceri... don't," said Tom, but she had already tugged the note from his fingers. Bending a little, she read the tiny handwriting that covered it:

My name is Moira Watson. On the bed in front of you, my body is the one lying to your right. To your left lies the body of my husband, Craig Watson.

We are the owners of this hotel. This was the realisation of our life's dream. But that matters naught. Not now.

When the plague—what they are jokingly calling The Millennium Bug; excuse me if I don't laugh or even smile—reached this place, we reacted immediately. We sent home the guests and staff. We locked the front door. If anyone had come, we'd have refused to open it.

It was not enough.

If you enter the adjoining room, there you will find our children. James was 14. A keen footballer and angler. A sharp scientific mind. Kathryn was 12. An accomplished rider. Showing promise as a pianist.

Craig, the strongest, was the first to go. I was too weak even to rise from my bed to comfort my bairns in their last moments.

Instead of allowing me to follow my loved ones, God saw fit to spare me. For what design I know not and care nothing.

I am weak, but the fever has passed. Why me? Why not sweet Kathryn? Or loving James? Or steadfast, loyal Craig?

My flesh can be restored. My spirit is beyond repair.

I reject God's design.

May He have mercy on my soul.

Ceri let go of the note. She glanced to the right of the bed. Lying on its side on the bedside cabinet was a large, medicinal-looking bottle. Empty.

She looked further to the right. In the far wall was another door. She took a step towards it.

"No!" Ceri felt Tom's hand on her arm. "Don't go in there," he said. "You don't want to see them."

A rushing sound filled Ceri's ears. Her vision blurred. All the terror, the pain, the horror, the guilt, all the things she thought she had conquered, came gushing back to the surface.

Pushing past Tom, she ran from the room.

Chapter Ten

Bri was not overwhelmed by Buckingham Palace. She had a mental image of how a palace should look and it didn't resemble this—not a turret or spire in sight. She and Will stood at the railings in front of the main building, clutching them like convicts. Though the gates remained shut and locked, the grounds were dotted with corpses. Civilians in the main, but military as well in full combat fatigues and body armour. Will wanted to scale the fence to fetch one of the soldiers' guns, but Bri dragged him away.

"They're not toys, Will. And you don't want to get too close to those bodies. You might catch something. Not a good idea. I doubt there are any doctors left."

Will did not protest too strongly. His trust in her appeared complete. Bri was unsure she wanted the responsibility of being the boy's mother substitute, but she would prefer that to not having Will around.

They strolled down The Mall to Trafalgar Square. Pigeons milled about the stone lions in the sort of copious numbers that tourists would have flocked there a month or two back. There was also a marked increase in the number of rotting corpses and, consequently, scavengers.

The bloated body of a woman floated facedown in the brown water of the fountain, hair spread out like weed.

"The water used to be blue," said Will, pulling a face.

Bri maintained the warding aura with minimal effort. If a rat scurried in their direction, it would veer quickly away when it drew within a few feet. Dogs gazed at them mistrustfully, but did not come near. The pickings were too rich to go to the bother of attacking food that might fight back. Even the pigeons, normally unconcerned at approaching within inches of humans, gave them a wide berth.

They walked down the wide avenue of Whitehall, past the Cenotaph, past Downing Street and to Westminster Abbey. The number of dead bodies increased so they had to weave between them. Bri made Will pull his scarf up to cover his mouth and nose; she did the same with hers. Flies weren't a problem—the temperature was probably a few degrees too low yet—but occasionally their passage disturbed a feasting gull or crow and it would take to the air with a startled cry, leaving behind a dusty, feathery wake Bri did not want them inhaling.

Although many of the corpses had been ravaged by claw or fang or beak, clothing and flesh torn indiscriminately, some remained untouched. Bri noticed the clothing worn by these corpses was similar: drab, old-fashioned, threadbare to the point of becoming ragged. String often took the place of belts. Hair on heads and on the swollen faces of the men was unkempt and sometimes thick with dirt. Empty bottles of spirits and wines with names she had never heard of lay among the bodies.

"Why are there so many, Bri?" Will asked while they walked past the Abbey. "Why didn't they go home to bed?"

"I don't think these people had homes, Will."

It was as though London's disenfranchised and destitute had at the last emerged from the deep, dank places of the city, determined to spend their final hours in the airy thoroughfares of the privileged where they had hitherto been shunned.

"I don't like it," said Will, clutching Bri's hand.

"Me neither."

They barely spared the Houses of Parliament or Big Ben a glance as they hurried by. Westminster Bridge, normally streaming with traffic and people, was dotted with corpses. Yellow-eyed gulls rose screeching at their approach, only to settle back onto their meals as soon as they had passed. Bri spotted a length of rope tied in a huge knot to the handrail, the other end disappearing from view over the side.

The London Eye stood still, as Will had predicted. The glass of one of the carousels was cracked and bore a large, dark stain as if something alive had exploded inside.

They left the bridge and descended steps to the river

embankment. Bri glanced back. A ragged corpse dangled from the end of the rope she had noticed on the bridge. The drop had almost torn the head from the torso. It was held tight by the noose while the body swung below it in the breeze, blackened feet facing in the opposite direction. Bri could too vividly imagine the body dropping to the muddy waters of the Thames as the sinew or whatever held it at last parted. The head would follow, a rotten cabbage tumbling into a murky stew. Would it sink, she wondered, or bob to the surface like some ghastly buoy? She gulped, hard, and turned away.

By unspoken agreement, they quickened their pace. The childish glee they had experienced only hours earlier when exploring Harrods seemed to have been prompted by a different city. *This* city had become sinister, birds and vermin menacing rather than merely bothersome, the silent buildings' magnificence lost beneath an air of brooding malevolence. Daylight was starting to leach from the sky, doing nothing to ease their sense of gloom.

"The cycle shop," said Bri, while they hurried south past Lambeth Palace. "Let's go straight there. I don't care about seeing any more sights."

Will nodded. He shot Bri a tight smile.

When they reached the next road junction, Will turned to the left away from the river. He led them down this street then that, never hesitating about which way to go. Bri wondered how close they were passing to Will's flat, but did not ask for fear of upsetting him again.

Once off the main tourist trails, the number of corpses they encountered thinned out dramatically. So, too, did the birds and animals, though Bri maintained the protective aura without having to think much about it, so second nature had it become.

Darkness fell, the sort of absolute dark that can only pertain in a land without artificial lighting, relieved only by weak starlight by which they could make out large objects sufficiently not to walk into them. The temperature dropped and they were again thankful for their new clothes.

"There," said Will, when they rounded a corner. He pointed across the road. "Mum would never let me go in. Said we couldn't afford for me to have a bike so there was no point drooling over them."

Bri found herself glancing in either direction before stepping out into the street. *Old habits die hard* she mused.

They stopped in front of the cycle shop. Plate glass window and a door mostly of glass. Will shook the handle.

"Locked," he said. "But look." He motioned to the shop next to it. "We can get in there."

The building next door also had a glass frontage, but most of the glass lay smashed on the floor inside, glittering faintly. Beyond, the rest of the shop lay in pitch blackness.

"Damn!" Bri muttered. "We left the candles and torch behind in that house. Did you pick one up in Harrods?"

Will shook his head.

"Neither did I." Bri wrinkled her brow in thought. A sharp twinge reminded her the cut was still tender. "Pass me one of those mobile phones. One with a camera."

Will frowned, but shrugged off his backpack and extracted a phone.

Bri fiddled with it for a moment, waiting for it to come on.

"Now then," she murmured. "Let's see… yes!"

Will blinked in the sudden white light illuminating the pavement. "Ah," he said. "A camera with a flash. Clever girl!"

"I'm not just a pretty face," said Bri. She glanced at the phone screen. "There's not much charge in this battery. We'd better be quick."

They stepped in through the broken window, Bri holding up the phone. The flashlight was bright enough to light the entire shop.

It had clearly been a chemist; it had also been ransacked. Boxes and packages lay on the floor. The secure cabinets behind the counter had been forced open and their contents removed.

"Ah," said Bri. She reached for a pink package standing alone on a shelf and quickly stowed it in her backpack. "Girl stuff," she said to Will's enquiring look. "Oh. Paracetamol. Even better." She grabbed the two boxes of tablets lying on the floor behind the counter. They would help keep the headache at bay for a few days.

No whiff of decay intruded above the normal sterile smells of a chemist shop. Apart from the broken glass and ravaged stock, nothing was amiss. Bri made for the back of the shop. A curtain hung there and she pulled it aside to reveal a fire door. She turned the key protruding from the lock and pushed the door open. Beyond lay a dark, narrow corridor.

"Come on," she said to Will, turning to the right. The door swung closed behind them. The corridor would have been cast into total darkness if not for the light from the phone. "That must be a shared toilet." Bri indicated a door in the wall opposite. She sniffed. "Smells like there's a corpse in there." She stepped forward and tried the door handle. "Locked. They must have died on the loo." She uttered a short, high-pitched giggle.

A few paces to their right was another fire door. Bri took hold of the grab handle. "Let's hope…" she said and pulled. It opened smoothly. "Phew! I thought it was going to be locked." She glanced back at the toilet door. "I guess the person in there is the owner of this shop." She swung the door wide and ushered Will inside, holding the phone up to light the way.

Will gasped. "Oh, wow! Bri, look at them all!"

Bri stepped into the shop behind him. She, too, gasped.

Floor-to-ceiling aluminium racks were affixed to every wall. Each rack contained a full complement of gleaming bicycles. Road bikes, mountain bikes, hybrids, they ranged from economy-priced, alloy-framed bikes to top-of-the-range, carbon-fibre racing models.

"Oh, oh, oh!" Bri squealed when a bike caught her eye. "It's Italian. These cost thousands." Handling it reverentially, Bri lifted the bike—easily, it had such a lightweight frame—down from the rack. For a few moments, she forgot about Will as she lost herself in wonder at such a perfect piece of machinery, adjusting the height of saddle and handlebars to fit her, itching to take it outside onto open roads.

When she remembered Will, she found him sitting astride a handsome boy's bike.

"Ooh, nice," she said and Will grinned. "We'd better make these backpacks a little lighter or they'll affect our balance. Let's open some of these tins of food. Shall we spend the night in here?"

"Okay. Bri?"

"Hmm?"

"Can we lock that door we came in through?"

From time to time, Tom glanced out of a window or the front door to check on Ceri. She had run from the hotel, across the lawn to the storm beach. She sat on the ridge of banked pebbles, gazing out to sea. Dusty had joined her and lay companionably by her side, Ceri's hand resting on his head.

Tom gave her an hour before stepping outside. Dusty glanced back as he approached and his tail began to wag across the pebbles. Tom sat down the other side of him and grunted while he made himself comfortable on the hard, shifting surface.

"Glad the rain's stopped," he said.

Ceri nodded, but did not look his way.

"Wind's not showing much sign of letting up," Tom continued. "Peter says it might later, though he expects it to be stormy again tomorrow."

"Did you find your guns?" Ceri turned her head towards him. Her cheeks were flushed from the wind but dry.

"Yep. Peter found a bunch of keys in that room." He took a deep breath. "Oh, we've locked that door and sealed the gaps with damp newspaper. We propped the front door open and the smell's all gone."

Ceri nodded. "What about the guns?"

"One of the keys was for the office. The guns were locked inside in a cabinet. The key for that was on the ring, too. Peter was right: there are rifles and shotguns. There's a walled garden to the side of the hotel—"

"I passed it when we were trying to find a way in."

"It has a firing range. Peter wants us to spend the afternoon in there getting used to the shotguns."

"Okay." She didn't look enthusiastic. "What about food?"

"There's tons. The kitchens were fully stocked ready for Christmas. Of course, all the fresh and frozen food has spoiled, but there's plenty of tinned, dried and preserved stuff. And we've found a barbecue, a huge one, with plenty of gas and spare bottles. We can eat like kings. So…" He tailed off awkwardly.

Ceri smiled. It was pale, a little forced, but a smile nonetheless.

"You're really not very good at this sort of thing, are you?" she said.

Tom moved his backside, trying to find a comfortable gap in the pebbles. "What d'you mean?"

"I mean you want to ask me how I am after my little bout of hysterics when we found that family, but you don't know how."

"Um, I wouldn't call them hysterics…"

"Oh, they most definitely were. If I hadn't run from the room when I did, I'd have started screaming."

"Oh." Again Tom shifted his backside. Of course, Ceri was right. He had always been hopeless at talking about feelings. He experienced a flashback to the last conversation he'd had with his mother. On the telephone, it had been, a couple of days before he'd driven to Swansea and found her dying. As the conversation drew to a close, he'd tried to tell her he loved her, but he'd hesitated and the chance had gone.

He glanced up. Ceri was watching him closely.

"Methinks I'm not the only one trying to keep painful memories under control," she said softly. "Want to talk about it?"

"Not really…" Tom tailed away again when he realised that he did, in fact, want to talk about it. *Needed* to. "Well," he began, "I found my mother in bed in a coma."

"Go on."

So he did. He told Ceri how he'd rung for an ambulance that

had never come, about his mother regaining consciousness at the end and speaking her last words, how he'd tried in vain to reach somebody who would take her body away and how he'd ended up burying her himself, wrapped in her duvet, in a hole he dug in her back garden with a shovel he stole from a neighbour's shed. By the time he'd finished talking, his cheeks felt raw from where the wind had whipped his tears dry.

"Oh, Tom," said Ceri. "That's awful." She reached across Dusty and squeezed his hand.

"But what about you?" he said. "I came out here to make sure you were all right, not to talk about myself."

"I'm fine now," Ceri said. "I wasn't earlier. Seeing that couple dead in their bed. Reading that poor woman's note. Imagining the children rotting in the other room…" She shuddered. "You were right to stop me going in there. Thanks."

"No problem."

"Thousands… *millions* of families must have gone through something similar." Ceri jerked her head in the direction of the hotel. "Seeing them brought it home to me that I'd have probably done exactly the same thing as that mother. If Paul and Rhys had been lying dead at home, instead of in a hospital mortuary, I'd probably have topped myself, too." She paused as if debating whether to continue, then sighed. "I had decided to kill myself anyway. I had made up my mind to do it the day you and Peter knocked at my door."

"I know. When Peter protected us from the Commune and later, when he showed us the ship leaving the distant planet and the dinosaurs dying and all the rest of it, he caught a glimpse of what you'd been planning."

"And he told you?"

"Yes." Ceri's face clouded with anger and Tom hurriedly continued. "He was concerned about you, Ceri. We both were."

"I feel as if I've been spied on," said Ceri, an edge to her tone. She breathed out deeply and her expression softened. "Still, I suppose he has looked out for us. If he hadn't protected us, we'd have ended up like that poor sod we found trying to walk to London through the snow wearing daps."

"Yes," said Tom, remembering the manic determination in the man's blood-drenched face and his irrational anger when Tom suggested he accompany them instead. "It's why I'm so keen on us being armed. I don't want to end up like that bloke." Ceri opened her mouth to say something and he hurried on. "I know having guns won't protect us from another Commune when the rest of their crowd gets here. And I know I'm not Rambo, but maybe, just maybe, we can try to do something to stop them. Fight back in some way." He sighed. "I don't know how yet, but there *has* to be a way."

They lapsed into silence. Waves ran up the beach, but stopped well short of the bank of pebbles. The tide must have turned, thought Tom.

"Come on," he said, starting to rise. "Diane and Peter were about to start cooking lunch when I came to find you. Let's eat, then I'll whup your arse at shooting."

He held out his hand and helped Ceri to her feet. Dusty leapt up and shook himself. The three of them headed up the lawn to the hotel.

Jason Grant, George Wallace and Lavinia Cram turned up that evening in Milandra's hotel suite at the appointed time of eight o'clock.

Milandra put aside the book she had been browsing which she had come across in the hotel lounge—*Ancient Pubs of Britain*—and raised her eyebrows. "The Chosen?"

Lavinia answered. "I *sent* a message to remind her. She replied to say she's gone with a team to South Ruislip. There's a shitstorm of rats emerging from the Underground tunnels and she's helping to clear them up. She sends her apologies."

Milandra thought for a moment. She had a shrewd idea how this meeting was going to go. Not having Simone present, with her ability to see more during a Commune than Milandra had given her credit for, might work in her favour. Although she hadn't yet fully decided on what she would do, the Chosen's absence left all options open.

She shrugged. "Sounds like Simone is usefully engaged elsewhere. We'll have to continue without her." She turned to Grant. "Jason, if I know you, you've thought of little else but this girl since we met lunchtime. You happy to chair the discussion?"

Grant nodded. "Sure." He glanced around the small gathering and sat forward, forearms resting on thighs. "Okay. This is what we have. A human girl. Between the age of fourteen and sixteen. She can keep a combined team of three out of her own psyche." He raised his eyebrows and received three nods. "So far, pretty straightforward. An adolescent mind with the strength to keep out three of ours. Unusual, but not unheard of. Let's move into unheard-of territory. This girl also appears to possess the ability to keep us out of another human's psyche. Not only that, but to remove us from a psyche a three-strong team has already penetrated and block the team from re-entering." Again he raised his eyebrows and received another three nods.

He sighed. "It gets worse. Before the team is ejected from the other human's mind, they see evidence the damage caused by the electrical treatment has been largely reversed. Healed. In the absence of any other candidate, I think we have to assume the girl is also responsible for that. Anyone disagree?"

Three heads shook in response.

"Okay. The first question we have to try to answer is this: *how* did this girl acquire these abilities?" Grant sat back in the chair. "Anyone want to shoot?"

Wallace was the first to clear his throat. "The traitor, Ronstadt? Maybe he's been in contact with the girl."

Grant shook his head curtly. "Unlikely. Ronstadt is probably in continental Europe by now. The girl's here in London. Too far apart."

"We have another traitor, then," said Wallace.

"There's no evidence of that. And even if there was, it doesn't overcome a fundamental obstacle. Let's imagine there was a human sitting here now before us." He nodded to Simone's empty chair. "Could we, all four of us acting in concert, impart into that human the abilities this girl has?"

Wallace opened his mouth, then closed it. It was his turn to give a curt shake of the head.

"Precisely," said Grant. "None of us would know how to impart such abilities to a human, or even if it's possible to do. If anyone would know, it would be the Keeper." He glanced at Milandra.

"To the best of the combined knowledge I hold on behalf of our people," she said, "the question has never even arisen. If such a thing is possible, none who has gone before us was aware of it."

"Any other theories?" asked Grant.

"Trauma," said Lavinia.

"Go on," said Grant.

"Well, maybe some traumatic event—like maybe seeing her parents die—has changed her brain in some way. Maybe."

"That's a lot of maybes," scoffed Wallace.

"Actually," said Grant, "that's kind of along the lines I've been thinking. The Cleansing was naturally traumatic to those who survived. I guess it's possible a young human girl—they can become quite hysterical at the best of times—was sufficiently devastated by the loss of loved ones for it to have wrought changes in her brain patterns or its chemical composition." He shrugged. "I'm no expert on human physiology. Perhaps it's similar to when someone demonstrates superhuman strength at a time of extreme stress. Like when a mother lifts a car that's crushing her child."

"That sort of shit is temporary, isn't it?" said Wallace. "The girl must have these abilities permanently. I mean, she obviously hasn't been treated so she must have been able to avoid the calling of the Commune."

"True," said Grant. "Either that or she suffered the trauma *after* being called, but before she could be treated. There have also been cases—documented cases—of humans awaking from comatose states after suffering serious injuries and finding they have developed psychic abilities. The power to read others' minds or to influence actions. Similar to our own abilities."

"*Documented* cases?" said Milandra. "Has someone been to a library this afternoon?" She smiled to show Grant she was gently teasing.

He smiled back. "There's a library a mile or so north of here in West Drayton. Probably not far from where the girl was spotted. Useful things, libraries. We ought to add them to our list of human artefacts worth preserving."

"I think you and Lavinia are probably right that the girl acquired her abilities through some sort of trauma," said Milandra. She did not voice them, but her thoughts kept turning to the cut and lump she had noticed on the girl's temple when viewing Luke's memory.

"Okay," said Grant. "Moving on to what I think is the next key question. Given that the girl has apparently healed the boy of the effects of our electrical treatment, does this mean she can heal any drone in the same manner?"

"Perhaps," said Wallace.

"Um, how can we even guess at that?" said Lavinia.

"I have a theory," said Grant. "Luke said the boy was aged around twelve or younger. Probably, then, prepubescent. Human boys often mature a lot later than their female counterparts."

"Yeah," said Wallace. "So?"

"Well, the boy's brain is probably still growing and developing, undergoing changes brought on by adolescence and puberty. Maybe the effects of the electrical treatment would have been reversed anyway, at least to some extent, through those natural changes. Maybe all the girl did was hurry them along."

"More maybes," said Wallace.

"Naturally," said Grant. "We can only speculate at this stage. My point is this: if she was able to heal the boy only because of his tender years, then she will pose no threat to the other drones.

The vast majority of them are adults. Even if she were able to get to them, she won't be able to heal them."

"That's possible, I guess," said Wallace. "But there's only one way to find out for certain."

"I had other questions for us to consider," said Grant, "but I have no objection to jumping ahead to the last one…" He glanced at Milandra.

"Might as well, now that Straight-to-the-point George has virtually asked it," said Milandra. She shot Wallace a brief smile to show she wasn't being disapproving, not that he would have much cared if she was.

"Okay, then," said Grant. "What, if anything, are we going to do about this girl?"

"That's the easy one," said Wallace. "We go after her."

He glanced at Lavinia. She nodded. "I see no alternative."

"When you say, 'go after her'…?" said Milandra.

"Capture her," said Wallace. "Examine her. Then we'll find out the answers to all these questions instead of pissing in the dark."

"A small team," said Lavinia. "Me, Wallace and…"

"Luke," said Milandra, before either of them could suggest Simone as the third member. "He knows what she and the boy look like, don't forget."

Wallace shrugged. "Fine by me."

"You only have three days," said Grant. "Then we leave for Salisbury and we need you two with us."

"Three days should be enough," said Wallace.

"London's a big city," said Milandra. "It might take you three days to even pick up a trail."

"Then we need to pinpoint her location," said Lavinia. "Like now."

Milandra kept her expression carefully neutral. The meeting had reached the point she had anticipated. She must tread carefully.

"I don't know," she said. "I'm a little weary…"

"Come on, Milandra," said Wallace. "There's four of us, she's not going to be more than a few miles away and we only need to find out her position. It's not as if we're going to try to persuade her to stay where she is. From all we've talked about tonight, that clearly wouldn't work."

"Indeed," added Grant. "It seems to me it would merely alert her to the fact she is being hunted."

Milandra looked at each of them in turn as though debating whether to agree.

"Okay," she said with a heavy sigh. "Gather a little closer then."

Bri lay in darkness, listening to Will's steady breathing. He had fallen asleep as soon as they settled down in the narrow space behind the counter of the cycle shop. There would have been more room to make themselves comfortable in the aisles formed between the racks of bikes and the central section stocked with bicycle accessories, but it would have made them visible from the street. The sense of unease which had seeped into them that afternoon had not yet fully dissipated.

It had been a long day, they had walked miles and Bri could feel her eyelids grow heavy. She closed them and slipped into the netherworld that precedes deep sleep.

Then snapped her eyes open wide when she sensed the invasion.

Be calm, child.

The voice came from inside her head. Acting instinctively, Bri expelled the invading intellects, leaving in place the protective yellow blanket that would stop them from re-entering. But the voice remained. Fighting down panic, Bri listened.

They have glimpsed your plans. They know you intend going south and then west to Cornwall. They are coming for you.

Leave immediately. Head north. To Nottingham. By the castle, an ancient pub: Ye Olde Trip to Jerusalem. *I will send someone who can help you. His name is Peter.*

You know how to shield your mind to keep them out. Protect the boy too.

Go. Now.

A fresh lance of pain stabbed her forehead. Gritting her teeth against it, Bri leaned across and shook Will.

"Huh?" he muttered, voice thick with sleep.

"Come on," said Bri. "We're leaving."

Ceri and Tom strolled down the lawn to the pebbles, picking their way carefully by the weak light of the torch Tom carried. Dusty loped ahead of them, nearly invisible in the darkness. As Peter had predicted, the wind had abated to a stiff breeze, but the sky remained cloudy, promising more rain tomorrow. They sat on the ridge of pebbles. The splash of waves sounded distant.

"Whup my arse," Ceri said musingly. "What precisely did you mean by that, Mr Evans?"

"Okay, okay, Annie Oakley," said Tom. "My shoulder's sore."

"Mine, too."

Tom reached to his right shoulder and rubbed it reflectively. "It's the one I hurt in the crash." He uttered a short laugh. "I was hopeless, wasn't I?"

"Well, look on the bright side, you can only get better."

Tom grunted. "I'm not so sure about that. To be perfectly honest, it scared the life out of me just holding one. I was terrified it would go off when I didn't mean it to. Maybe this wasn't such a good idea."

"It'll be fine. So long as we follow Peter's instructions. Never carry them loaded and always have the barrel broken except when you intend to use it."

"I suppose." Tom didn't sound convinced. "Perhaps I'll improve tomorrow." He gave a great yawn. "It's chilly out here and I'm knackered. You must be too. Ready for bed?"

"Yes, I am. But I asked you to come for a walk for a reason. I want to ask a favour and I didn't want them, *her* especially, to hear."

"Okay."

Ceri inhaled deeply. "Don't take this the wrong way, but would you mind if we shared a room tonight?"

In the darkness, she heard Tom's sharp intake of breath.

"Really," she said. "Don't take it the wrong way. I'm not ready for *that*. Don't know if I ever will be. But the thought of lying on my own in the dark, thinking about that poor family… I'm dreading going to bed. Look, I'm not even asking you to share a bed. Only a bedroom. I can't be on my own in there."

"There's a family room," said Tom. "It's got a double bed and two singles."

"Sounds perfect." Ceri breathed out heavily. She hadn't been looking forward to this conversation, but it had proved a lot easier than she'd imagined. "Hey, you don't snore, do you?"

Tom chuckled. "A little, according to Lisa…" The chuckle faded. "Mind you, Dusty can pump out the snores. And, er, he can be a little, um, *windy*. I'm not sure all this tinned meat is agreeing with him."

Ceri laughed. "Yeah, that's right, you blame it on the dog. Seriously, though, thank you. Shall we go, then?"

They stood and Tom whistled for Dusty, who came lolloping out of the darkness. Side by side, they strolled back to the hotel.

Dusty started to follow the humans across the lawn, but stopped when a sound reached his ears. A rushing, bubbling sound, coming from behind them. But faint; the humans hadn't heard it. He turned to face the bay, ears raised, tail stiff.

He uttered a low, curious *whuff* when he sensed something different, something unusual, out there in the darkness.

Whatever it was, Dusty instinctively knew it lay beyond his reach. He stared out to sea for a few moments longer, senses pinging, but unable to see anything untoward.

If he possessed shoulders, he would have shrugged. He about faced and trotted after the humans.

Part 2: Pilgrim Through This Barren Land

Chapter Eleven

Seagulls and rats had taken over the streets of Dublin. Dogs, too, gathered in small packs, scavenging and hunting together. Colleen O'Mahoney carried a golf club whenever she ventured outside and banged the ground with it to warn off any bird or rodent that came too close. If she saw a pack of dogs, or even one on its own, she'd duck into a building until they had passed.

Her flat—and Sinead's she had to remind herself; if anything, it had become Sinead's alone—was situated in the Rathmines area of the city. When the world had gone to hell, she and Sinead had locked themselves away in a doomed attempt to avoid catching whatever it was that was killing people.

Sinead's eyes, red and running and haunted, had told her more eloquently than words that they had been too late. When Colleen's limbs became too heavy to hold up unaided and daylight made it feel her head would explode, she had taken to their bed alongside Sinead and descended into delirium.

She awoke, she didn't know how much later, to darkness and stench. The darkness was no surprise—they had taped black plastic to the windows to keep out even a chink of light—but the stench… Tentatively, she reached out a hand to the other side of the bed, and withdrew it with a whimper when it encountered something cold and moist.

Sinead must have been dead for days. Her body had bloated and blackened. Fungus spores had started to appear on her face. In places, her skin was beginning to slough away. Colleen saw this in the pale winter's light entering the bedroom once she had torn away the plastic from the window. While she stood and gazed at her lover's corpse, her mind loosened a little.

Weak and thirsty and filthy though she was, Colleen knew she could not stay in the flat. She paused long enough to pack a bag with clean clothes, a towel, a few toiletries and her toothbrush. In the kitchen, she downed a bottle of water, then promptly brought it back up when the image of Sinead lying in their bed flashed into her mind. She left the flat, pulling the door locked behind her, before attempting to drink another. By sipping, not swigging, she kept the contents of the next bottle down.

Barefooted, clad in a stained and stinking nightdress, Colleen tried the doors of adjoining flats until she found one unlocked. Nobody answered her tentative call. The hallway of the flat was dim and shadowy. She flicked a light switch, but nothing happened. She opened a door that led into a bedroom. The waft of foetid air made her step back in a hurry, coughing. The room beyond was cast in deep darkness and silence. She quickly closed the door.

In the kitchen, a cupboard yielded an unopened six-pack of lemonade cans and a slab of cooking chocolate. The chocolate was bitter, but she devoured it anyway. While she sipped the lemonade, the image of Sinead began to intrude and she was nearly sick again. With a huge effort of will, she thrust the image away but, in the process, her mind loosened a little more.

Another door led into a bathroom where she found a bath partly-filled with cold, but clean, water. Nothing came from the taps when she tried them. The toilet flush didn't work.

Colleen stripped off the nightdress and threw it into a corner. Gasping at the cold, she stepped into the water and slowly lowered herself in. Fifteen minutes later, clean and clothed, still shivering, she left. With only the briefest glance at the door of her and Sinead's flat, she walked out of the building.

She had no idea what day it was or the time of day, except that it wasn't night-time. Grey clouds filled the sky, giving the city the pall of a black and white photograph. Other than the occasional rustling of litter disturbed by breeze, nothing moved. She made her way through streets that normally thrummed to the bustle of people and traffic, but that were now still.

A body that hadn't been fed and legs that hadn't been exercised in days meant she couldn't go far. *The Burlington Hotel* was at the limit of her endurance and she struggled to force her way through the revolving door.

The lounge and reception area, the bar, all were empty. Her voice, when she called out, sounded lost and forlorn. Nothing, not even an echo, replied. She didn't call out again.

Dumping her bag at the foot of the stairs leading up to the guest bedrooms, she walked through the dining room and into the hotel kitchens, all chrome and stainless steel. Most of the fresh and frozen meat and produce had spoiled, but the smell was tame compared to that of rotting corpses and barely made her wrinkle her nose. A little exploration of the kitchens provided her with a loaf of soda bread that was edible when stripped of the stale outer layer of crust, a chunk of bright yellow, sweating cheese, a serviceable side of ham, a pat of butter that had not yet turned rancid and a catering-sized jar of mixed pickles. She sat at a gleaming work surface and ate her fill.

The wine storage area was locked. She found sufficient bottles of mineral water and cartons of fruit juices in one of the walk-in pantries to last her weeks; enough canned, jarred and dried food to march an army to Belfast.

Clutching a jar of Russian caviar and a box of crackers under one arm, she retrieved her bag and trudged upstairs. In the first room she found unlocked that didn't emit a stench, she lay on the bed and fell into a fitful sleep.

It had fallen dark outside when she awoke screaming and thrashing, imagining she was trying to get away from the dead form of Sinead, sweet Sinead, who had become a monster that stalked her dreams.

Weak and fatigued, Colleen stumbled downstairs. The bar at *The Burlington* was long and oval, like a Cuban cigar. She fumbled at a bottle hanging upside down in a clamp, attached to an optic. As her eyes adjusted to the darkness, she could make out freestanding bottles in rows on glass shelves. Grabbing a full bottle of Bushmills and a tumbler, she settled into a sofa in a dark corner of the bar.

An hour or so later, numbed by whiskey, she fell into sleep

once more. If she dreamed about Sinead this time, she could not remember when she awoke, bleary-eyed and thick-headed, in dawn's pale light.

She giggled. It made her head hurt more, but she didn't care. She had discovered a way to get through the nights.

A band of low pressure hovered over the North Sea, bringing strong winds and rain lashing onto the north-eastern tip of Scotland, and prompting Tom to dub Peter 'The Weatherman' for so accurately predicting the storms.

Since there was a ready supply of food and each of them enjoyed walking around the bay in between downpours, watching waves come crashing up the beach, they decided to remain in the hotel for a few more days. Even Ceri had seemed happy to agree, although Peter noticed that she picked up her stride and looked studiously in the other direction whenever she passed the sealed door behind which the Watson family had met its end.

Peter supervised a couple more practice sessions for Tom and Ceri to hone their shooting techniques. He had not been able to get the pigeon trap working so improvised by standing behind the shooter and throwing the clays into the air. They also shot at ornaments and vases Peter purloined from empty guest bedrooms. Tom had improved his aim at these static targets, but missed most of the clays. Ceri, on the other hand, impressed Peter. She possessed a good eye and steady hand. Still, he reminded himself, it didn't mean she would be any good in a hunting or combat situation; it was one thing to shoot a lump of clay out of the air, quite another to press the trigger when sighting on a warm, breathing creature. That took the ability to detach oneself from the impulse to empathise with the victim.

When not engaged in target practice or in another unexpected activity of which the others were not yet aware, Peter found himself in reflective mood during those stormy days. Often, he would retire to his bedroom on the pretext of reading a book, instead to lie on his bed, gazing at the photograph of Megan in the heart-shaped locket that had once adorned her neck, but that now hung around his own. His gaze usually strayed to the other side of the locket and its treasure of one golden lock. How he yearned to remove the protective glass cover and stroke her hair once more. But he dared not. The lock of hair was precious beyond measure; his last remaining physical piece of her. He would not risk destroying it for the sake of a moment's euphoria.

Sometimes he cursed himself for a fool, for allowing himself to have become involved with a human, knowing it could only end in death for her and heartache for him, yet neither did he regret one moment he had spent in her company. It had cost him his sense of oneness with the rest of his kind, had imbued him with alien passions, but to experience such overwhelming trust, companionship and loyalty to only one other had made it all worthwhile. Love, they called it. Such a small word for such an all-embracing emotion.

He reflected, too, upon his decision not to take part in the Cleansing. The silvery canister resembling a vacuum flask nestled, unopened, in a zip-up holdall under his bed. He harboured no regrets, except he wished he could have found a few more survivors to save from the calling of the Commune.

Peter had grown fond of Tom and Ceri. It made it harder to try to persuade them to accompany him to mainland Europe, yet try again he must. He waited until the evening of the second full day of the storm, their third evening at the hotel.

Stomachs full, they retired to the cosy lounge, warmed by oil-fired heaters, and illuminated by candles and paraffin lamps of which the hotel had an abundant supply. Ceri and Tom had raided the well-stocked wine cellar and sipped vintage burgundy. Peter took occasional swigs from a bottle of beer; he enjoyed the taste, but not the debilitating effect alcohol had upon him so rarely drank more than two. Diane seemed content with orange juice.

"The wind should drop tonight," Peter remarked. "And the rain will clear. I expect a fine, dry day tomorrow."

"How can you know these things?" asked Tom. "Is this one of

your, ahem, *special* abilities?"

Peter smiled. "I spent many years at sea. Clippers, dhows, schooners—you name it, I've probably sailed in it. Indian Ocean, South China Sea, Coral Sea—you name it, I've probably sailed on it. Explorer, spice trader, tea trader, rubber trader, a brief though memorable stint at piracy, and then many years in the British merchant navy. Every sailor, even those with much less experience than me, gets a feel for the weather. It becomes instinctive. We don't need barometers to tell us when the pressure is changing. And it's changing now. It won't surprise me if we experience a week of settled weather."

"Okay," said Ceri. She blew cigarette smoke lazily towards the ceiling. "The weather's going to be nice. So what?"

"Well," said Peter, knowing that if he didn't convince them now he never would, "we may not have a better opportunity to cross the North Sea in safety than in the next few days."

For some moments there was silence, broken only by a grunt from Dusty while he changed position on the thick rug he occupied in front of a heater.

"I don't get it," said Tom. "All of your people, yours and Diane's, are here in Britain. They're going to set off a beacon here. The rest of your civilisation is on its way and I assume, because of this beacon, is likely to arrive somewhere near here. If we—me and Ceri—have any chance of doing something to save ourselves, surely it must be here in Britain. Yet, Peter, you seem intent on persuading us to leave. I don't get it."

"Tom, if you and Ceri have any chance of doing something to save yourselves, you need help. You need to find more humans. We can find more in Scandinavia and the Netherlands. Belgium, France, Spain. Come back with... yes, why not? Come back with a small army."

"A small army?" Ceri sat upright and stubbed out her cigarette in a saucer. "How long do you think that will take? I don't speak Swedish or Dutch or Spanish. My French is passable, but not enough to make a Frenchman understand why he needs to accompany us back here. And how spread out will the survivors be?"

"Well," said Peter, "I can speak a number of European languages, and many of the survivors will have banded together by now. We'll merely have to find each group."

"Won't work." That was Diane. Peter stared at her; she was the last person he expected to raise objections to his plan.

"What do you mean?" he said.

"The survivors won't have banded together."

"The Commune…?"

Diane nodded and Peter sighed.

"Um, hello?" said Tom. "Would you like to explain to us what you're talking about?"

Peter waited to allow Diane to speak, but she was fiddling with a fresh bottle of orange juice and seemed disinclined to say any more.

He turned to Tom and Ceri. "During the Commune, when all the strength of our people, bar mine, joined together and called the survivors of Britain to London, it also made contact with every other survivor in the world."

"They can do that?" said Ceri. "Spread their minds around the entire planet?" Peter nodded and she whistled. "That's a powerful trick."

"Not powerful enough to force those further away into doing something that's completely contrary to their will."

"Like committing suicide?" said Tom.

"A Commune five thousand strong, nope," said Peter. "Seventy-five thousand… You already know the end of that sentence. Instead, the Commune would have planted some suggestion in the survivors' minds, one that would not go totally against the grain and which they therefore would be strongly persuaded to obey."

"What sort of suggestion?" asked Ceri.

Peter looked at Diane. "You took part. What message was given to the survivors outside this island?"

"To stay where they are. Not to seek out others. To burn bodies." She shrugged. "That's it, but it was probably enough."

"Ah," said Peter, "it would have been enough at first, yes, but would not last indefinitely. It's likely already wearing off."

"Not sure it's likely, but it's certainly possible."

"Then they will be starting to band together," said Peter. "We'll be able to find them."

"Europe's a pretty big place," said Diane. "They'll be spread out, far apart from each other. It will take them months, probably longer, to find more than one or two other survivors."

"Peter," said Ceri, a determined tone in her voice. "Tom and I have already made it clear we don't want to leave the U.K. because this is our home and…" She took a deep breath. "If we have to meet our end, we want to do it here. All right, you know lots of languages so if we did sail over to the continent communication won't be a problem. Besides, most Europeans can speak some English. It's only us Brits who are monoglots."

Tom grunted in agreement.

"But," continued Ceri, "and this settles it as far as I'm concerned, *we don't have enough time*."

Both humans looked steadily at Peter and he could see in their eyes he had lost this battle. He glanced at Diane.

"They're right," she said. "I think you already knew."

Yes, he thought, *but I had to try. I owe it to Megan.*

He allowed his shoulders to sag in resignation.

"Mind you," said Tom, "I also agree we need to try to get more people. Isn't there a way, er, you and Diane, can't you join your minds, or whatever it is you do, and call the European survivors to us?"

"Ooh," said Ceri, as if someone had trodden on her toe. "What about America? Can you reach the American survivors?"

"Whoa," said Peter. "Slow down, you two. And, please, lose those expectant expressions because I'm afraid we have to disappoint you." He glanced at Diane who nodded for him to go on. "I'm sorry, but what you're suggesting simply isn't possible.

Unlike Milandra and her Deputies, Diane and I are not adept at reaching. Even if our combined psyches were powerful enough to travel to mainland Europe, which is extremely doubtful, the most we'd be able to do is pass a brief message to any survivors who happen to be on the coast. Not a very long stretch of coast, at that. There's no way we'd have the power to compel them to come here. As for reaching across the Atlantic? Forget it. We'd never make it that far."

Tom, and Ceri in particular, looked so crestfallen that Peter felt like offering them some crumbs of comfort, however small. But he had none.

"Milandra," said Diane.

All three looked at her quizzically.

"She could help us do it," said Diane. "Reach Europe and probably the States, too. At least the eastern seaboard."

"Yes," agreed Peter, "she probably could. Any Keeper could and she's a mighty powerful one. But she's hardly likely to help, is she?"

"We could kidnap her," said Tom, a fresh look of excitement and hope lighting his face.

Peter shook his head. "Tom, now you can fire a shotgun, it *still* doesn't make you Rambo. Look, even if the four of us could walk in and snatch the Keeper from under the noses of her Deputies—which, trust me, we can't—there is nothing we can do that would force her to help us. Nothing." Again, Peter glanced at Diane for back-up.

"No," she said, "you're right. There isn't a way to force her. But we could *ask* her."

Again Tom grew excited. "Yes! She's only in London. The two of you could reach her there. With your minds, I mean."

Peter frowned. The three of them looking at him expectantly. He hadn't planned on coming clean, not yet, but if he didn't tell them now he would not have any excuse if they later found out.

"Diane and I *could* join forces and try to contact Milandra," he said. "But there's no need." He looked down for a moment. When he looked back up, the others wore puzzled expressions. "The truth is," he continued, "that two nights ago *I* was contacted. By Milandra."

It had been many years since he had gazed upon the ocean. Zach stood on the cape, watching gulls and cormorants swoop and squabble, tasting the salty air, listening to the *swoosh* of waves.

Two days it had taken him to reach the coast, during which he had stocked up on food and water, oil and gasoline, and greatly expanded his arsenal. He had acquired all the ammunition he was ever likely to need for his hunting rifle from his usual supplier, though he'd had to break in and serve himself since there was no sign of human life in the town. While making his way due east, in the direction of Augusta, he came across an army convoy. Six covered trucks, two armoured trucks. Quite why they had stopped at the side of the road, facing away from Augusta, he could not tell.

Some of the soldiers' bodies had been dragged from the trucks, lying tattered and torn by the side of the road, but he suspected this had occurred after death. On the many corpses still occupying the trucks, he saw no evidence of violence. Indeed, most appeared to have died peacefully, supine on the truck floors or propped against each other on the side benches.

Any suspicions that the mutilated corpses had been dragged from the trucks by people were firmly banished when he found the intact supplies and weaponry, for surely only wildlife would not have bothered looting the hardware.

When he drove away from the convoy and headed south, the passenger seat and footwell of his pick-up contained, in addition to his hunting rifle, three 5.56-millimetre assault rifles, two 12-gauge pump-action shotguns, and ammunition boxes containing shotgun shells and magazines for the rifles, with cartridges and a spare magazine for the 9-millimetre Beretta pistol tucked into the inside pocket of his hunting jacket.

Now and again while he drove, he cast a glance at the assault rifles. When first picking one up, he had almost dropped it as if it was hot. The dark days of his early twenties crowded his mind and he'd had to struggle to quell the memories. And worse: the weapon felt good in his hands, natural, as though it somehow completed him. He didn't like that feeling. He didn't want to be that person, that youthful dealer of death, and had fought for over forty years to escape him.

He almost decided not to bring any assault rifles. Almost. They were insurance policies, he told himself. He would take them along in hope he would never need to use them; he was unlikely to encounter a situation he couldn't handle with the pistol, shotgun or hunting rifle.

Zach still didn't know whether he was the last surviving person. He had noticed no evidence of extant human life during his two-day drive to the cape south of Portland—no sound of engines or gunshots, no sight of smoke or moving vehicles, no smell of cooking. He didn't know how he would react if he did come across another living person; probably by avoiding them if at all possible, but he wasn't completely decided. It wasn't that he had developed a craving for human company, only that he could not help but feel a creeping curiosity as to why he and any others had survived, when clearly they were greatly in the minority. Perhaps speaking to another survivor would reveal an answer.

It wasn't something he dwelt upon—unless and until he actually saw someone else, it was a moot point.

His stomach rumbled. The back of his pick-up contained a variety of canned goods, but he hadn't travelled to the ocean to eat from cans. A dozen or so tiny buoys bobbing in a sheltered cove caught his eye. He was no seaman, but reckoned he could manage to row one of the small boats resting on the sand out to the buoys with little difficulty. A restaurant on the main drag had already been explored and a range of cooking pots discovered. All he needed was to build a fire of driftwood and he would be eating lobster for dinner.

As Zach strolled towards the cove, he started to whistle.

Reputed to be the oldest public house in England, a distinction claimed by around twenty other pubs, *Ye Olde Trip to Jerusalem* was partly built into caves formed from sandstone at the foot of Castle Rock in Nottingham. The air temperature was already winter-low; inside the pub, the stone kept it cooler still, acting like a refrigerator, discouraging flies. The process of putrefaction had struggled to gain a firm foothold and, at a glance, the dozen or so men arranged around the cave appeared to be sleeping, an impression reinforced by the pint glasses standing on the tables before them, many still holding brown or amber liquid.

Bri gasped and came to a halt. Will tucked into her side.

"Are they dead?" he whispered.

"I'm not sure…"

The fading late afternoon light struggled to impose itself through the small window set high in the rocky wall and the men were cast in gloom. If one or more was still alive, Bri and Will would not be able to see the rise and fall of a chest or the flutter of eyelids.

Bri drew in a deep breath and detected it. She hadn't noticed it immediately due to the shock of coming across the bodies, but it was there, faint and familiar.

"Can't you smell them?" she said. "They're dead."

She stepped forward and grabbed hold of the nearest table. It consisted of a wooden top attached to a cast-iron frame and legs. It took all of her strength to drag it backwards into the doorway to block the opening. The scraping of iron on stone was shockingly loud and echoed in the cavernous ceiling space.

She gave a nervous giggle. "If they weren't dead, that would have woken them."

"Bri," said Will in a small voice. "I don't want to stay here."

"Neither do I. And we won't sleep in this room. But I think we need to stay somewhere in this pub. Peter, whoever he is, is coming to help us. At least, that's what the Voice said."

The Voice, as Bri had come to think of it, had not spoken to her since. Neither had she felt any further attempt at invasion of her mind. She had done as the Voice suggested: enveloped both her and Will's psyches in a dense, yellow fog, like a three-dimensional blanket. Each evening before closing her eyes to sleep, she renewed the protection. At a cost. Each time the headache returned, stronger and more insistent. She would soon need to think about obtaining a fresh supply of painkillers.

Bri shrugged off her backpack and took out the large torch she had acquired in a small town on their way north. Biggleswade. Will had found the name amusing. Bri's backpack had grown heavy again with the weight of the spare batteries. Will's pack contained another torch and more batteries. They were determined not to be without light when they needed it.

Darkness fell. They explored the rest of the pub by the powerful beam of Bri's torch. They found no more bodies, although could detect the odour of decay coming from the cracks of a locked wooden door behind one of the bars. Bri suspected the door led to living space, but made no attempt to investigate further.

They decided to make beds for the night in an eating area at the end of the pub furthest from where they had found the bodies of the men. This part of the building felt more modern, though still many centuries old. A blackened stone fireplace occupied a third of one wall. Bri unceremoniously kicked a chair until the legs snapped and piled the wood in the hearth. While Will tore up an old newspaper and stuffed crumpled wads into the gaps between the wood, Bri rummaged around behind the bar until she found a box of matches. Soon, the crackle and spit of flames, and the oaky scent of charring wood, filled the room.

Bri went outside to where they had left their bikes and wheeled them both inside. She shut and bolted the pub door behind her. Except for the sound of a distant engine that had come from the west while they crept northwards through the black streets of Lambeth, they had heard no sound of pursuit, but Bri did not want to take any chances. The thought that the Voice had lied, had directed them into a trap, occurred to her, but she dismissed the notion. Why send them all the way to Nottingham when they could more easily have been captured in London? And the Voice had not *felt* deceitful.

When she returned to the far end of the building where they would spend the night, Will had smashed another chair against the floor and was feeding more wood onto the fire. As she walked in, closing the bar door behind her, he pointed to a bronze scuttle, standing to one side of the hearth, that she had not noticed before.

"Coal," he said. He grinned.

"Excellent! Chuck some on."

Bri dragged two long, high-backed benches in front of the fire. They had padded seats and would do for beds.

Flames licked up the ancient stone chimney and threw blazing heat into the room. With the fire banked with coal, it should give out heat for most of the night. They both stripped down to their underwear, but kept their clothes nearby. As the fire died, they would want to add more layers.

"Bri?" said Will.

"Yes?"

"My bum's sore."

She chuckled. "So's mine."

They had pushed the bikes from the cycle shop and through the streets of Lambeth. Clouds had covered the stars and it had become too dark to risk riding them. The thought of gashing skin or breaking bones made Bri shudder; even a shallow cut like the one to Will's calf would be no joke in this doctorless new world if it became infected.

Will led them unerringly north through dark streets and across the river by way of Blackfriars Bridge. For an hour they had kept going, until exhaustion forced them to grab a few hours' sleep in the lobby of a block of flats in Islington.

At first light, they crept out of the building and mounted their bikes. Bri had delayed long enough in the cycle shop to make sure they were each equipped with a well-fitting helmet, but had abandoned her plan to kit out the bikes with lamps; they would have to pick some up along the way.

Balancing body weights with the additional burden of backpacks took some getting used to, but ungainliness was soon overcome by the joy of cycling on traffic-free roads. Fear of pursuit was quickly forgotten in the thrill of riding top-notch bicycles. Bri's Italian model handled every bit as well as she had hoped. Judging from Will's ecstatic expression and the easy way he managed the bike, his did, too.

They rode north along the A1, having to deviate around the occasional knot of abandoned vehicles, but otherwise making good time. They turned west for Nottingham in the afternoon of the second day. Will suggested they follow the M1, which would have taken them almost directly to their destination, but Bri felt a certain reluctance.

"If they realise we've come north instead of south," she said, "they're more likely to think we've gone on the motorway. It might be safer to avoid it."

Will didn't argue; merely regarded her with wide-eyed trust that gave her another twinge of discomfort.

They reached Nottingham when the afternoon was winding down to evening. The castle was well signposted and they found *Ye Olde Trip to Jerusalem* with a few minutes of daylight remaining.

"Bri?" came Will's voice, now heavy with drowsiness.

"Hmm?"

"Who's Peter?"

"I don't know. But I think he's a friend."

"Bri?" Little more than a whisper.

"What?"

"Will you always look after me?"

"Of course I will." She hoped she sounded more confident than she felt. She was only sixteen and unsure whether she would be able to look after herself. "Go to sleep now."

"G'night."

"Goodnight."

Bri closed her eyes. She renewed the yellow fog, imagining it settling over them both like Harry Potter's invisibility cloak. Grimacing at the fresh pain coursing through her head, she dry-swallowed two painkillers.

She lay in the semi-darkness, warm in the glow of the fire, waiting for the pain to recede and sleep to claim her.

Chapter Twelve

Milandra wrestled with her conscience. It had been forty-eight hours since she and the Deputies had located the girl. Two days during which she had at turns berated and congratulated herself for sidestepping the girl's impressively robust defences.

Tomorrow the salt trucks would be leaving for Salisbury. The next day, the buses and coaches would be loaded with drones and a thousand people, and would follow the trucks. Jason Grant had all the arrangements in hand. There was little for her to do.

She could afford to be introspective; could take time to ponder the girl.

Milandra was deeply intrigued. If there had been any doubts in her mind after listening to Luke's tale and viewing his memories, they were banished at once upon entering the girl's psyche. She marvelled at how the girl had detected their presence immediately and how deftly she had ejected the Deputies. Never had Milandra witnessed such abilities in a human.

Her name was Brianne, Milandra had seen, but she preferred to be called Bri: like the cheese but without the e. Milandra had kept that knowledge to herself and had not tried to contact Bri since, but felt it safe to assume the girl had followed her suggestion to flee London to the north. Certainly, the small hunting party of Wallace, Lavinia and Luke had discovered no trace of her or the boy, apart from some empty food cans at the back of the cycle store.

The Chosen had become petulant when she returned from Ruislip to discover she hadn't been included in the search for the girl.

"Why didn't they wait for me?" she asked, her mouth turning down at the corners.

"Well," said Grant, "they wanted to leave immediately and you weren't here."

"They could have *sent* for me."

"They could have," agreed Milandra, barely managing to conceal her enjoyment at Simone's annoyance. "But you *chose* to chase rats instead of involving yourself in our discussions about this girl. *You* excluded yourself. Don't try blaming anyone else."

Simone's eyes narrowed and Milandra set her jaw firm, ready for conflict if that's what the girl wanted. For a few charged moments, they stared at each other.

"Er…" Grant cleared his throat. "Ladies?"

Simone held Milandra's gaze for a moment longer before looking away. She tittered. "Getting rid of rats is fun. Snap, crackle and pop!"

The Chosen flounced from the room, twittering something about coming back in time for the trip to Salisbury. Milandra was glad to see her go. She didn't want Simone mooching about the place, forcing her to be guarded at a time when she needed to be pensive without anyone watching her. Regarding her. Measuring her.

Milandra put Simone from her mind. For now. If there was a time for reckoning between them, it would be later.

Now she had other concerns. Such as whether she had put in motion a chain of events that would generate their own momentum, like the first drop of water squeezing from a breached dam.

She felt no guilt about contacting the girl. Bri was an enigma, right enough, and Milandra was as keen as anyone to know more about how she had acquired her undoubted abilities, but she saw no reason why Bri should be studied against her will. Helping the girl evade capture did not make Milandra a traitor to her own people, or so she told herself. But contacting Ronstadt… that might be a different matter.

Peter held up his hands to quell the barrage of questions.

"Okay, okay," he said. "If you let me speak, I'll tell you." He paused, considering for a moment. Ceri and Tom both regarded him with a mixture of hope and apprehension; Diane with suspicion. "It's not that surprising Milandra has contacted me. After all, she warned me during the Commune someone would be coming after me."

"She did?" said Diane.

Peter nodded.

"But why would she do that? They consider you a traitor."

Peter smiled tightly. "If refusing to take part in mass slaughter makes me a traitor, then I guess that's what I am. But Milandra clearly doesn't see it that way."

"She lied about you. Said you intended heading south from Cardiff, not north. But the Chosen saw the truth and told Bishop."

"That's how you found us so quickly. I did wonder. Anyway, two nights ago I was about to go to sleep—"

"You sleep?" Diane sounded incredulous.

"Yes. It's something I taught myself to do. I quite enjoy it."

"But—"

"Diane! Hisht!" said Ceri. "Let him tell us what Milandra said." For a moment, the two women glared at each other. Then Ceri turned back to him. "Carry on, Peter. Please."

"Okay," said Peter. "I was about to go to sleep when Milandra came." He looked at Tom and Ceri. "It's difficult to explain. It's a little like hearing a voice in your head, but it's more than that. It's as though the other person—their complete personality—takes up temporary residence." He glanced at Diane for confirmation.

"Yes, I suppose that's as good a way to describe it as any. But—" she shot Ceri a pointed glance "—this needs to be asked—how did she get past your barrier?"

"That's the first thing I asked her," said Peter. "She replied that being the Keeper has some compensations. The ability to communicate with any of our number within reasonable distance, no matter how strong the barrier they've erected, is one of them."

"So what did she want?" said Tom, an impatient edge to his voice.

"She asked after Diane. Whether she had recovered from her injuries." He turned to Tom and Ceri. "Then she asked about you two. How you were coping with your grief."

Ceri snorted. "Bloody hell! Of all the hypocritical…" A flush of high colour blazed in her cheeks.

"For what it's worth," said Peter, "I believe she is genuinely concerned. I was guarded in my responses, but truthful."

"That's all well and good," said Tom, "but she didn't contact you to enquire about our health. Seriously, Peter, get to the point."

"I'm trying to. As you know, apart from you two, the survivors of mainland Britain were called to London where they were subjected to electrical treatment—"

"Mutilation," Tom interjected.

"I won't argue," said Peter. "The survivors have been mutilated to make them more pliable. They have been put to work clearing and burning corpses. They are also going around London switching off electrical appliances in readiness for the city being reconnected to the Grid."

Ceri uttered a small gasp.

"But Tom and Ceri aren't the only survivors in Britain outside the control of our people. There are two others: a young boy and a teenage girl."

This time, Ceri's gasp was louder and was joined by one from Tom.

"The boy has undergone electrical mutilation; had been under control. But somehow—Milandra doesn't know how—the girl has healed him."

Peter paused to allow this to sink in. Diane wore a puzzled frown. Tom and Ceri were sitting forward in their seats, eyes shining.

"There's more," continued Peter. "A small group of three of our people came across the girl and boy in West London. The girl's psyche was attacked by their combined force. She kept them out easily. The people were able to take control of the boy, but she ejected them from his mind. She protected the boy so that they couldn't get back in. Much like I protected your minds during the Commune, and since. Somehow—and Milandra is making out she is clueless as to how—this girl has developed the ability to do many of the things we can."

"What do you mean that Milandra is 'making out'?" asked Diane.

"Well, I think she has a suspicion, but won't reveal it."

"What does this mean?" asked Ceri. "Could…? No." She shook her head fiercely, as though to dispel a false hope.

"I don't know what it means," said Peter.

"If she contacted you two nights ago," said Tom, eyes narrow, "why haven't you told us this sooner?"

"I wanted to mull it over myself, though I haven't been able to come up with any answers, only suppositions that I'd prefer to keep to myself for now. And I expected you—you, Tom, in particular—to want to go and fetch them immediately. But they are on bicycles and it will take them at least two days to reach Nottingham."

"Nottingham?" said Tom. "What are you talking about?"

"Milandra's Deputies want to capture the girl. Study her to find out how she has developed these abilities. Milandra warned the girl and told her to flee London for Nottingham. She wants me to go and fetch her. The boy, too. Bring them back here where they'll be safer."

"It's a trap," said Diane immediately.

Peter shook his head. "There was no sense of deception in Milandra. Only doubt. She thinks she's doing the right thing, but isn't certain."

"Nottingham's not a tiny place," said Tom. "I went to uni there. How are we supposed to find them?"

"Milandra told the girl to go to a pub. Um, something about Jerusalem."

"*Ye Olde Trip to Jerusalem*?" said Tom.

"Yes, that's it."

"I know it well," said Tom. "It's by the castle. What are we waiting for?"

"We?" said Diane. "Milandra wants Peter to fetch them. Do we all need to go?"

"Absolutely," said Ceri. "No matter what, we stick together. Bad things happen when small groups start splitting up. Don't you ever go to the movies?"

"Ceri's right," said Peter. "We either all go or none of us go."

"Not going isn't an option," said Tom. "We're talking about two children who will likely be exhausted and terrified. Despite what you just said about not splitting up, I'm going to Nottingham even if I have to go alone."

"I'm going too," said Ceri. "My son was eleven. If he had survived, I would hope someone would try to help him. Do we know how old the boy is?"

"No," said Peter. "I know the girl's name. It's Brianne, though she goes by Bri. Okay. We'll need to take food and water. There's enough spare petrol in the boot—that's the trunk, Diane—and we can top-up as we go. Anything else?"

"Flashlights," said Diane.

"First aid kit," said Ceri. "Blankets. We don't know what condition these kids are in."

"Shotguns," said Tom. "Just in case."

"Okay," said Peter, "but they stay in the boot. You know how to find this pub?"

Tom nodded. "Not so sure how to get to Nottingham from here, though all we need to do is follow the main roads south from Edinburgh. It will be signposted when we get nearer. I can guide us to the pub once we're there."

"You're up front with me, then," said Peter. "It's been dark for, what, two or three hours? It's probably around eight o'clock. Provided we don't encounter too many obstacles that force us into going the long way around, we should be in Nottingham by early tomorrow morning."

Colleen O'Mahoney had long fancied staying in *The Burlington Hotel*, but it would have been an extravagance she could ill afford. Now that she could stay there, she found it didn't meet her expectations. Mind, those expectations had been founded on there being a body of staff and other guests present. Of course, she giggled, there was *the* occasional body present, though whether staff or guest she couldn't tell and, truth be told, they weren't good company. They tended to merely lie around exuding foul odours.

After a few days of confinement, of eating as often and as much as she wanted, of drinking fruit juice all day and whiskey all evening, she felt stronger in body if not in mind. *That* wavered between frivolous hysteria and dark chasms of madness, which threatened to swallow her whole unless she drank more whiskey.

Clutching the golf club she'd found in one of the hotel bedrooms, she began to venture outside. At first, she managed only a few hundred yards before becoming overwhelmed by the feeling that unseen eyes were watching her. Contemplating her. With a cry, Colleen fell to the ground, the golf club forgotten, and wrapped her arms around her head. Tucking her knees to her chest, she waited for the owners of the eyes to come for her.

All that came was a rat. She felt its whiskers brush her hands and recoiled in revulsion. Grabbing the golf club, she bounded to her feet and swung wildly. The rat scooted out of reach with an indignant squeak.

Each day she ventured a little further, always making for the river and one of her favourite areas of the city, before turning back to the hotel. In this manner, daring to travel a little more each time, it took her five days to reach Temple Bar.

Many of the pubs were unlocked, but occupied. She had become so accustomed to the smell of death, she would have been willing to share with a few leaking corpses if she hadn't found the door to one of her favourite watering holes, *The Quays*, firmly locked. Using the club to smash the glass of the front door and remove the shards, she had been able to wriggle inside without cutting herself. Loose her mind might have become, but she retained sufficient self-awareness to realise that sustaining a serious wound would not be advisable in these days of solitude. Another thought followed hard on that one's heels: might she be the only person still alive?

She was certainly the only living person in *The Quays*. Thankfully, she could detect no signs of formerly-living persons either. She made her way across the echoing wooden floor and around the bar. It had been a long walk from *The Burlington*, interrupted by heart-pounding dashes into doorways or behind parked cars until the dogs had passed by. One had spotted her cowering in an alleyway between two locked buildings and trotted over to investigate. While she held the club shakily towards the dog in sweat-slickened hands, it had uttered a faint *rowf?* and gone on its way without a backward glance.

It was mid-afternoon, a few hours before she usually indulged, but she felt she deserved a whiskey or two.

She found a glass and held it up to the Jameson's bottle. No sooner had she pressed the glass against the optic to release the amber liquid than her grip slackened and the glass fell to the counter below, smashing to pieces.

Colleen groaned. She had suspected she was on the verge of insanity; here was the proof. A voice was speaking inside her head. She didn't believe it was real, yet had no choice but to listen.

When the voice fell silent, she glanced wildly around. The pub remained empty and still.

Bodies. She must burn bodies. She giggled. That shouldn't be a problem. The pubs around here were full of them.

She mustn't go far. The voice had been quite clear on that. It might not be real, but neither was it a voice that could be readily disobeyed.

Colleen shrugged. There were plenty of snacks behind the bar. And whiskey. A lot of whiskey.

She reached for another glass.

They took a couple of pillows with them. Tom propped one of them between his head and the front passenger door. They had not travelled more than fifteen minutes from Wick along the coastal road when he began issuing soft snores. Peter turned on the CD player and hummed along to some classical tunes Ceri didn't recognise. He did not turn it up very loudly and it provided a pleasant background noise. Soothing.

Ceri sat behind Peter, Dusty pressed against her left leg to keep as far from Diane as he could. They had made room between the containers of petrol, shotguns and provisions in the rear compartment for his basket, so he would be able to curl up there on the way back. Two children should be able to squeeze comfortably into the rear seat between Ceri and Diane.

Eyelids growing heavy, Ceri was about to prop the other pillow in the corner by her head when Diane spoke to her. Softly, so she could only just hear her above the music and the purr of the engine.

"You had children?"

"Only one. A son. Why?"

"What was it like?"

"What was what like?"

"Being a mom."

Ceri glanced at the other woman. In the muted light given off by the dashboard display, she seemed to be watching Ceri closely, intently, as though she was genuinely interested in Ceri's reply.

"It was wonderful," she said. "Rhys gave my life new meaning. New focus. He made me complete." She raised a hand and pinched the bridge of her nose between finger and thumb. "Why do you ask? Have you never had children?"

Diane shook her head. "We do not possess your urge to procreate. Did it hurt? Giving birth?"

"It was the most excruciating twelve hours of my life."

"Yet many women put themselves through the ordeal many times. If it is that painful, why have more than one child?"

"It *is* painful. It was also the most rewarding experience of my life. To hold my son for the first time…" Ceri wiped at the corner of her eyes as they misted with memory. "We remember the feeling more than we remember the pain."

"The pain was designed to limit your urge to reproduce. Although it was desired that you should expand your population, it was deemed prudent to put in place a check to limit that expansion within reasonable bounds. It clearly did not work." Diane uttered a short laugh. "But you did not put yourself through it again?"

"I've already told you, I only had one child." Ceri did not want to tell her any more. She did not trust Diane; doubted she ever would. "Tell me why you've never had children."

"There are no children among our species."

"No children? How can that be?"

Diane shrugged. "Children are weak. Vulnerable. Needy. They take away from the whole, not add to it."

"Well, they are certainly needy," said Ceri. "They take over your life. But that's what being a parent is all about. Nurturing and protecting your children until they can fend for themselves. Unless they're snatched away from you, that is…"

Ceri glimpsed an expression pass across Diane's features she had not seen there before. Guilt. Maybe even shame. She felt a stab of vicious pleasure. *Suffer, you bitch, if only a little, for what you and your kind have done.*

"Tell me," said Ceri, "if you don't have children, how *do* you reproduce?"

"You were made broadly in our image, you know."

"So I've heard."

"Then you'll realise your reproduction processes are broadly similar to our own. The key word here is 'broadly'. We don't derive physical or sensual pleasure from the act of fertilisation. We don't have a sexual drive. We don't experience orgasms. We reproduce when, and only when, it is considered to be for the greater good."

"I almost feel sorry for you. Almost. But why, then, do *we* have libidos and orgasms?"

"You were genetically programmed that way to encourage population growth. You were brought to this planet to begin to colonise it in preparation for the Great Coming. Had we known it would take five millennia for that to happen, we wouldn't have made you quite so, er, *rampant*."

Diane smiled. It was brief, but transformed her from dour sourpuss to something more… human. Perversely, the thought reminded Ceri that she regarded Diane as *in*human and drove the impulse to return the smile firmly away.

"So," said Ceri briskly, "the sexual act to you is, what, mechanical?"

"Oh, totally. We derive infinitely more pleasure from eating. Reproduction is a purely functional process for us, which is why we can choose *not* to reproduce. The last birth among my people here on Earth Haven occurred more than two thousand years ago."

"Earth *Haven*?"

"Where we come from is Earth Home."

"If you say so. Why no births for that long?"

"When we first arrived and landed in the Atlantic Ocean, some of our number were lost in the attempt to reach land."

"Peter has told us the tale. How most of those who survived congregated on Salisbury Plain. And built some sort of beacon."

"Had we landed in the Pacific, Stonehenge, or something very like it, would have been constructed in California or Chile or on one of the Japanese islands. And that is where we would now be preparing to reactivate it." She shrugged; apparently her favourite gesture. "But most of us landed on this island so this is where the beacon was built. Although humanity had multiplied and started to spread across the planet, there remained great swathes of unpopulated land where we could replace some of our lost people in safety. We still held dominion over humans and could keep them away from the nurseries."

"What d'you mean, 'in safety'?"

"You need to understand how we reproduce. The act of fertilisation is essentially the same as humans'. The male produces semen used to fertilise an egg *in utero*. However, the female produces one egg—only one—at will, and can choose never to produce one without any ill effects."

"No periods…" said Ceri.

"None. The male produces semen at will. No ill effects if he never produces any."

"No wet dreams."

"No pent-up aggression, sexual frustration, desire to dominate, or rape. Sex is a constant undercurrent in human society. It is irrelevant in ours."

"Okay. So suppose you choose to become pregnant. What then?"

"The gestation period in the womb is around two weeks. The foetus will be much further developed than a human foetus of the same age, but can still be expelled comfortably without distortion of the cervix. The contractions necessary are not painful, so I understand. The placenta is thicker and tougher than a human's. A little like a sheep's bladder. It is expelled whole and continues to expand while the foetus grows. As the foetus becomes a person, the placenta thins and becomes more like a shroud. It dries out as its occupant's need for nutrients decreases. When the new-born is ready to emerge, he or she will pull back the placenta like shrugging off a sheet."

"How long does it take? From when the foetus is expelled, as you so charmingly put it, to when the new person emerges?"

"It varies depending on what sources of energy are available to nurture the new-born. On Earth Home it could take up to six months. Here, with such a powerful sun, it takes half that."

"And the new-born, when it emerges… how old is it?"

"He or she will be three months old, but will emerge fully developed and matured. They will appear to be, in human terms, anything from mid-twenties to early fifties. Physical beauty is unimportant to us. Some of our new-borns are white, some black, others in between. Some will look Caucasian, some Oriental, some Negroid or Hispanic or Latino or Aboriginal. Others Slavic or Aryan. Like your ancient architecture echoes that on Earth Home, so the different physical characteristics of humans reflect their creators."

"Does Earth Home suffer from racial tensions?"

"Have you not been listening? Looks do not matter. The only difference a person's skin tone makes is the darker the colour, the more suited the person will be to working on the planet's surface where solar rays and winds can quickly damage lighter skin."

"Sounds almost utopian." Ceri thought for a moment, wrinkling her brow in concentration. Strong as her distaste for this woman ran, she had long held a fascination for science fiction. Diane's tale intrigued the side of her personality that had driven her to seek out recordings of old BBC series like *Dr Who* and *Blake's Seven*, and sit absorbed in them long after her husband had gone to bed. "Okay, let's see if I have in fact been listening." She took a deep breath. "You off-world types don't get it on like us mere mortals. At least, not for the last couple of thousand years. When you did, it was a little like taking the car for an MOT: served a purpose, but not much fun. No passion, pleasure or pain. No post-coital cigarette."

Diane nodded. She gave no hint of a smile.

"Then," continued Ceri, "your fertilised ovum develops into a foetus in only a couple of weeks and is born with the placenta still intact. Within less than three more months here on Earth—oops, I mean Earth *Haven*—a walking, talking, fully-functioning grown-up emerges from the placenta."

"That's pretty much how it works."

"Okay. But how does the new-born emerge with the ability to talk? How does it acquire knowledge and skills if it's not even connected to its mother?"

"Do you know about the Keeper? What she does?"

Ceri thought for a moment. "Doesn't she act a little like a hard drive, storing your people's knowledge and experiences?"

"Milandra would be amused to hear herself described as a 'hard drive' but, yeah, that's essentially it. She is permanently linked to every one of our people here on Earth Haven. If one of us dies, that person's memories, knowledge and experiences pass to Milandra and are absorbed into the whole. This is what would

have happened when the helicopter exploded and Bishop burned.
I doubt his memories were altogether pleasant. Couldn't have been
much fun for Milandra."

"My heart bleeds. But what has this to do with the new-
borns?"

"When they are approaching maturity, almost physically ready
to emerge from their cocoons, the Keeper will awaken their
consciousness. She will impart basic skills like speech and mobility,
together with knowledge of our history and culture. In turn, each
new-born will become linked to the whole through the Keeper."

"Each one is born with the same level of knowledge and
skills?"

"Not necessarily. If it is desired that a new-born should acquire
a particular specialism—engineering, say, or quantum mechanics—
someone possessed of the necessary knowledge will attend the
nurseries and impart the knowledge to whoever has been chosen
to receive it."

"How is the knowledge imparted?"

"By placing hands on the placenta—contact isn't necessary, but
it makes the connection easier—and entering the new-born's
intellect. Then it's merely a case of sharing the knowledge. To
borrow your analogy, it's a little like copying a file from one
computer to another."

"What role do the parents play in all this? I mean, once the
baby, or whatever it is, has been born and taken to the nurseries?"

"None. We possess neither maternal nor paternal instincts.
Once the foetus has been expelled, the host female has nothing
further to do with it. The sperm provider will not be aware that
expulsion has taken place."

Ceri shook her head slowly. "I can't imagine what that must be
like. What about later, when the new-born has emerged as a
grown-up. Won't they know who their parents are?"

"No. And the parents won't know which new-born they sired.
Usually we determine that a certain number of new-borns are
needed to replace gaps in the population. When that number of

foetuses has been produced, they are taken to the nurseries—that is merely what we call places of safety, normally places which receive plenty of sunshine, where the new-borns can develop without interference—and nurtured together. There will be nothing to mark an individual as having come from a particular female or having been sired by a particular male. The parents won't even know which gender they produced."

Ceri was aware her jaw was agape and closed it. "That's awful. Doesn't anyone ever try to find out which child is theirs? Or who their parents are?"

Diane shook her head. "Why would we? Humans are selfish, thinking only of themselves." Ceri stiffened and Diane raised a hand in a placatory gesture. "It is not your fault; it is how we created you. We, on the other hand, are not limited to the space within our heads. We are each part of a greater whole and we all work towards the betterment of the whole, not the individual."

"Do you have life partners, others to whom you are attracted and want to spend the rest of your lives with?"

"Physical or sexual attraction has no meaning to us. We are attracted to others based on the nature of their intellect, but it is rare for us to want to live together in the sense you mean."

"What a sad and lonely existence it must be."

Diane shifted a little in her seat. "It *has* been difficult living apart from my kind for so long, but it was out of necessity." She sighed. "We are each part of the whole and work for the greater good."

"Yeah. So you said. I have to ask: how was putting a stop to Bishop for the greater good?"

There was only the slightest pause before Diane replied. "Bishop had become ambitious, greedy, selfish. He hated humans but had become akin to them." If Diane noticed Ceri stiffen again, this time she ignored it. "We are better off without him."

Ceri's hackles had been rising for the last few minutes. She did not try to keep the contempt from her tone. "The irony is, Diane, that you speak of lofty ideals, of working for the greater good, all high and mighty, so fucking altruistic. Yet you can kill seven billion humans, people you have lived amongst for thousands of years, without batting an eyelid. That takes a special kind of ambition. An ugly kind of greed. One that we humans, who you regard as so beneath you, would not be capable of."

Turning to the window, Ceri raised the pillow from her lap and sank her head into it. She closed her eyes and allowed the rhythm of the road to carry her away.

Chapter Thirteen

Zach was no longer alone. The other person was yet to reveal himself, but he was there, lurking in the shadows, watching him. At least now he knew his fanciful notion of being the sole survivor of the Millennium Bug was precisely that: fanciful.

Zach went about his business, which largely consisted of stockpiling canned and dried foodstuffs, and bottles of water, in the back of his pick-up. He made mental note of every item and its position. So far, nothing had been moved. The cab of the truck containing the rifles and shotguns he kept locked, and he rarely strayed beyond earshot of anyone attempting to smash the glass of the windshield, or side and rear windows—they were fitted with tempered glass and could not be broken without raising a ruckus. His jacket he kept open, despite the cold, for ready access to the Beretta nestling in his inside pocket.

The good folk of this township had been fond of reading, judging by the wealth of books Zach found in bookcases in hallways and studies and living rooms. There would probably be more in the bedrooms, but he avoided them; it was where the bodies tended to be. Soon, he had acquired a sizable store of reading materials that would keep him occupied during stops on his journey south. Heck, he had enough books to keep him occupied to the southernmost tip of Chile if he had a notion to go that far.

The other person was not adept at covert surveillance. Zach caught numerous glimpses of movement from the corner of his eye or reflections in shop windows when the other darted out of sight.

A gallon of cooking oil also sat in the back of the pick-up. Zach used a little to grease an iron skillet and began to fry slices from a can of corned beef over a driftwood fire on the beach. He sat looking out at the ocean, his back to town, the pick-up parked within sight if he turned around. The other person was trying to make no noise, but Zach could hear the soft scrunching of sand while he approached. The sound was louder on alternate steps as though one leg was being favoured. He waited until the other person was within two yards before turning, pistol in hand.

The other person wasn't a he. Zach wasn't good at accurately estimating people's age, especially women's; he put her at around thirty, but knew he could be way off the mark. Her hair was dark, thick and matted. It hung around her face in tangled folds, like a moth-eaten curtain. In her hands she clutched a short lump of wood.

Zach raised his eyebrows. "You fixin' to whack me with that?"

The woman glanced down. "No!" She dropped the wood to the sand with a dull thud. "It's for your fire."

"You armed?"

The woman shook her head. "Dunno how to use a gun."

"Got a blade?"

Again she shook her head. She kept looking at the pistol with wide eyes, in as much as Zach could see of them through her hair.

"Mind if I frisk you? No offence, miss, but you're the first living person I've seen since this world went to hell in a hand cart."

Her eyes opened wider. "You're not... not a perv are you, mister?" It came out in little more than a whisper. Zach had to strain to hear above the lap of waves, crackle of flames and sizzle of frying meat.

"Nope," he said. "If you don't want me to frisk you, that's your prerogative. I won't force you. But you'll need to turn around and walk away. Hurry up and decide. My beef's burning."

Her glance darted to the skillet and her tongue came out to lick her lips.

"Okay," she said.

Zach replaced the pistol in his jacket pocket and rose to his feet, never dropping his gaze from the woman. He patted her down. She was clean only in the sense that she wasn't carrying a concealed weapon. Otherwise...

"You smell near as bad as the corpses in those houses," he remarked.

The woman flushed. "Don't know if it's escaped your attention, mister, but there ain't no running water."

Zach raised his hand to indicate the sea. "There's the ocean."

He turned back to the fire and tended to the skillet. After a few moments, the woman stepped up to the fire. She had retrieved the lump of wood. She looked down at him enquiringly and he nodded. She bent forward and dropped the wood onto the fire, raising a cloud of sparks. Zach hurriedly pulled the skillet away to avoid getting ash on the meat.

"Oops," said the woman. "Sorry." She stood watching Zach eat the slice of fried meat. "Can I sit down, mister?"

Zach grunted. "Only mind to sit downwind."

She lowered herself to the sand on the other side of the fire. She winced as she did so.

"You hurt?" said Zach, around a mouthful of meat.

She nodded. "I live in Portland, in the north of the city. Done something to my knee walking here."

The woman looked as though she wasn't accustomed to exercise, Zach thought. When he'd frisked her, she felt flabby.

"Prob'ly a shock to the system," he said, "all that walking. You could shed a few pounds."

The woman's face contorted and tears began to run down her cheeks, cutting paths through engrained dirt.

Zach cut another slice of meat and placed it on the skillet. He busied himself frying it. When it was ready, he glanced at her. She was looking down at her lap, shoulders convulsing while she sobbed quietly. He sat back to enjoy the meat. When he looked at her again, she had stopped crying and was regarding him sullenly.

"You got a mean tongue, mister," she said.

"And you've been eyeing my lunch since you got here." He waved a hand towards the town. "There's plenty of food simply lying around. No need to go hungry. What you been living off?"

She shrugged. "Potato chips. Twinkies. Candy."

"Them's snacks," said Zach. "Know what I had for dinner last night? Lobster." He nodded towards the cove. "See the buoys beyond the water's edge? I dragged 'em in last night. Four more prime New England lobsters waiting to go into my pot."

The woman looked back at her lap, fingers twisting and untwisting. She muttered something.

"What's that?" said Zach.

"I said I don't know how to cook." She glared at him, chin jutting and bottom lip quivering.

"How old are you?"

"Twenty-four."

"Twenty-four and you can't cook?"

"My momma did all that."

"And she never taught you?"

The woman shook her head.

Zach sighed. He cut another slice of corned beef and placed it in the skillet.

"You want this one?" he said.

Will's eyes flickered open, blinked a few times, then grew wider—he had no idea where he was. A faint grey light was coming from somewhere behind him. Not much, but enough for him to see the girl sleeping a few inches away on a wooden bench.

A pub. An old, scary pub. That's where they were.

Will shivered. The fire had died. He reached to the floor for his clothes. At some point in the night, he had donned his tee-shirt. Now he yanked his Harrods hoodie on and stretched for his jeans.

He froze at the sound.

For a few seconds, only his eyes continued to work. They swivelled towards Bri. Her eyes were open now, too. Wide and uncomprehending.

The sound came again. A harsh, rasping scrape, too fleeting to make out its source, over nearly as soon as it had begun.

Will could only think of one thing that might be making such a sound and his bladder almost let go. He reached towards his groin, breaking the momentary paralysis, and clutched at himself.

"Will?" said Bri. "What was that?"

Before he could answer, it came again, only now it was a noise, a long, grating grind of metal on stone.

"The table, Bri!" Will's voice came out in little more than a squeak. "They're moving the table."

He shrank back against the bench, pinching himself to stop urine splashing out in a warm gush.

"Huh?" said Bri. "That's not possible…"

"They weren't all dead, Bri. Or maybe they were."

Will moaned. He glanced fearfully at the door. The room had lightened, or his vision had acclimatised, enough for him to see the iron latch lifting.

"They're coming! Oh bloody hell, they're coming…"

He threw himself onto his side and buried his face into the musty old cushion covering the bench. He was still clenching himself tightly; a detached part of his mind told him he might as well let go, that peeing himself was the least of his problems.

Will did not let go. Even if he was about to die at the pale hands of the dead men from the cave bar, he was not going to shame himself in front of Bri.

A creak came from behind him and he heard Bri gasp.

Then a deep voice said, "Hello. Is your name Brianne?"

"Peter?" Bri's voice sounded small.

"Yes. I'm Peter."

Will let his breath escape in a hot rush and sat upright. Even greater than his relief at not being eaten by dead men, he found he could let go of himself without spurting like an untended hosepipe.

A man stood in the open doorway. *An old man,* thought Will. *Ancient.*

The man stepped forward and three other people shuffled in behind him. Another man, younger than the first, but still quite old to Will. Two women: one had a lined face and twinkling eyes; the other stood to one side as though feeling awkward.

The ancient man spoke.

"This is Tom." He inclined his head towards the younger man, who smiled. Will thought he looked kind. "This is Ceri." He nodded at the woman with twinkling eyes. "And this is Diane." The awkward-looking woman didn't smile or acknowledge them.

Something else came through the door, pushing past the ancient man's legs. Immediately, Will's need to pee returned and he clutched at himself again. He uttered another low moan.

"This is Dusty," said the man called Tom, bending down to ruffle the ears of a large, black dog.

The dog noticed Bri and Will, and bounded forwards. Will could not help himself. Although still he managed to retain the urine, he could not hold back the whimper.

"Please!" said Bri. "Keep the dog away! Will's terrified of them."

The man called Tom frowned, but stepped quickly forward and grabbed the dog by the thick fur behind its head. He turned the animal and led it from the room, muttering something to the ancient man while he passed.

"Bri," Will whispered.

She did not look at him. She seemed transfixed by the sight of the three people standing by the door.

"Bri!" he whispered more urgently. "I have to pee."

Without taking her eyes from the strangers, she nodded to the bar. "There's a low sink. Go in there."

Will slipped off the bench and padded to the bar. The sink was behind it, underneath the stained wooden counter. It was there for the convenience of bar staff, but it did nicely as a convenience for a ten-year-old boy. Will pointed and let go with a deep sigh. The counter of the bar came up to his nose, allowing him to peer over. Bri was regarding the grown-ups gravely. Two of the three remaining adults were looking at her. The twinkly-eyed woman—he couldn't remember if her name was Ceri or Diane—was watching him, a strange look on her face.

Feeling self-conscious, Will bent his knees a little to bring his eyes down below the counter.

As he finished peeing, a thought occurred to him. These grown-ups had come here for Bri; they weren't interested in him. They might take her away and leave Will here, alone with the dead men.

He almost ran back to the benches and tugged on his jeans and trainers; if they tried to make a break for it without him, he would be ready to follow.

The ancient man—Peter—was speaking, addressing Bri.

"… come back with us. You'll be safe. We'll be far away from the people who are chasing you."

Will shifted a little on the bench and watched Bri closely. Surely she wouldn't agree to leave him behind?

"Who is chasing us?" she asked. She hadn't looked at Will since the people had appeared. "And why?"

Peter smiled. He didn't look quite so old when he did that. "We'll be able to answer most of your questions," he said. "But when we get back. It's a long drive."

"Where are we going?"

"Scotland."

"We're staying in a castle," said the twinkly-eyed woman. Her voice had a lilting quality. She was looking at Will and smiling, though somehow Will thought she looked sad. "There are loads of spare bedrooms. You can each have your own or you can share. Whichever you want. And there's a fantastic beach outside the front door. You'll love it."

"I'm coming too?" said Will.

Bri turned to him. "Of course you're coming, you doughnut. You didn't think I'd go without you, did you?"

Will suddenly felt silly and looked down at the floor, his face burning.

"Oh, love!" he heard someone exclaim, and the next moment he was enveloped so tightly he gasped. Twinkly-eyes had rushed forward and thrown her arms about him. She smelled smoky. When she pulled away, Will looked up into her face and saw tears flowing down her cheeks. "I'm sorry," she said, wiping at them with her hands. "Ignore me."

"It's okay, er…"

"Ceri," said the woman.

"It's okay, Ceri. I don't mind if you have to cry."

For some reason Will couldn't fathom, his words made her cry harder and she backed to the door, her face crinkling, sniffing. He glanced at Bri, wondering if he'd said something wrong, but she smiled at him.

"We'll let you two get your stuff together," said Peter. "We'll be outside."

After the three grown-ups had filed out—awkward woman, who must be Diane, hadn't said a word—Bri swung her bare legs off the bench and grabbed Will's hands.

"Are you happy if we go with them?" she said, staring intently at him. "Peter and Ceri seem really nice. Tom looks nice, too, but I'm not so sure about the other woman."

Will wrinkled his nose. "Me neither."

"If you don't want to go with them, we don't have to."

"I want to stay with you, Bri."

"And if I want to go with them?"

"Then I want to as well."

She stared at him for a few more moments before nodding. "Okay then. We'll go. I need to know what's been going on. Why I can suddenly control dogs and hear voices. Who those people were that chased us. I think we'll find out…" She sighed. "Though I don't think we'll like what we hear."

Bri let go of his hands and began to pull on the rest of her clothes. Minutes later, they stepped from the bar to the front door. It stood open. A fresh breeze struck Will's face, making him gasp.

Beyond the door, Peter stood waiting. He grinned when he saw them.

"How did you get in?" asked Bri. "The door's not broken and I bolted it."

"There's a side door," said Peter. "It was unlocked."

Will followed Bri outside, then stopped in his tracks when he noticed the black dog sniffing at the base of the rocky wall that rose beyond the pub. Bri stepped back to his side.

"Will?" she said. "Have you always been afraid of dogs? I mean, were you afraid of them before they chased you a few days ago?"

He shook his head and bit his lower lip, knowing he was being a pansy, but powerless to be anything else. The memory of the snarling as the dogs caught up with him was the only complete memory he had of that time before Bri made the fog go away. It was a strong memory, a crippling one.

"Had a puppy," he managed to say, not taking his eyes from the black dog. "Pongo."

"What happened to it?"

Will shook his head. "I don't know."

He could remember feeding Pongo when his mum and sister were in bed, too ill to do anything except lie in the dark, coughing and wheezing. Pongo had still been there when he had gone to the bedroom he shared with his sister and climbed into bed, too weak to undress.

Poppy had not been coughing by then. She had been silent and still; too still. When he had woken up feeling a little better, his mother was still, too, and there was no sign of the puppy. The door to the flat was ajar, although Will could not recall leaving it open.

"Okay," said Bri. "Do you remember I made the bad dogs leave you alone?"

Will nodded.

"The thing is," she continued, "they weren't really bad. They were *very* hungry and had been without their masters for too long. They had turned wild." She pointed at the black dog. "See him? Dusky, was it?"

"Dusty," said Will promptly.

"That's it. Dusty. Well, Dusty isn't wild. He's friendly, like Pongo. You don't need to be afraid of him."

Bri glanced behind her at Peter, who nodded. The younger man—Tom—came and stood next to Peter. He smiled at Will.

"Brianne's right," he said. "Dusty is lovable and soppy. He likes having his tummy tickled." Tom spoke in the same lilting tones as Ceri. "He'll help to keep you safe and will never hurt you." Tom's smile grew wider and Will tentatively returned it. "Unless you count trying to lick you to death."

Will grinned.

Tom held out his hand. "Come and meet him?"

Will glanced at Bri. "Will you come, too?"

For answer, she grasped his hand and they stepped forward together. When they reached Tom, Will grabbed his outstretched hand. It was warm and strong and comforting.

Tom whistled to Dusty. The dog's ears pricked up and he bounded towards them. Will stiffened, but did not try to back away.

Dusty bumped into Tom's legs, trying to lick his face when Tom reached down with his free hand to pat his side.

"Come here, you big softie," said Tom affectionately. "There's someone here you're going to love."

Releasing Will's hand, Tom crouched and placed his arms around the dog's back, encircling its chest so it could not jump up. He looked at Will, smiled and nodded.

Still clutching Bri's hand, Will stepped hesitantly forward. He took a deep breath, then another pace. With his free hand, he slowly reached out and touched the top of the dog's head, ready to whip his hand away if the animal growled or tried to bite him. The fur felt smooth and silky. He moved his hand to the dog's ear and ruffled it gently.

Dusty lifted his head, making Will take a sharp breath, but he only wanted to sniff at Will's wrist where the sleeve had pulled up. His tongue came out and licked the exposed skin. Warm, wet and slightly ticklish. Will began to giggle.

He let go of Bri and crouched next to Tom. Dusty immediately licked his cheek, making him giggle more.

Within thirty seconds, Will had made a new friend.

Milandra and Jason Grant walked briskly to the parking lot. Although it was a couple of hours after dawn, the streets glistened under a coating of frost.

"If it's like this tomorrow, we'll be glad those salt trucks went out today," said Milandra, a little breathlessly; she wasn't built for brisk walking.

"Especially with novices behind the wheels of the buses," said Grant. "I think Rod Wilson should take charge of the lead bus. All the others have to do is follow him."

"The roads ought to be clear of stalled vehicles. The 'dozers and crane got through safely?"

"Yup. They've offloaded the crane at Stonehenge. They're making themselves comfortable in the town until we join them."

They walked in silence for a while. Milandra glanced at Grant now and again. He seemed distracted.

"Jason? What is it?"

"Huh?"

"Come on. I know you. There's something on your mind."

"Am I that transparent?" Grant gave a thin smile. "You're right. There's something worrying me. Maybe that's a little strong. Perhaps 'concerning' would be a better word."

"So, give."

Grant sighed heavily. "Okay. We've been away from Earth Home for a long time."

"Almost five millennia," agreed Milandra.

"During which we've been out of touch. Apart from receiving the message to say they're on their way, we've had no contact with them since we sent the first pulse from Salisbury Plain."

"Ye-es. You know the distances involved are far too great for communication. To send the message would have taken a vast amount of resources and the combined strength of all seventy thousand of our people."

"I know. It was agreed before we left that the message to say they were following was the only one that would ever be sent."

"So…?"

"Five millennia is a long time. It hasn't felt so long here. The sun enables our cells to regenerate so fully and efficiently, it sometimes feels like we're re-emerging from the placenta."

"And?"

"We enjoy an extraordinarily long life here on Earth Haven. Much longer than we would have on Earth Home."

Milandra nodded. "We'd probably both have died centuries ago."

"So will many of those we left behind. New people will, of course, have been produced to replace those gone."

"Yes. The nurseries are likely to have been fully occupied. Jason, what's your point?"

"Well, what if the new people, the ones we don't know, are somehow different? What if there have been fundamental changes?" Grant shrugged. "I don't know. Ideological changes."

"Are you forgetting that each new person born on Earth Home will be part of a greater whole?" said Milandra.

"Of course not. But what if they see us as having lived among humans for too long? That *we* are no longer part of the whole?"

Milandra considered for a moment. "I don't think that's worth worrying about. When they arrive, the incoming Keeper and myself will merge their joint consciousness with ours. Any, er, abnormalities in ours will be subsumed into the greater whole and will realign."

"Are you sure?"

"Yes."

Milandra sounded more confident than she felt. Something in Grant's line of reasoning bothered her. Something she needed to ponder when she was alone. She filed the thought away for another time.

They had reached the parking lot. Milandra could hear the steady chug of the engines of the salt trucks waiting for her and Grant to arrive so they could set off. She stopped and grabbed

Grant's arm.

"Have you communicated with Wallace and Lavinia today?"

He nodded. "They're in a place called Worthing. It's a little along the coast from Brighton. They've found no trace of the girl."

"When we've finished here, I'd like you to send them another message. They have until midday—if they've not found her by then, they are to come back. Luke can continue the search alone if he wishes, but we need the Deputies back here by this evening."

"Yeah, sure. I have the feeling they've had enough anyway. George is spitting feathers. He can't understand how two kids have evaded him."

He favoured Milandra with such a keen glance that she almost blushed.

"Come on," she said, stepping forward. "Rod's waiting for us."

Rum helped the bodies to burn. Colleen wasn't fond of gin, but positively detested rum so that's what she used. She wasn't sure for how long she would be confined to Temple Bar—there were far worse places she could have been when the voice came; a place without any pubs, for instance—and wasn't about to waste anything she enjoyed drinking.

She had found a box of disposable latex gloves behind the bar of *The Quays* and a bundle of cleaners' overalls in a cupboard. She fashioned a rudimentary mask from a towel, and used plastic shopping bags to cover her boots and hair. As protected against swarming flies and any nasty diseases forming on the corpses as she felt she could be, she went to work.

It was heavy, stinking work. The stench easily made it past the makeshift mask until she hit on the idea of soaking it in spirits. Gin, with its perfumed fragrance, worked well. She just had to remember to remove the mask before lighting fires.

Skin and flesh and God-only-knew-what sloughed away and leaked from the first few bodies she dragged into the street. A skip in a side alley yielded a piece of heavy-duty plastic sheeting as large as a rug. By dragging each body onto it, and then dragging the sheet, the work became less messy.

Gradually, over days and weeks, she cleared Temple Bar of its dead. A mound of ashes and scorched bones in the central square attested to her diligence.

As the number of corpses in the pubs diminished so, too, did the compulsion to remain where she was. At first, she had felt unable to walk beyond the end of the road where *The Quays* was situated. An unseen yet powerful restriction made her legs not want to carry her any further and her brain not want to force them to. Only as the constraint loosened was she able to wander further afield.

She always took the golf club with her and still avoided packs of dogs, once by ducking into the back of a parked car. A parked car thankfully free of human remains. The dogs did not hang about for long. There were probably too many rich pickings elsewhere to be bothered hanging around for prey that may or may not emerge. That might change, she suspected, when the corpses had all rotted away, but she spent no time fretting about it. Not much point thinking months ahead when unsure whether you'll see tomorrow.

The day she awoke and found she no longer felt the urge to look for bodies to burn was the day she saw the man. The morning was fine and she decided to take a stroll to O'Connell Bridge. The bridge stood at the limit of where she had hitherto been able to wander and she wanted to test whether that limit had faded away like the need to dispose of corpses.

She reached the bridge and spent a moment staring down at the brown waters of the Liffey. Then she raised her head and looked across to the other side.

"Shit!"

Colleen was barely aware she had spoken aloud. She almost took to her heels, but forced herself to stay still. Her knuckles whitened where they gripped the golf club.

The man was standing at the other side of the river, looking at her. He began to walk across the bridge.

Colleen watched him, poised to run at the first sign that he might present a threat. He drew nearer and she was able to make him out a little better. Not a big man, huddled against the fresh breeze inside a coat that looked two sizes too large. Hair grey and receding. Spectacles.

"Hold it right there!"

She held out the club like a sword. Her hand shook. She could only hope the man didn't notice.

He took his hands from the pockets of his coat and held them up, palms out, to show her they were empty.

"Please," he said. "I mean you no harm. You're the first living person I've seen in…" His face creased into a frown. "I don't know how long."

"You don't sound local."

"I'm from Lincolnshire originally, but I married an Irish girl. My name is Howard."

He took a step forward and Colleen took one backwards. He stopped.

"Please," he said. "Won't you at least tell me your name?"

"Why do you want to know my name?"

"Isn't that what strangers do when they meet—tell each other their names? So they're not strangers any more?"

Colleen thought furiously. She hadn't had to engage her mind in deep cogitation for quite some time and found her thought processes had slowed. Either that or they had become sluggish through over-indulgence in the *uisce beatha*.

"I'm Colleen," she said at last.

"Pleased to meet you, Colleen," said Howard and smiled.

He had a friendly smile and Colleen found some of the shock at seeing another living person wearing off. She allowed herself to relax, only a little, enough to enable her to lower the club.

"Tell me," said Howard, still smiling, "have you ever sailed a yacht?"

Chapter Fourteen

As though rejoicing in the absence of people, black guillemots ventured closer to the shore. Zach watched them diving out beyond the shallows of the cove while he listened to the woman talk.

Her name was Amy Kerrigan. The product of a broken marriage, she had not seen her father since he walked out when she was four.

"Papa used to beat on Momma," she told Zach. "We was better off without the bastard."

Amy had lived with her mother in a two-bedroom apartment in North Portland. Although she spoke falteringly, her story did not take long to tell. Dropping out of high school, she had gone to work in the same place as her mother, embroidering motifs onto school sweaters and sport wear. When not working they stayed in, watching soaps and old films. Once a year they took a Greyhound to New Jersey to spend two weeks with Amy's aunt.

"I hate New Jersey," she said. "Made me sweat some."

The Millennium Bug had struck them both down at the same time. Amy had awoken; her mother hadn't.

"I knew she was dead," Amy said, her bottom lip quivering. "She smelled bad. When I shook her shoulder, my fingers sank in…"

Since then, Amy had been scavenging anything she could eat without cooking, avoiding dogs and vermin, sleeping in the caretaker's tiny basement apartment.

Later that evening, when they had left the beach and Zach had broken into a ramshackle clapperboard house on the seafront, she resumed her tale.

The voice Zach had heard compelling him to remain where he was and burn corpses had also come to Amy. Grimacing, she recounted her struggles to drag rotting bodies down narrow staircases and out into the street. She had tried setting them alight, but did not know how to make them burn, and had ended up leaving them for the seagulls, rats and dogs.

When the compulsion to stay in one place began to wear off, Amy fled the piled corpses and the stink, making her way slowly through the city.

She heard the engine of Zach's pick-up from afar and hurried to the cape, twisting her knee in her haste.

"And now here I am," she said. The flickering candle light gave her grubby face a haunted, demonic look. "Can't cook. Can't drive. Can't use a gun. Can't do jack shit."

Zach yawned. "Well, I'm turning in for the night. Heading south at first light."

She turned pleading eyes to him. "In the morning… Take me with you, mister."

Zach shook his head. "I travel alone."

"The President, he said we gotta stick together. Help each other."

"I never voted for him."

"*Please*, mister. If you're gonna leave me here, may as well put a bullet in my brain for you'll just as surely be killing me."

Earlier, Zach had shared his lobster supper with the woman. She had eaten greedily, wiping her fingers on her already-filthy clothes. She was difficult to warm to, the sort of person he doubted he'd have liked even before he went to 'Nam and was instilled with the need to be apart from everyone.

He stood and lit a spare candle. She stared up at him, imploring.

"I travel alone," he repeated.

The Range Rover crested the tip of the headland and came to an abrupt halt.

"We have company," muttered Peter.

Tom, sitting behind the passenger seat, leaned a little to his right to see through the windscreen between Diane and Peter. His weight pressed against Will, who didn't seem to mind in the slightest. The boy was sitting forward, pointing excitedly.

"A submarine," Will said, awe lending gravitas to his unbroken voice.

To Will's right sat the teenager, Bri, and beyond her, Ceri. They, too, strained forward to see the bay below.

The wind had dropped and the sun shone from a faded sky. The waves had none of their power of the previous days and broke half-heartedly on the sand, losing impetus barely a quarter of the way to the line of storm pebbles.

In the centre of the bay, maybe half a mile from shore, a submarine rode the mild swell. Long and dark and sleek, it lay half-submerged like a heavily-dorseled whale shark. Figures of men clustered on the narrow conning tower and exposed decks. The sunlight glinted and flashed from binocular lenses when the figures turned to look at the Range Rover.

A little way up the beach, just beyond the reach of the waves, three men in dark clothes stood near a bright yellow dinghy. One was pointing up at them while another followed his gaze. The third took off up the beach, sprinting towards the hotel. He looked as if he was shouting.

They had closed the front door of the hotel when they left for Nottingham, but hadn't bothered locking it. A fourth figure emerged from the doorway. It was clad in a full-head and -body environment suit that reminded Tom of the suits the soldiers had been wearing outside the sports centre in his home town. Except this one wasn't in drab army khaki but a buttercream shade that would look less incongruous in a sterile laboratory than on a beach in the eastern Highlands of Scotland.

The suited figure paused outside the hotel entrance and turned in their direction. For a moment, he seemed to peer at them with a blank-faced glare before turning and breaking into an ungainly, loping run towards the beach.

The man who had been sprinting to the hotel stopped when he saw the suited man's approach. He turned and ran in the opposite direction, back to the dinghy.

"Quick, Peter!" said Ceri. "Get us down there."

Peter drove down the road to the hotel. By the time they reached the gravel approach, the suited man had disappeared from sight behind the bank of pebbles.

The door next to Ceri had buckled and was a little difficult to open since its close encounter with a drystone wall in Herefordshire. Nevertheless, she was out of the vehicle and running down the lawn before Tom. He set off after her.

"Wait for me!" he called, but she ignored him.

Tom crossed the lawn and started up the bank of pebbles, treading cautiously to avoid turning his ankle. Ceri was already disappearing over the lip.

He stopped moving when he heard the gunshot. Fear rooted him to the spot. The sound of the second shot reanimated him. He whirled around.

"Keep the kids back!" he yelled at Peter, who was out of the car. "And Dusty!"

Forgetting to be cautious, Tom turned and ran up the bank, pebbles shifting and cracking beneath his feet. He gained the summit and gazed down at the beach.

The cream-suited man had almost reached the dinghy and had turned to face back up the beach. Slightly behind and to either side of him, the three darkly-clad men formed a rough semi-circle in front of the dinghy. All three of them held to their shoulders black rifles that looked mean and businesslike. One of the rifles was pointing directly at Tom. He gulped and tore his gaze away to where the other two rifles were trained.

Ceri was crouched at the foot of the pebble bank, chin to chest, arms clasped around head.

"Are you all right?" Tom shouted. "Ceri! Have you been hit?"

She didn't respond.

"Stay where you are!" came a stern voice from the beach.

Tom glanced at the men. The one pointing his gun at Tom took his left hand off the barrel and held it out, palm flat, in a 'Halt!' gesture.

"Stay where you are!" the man called again.

Tom held out his own hands in what he hoped was a placatory manner.

"Please," he said. Unsure whether they had heard him over the hiss of the waves—the men were around a hundred yards away—he spoke louder. "Please! I'm only going to check that my friend is all right." He pointed at Ceri, who still hadn't moved. "I won't come any closer than that, okay? Neither of us will."

Taking a deep breath, he edged forward. The man who had called out to him replaced his left hand on the barrel of the rifle. One of the other men raised his rifle from Ceri to train it on Tom.

He tensed, wondering what it felt like to be shot. He had read somewhere you didn't hear the shot that killed you. Maybe he would die in blissful unawareness of having been hit.

He continued to edge towards Ceri and concentrated all his attention on her. Staring at the rifles wouldn't deflect the bullets or make them do less damage.

The pebble bank was gently sloping on the sea side that made it easier to move down without lurching into an ankle-twisting slide. He slowly but steadily closed the gap.

"Ceri," he said, as much to calm himself as her, "I'm coming to you. Don't be startled or make any sudden movements. And don't move any further forward, whatever you do. Just keep still, as you are. I'm nearly there."

Tom reached her and deliberately lowered himself to the pebbles by her side. His legs had started to shake. Gently, he placed an arm around her shoulders and hugged her to him. She was trembling.

"Are you all right?" he said in a low voice. "Have you been hit?"

Ceri lowered her arms and raised a pale face to his.

"They shot at me, Tom. Why did they shoot at me?"

"I don't know. Were you hit?"

She shook her head and Tom let out a long sigh.

"Thank God. They must have been warning shots. I get the

impression that if these men want to shoot you, they don't miss."

Ceri looked down the beach where three rifles were now trained on them both. The person in the environment suit had turned and seemed to be engaged in a conversation with the rifle-toting men.

"That's what they are, aren't they, Tom? Men? Like us. Not like Peter and Diane."

"Yes, I think so."

"Then why did they shoot at me? I only wanted to talk to them."

"I don't know. But maybe we're about to find out."

The suited figure started to walk up the beach towards them. The three men fanned out behind, their guns still pointing at Tom and Ceri. When they had halved the distance between them to about fifty yards, they stopped. Two of the men fell into a crouch, rifles aimed unwaveringly at Tom and Ceri. The third man remained standing, rifle pointing towards the pebble bank, sweeping slowly back and forth as though expecting attackers to appear over the ridge like Comanches in an old cowboy film.

The figure in the environment suit continued on, coming to a halt around ten yards away. The sun, weak as it was, hung over Tom's shoulder and reflected off the visor of the suit's mask so he was unable to make out the occupant's features.

"I am Acting Lieutenant Commander James Irving of Her Majesty's Submarine *Argute*," came a tinny, yet authoritative, voice from behind the mask. "Please identify yourselves."

"Um, my name's Tom Evans. And this is Ceri… Ceri, er…"

"Ceri Lewis." Her voice sounded a little stronger as if she had recovered her poise. "Why did you shoot at me?"

"Please identify any weapons you are carrying," said Irving as though Ceri hadn't spoken. "Do not move your hands towards them."

"We don't have any weapons," said Tom. "At least, not on us."

"Please stand, sir," said Irving. "Slowly, keeping your hands in full view at all times."

"What is this?" said Tom. "Why are you treating us like terrorists?"

"Sir. Please stand."

"I want to know—"

"*Sir!*"

Tom bit down on his lip to stop himself from arguing. Irving's faceless visage was unnerving; the steadily trained rifles added to the feeling of helplessness threatening to overwhelm him. Another thought passed through his whirling mind: Peter or Diane could appear over the pebble banking at any moment. Tom needed to defuse the tension before there was any more shooting.

On legs that still shook, he rose to his feet.

"Lift your jumper."

Before Tom could obey, a voice came from behind him.

"Tom? Ceri? Are you okay? What's happening?"

Tom addressed Irving. "Let me call to him. Tell him to keep back."

"How many are there?" said Irving.

"Four. Two adults, two children. Though the girl's sixteen, not really a child—"

"*Tom!*" Peter's voice sounded closer.

"*Please.*"

Irving nodded. He looked back and motioned to one of the crouched men. The man stood and began to circle to his right, maintaining the fifty-yard distance from Tom and Ceri.

"Peter!" Tom called. "Don't come any closer. Get Diane and the children and go into the hotel." The armed man had started moving towards the pebbles. Tom had a clear vision of Dusty bounding excitedly up to the man and receiving a bullet to the head. "And, Peter, leave Dusty in the car. Make sure the doors are closed so he can't get out."

"Dusty?" said Irving.

"He's a dog," said Tom.

"Tom?" came Peter's voice. "Is Ceri all right?"

"Yes. She's fine. We're both fine. All four of you go into the hotel. Do it now, Peter, okay?"

"Okay." Peter sounded uncertain.

After a few moments, there came the clunks of car doors closing. Tom thought he also heard a muffled bark and hoped that Peter had done what he'd asked.

Irving looked to his right. The armed man had made it to the top of the bank of pebbles and was peering over the ridge, rifle poised. Tom also watched him, holding his breath. He let it out in a deep sigh when the man lifted his left hand, thumb pointing upwards.

"Mr Evans," said Irving. "As I was saying, please lift your jumper."

Tom did as he asked. The weather might have calmed, but the air remained cold and he gasped as he felt the skin on his torso pimpling. Both his and Ceri's jackets were next to Dusty in the back of the Range Rover.

"Please turn around," said Irving. "Slowly."

Again Tom obeyed.

"Now," said Irving, when Tom was once more facing him, "pat down your trousers."

Tom lowered his shirt and jumper. He bent and smoothed down his jeans, showing Irving there was nothing bulky concealed within.

"Thank you. Please sit as you were."

Tom lowered himself to the pebbles beside Ceri. She had watched him obey Irving's commands, bewilderment etched into her features.

"Now, Miss Lewis—" began Irving.

"It's Mrs Lewis," said Ceri.

"*Mrs* Lewis. Please stand and do the same."

Ceri hesitated and, for a moment, Tom thought she was going to tell Irving where to go. But then she stood, bewilderment replaced by a look of grim determination, and repeated the actions he had performed. When she resumed her seat next to him, she was shivering, but this time Tom thought it was from cold, not shock.

"Thank you," said Irving.

It was difficult to be certain behind that suit, but Tom fancied the man's bearing had become more relaxed. The same could not be said for his colleagues. They remained tensely watchful, two rifles trained on him and Ceri, the third held ready by the man on the ridge of pebbles.

"Why did you shoot at me?" asked Ceri.

"We were warning you to keep back," said Irving. "I am sorry if it frightened you, but you were running and appeared excited. You may not have heeded verbal commands."

"Commands?" Ceri's tone dripped scorn. "I'm not in your fucking army."

Again it was difficult to be certain through the suit, but Irving seemed to straighten. "This is not the army, madam. We are in Her Majesty's navy. Or, at least…" This time Tom was sure the shoulders within the suit sagged. "… what's left of it."

"But why did you want us to keep back?" Tom knew the answer even as he asked the question. "The Millennium Bug. You're afraid of catching it."

"Are any members of your party unwell?" asked Irving. "Sniffles, coughs, colds?"

"Ceri and I both caught the virus," said Tom. "But we recovered. The same happened to Brianne and Will—they're the two children."

"And the two other adults?"

"Ah. That's where it gets a little complicated."

George Wallace and Lavinia Cram arrived back in London mid-afternoon. Luke returned with them, but did not come to the hotel.

"I don't understand it," raged Wallace. "How could two kids, two *drones*, outwit us? We saw the girl's plan to head south to the coast and then west. We went to the cycle shop where they was holed up. They had been there all right and hadn't long left. The scraps in the food cans hadn't had time to dry up. We should have caught them up within minutes."

Lavinia was more circumspect.

"They must have heard our engines," she said. "Changed their minds about going to the coast. Then she kept us out when we tried to find her again. That's one smart cookie."

Wallace glanced at her sharply. "Sounds almost as if you admire the little bitch."

Lavinia shrugged.

Seeing that the gesture only made Wallace madder, Milandra stepped in.

"George, it doesn't make much difference how they escaped," she said in a soothing tone. "Fact is, they're gone. Forget about them. Tomorrow we head for the Beacon. I need you to refocus."

Wallace glowered and muttered something under his breath.

Milandra turned to Grant.

"Jason, where is the Chosen?"

"She's been out at the Burning Fields."

"Again."

"Yup. I've told her to make sure she's back here this evening so we're all ready to go in the morning."

"Okay. Good." She glanced at Lavinia and Wallace. "You must be tired after two days on the road. I've made sure there's plenty of food ready for you. Go eat. Rest. Be strong again."

"Cool," said Lavinia. "I am kinda hungry."

Wallace grunted.

"You too, Jason," said Milandra. "I want you in top condition tomorrow."

Grant grinned. "Hey. I'm always in good shape. But, yes, I'll go feed myself up. See you bright and early, Keeper."

Milandra waited until she was alone. Then she stepped over to the sun lamp and switched it on. With a series of clicks, the room became bathed in cold, white light. Milandra drew up a chair and sat in the full glare of the light, uttering a sigh of contentment. She had done the same thing for a couple of hours after communicating with Ronstadt and replenished the energy she had expended far more efficiently than through eating.

She had also utilised the lamp's regenerating rays after another exercise she had performed—one more arduous than communicating with Ronstadt. It had left her exhausted, but she had been prepared. Two trays of food stood by the side of the chair and she had scoffed them down while soaking up the lamp's light. The hotel kitchens were stockpiled; if anyone noticed that such a large amount of food had disappeared, no one commented.

An hour in front of the lamp should suffice now. Then she would be ready for the Beacon.

Colleen found herself at ease in Howard's company. She had not appreciated how much she had missed the companionship of another person, seeing another face, hearing another point of view, until she experienced them all anew.

He had been a G.P., working and living the other side of the Liffey in the Clontarf area of the city. When, in *The Quays*, he recounted the tale of his wife and children dying in hospital of the Millennium Bug during the first days of the outbreak, Colleen held his sobbing frame and in that moment realised she had also missed the touch and scent of another human. A warm, breathing one.

She declined his suggestion that she should go to Clontarf with him. He accepted her invitation to stay in Temple Bar.

"I like a drop of the amber stuff myself," he said with a grin. "What food do you have?"

On learning that she survived on crisps and pork scratchings, he had insisted on returning to his home to fetch as many cans of food as he could carry. Colleen did not offer to accompany him and he did not ask her to. Still reeling from the discovery that she wasn't the last living human on Earth, she was not yet ready to quit Temple Bar and the sense of security, no matter how superficial, she felt there.

"I circled around the Bar," he said, when he arrived back with a rucksack bulging with cans. "I found a supermarket that hasn't been looted. The shelves look full."

Howard also brought a supply of candles with him. Colleen hadn't bothered looking for any; she could find her way to the whiskey bottles in the dark.

They sat long into the evenings, sipping Bushmills or Jameson's, telling each other about their lives before the Millennium Bug. His as a partner in a general medical practice; hers as a lecturer in media studies in Trinity College. Although they came from widely differing backgrounds and had moved in social circles that were many miles apart in creeds if not in geography, they found themselves comfortable in each other's presence. Maybe, Colleen suspected, it helped that Howard had had a daughter roughly her age and so there was no hint of sexual attraction towards her that might result in awkwardness or worse. For her part, she felt purely platonic towards him; for a start, he was the wrong sex.

In his company, her mind that had worked so loose on discovering Sinead lying dead beside her, gradually began to tighten.

"So," said Howard on the third evening after he had moved in to Temple Bar, "I have a yacht."

"As indeed you informed me when we first met," said Colleen. "It's moored in the marina in Dun Laoghaire, is it not?"

"Aye. And there, I thought, it would have to remain. Ridiculous as it sounds, I was afraid I might be the only survivor... You're nodding. You thought the same?"

"Yes. I hated the thought." Colleen glanced down at the glass in her hand. "I had sort of decided to drink myself to death. And then you came along. Now, I still might drink myself to death, but at least I can do it in company."

Howard smiled, the sort of smile tinged with sadness. "I might join you in that quest," he said. "But not yet. You see, finding you has moved the goalposts somewhat."

"How d'you mean?"

He shifted a little as though uncomfortable with what he was about to say. "A few weeks ago, I, er… I heard a voice."

"'Stay here. Burn bodies.' That sort of thing?"

"You heard it too? Thank God! I thought I had gone nuts."

"Maybe we both have."

"Maybe. I had considered the possibility of the voice being real. I mean, I heard it inside my head, but what if it came from an external source? Like a radio wave or something."

Colleen shrugged. "What if it did?"

"Then it would mean that *someone* must have transmitted the signal or whatever it was. There must be other survivors." He took a large sip of whiskey. "I didn't really believe that. Until I met you. You're proof that there are other survivors."

"Well, I'm proof that there is *one* other survivor, though I'd have to agree it seems likely there will be others, too. *We* both fell ill; *we* both pulled through."

"Precisely. The Millennium Bug wasn't fatal to us. It's a near certainty there will be others throughout the world who also survived it."

"Hmm." Colleen drained her glass and rose to fetch a refill. "I must ask," she said, when she had returned with a full glass, "what all this has to do with your yacht?"

"Ah, yes, my yacht. You see, I would dearly like to sail across the Irish Sea to Britain. Take a look to see if we can find other survivors. And, well, I had family in Lincoln. While I'm there, I'd like to be certain…"

"I had family, too," said Colleen. "In Shannon. They disowned me for moving in with Sinead. Her family did the same. That's why we came to Dublin." She looked at Howard and felt her eyes well. "I hope they're all dead. I don't need to be certain."

Howard reached out and gripped her hand. He squeezed it briefly. Colleen did not want to cry so set her jaw to hold the tears back. It was a trick she had mastered many years back and it did not let her down now.

"Well, then," said Howard, "how would you like to sail to Britain with me?"

"Why cross the Irish Sea to look for survivors? There must be some here in Ireland."

"Undoubtedly. But Britain's much bigger and was more densely populated. There are likely to be many more survivors there."

"I can see you may be right. But why didn't you go sooner? Before you heard the voice?"

"My yacht. I've managed it on my own around the coastline, but it will take at least two to handle it across the Irish Sea."

Colleen grunted. "I'm no sailor."

"Doesn't matter. You just need to be able to pull and tie off ropes. Obey simple instructions. With two of us, and a fair wind, we'd make it across."

"I don't know. I'm an Irish girl through and through. Lived all my life on this island. Now at the end of life, do I want to be leaving my homeland? Howard, I'm sorry. I'm not sure that I do."

"At least think about it, please? You see, there's something else nagging at me. Something I can't quite get a handle on. You don't feel it yet, but maybe you will. A weird sensation has been growing in me of late. Since the urge to burn bodies has started to fade, it's being replaced with another. Perhaps one that will grow to be even more compelling." He paused.

"Nope," said Colleen. "I have no idea what you're talking about."

"Let's wait and see if you start to sense it as well. If so, you too are going to feel that we *need* to go to Britain."

It is tricky to express disdain from behind a reflective full-head mask, but Acting Lieutenant Commander James Irving was making a good job of it.

"Aliens?" he said, his tone even flatter than the mask normally made it sound. "Mind-controlling aliens who have lived amongst us for thousands of years, but who suddenly decide to spread a deadly virus—one they've created themselves, no less—in order to get rid of us pesky humans. That's what you're asking me to believe?"

Tom sighed. "I know how it sounds. I still have trouble believing it myself."

"Tom!" exclaimed Ceri. "How can you say that after all we've been through?" She turned to Irving. "Yes, it sounds completely bonkers. It also happens to be true, but there's probably nothing we can say that will convince you. Peter might be able to, though. He could *show* you."

"Peter, who's one of these aliens, though you can't tell by looking at him?"

"*Yes.*" Ceri could feel her frustration mounting. "You link hands and he'll play pictures in your mind…" Ceri tailed off; she didn't need to see Irving's features to know what expression he was making. "Okay. If you can't believe our story, how do *you* explain what's happened?"

"Well, this isn't official naval policy, you understand…"

"There is no official naval policy," said Ceri. "Not any more. There's no official anything."

"As you say, madam. Our best guess is that the virus lay dormant within a fragment of meteor that impacted on Earth. Something happened to release it into the atmosphere; maybe a seismic event."

"Well, Acting whatever-you-are Irving, that's no less bonkers than our story."

"Wait a minute," said Tom, a thoughtful look on his face. "You must have felt the effects of the Commune. You weren't on mainland Britain when the Commune was held, but Diane said that a message was sent worldwide, to every survivor on the planet. Something about staying put and not trying to find other survivors." He looked questioningly at Irving.

"Sir, I'm sorry but I have no idea what you're talking about."

"Where have you been?" asked Ceri. "How have you survived?"

"I'm afraid that's classified, madam."

Ceri half-rose to her feet. Immediately the two soldiers behind Irving, who had relaxed their stances somewhat while the conversation wore on, came to alert. Once more, Ceri was looking at two guns pointing in her direction. She sank back to the pebbles, although her irritation had not abated.

"*Classified?*" She almost shrieked the word, so strong was her indignation. "Listen to yourself. And look around." She threw her arms wide, almost clonking Tom in the face. "There's nobody left. No government. No military. No civilians. Who, in all that's mighty, are you keeping it classified from?"

Irving said nothing for a few moments. Then, "Please wait here. I'll seek orders. Commander Napier will be expecting me to report back by now in any event."

He turned, nodded at his colleagues and walked back towards the dinghy.

Ceri and Tom watched him go. They didn't speak; for now, there was nothing left to say.

Chapter Fifteen

When in Wick looking for tools, Peter had picked up a pair of binoculars and slipped them into his pocket. Travel binoculars, not much bigger than opera glasses. He used them to track the creamy-suited man's progress down the sand.

"What's happening now?" asked Diane.

"He's taken his mask off. Not sure why… oh, he's talking to someone on a walkie-talkie. Hold on a moment…" Peter raised the glasses and focused on the submarine. "Yep. He's talking to a man on the tower of the sub. These binoculars aren't powerful enough to make out much, but I'm guessing he's the Commander."

He brought the focus back to where Tom and Ceri sat at the foot of the pebble slope. From his vantage point of a top-floor bedroom at the front of the hotel, Peter was high enough to see over the lip of the storm beach.

An armed man remained in position on top of the pebbles, affording him a clear view of the hotel entrance. The other two men remained on the sand, covering Tom and Ceri with their rifles.

Peter felt a surge of helplessness. He wanted to be out there talking to the submariners, not stuck in here babysitting. He glanced at the holdall he had retrieved from his bedroom and brought here in case he was able to go outside and join in. If so, and it was going the way he was afraid of, he wanted to have the holdall, and what it contained, close to hand.

He felt a tug at his jumper and looked down.

"Please, Peter," said Will. "Can I have a go?"

Peter smiled at the boy. "Of course. Here, let's push the lenses a little closer together so you can see properly." He showed the boy how to turn the focusing dial to gain a clearer view. "There you go. You should be able to see the submarine a lot better now."

Peter turned back to the room. Diane occupied a chair in a corner. As usual, she was expressionless and hadn't spoken much except to ask for the occasional update.

The girl lay on the bed, looking pale and drawn. Peter approached the bed and sat down.

"How are you feeling, Bri?" he asked. "That's a nasty-looking cut on your forehead."

"I'm okay," she said. She tried a smile, but it seemed forced. "My head does hurt a lot, but I have painkillers."

"We're sorry we've brought you back to this. We had no idea that submarine would be there."

"I know." This time Bri's smile was more successful. "Will the men from the submarine stay?"

"Doubt it. Except for the one in the enviro-suit, they're keeping well back from Tom and Ceri, and it's clear they don't want any of us to go out there. I think they're afraid we might be contagious."

"With the Millennium Bug? Maybe they're right. Both me and Will caught it."

Peter shook his head. "The virus dies with the host. In your case, and Will's, Tom's and Ceri's, the contagious period had ended by the time you woke up feeling better. So, no, they can't catch the Millennium Bug from you."

Bri frowned. "How do you know that? I watched the President of the United States speak on telly. He said we didn't know enough about the virus. That's why everyone died."

"Ah. There are some things we'll need to explain to you. Better wait for Tom and Ceri to be here, too."

"Does it have to do with those people in London, the ones who chased me and Will?"

"Yes."

"They did something bad to Will. When I first met him, it was like he was brain-damaged or something."

"But you fixed him?"

Bri's eyes widened. "How did you know? Don't tell me, you'll explain later."

Peter couldn't help but smile. "All will be explained. And there

are some things you'll need to explain to us. Like how you fixed
Will."

"I'll try, but I'm not sure I know how."

"Just do your best. No one can expect more. I'll have a favour
to ask you, too. I need to try to see what's causing your headaches.
I don't know whether I'll be able to do anything to help like you
did for Will, but it's worth a look."

"Are you a doctor, Peter?"

"No. But maybe I can do something." He glanced across at
Diane, who was watching them. "Or maybe Diane can. Or
perhaps both of us." Diane shrugged and looked away.

Bri opened her mouth to say more, when an excited shout
came from Will.

"The man in the suit! He's coming back!"

The bed was firm where it needed to be and soft where it didn't.
Zach slept soundly, lulled by the distant lapping of the ocean.

He awoke to the raucous cries of gulls and wondered for a
moment where he was.

A full, burning bladder drove him out of bed. He had secured
the door by placing the back of a chair underneath the handle. It
wouldn't have kept out a determined intruder, but Zach would
have received warning enough to grab the pistol from the bedside
table. He didn't think the woman, Amy, had sufficient wit to try
anything, but he hadn't survived for forty years alone in the wilds
without exercising caution.

A large vase containing the stalks of long-dead flowers and an
inch of stagnant water served as a chamber pot. Zach sighed
deeply while he emptied his bladder.

He opened the drapes and looked out at a sunlit Atlantic
Ocean. Waves rushed in to break on rocks in front of a small
lighthouse. Foam whipped into the air. Gulls soared. It looked a
fine but fresh day. Mid to late morning, judging by the height of
the sun.

There was no sign of Amy downstairs. Zach grunted. Must

have moved on in the night. A twinge of something tugged at him. He pushed it away before he could acknowledge it might be regret.

He breakfasted on cold beans straight from the can, washed down with pineapple juice left over from supper.

A creature of habit when it came to bodily functions, there was one last thing Zach needed to do before he set out. That accomplished—there had even been enough water in the cistern to flush his doings away—he headed outside.

The stiff breeze was strong enough to qualify as wind. It caught his jacket, blowing it out behind him like a cape while he walked. If he didn't keep his grey hair tied back in a pony tail, it would be swirling around his head like a gorgon's serpents.

He strolled to where he'd left the pick-up, enjoying the air and sun on his face. He carried two bags of canned food and bottled water he'd found in the house. Arriving at his pick-up, he walked around to the back to deposit the new acquisitions to his stock.

Zach came to a dead stop. Eyes narrowing, he stepped back and lowered the bags to the asphalt. He tugged his jacket closer and did it up so it wouldn't snag or impede him if he needed to move quickly. He extracted the pistol before zipping the jacket over his chest.

Treading lightly on the balls of his feet, Zach moved back to the truck. Holding the pistol ready, he peered into the flatbed.

The bed of the truck behind the cab was covered in a blue tarpaulin. Beneath it he stored items he wanted to keep dry. Things like blankets, sacks of grain and dried food in cardboard packaging. Wooden toggles secured the tarp to the truck bed. At one corner, four of the toggles were unfastened. Enough to allow a person to crawl underneath.

Training the pistol on the tarp with his right hand, he reached out with his left and undid the three toggles that still secured one side of the material to the bed. He flipped back the sheet and took half a step back.

A face looked up at him, blinking in the sunlight.

Zach sighed and lowered the pistol.

"Amy. What are you doing?"

She sat up, shielding her eyes with her hand. There was something different about her.

"Must have fallen asleep," she mumbled.

"Get out of my truck."

"I'm cold." She clutched her arms about her torso and shivered.

"Out."

Zach watched her scramble unsteadily to her feet. She placed her hands on the truck's side and looked at him.

"Help me?"

Breathing a deep sigh, Zach unzipped his jacket and stowed the pistol. He stepped forward and held out a hand. Amy gripped it and used it to slow her fall. She drew in breath in a sharp hiss when her injured leg made contact with the ground, and took an involuntary stumble forward against Zach.

He shoved her away, though not roughly. She had only been against him for a few moments, but they had been long enough to tell him…

"You smell better," he said.

He looked closely and could now see what was different. Her hair had been brushed and no longer looked thick with dirt and grease. It gleamed a little in the sun like burnished teak. She, too, had tied it back in a pony-tail, revealing a face that no longer bore streaks of grime.

"You look younger," he said.

She smiled, shaving a few more years off her appearance. The outfit of clean clothes and new boots added to the overall improvement.

"Heeded your advice," she said. "Took a dip in the ocean. Golly, it was cold!"

Despite himself, Zach grinned. He didn't know anyone still used the expression 'golly'.

"It was worth it," he said.

He busied himself unpacking the contents of his bags and resecuring the tarpaulin. When he'd finished, she hadn't moved from the side of the truck. She was watching him closely, chewing on her bottom lip.

"Where you headed?" she asked.

"South. Maybe fetch up in one of the Carolinas. Perhaps as far as Miami." He shrugged. "I ain't tied to no schedule."

"Take me with you."

She didn't plead with her voice, but with her eyes. Now her hair didn't hang in matted strands obscuring her eyes, Zach could see that the latter were as rich a brown as the former.

He turned away and stepped to the driver's door. Taking his keys from his pocket, he unlocked the door and climbed in, pulling it closed behind him. The truck started first time and he rode the throttle, enjoying the powerful roar of the five-litre engine.

He glanced to his right. She was standing a few paces back, expressionless except for the yearning in her eyes.

The passenger seat and footwell were strewn with rifles, shotguns and ammunition. Zach moved them into the storage space between the bench seat and the cab wall, concealing them beneath a travel rug he kept there. The floor of the space was raised, enabling him to reach the weapons without having to heave himself over the back of the bench. He placed a shotgun and box of shells on top of the rug; he could reach back for them by only half-turning in his seat.

He looked again out of the passenger window. She hadn't moved.

"Golly!" he muttered.

Zach leaned across and unlocked the passenger door. He opened it.

"Get in," he said. "Before I change my mind."

Acting Lieutenant Commander James Irving of HM Submarine *Argute* walked up the beach, securing the helmet as he went. It was stuffy with the helmet on and it had been a relief to remove it to use the walkie-talkie.

He had reported on what he'd found, and briefly recounted the couple's strange tale of alien mind control and dissemination of deadly disease. Commander Napier's assessment had been short and brutal: poppycock. He had been ordered to return to the craft. Reluctantly, and only after Irving had repeated the points the woman had made, except in a more diplomatic manner, the Commander had agreed to dispense with protocol and allow him to reveal their movements of the past month.

Irving nodded to his men as he passed them. He continued until he was ten yards from the couple. They watched him approach every step of the way. The man looked anxious; the woman resigned.

"Okay," he said. "Commander Napier has authorised me to disclose anything you want to know. Within reason. So?"

"Where were you when the Millennium Bug broke out?" asked the woman.

"Engaged in deep-water training exercises in the Norwegian Sea. The Admiralty recalled us, but we were ordered to remain submerged at depth. We laid up south of the Faroe Islands awaiting further orders."

"What were those further orders?"

"None ever came."

"What about the other subs?" asked the man. Tom, Irving remembered. The woman was Ceri. "I take it we had more than one?"

"Yes. The other craft were also recalled. They were deployed in strategic defence when nuclear war was threatened."

"Where are these other craft now?"

Irving shifted his feet in the sand. Despite authority from his C.O., despite the dismantling—nay, obliteration—of the previous world order, it still felt wrong to be discussing sensitive naval matters with mere civilians. Maintaining secrecy had been ingrained in him since he joined the service as a seventeen-year-old rating.

"Really?" said Ceri. "Still clinging to 'classified'?"

"Yeah, all right," said Irving. "The last report we received was that the crew on every other craft had fallen ill. When all went silent, we tried reaching the others on frequencies only they would tune into. Nothing."

"Had they been ashore?" asked Ceri. "When they were recalled at the outbreak. Did the crews come ashore?"

"Some may have. The senior officers, at least, to receive briefings. Fresh stores would have been taken aboard."

"Whoever came ashore became infected," said Ceri. "Then carried the virus aboard with them."

"Not possible," said Irving. "This was within a few days of the first outbreak. No virus could spread that quickly and be so contagious."

The woman snorted and spread her arms. "Again, take a look around. The proof that what you just said is bullshit is everywhere. In the abandoned cars, the empty towns and cities, the silent schoolyards."

"Have any of your crew been ill?" asked Tom.

"No. At least, none of those who remain."

"Remain?"

"Yes. It's why we only have one inflatable left." Irving sighed; this part was even more difficult to relate to two civilians. "Despite the lack of orders from Admiralty, we listened to what was happening around the world. When it became apparent a deadly pandemic was sweeping the globe, that nowhere was safe, there was almost a mutiny. Men wanted to be with their loved ones. Commander Johnstone—"

"Thought your commander's name is Napier," Ceri interrupted.

"Commander Napier was then Lieutenant Napier. I was Warrant Officer Irving. Not eligible for non-commissioned ranks, thus *Acting*, see."

"So," prompted Tom, "Commander Johnstone…?"

"He was the reason there was no mutiny. Commander

Johnstone had recently become a grandfather for the first time. He was as anxious as anyone to return to his family. He ordered us to surface and we made for Clyde. We did not get too close to shore—it already looked deserted, but we weren't about to risk infection for those who were staying—and anyone who wanted to leave was given permission to disembark. Around half the crew left in inflatables."

"But not you?" said Ceri.

"I lost touch with my family many years ago. No wife or kids." He sighed. "We had enough men to continue to be operational. We've been submerged nearly ever since. Worked our way down the coast of Europe, looking for signs of survivors. Groups of survivors. We've seen the occasional individual fishing or building fires on the beach, but only on the continental mainland. We came back up the west coast of Britain, past Cornwall, Wales, Lancashire and Cumbria—the *Argute* was constructed in Barrow-in-Furness, you know—and around Scotland. The weird thing is that we haven't seen so much as a single person in Britain until we found you."

"That's not weird," said Ceri. "We told you why. Everyone was called to London. If you'd gone there, you'd have seen thousands of people."

"E.T. and his chums, too, no doubt."

The woman coloured, but stared defiantly back at him. Irving found himself warming to her; she showed spunk. Pity she and the man were so deluded.

"How did you find us?" she asked, clearly choosing not to pursue the nonsense about aliens.

"We heard the sound of gunfire."

"That was us learning how to use shotguns," said Tom.

"We came as close as we could in the heavy swell and listened. We heard a vehicle drive away last night. When the sea calmed this morning and we couldn't see or hear any sign of life, we decided to take the risk of coming ashore. I was investigating the building when we heard you coming back and, well, the rest you know."

"The water," said Tom.

"Beg your pardon?"

"That's why you didn't receive the message. You must have been submerged in deep water when the Commune was held. I wonder… what about other countries? They have submarines too, don't they?"

"Only a handful of countries have subs like the *Argute*. Nuclear-powered subs. Traditional subs can't stay submerged for long. We can stay under for months on end."

"What's happened to the other countries' nuclear subs? Are there any still about?"

"Most were in port when the Millennium Bug began. Nuclear-powered subs are incredibly expensive to operate. In days of downturning economies, they are employed frugally. Those that were out conducting sea trials or on ops were recalled by their governments when the nuclear shit looked about to hit the fan. Just before the crisis, we were in contact with one American sub, USS *Vermont*, but last we heard she was heading back to port in South Georgia for refitting. The only other sub we've been in contact with since is a Russian craft." Irving shrugged. "That was two weeks ago. They were operating on a skeleton crew, like us, but it sounds as though the situation has, er, got to them. They were heading home to stock up on more vodka."

"Ha!" exclaimed Ceri. "They've got the right idea."

"What weapons do you have on board?" asked Tom.

Irving considered refusing to answer. He didn't much like the look in the man's eye while he asked the question. Then he remembered his own argument for disclosure to Commander Napier: what harm can it do to tell them everything they want to know? They're merely six people and a dog; it's not as if they can do anything with the knowledge.

"Tomahawk cruise missiles," he said.

"Nuclear warheads?"

Irving shook his head. "We're Astute Class. Only Vanguard Class carry ballistic missiles."

"These Tomahawk missiles… from how far away can they hit a target?"

"Assuming all satellites are still operational, they're accurate to within a few metres for up to two thousand kilometres."

Tom gave a low whistle. "So dropping a couple of missiles on, say, Stonehenge from here would be a breeze?"

"In theory, yes."

"That's where they're making some sort of beacon, to guide the rest of their civilisation to Earth… Um, what do you mean 'in theory'?"

"I mean that it's not going to happen in practice." Irving held up a hand to forestall Tom's further words. "I have told you all I can. Now my men and I must return to the *Argute*. Commander Napier wants to head out into the Atlantic this evening. We're going to Kings Bay in southern Georgia to ascertain whether the United States Navy is still in existence."

"No!" said Tom. "Please. If you blow up Stonehenge, it might give us some chance—"

"Enough!" Irving felt that if he heard any more, the craziness might start to wear off on him. "I understand that you've been through a hard time and trauma can affect people in many strange ways, but if you think we're going to waste missiles blowing up one of our nation's most ancient monuments to fit in with some hare-brained conspiracy theory, then think again."

"But—"

Tom rose to his feet and Irving took a pace backwards, hearing the smooth ratcheting sound of a round being chambered behind him, but Ceri grabbed the man's arm and pulled him back down.

"Tom! Leave it!" she hissed. "There's no way we're going to make them believe us. He's right. It *does* sound completely crazy. The only way he'd understand is by letting Peter show him, but that's not going to happen while they're afraid of catching something." She sighed and turned back to Irving. "Go on, go. Go to America. I hope you find what you're looking for. Either way, come back to Britain when you're done, okay? Make sure you're back by May at the latest. It might still not be too late to prove you're not a complete arsehole."

As Irving walked back to the inflatable, his three men fanned out beside him, he removed the suit helmet and glanced back. The couple had not moved from the base of the pebble bank. They watched him walk away, their arms around each other. The woman was sobbing.

The compulsion that Howard spoke about, of needing to go to Britain, did not materialise in Colleen. On the contrary, she had never left the shores of the Emerald Isle and the thought of doing so now terrified her. There would be no coastguard or shipping to call upon if they hit trouble. Even if they made it safely to Britain, then what? Any survivors they encountered would likely be scared and suspicious, like she had been when meeting Howard.

Colleen had not always been afraid. There had been a time when she had looked the world in the eye, daring it to cow her. With Sinead at her side, she'd felt ready to face anything life might throw at her. She'd have paddled to Britain in a rowing boat with Sinead, and strode through England's green and pleasant land with chin jutting and fists clenched.

That was then. Life had at last beaten her down. Rather, death had.

In the weeks since she had fled their flat in Rathmines, the dream image of Sinead as a grasping monster had receded. Colleen suspected she might now during her sleep be able to remember Sinead as the loving, laughing girl she had been even without whiskey to drive away the terrors. But that was merely one reason to stop drinking. There were a million and one other reasons to carry on.

Although once or twice she caught Howard looking at her with concern—his doctor's face—he was quick to alter his expression and did not once voice his disapproval at her drinking herself semi-comatose each night.

It was the appearance of the man calling himself Clint that

made Colleen curb her drinking. She did not want to lose control of her faculties with him around.

Howard had decided to return to his surgery to collect his doctor's bag and as many medical supplies as he could carry.

"I meant to bring my case when I first returned," he explained, "but didn't have room to carry it with all the food I brought back."

"Sorry," said Colleen. "I should have come with you."

"Nonsense." Howard gave her one of his reassuring smiles. He must have been popular with his patients if his bedside manner was as disarming. "And you needn't come with me this time if you'd prefer to remain this side of the river."

"I *would* prefer that. I'll wait for you this side of O'Connell Bridge. Where you first saw me."

Howard had been gone about an hour, time Colleen had spent gazing down into the Liffey. It might have been her imagination, but she fancied that the water below, normally brown and greasy, already looked to be running purer without man depositing filth into it. Occasionally she glanced about, golf club at the ready in case any rats or dogs were taking an interest in her.

A light drizzle began to fall from a sky the colour of porridge. Colleen didn't mind; her hair could do with a rinse.

She heard him before she could see him. *Click-clop... click-clop...*

A man appeared at the far side of the bridge, walking up the centre of O'Connell Street. It wasn't Howard.

Whether her self-preservation instincts were dulled after a few days in Howard's company or the whiskey had made her soft in the head, she didn't think to duck out of sight until it was too late.

The man had started to cross the bridge, but came to a halt when he noticed her. At the same time that he stopped, so did the clicking noise. He resumed walking: *click-clop... click-clop...*

Jeans tucked into knee-high, leather cowboy boots. The toes of each boot *clicked* on the road an instant before the heel *clopped*. A leather jacket zipped tightly against the rain; it strained a little against the girth it had to contain. A wide-brimmed Stetson, as though he were in Texas not Dublin. A black holster on one hip. Jeans, boots and jacket looked new and stiff. Unworn and uncomfortable.

She stayed still while he approached, but gripped the club a little tighter. He drew close enough for her to make out his face beneath the brim of the Stetson. Pasty jowls, eyes dark and narrow like fissures in stone; they stared at her, sizing her up. His lips were full, too full as though over-Botoxed, and orange-stained from the unlit cheroot dangling from one corner.

"That's far enough," Colleen said when he was about ten yards away. She did not raise the club; her glance kept returning to the black holster at his hip. It had a flap concealing whatever lay within. Her tongue darted out to lick nervously at her lips.

One corner of the man's mouth turned up in a smirk and he took two more paces before coming to a stop.

He extracted one hand from his jacket pocket and raised it to his mouth to remove the cigar. Like the rest of him, his hands looked big.

"So," he said, "I'm not the Omega Man, after all." His accent was soft and Irish; a local man.

"I'm not alone," said Colleen.

He moved his head to look about, exaggerating the movement for her benefit. "Your friends must all be hiding." He smirked again and his gaze moved to the golf club. "Going to play a round?"

Maybe it was adrenaline brought on by apprehension, but Colleen felt a surge of the old indomitable spirit return. She hefted the club.

"This?" she said. "No, this isn't for playing with. It's to keep vermin away." She felt her jaw jut out in her once-familiar gesture of defiance.

Although Colleen wouldn't have thought it possible, the man's eyes narrowed further. His smirk disappeared.

Colleen was fed up of being afraid. Afraid of solitude, of unfamiliar places, of sleeping. Now this stranger had come and made her feel afraid again. She'd had enough.

"What's with the Stetson and boots?" she said. "Playing at cowboys? That a six-shooter you're packing on your hip?"

The man replaced the cheroot between his lips. When he spoke, they moved around it.

"That's quite a mouth you have," he said. "I'm sure you can be friendlier than this. A *lot* friendlier."

His gaze moved down her body and Colleen felt her skin crawl as though a bucket of woodlice had been tipped down her neck. Involuntarily, she took half a step back.

The man smiled. His lips were too thick, out of proportion with the rest of his features. They made his smile sinister, like the grin of a clown with teeth filed to points. Colleen had to stop herself taking another backward pace.

"Would you like to see my pistol?" The man's tone dripped with innuendo and he chortled as though pleased with his wit.

Colleen did not reply. The fight-or-flight instinct was raging within her, flight winning hands down, and it was taking all her willpower not to run.

He undid the flap on the holster and withdrew a pistol. Colleen knew nothing about guns, but had seen pistols like this on television. Usually in war films.

"That's a…"

"A Luger," he finished for her. He held the gun against his cheek and sighed. "So cold. So symbolic."

"Hmm. A nazi-cowboy fetish," said Colleen. She had tamed the impulse to run. The man no longer scared her. In fact, she was starting to find him vaguely ridiculous. With a sudden certainty, she knew… "It's not real. That gun's fake."

The man's pasty cheeks flushed with colour. He pointed the pistol at Colleen's face and her certainty evaporated when she stared down the barrel. She felt an urgent need to empty her bladder. He pulled the trigger.

Click.

"You're right," he said. "It's imitation. I've tried to find a real one, but no luck yet." He reholstered the gun and reached behind him. "This, however, is very real."

He brought his hand forward. Something metallic glinted. There was another *click* and a blade appeared. Wickedly long and pointed, stained a blackening red. He turned it this way and that for Colleen's inspection.

She stared at the blade. The black-red started to run as drizzle soaked into it.

"Tsk, tsk," said the man. "Forgot to clean it after my last kill. Naughty Clint."

"*Clint?*" Colleen couldn't help herself. She snorted.

The man's face coloured again and he scowled. Still holding the knife out, he took a step towards her.

Colleen didn't react. She was no longer even looking at the man, but beyond him.

She waved. Howard's hands were too full to wave back.

Chapter Sixteen

The sun rose over London into a clear sky. It shone onto a thick hoar frost, making road surfaces glitter as though truly paved with gold. Without industry and traffic and people to generate heat, the frost had taken firm hold. Spider webs hanging between railings looked as if they had been spun from sugar, not silk. Grass, shrubs and twigs might have been crafted from white glass.

Walking from the hotel to the parking lot in the early morning light was no easy task. Milandra clung to Jason Grant's arm. The last thing she needed was to lay herself up with a broken ankle.

"These sidewalks are treacherous," she commented. "The pavements look equally as bad so it was as well you had the foresight to send out those salt trucks yesterday." She gripped Grant's arm tighter. "Go, you."

"This is kind of fun," said Simone Furlong. She bounded forward and planted her feet on the ice-encrusted paving stones, shooting forward for a few yards in a slide. "Wheee." She sounded like a teenager.

"Friggin' cold," muttered George Wallace, tugging his jacket tighter. "Why couldn't we have landed somewhere tropical five millennia ago?"

"I quite like it," said Lavinia Cram. "Makes a change from the Florida humidity."

"You can keep it," said Wallace with a scowl. "When this is over, and the traitor is no more, I'm heading for warmer climes and staying there."

"Still intent on going after Ronstadt, George?" said Milandra.

"Yep. Though I been doing some thinking. May not be any need for me to go chasing around Earth Haven hunting him. The Commune can get him to come to me."

"I doubt that even a Commune of seventy-five thousand can force one of our number to act against his will," said Milandra. "At least, it's never been tested."

"Then about time it was," said Wallace.

The rumble of engines reached their ears long before they arrived at the parking lot. Twenty-two red double-decker buses and twenty coaches stood idling, exhaust fumes turning the cold air grey.

The surface of the lot had been gritted and rock salt crunched beneath their feet. It was a great relief to Milandra to feel she could walk without her feet wanting to slide out from under her.

Drones had started to arrive, shepherded by teams of three people. The shepherds were armed, but merely as a precaution. The drones were docile and pliant, shuffling along to wherever their herders indicated. If a drone showed an inclination to act as an individual, the team quickly combined mental forces and nudged the errant drone back down the subservient path.

A sandy-haired woman directed the arriving teams. Milandra recognised her; she had co-piloted the airplane Bishop had flown in from Australia.

"Fifty drones to each red bus," she called. "One team of three onto each bus for control purposes. The rest of the teams, onto the coaches." The woman caught sight of Milandra's group and strolled over. "G'day," she said. "I'm Tess Granville."

"I know," said Milandra. "You came in with Troy Bishop."

"Yes. I heard that he passed. Shame."

"Hmm. Which coach are we on?"

"That black one on the end. Have a good journey and I shall see you in Salisbury."

"Indeed." Milandra turned to her Deputies. "You all get on. I'm going to watch for a little while."

"I'm staying out here, too," said Grant. "Make sure everything runs smoothly."

"Fine," said Milandra. "But don't feel you have to stay by my side. I know you're itching to get involved."

Grant smiled. "You know me too well."

He walked off to talk to Rodney Wilson, who was standing by

the line of red buses.

"Well," said Wallace. "I ain't staying out here in this cold. See ya on the bus."

"Those single-decked ones are called coaches over here," said Lavinia.

"Whatever," said Wallace.

Simone and Lavinia went with him and disappeared onto the black coach.

Milandra walked over to where Tess continued to direct the arriving groups. The drones had been taken off work details the previous day, stripped of their stinking clothes and sluiced down with rainwater to remove the worst of the filth covering them. Each drone had been provided with a clean set of clothes, although not much attention had been paid to sizes judging by the way shirts hung loosely like limp sails, while trousers barely reached ankles.

"Fifty drones to each red bus," called Tess. "Count them on, please. Oh, I remember you. Fresh little bugger, you were. Well, mate, your groping days are over."

Tess was directing her comments to a slack-jawed youth who had arrived in a larger group of drones. He looked towards the sound of her voice with a vacant gaze, but no recognition showed in his dull features.

Although the expressions on the drones' faces in this larger group were as blank as those who had already clambered onto buses, their bearing was straighter and they marched rather than slouched. Cleaner, too, than the others, they wore clothes that fitted them well. Milandra guessed who these were immediately: the hundred who had been spared work, had been kept well-fed and healthy, exercised regularly. Sixty-three of their number would be instrumental in restarting the Beacon.

Milandra watched while the hundred were marched to two buses designated as theirs. Whereas the destination boards at the front of the other vehicles were blank, these two buses displayed the number 100.

The drones boarded and were joined by teams of six on each bus. Since the hundred were fitter and healthier than the rest, any problems they might cause by becoming unruly on the journey could potentially be more serious. Grant had therefore insisted on them being minded by larger teams, who were under orders to clamp down instantly on the slightest show of individuality.

Milandra shivered. Now she had stopped walking, the icy air was seeping into her ancient bones like ink on blotting paper. She stamped her feet and breathed onto her hands before thrusting them deep into her coat pockets. Wallace had been right: why hadn't they landed further south instead of on this freezing island?

Smiling wryly to herself, Milandra made for the black coach.

The fluttering sensation inside Bri's head did not feel particularly unpleasant. Perhaps it was because she knew she could eject the invaders any time she chose that made the intrusion bearable.

Bri held hands with Peter and Diane. She found it difficult to think of them as non-human, despite what Peter had shown her and Will the night before, after the submarine had left.

A 'montage' he'd called it; a series of images, flickering at first then growing so intense it was as though Bri was actually experiencing the events herself. A vast craft leaving a red-tinged desert planet of black sand; gigantic creatures gazing in terror at the skies; a tidal wave that swept away everything in its path; rows of hairy, sleeping people who only looked vaguely human.

Will had grown wide-eyed with wonder. He'd chattered about spaceships and aliens and dinosaurs for the rest of the evening until even Ceri, who seemed to have taken a real shine to the boy, had grown weary.

Then Peter told her another tale. About the deliberate spread of a deadly virus. By the time he had finished speaking, Bri had been sobbing.

She did not know what to believe. Ceri said she was certain that what Peter had shown and told them had actually happened; Tom seemed less sure. If it was true, Bri was now holding the hands of people who had been instrumental in the deaths of her parents and brother. If 'people' was the correct word.

She liked Peter. He sometimes said funny things that made her laugh and he appeared genuinely concerned for her well-being. When he had asked if he could take a look to see if he could discover what was causing her headaches, she agreed immediately. Hesitation only came when he suggested that Diane also take a look.

That was an entirely different prospect. Diane had barely spoken three words to her or Will. She seemed aloof, not truly a part of the small group which had found them in Nottingham.

Diane noticed Bri pause.

"It's okay," she said. "I understand if you'd rather not have me inside your head."

Bri considered her for a moment. Aloof, yes, but she didn't get the sense that Diane was a bad person. And, according to the story Tom and Ceri had related to her last night, Diane had saved the lives of the other three.

She shrugged. "If Peter thinks that it's better if you look, too, that's fine."

Diane had given her a tight smile. It hinted that she could be an attractive lady if she smiled more often.

Ceri and Tom stood watching, both wearing apprehensive expressions. They looked more worried than Bri felt. Will was playing outside with Dusty, under strict instructions not to go down to the beach and to come running if he saw anything unusual, especially out in the bay.

The inspection, or whatever it was, of her mind didn't last long. Bri could have looked back at the invading intelligences, subjected them to the same sort of scrutiny to which she was submitting. Instead, she remained passive, sensing the invasion as a sunbathing person might sense an insect crawling over her back, but tolerating it.

Then it was over. Their hands let go of hers. She felt the minds withdraw and looked from Peter to Diane. As usual, Diane's expression was neutral, but it seemed more deliberate this time; forced. Peter, with his open features, would have more difficulty maintaining a neutral expression and didn't look as though he was even trying to. His face crinkled into a frown.

"Peter?" Bri's voice sounded tiny.

Peter shook his head. He chewed on his bottom lip.

"*Peter*?" Bri could not keep the hint of panic from her voice. She suddenly felt sick.

Tom and Ceri both came forward.

"What's wrong?" Tom's voice was higher-pitched than normal.

Peter glanced at Bri and must have noticed the effect he was having on her. He forced a strained smile to his lips and placed his hand on her forearm, gripping it reassuringly.

"I'm sorry," he said. "I didn't mean to alarm you."

"What did you see?" Bri asked.

Peter's smile faded and he let go of her arm. He rose to his feet. "I need to discuss this with Diane first," he said. "Try to make sense of it." He looked at Diane and jerked his head towards the door.

She stood and followed him from the room.

Clint had retracted the switchblade and secreted it somewhere behind his back by the time Howard reached them. Colleen wanted to rush forward and hug Howard, but that would mean passing close to the newcomer. She stayed where she was.

In his right hand, Howard clutched a black case the size of a small suitcase. In his left, he carried a bulging canvas sack, and on his back a rucksack, also bulging.

He drew level with Clint and stopped. Colleen was struck by how small Howard looked. Like a jockey standing next to a heavyweight boxer.

"Hello," he said with a smile. "I'm Howard. Pleased to meet you." He lowered the black case carefully to the ground and held out his right hand.

Clint's pasty features drew together. He took a step away and did not reach for Howard's hand.

"I'm Clint," he said. He shot a dark glance at Colleen, who bit the inside of her cheek to prevent the chortle escaping.

If Howard found anything comical about the man's name, he hid it well. Without making any show of Clint having ignored his proffered handshake, he bent and picked up the case.

"Will you come and eat with us?" said Howard. Colleen's heart sank. "We have plenty to go around. And I could do with getting out of this drizzle."

"Er, I have my own pad back yonder..." Clint inclined his head to the north of the city. Again, Colleen had to struggle to avoid showing her amusement; he was now even sounding like an Irish cowboy. "Where are you folks staying?"

Colleen's urge to giggle vanished. She glared at Howard, willing him not to say any more, but he wasn't looking at her.

"*The Quays*," he said. "In Temple Bar. Not far."

Clint raised his hand to the brim of his Stetson and tipped it. "Lead on, pardner," he drawled. Colleen no longer found it funny. He was starting to creep her out again.

Howard walked towards her.

"Here," she said, "let me take that sack from you." When she leaned in to him, she whispered, "Be on your guard. There's something not right about him. He has a switchblade with blood on it."

She straightened, holding the sack. It was surprisingly light.

Howard's eyes widened and his mouth briefly contorted into a grimace of apology. He gave the slightest of nods to show that he understood.

Colleen headed for Temple Bar, walking slowly, taking a circuitous route, reluctant to lead Clint to the one place she felt safe. Howard hung back and she could hear the men talking.

"What did you do before the Millennium Bug?" Howard asked.
"I was a doctor, a G.P. Colleen there was a university lecturer."

"Oh, I was a personal bodyguard. To a famous Irish actor." Colleen noted he was forgetting to drawl.

"Really?" said Howard in a tone suggesting he was both delighted and fascinated in what Clint had to say. "Which one?"

Colleen smiled wryly to herself. She had found herself opening up to Howard; he had that way about him, that he was genuinely interested in whoever he was talking to. It was clearly working on Clint, too.

"Um," said Clint. "I'm not supposed to say. Client confidentiality, you know."

"I understand. Similar principles bind me. Doctor-patient confidentiality and all that. Although I have to say I doubt such ethical considerations apply any longer. I could tell you all about Mrs McGilliguddy's rheumatism, were you interested, and it wouldn't matter one iota. Mrs McGilliguddy, bless her soul, certainly wouldn't object."

"Ah. Of course you're right," said Clint. "Well, okay. I worked for…" He named an actor.

"*Really*? Wow! I've seen lots of his films. Superb actor."

"Yeah. The best. Great guy, too. Lovely to work for."

"And you were his bodyguard… That's quite a responsibility. Must have been dangerous."

"Oh yes. But, you know, I can handle myself."

"Yes. I can see that. And I expect you had a gun."

"Oh yes. A Magnum. Like Dirty Harry's."

"Go ahead, punk, make my day," said Howard in a passable impersonation of Clint's namesake.

"Yes. Very good." Colleen detected irritation in his tone; Clint did not like to be upstaged.

"I expect you had to leave the Magnum in the States," continued Howard.

"Yeah, er… how d'you mean?"

"Well, when you returned to Ireland. You wouldn't have been allowed to bring the Magnum with you."

"Oh, I see. Yes, of course, he lives in the States."

"In Los Angeles?"

"Yes. Er, no. He has a ranch. In Wyoming. I help out with the horses. Mustangs."

"Wow! What a life you must have led. So why were you in Dublin? On leave?"

"Yes. He's very generous with leave. Pays my air fares and everything." He sighed wistfully. "Business class, of course."

Colleen wanted Howard to stop. One glance at Clint's face and hands, the flesh as pale as the underside of a mushroom, gave instant falsehood to his claims to have been living and working under the Wyoming sun. At some point, Clint was likely to come to the realisation that both she and Howard were fully aware he was lying. Colleen did not think it would be a good idea to be around him when that happened. She thought of the blood-stained blade and repressed a shudder.

"We're here," she said.

She opened the door and the three of them stepped into *The Quays*.

The convoy of forty-two buses and coaches wound its way slowly through West London, following the trail laid by the bulldozers and gritters. They had done a good job. Abandoned vehicles had been shunted aside, leaving wide, empty lanes for the drivers, many of whom had only sat behind the wheel of a bus for the first time five days previously. The road surfaces glinted, but it was crystals of salt, not ice, that reflected the sunlight and the journey was unhampered by the heavy frost.

On one of the red double-deckers, one that bore the number 100, sat Joe Lowden. He was a northern lad, but was no longer consciously aware of the fact. He was no longer consciously aware of much at all. His mind lay shrouded in fog like a cemetery in a Hammer film.

Unconnected images of his past played randomly across the scrambled surface of his psyche. A young boy standing on the wooden deck of a boat, staring open-mouthed at open-mouthed fish. A polythene bag containing round violet pills. A woman wearing scarlet lipstick holding out a ten-pound note. A filthy man reaching out a hand to tousle a young boy's hair.

He didn't know who the open-mouthed young boy was, or the man and woman. He no longer remembered his own name. It was lost within the swirling fog.

Had Joe Lowden still been capable of complex thought, he might have appreciated the upsides to his current predicament: he was fitter than he had ever been; had filled out from all the food he had been eating; he no longer craved chemical stimulation.

Joe sat quietly, dozing occasionally when the motion of the bus lulled him, staring at the back of the woman's head in front of him when his eyes opened, now and then glancing without interest at the white fields passing by the window.

The buses carried Joe and over a thousand like him to Salisbury.

Peter strode down the corridor and entered an empty bedroom. When Diane had followed him in, he closed the door and turned the lock.

"Did you see?" he said. "All those new pathways and active areas? Her brain is lit up like Blackpool."

Diane nodded. "I don't know what Blackpool is, but she's using parts of her brain that are dormant in other humans."

"It must be the head trauma. It's somehow activated neural links that have in turn awoken areas of the brain they haven't previously been able to access."

"I think…" Diane spoke slowly, as though voicing a thought not yet fully formed. "I think that their brains have evolved to be like ours. After all, they *were* created in our image. Those newly-active areas of her mind… they were dormant before she was struck on the head, but they *existed*. They weren't present at all in the original drones. These areas must therefore have gradually developed since the first drones arrived here. Perhaps through interbreeding with the native bipedal species. Perhaps through a genetic memory of the drones' creators. Maybe a bit of both. Doesn't really matter. What matters is that these areas of the brain exist and are ready to be used when activated." She paused for a moment. "I think that within a generation or two, perhaps three or four—again, it doesn't really matter—humans were going to find they could tap into those unused portions of their brains without having to suffer a head trauma first. They are on the verge of evolving to that stage."

"To becoming us," said Peter. "I think you could be right." He sighed. "If putting aside the love of violence and conflict would accompany that evolutionary step, it might not be necessary to get rid of them all. Sadly for them, we'll never know."

"Did you notice anything else about the girl?"

"That she needs urgent medical treatment?"

Diane nodded. "I have an idea what her condition is, but she needs a doctor."

"Yes," said Peter. "It's why I wanted us to be alone. I need to speak to Milandra."

Diane's eyes widened. "You can't reach London from here, surely?"

"Not on my own. But maybe the two of us…?"

"Okay."

"Really? I anticipated having to talk you into it."

Diane shrugged. "I can see the girl needs help that no one here can give her. And I've had my fill of killing humans. I don't even think of them as drones any more. If I can help save the girl, I'm in."

"Thank you." Peter reached out and briefly gripped her hand. She did not return the squeeze, but neither did she pull away. "This is going to be exhausting. We'll need to go straight to the kitchens afterwards and eat like teenage boys. Come. Let's sit on the bed."

They sat side by side.

Peter glanced at Diane. "Ready?"

She nodded.

"Right then. Let's do this."

Peter took a deep breath and closed his eyes. He let his mind slip free and found Diane's. Combining into a whole more powerful than the sum of its parts, Peter *reached…*

With the heating system turned up high, the interior of the executive coach was as warm as slippered feet by the hearthside. Although the coach's occupants did not need to sleep, except when recovering from physical injury or great mental fatigue, many felt their eyelids growing heavy. Lulled by a combination of cosiness and gently rocking motion, some gave in and dozed, chins lolling on chests.

Seated around a table near the front of the coach, three of the Deputies played poker. The game was punctuated by accusations from Wallace and Lavinia that Simone was using her powers as the Chosen to peek into their minds when they were concentrating on their hands. For chips, they used diamonds, rubies, emeralds and sapphires they had found in a suitcase in Bishop's flat. Troy Bishop had been a keen hoarder of precious gems.

Milandra and Jason Grant sat across a table from each other on the opposite side of the aisle. Grant's eyelids fluttered closed occasionally and he'd jerk his head upright whenever it dropped forward. Milandra smiled at his latest wide-eyed snap back to full consciousness.

"Why fight it?" she said. "I know how hard you've been working to get the Grid ready to be switched back on and to make sure today runs smoothly. Have a nap. Revitalise."

Grant returned her smile. "You know, I might just do that. It's snug in here."

He reached down to a button at the side of his seat and reclined the back rest. Folding his arms across his chest, he closed his eyes.

Milandra watched his breathing slow. Then she turned her attention to the white scenery outside. The frost was so thick in places it looked like snow.

She became aware of the other presence as soon as it appeared, pressing against the barrier around her mind, requesting an audience. She allowed it to enter.

Milandra?

Wait! There are others near. Let me pretend to doze off…

She glanced around. The three Deputies were too engrossed in their game to pay her any attention. Grant's mouth had opened slightly to emit soft snores.

Milandra gave a great yawn and turned her head a little towards the window. Crossing her arms over her ample bosom, she closed her eyes.

Okay. So, Peter, you're not alone.

Diane Heidler is with me.

Fully recovered from her injuries, I trust?

Yes. She says thank you.

And the reason for your visit?

The girl. Brianne. We've looked inside.

And?

As you suspected. She is accessing areas of her brain that are dormant in other humans. Fresh neural pathways have opened, connecting the newly-functioning areas with the regular parts of her mind. The new pathways begin at the site of the trauma to her temple.

I knew that injury must be connected to the girl's abilities. How did she sustain the trauma?

She can't remember. That part of her memories is obscured.

And how is she physically?

There's a lot of damage. She needs medical treatment.

If any doctors survived on the mainland, they'll be of no use to anybody now.

We sense you have already anticipated this need and acted upon it.

Your senses do not fail you. I noted the injury when viewing the girl through another's memory and suspected she would require medical attention. I began to scan our memory bank for medical knowledge, but it is like hunting for one shrimp in an ocean without being sure the shrimp is even there. It is uncertain whether any of our people gained the requisite knowledge to heal humans of physical harm. We have certainly never required such knowledge for ourselves. Only the geneticists would know.

And they were all left behind on Earth Home.

Indeed. So the knowledge of any who have since died has not passed to me. I considered the team who created the virus, but its activities were confined to the cellular level. I doubt any of them will possess the necessary know-how to treat a head wound. No. Our collective memory, vast as it is, will not provide the answer.

Then how?

Even on my own, I am able to extend beyond the shores of this island. But my reach is limited. I looked to islands lying near this one and got lucky. There is a doctor in Dublin. At that range and alone, I could only suggest, not compel, but I sensed he already possessed the desire to travel to mainland Britain. Look for him in Holyhead. That's in—

North Wales. I know… Er, Diane wants to know why you're doing this. Helping to save the girl.

Milandra paused before replying. She had been avoiding asking this question of herself.

There is no guarantee the Great Coming will succeed. Our previous journeys here, and that of the ancients before us, have demonstrated that manoeuvring within the gravity of a planet a craft built for interstellar travel is fraught with danger. If it fails, we shall need to reconsider our attitude towards the surviving humans. Even if it succeeds, some—we three are examples, and I suspect there will be more—may urge a display of compassion. Before the girl became known to us, such pleas were doomed to fail. Now the girl and her abilities might lend greater weight to those who would see the continuation of the human race; an improved, maybe enlightened human race.

You mean the girl herself could stand as a beacon of hope for the human race surviving?

Hmm… a beacon? Yeah, maybe. Provided she survives herself, of course. So look to Holyhead.

One last thing. The Beacon—the other *beacon—when do you intend to reactivate it?*

Within the week. Earth Haven and Earth Home will be in the necessary alignment at around five in the morning. There are a thousand of us on our way to the site now and another thousand or so drones. Do not try to interfere.

We *won't. But the two adult humans might.*
Prevent them if you can. It will not go well for them.
We shall try. Have to go now. Exhausted. Thank you, Milandra.
They were gone.

Milandra kept her eyes shut so she could think without distraction. She had told Peter and Diane that she had started to scan the collective memory, looking for medical knowledge. What she hadn't told them was that she had abandoned the search as a waste of time almost immediately, but had continued to sift through the depths of accumulated wisdom and experiences like an internet surfer, pausing at any items that looked interesting, passing quickly over those that held no attraction.

It had been a while since she had ventured into that realm; it was easy to forget quite how vast the stored information had become.

A notion still nagged at her, triggered by something Jason Grant had said, that she should spend time trawling the memories, looking for she knew not what, but that she would recognise it when she found it.

It would have to wait. Everything was secondary to the Beacon.

Chapter Seventeen

While they waited for Peter and Diane to return, Tom and Ceri told Bri everything they knew about the Beacon. From outside came the occasional bark from Dusty. Tom crossed to the window frequently to check that dog and boy were okay. Whilst there, he glanced out at the bay, hopeful the submarine would return; if the crew hadn't changed its mind about bombing Stonehenge, he'd welcome another chance to persuade them. The sea remained placid, but empty.

"So they're going to mess about with Stonehenge," said Bri. "Rebuild it as a circle with only the smaller stones."

"Yep," said Ceri. "The bluestones."

"And that's it?"

"There is more," said Tom, "but we haven't quite got to the bottom of it. Apparently the stone circle has to be activated in some way before it becomes a beacon. We don't know how it's activated."

"But once it is, the others like them will come?"

"I think the others are coming anyway," said Tom. "The idea of this Beacon is to make sure they arrive at the right planet in the right solar system. Ceri will correct me if I'm wrong, but even without the Beacon the others are due to arrive in May or June."

"Tom's right," said Ceri. "They don't *need* the Beacon to get here, but it will limit the possibility of something disastrous going wrong."

"And we don't want to limit those possibilities," said Tom.

Ceri sighed. "No, we don't. But there's nothing we can do."

"So Peter keeps saying." Tom threw his hands up in exasperation. "I can't simply sit here and do nothing."

"Peter wants the Beacon to work," said Bri softly.

Tom glanced sharply at the girl.

"What d'you mean?" he asked.

"When they examined my mind earlier, I caught a glimpse of

Peter's thoughts. I wasn't trying to look… it just happened."

Tom nodded, remembering Peter telling him something similar about seeing some of his and Ceri's thoughts when showing them the montage of spaceships and tsunamis.

"Are you certain?" asked Ceri. "That he wants the Beacon to work?"

Without hesitation, Bri nodded.

"But why?" said Tom. "I thought he was on our side."

"I only saw that he wants the Beacon to be activated," said Bri. "I didn't see why."

Ceri shook her head slowly. "The sly bastard. That's why he was so keen on trying to get us to go to Norway. So we'd be out of the way. And he was the one pressing for us to get back up to Scotland when we'd found Bri and Will in Nottingham."

"Yes, he was," agreed Tom. "He insisted on leaving their bikes behind when I offered to find a van and bring them back with us."

"He promised he'd find us cycles just as good in Wick." Bri sighed wistfully. "That was the best bike I've ever ridden."

"Maybe he's afraid," said Tom. "Afraid we'll stop the Beacon being activated. Which must mean there *is* something we can do."

Ceri frowned. "I still don't see what."

"What will happen?" asked Bri. "When the rest of them come. What then?"

Tom shot Ceri a glance and gave a brief shake of his head.

"No," said Ceri. "She's entitled to know."

"Entitled to know what?" Bri's eyes grew wide.

Tom sighed. "Okay. Bri, you know why, according to Peter, the Millennium Bug was let loose?"

She nodded. "We'd become too many and too violent."

"Exactly. Well, the rest of their civilisation are coming to Earth—Earth Haven they call it—to make it their new home."

Bri's eyes grew wider still. "They won't want us around getting in their way."

"Something like that. It won't be decided until they're all here, but it seems highly likely they won't want to take a chance on humans growing strong again, becoming too many for them to control."

"And they'll get rid of us." Bri brought one hand up to her mouth and her eyes filled with tears. "How will they do it?"

Tom glanced again at Ceri, who nodded for him to go on.

He took another deep breath. "Peter thinks they will hold a Commune. It's what they call it when they all get together and combine their minds. Remember the voice you felt inside your head telling you to go to London? That was merely five thousand of them. When the other seventy thousand of them get here, they'll hold another one. With the combined force of seventy-five thousand minds, Peter is certain they'll be able to control all the surviving humans throughout the world. They'll make us kill ourselves."

"That's awful." Bri's eyes brimmed over and she swiped at the tears running down her cheeks. "We must do something," she said. "Starting with this beacon thing."

"I agree," said Tom. "We have to at least try."

"Oh, shit," said Ceri. "I suppose you *are* right. But, Tom, just me and you, okay?"

He nodded.

"Wait a minute," said Bri. She sat up straighter. She had already stopped crying and Tom felt a surge of admiration. If he had been told when a sixteen-year-old he had mere months to live, he would have fallen to pieces. "I'm part of this. So is Will."

"No!" said Ceri. "He's only a boy."

"And you're injured, Bri," said Tom. "You told us they have guns. We can't take you and Will into that sort of danger."

"That's not your decision," said Bri, her chin jutting out. "You're not our parents. They're dead."

"No," said Ceri, "we're not your parents. But I had a son. Rhys. He was the same age as Will. I could do nothing to protect him. I'm going to do all in my power to protect Will. And you, Brianne."

"If the others come, we're going to die anyway," said Bri. She shrugged. "Die now trying to stop them. Die later. Same difference."

"Maybe," said Ceri. "Nevertheless, you and Will can't come with us. And that's final."

Bri said nothing more, but Tom recognised the spark of defiance burning bright in her eyes.

The only time Clint became animated was when, at Howard's prompting, he fantasised about his life as a bodyguard in Wyoming. Colleen didn't join in. She knew she would be unable to keep the scorn from her voice and had no wish to antagonise the man.

For the rest of the time, Clint remained aloof and watchful. He seemed particularly fond of watching her. Whenever there was a lull in conversation, or while they cleared away the dinner things, Colleen felt his regard upon her like an itchy rash. She grew increasingly uncomfortable and resolved not to drink heavily while in his presence.

Clint did not appear interested in alcohol. When Howard offered him a shot of whiskey or whatever else took his fancy from the array of bottles behind the bar, Clint shook his head curtly.

"I don't indulge," he said. "Part of my discipline as a bodyguard, you see."

Howard nodded knowingly. He really was very good at leading the man on. "Ah, yes. Must maintain control at all times. Wish I had your will-power."

Howard helped himself to a double shot of Jameson's. He remained behind the bar and Colleen could hear him rooting around on the shelves.

"A-ha!" he exclaimed. He came back to where they were sitting, clutching a packet of cheap cigars and a box of matches. "Your cheroot reminded me," he said to Clint. "Every Christmas Day, after dinner, I smoke a Cuban cigar. Except for the Christmas just gone. For obvious reasons." He glanced at the packet of cigars.

"These aren't exactly Cuban, but they'll do."

He extracted a cigar from the packet and unpeeled its cellophane wrapping. After a few false starts—the matches were a little damp—he managed to light the cigar and the bar became redolent with the earthy aroma of tobacco smoke.

Clint cleared his throat. "Where do you folks take care of, um, business of a personal nature?"

Colleen nodded to the main door.

"The pub across the road. There are some bowls and pans outside which should have rainwater in them. Use one to flush away afterwards. Then leave it outside to fill up for next time."

After the door had closed behind him, Colleen peered out. She watched him locate a bowl, pick it up and disappear into the pub opposite.

She turned back to Howard.

"He gives me the creeps," she said. "He keeps watching me. And that knife… he hasn't even told you he's got it. He must know I'm bound to tell you."

Howard breathed out a cloud of blue smoke. "He couldn't keep his eyes off you on our way here," he said. "I fear you have become part of his fantasies." Howard took a deep sip of whiskey. What he said next chilled Colleen. "When he comes for you, I'm not going to be able to stop him. Even if I was handy with my fists, which I'm not, he's too big."

"Then let's do something to him first." Colleen glanced at Howard's black case. "Don't you have something in there we can give him to knock him out? Better yet, kill him?"

Howard shook his head slowly. "There are drugs in there that could do him serious damage. Probably even kill him. But I could no more administer them than I could stick a knife in him. I'm a doctor. I extend life, not shorten it."

"Things have changed."

"Yes. But *I* haven't."

Colleen let her shoulders sag. The sense of security she felt in Temple Bar had dispersed like dust in wind. "What can we do then? Run away from him?"

"That's the only thing we can do. But he'll come looking for us. I sense a controlling, manipulative man beneath that ridiculous outfit. That sort won't simply let us walk away. He has no one else over whom he can exert control or with whom he can play out his fantasies."

Colleen shuddered. "I've known his type. But this is a big city. He'll not find us easily."

"True enough. He'll not give up easily either. Do you want to spend the rest of your days looking over your shoulder?"

"Then let's leave the city. Go up to Belfast or down to Waterford."

"Or leave Ireland. That's the only way we'll be sure he's not following us."

With a sinking feeling, Colleen realised Howard was probably right. She had met men, and women, like Clint before. Not content unless they had some sort of hold, some power, over others. Although they had not been in Clint's company for long, she recognised the signs as much as Howard did: the reluctance to take instruction, the close watchfulness, the need not to relinquish control of his faculties.

"Okay," she said heavily. "We'll go to Britain in your boat. When?"

"I doubt he'll try anything tonight. Too soon. He'll want to be sure of his ground first. Tomorrow is when he's likely to feel secure enough to act. We must leave before he does. Can you drive?"

"No. Sinead drove. I took the bus."

"I drive, but I can't get to my car. There was rioting in my street and it's blocked. I'll have to find one nearby. When he's back, I'll nip out on the pretext of using the loo…"

"No! Don't leave me alone with him."

"Okay, although I really will have to use the loo. I'll be quick." They both looked towards the sound that came from the door. Howard raised his finger to his lips.

Clint came back in. The cheroot still dangled unlit from the corner of his mouth.

"Where are you folks spending the night?" he enquired.

"Here," said Colleen.

He snorted. "There are better places than this, you know."

"We like it here."

"There are places that have, you know, beds and stuff."

"We like it here," repeated Colleen.

Howard waved his arms towards the bar. "Yeah, places with beds don't tend to have such well-stocked bars. So, Clint, you heading on back to your pad?"

"Thought I might hang out with you guys for a day or two." He looked pointedly at Colleen and she felt her skin crawl with revulsion. "The view here is a lot pertier."

Pertier? Colleen thought. *He actually said 'pertier'?*

Howard glanced regretfully at his empty whiskey glass. He took a last puff on the cigar and stubbed it out in the bottom of the glass. "Well, it's time to hit the sack for me," he said. "I have to pay a short visit across the road first."

While he was gone, Colleen busied herself preparing the sleeping area. They had dragged in two mattresses, which occupied a space on the wooden floor that might once have been used for dancing. She pushed her mattress tight to the wall and nudged Howard's a little closer so Clint would have to clamber over him to reach her. She could feel him observing her while she worked.

She nodded towards a padded bench running along the wall opposite her mattress.

"You should be comfortable enough there," she said.

He smirked. "Would be even comfier sharing your bed."

The candlelight glinted off something in his hands. With a start, Colleen realised he had extracted the knife. The blade was once more extended.

"What are you going to do with that?" she asked with a little difficulty: her mouth had abruptly dried.

"Oh, I like the feel of it in my hand. It's comforting. Not as good as a woman's tit, but nice enough for now."

The door banged shut behind Howard when he came back in. Clint made the knife disappear, but the smirk remained on his thick lips.

The oldest continuous settlement in the U.K. is the town of Amesbury, seven miles north of Salisbury and a mile or so from Stonehenge. Inhabited since the end of the last ice age, it took the Millennium Bug to all but empty the town of humans. The sole survivor, a woman in her forties, stepped into her car one rainy day in late December, called by the Commune. When she passed beyond the town limits heading for London, so Amesbury became devoid of human life for the first time in more than ten thousand years.

Now, late on a bitterly cold January afternoon, humans were returning, in red double-decker buses. That is, an approximation of humans, with muddied minds and vacant stares.

The caravan of buses and coaches had left the M3 near North Waltham and joined the A303, which led to the chalk plateau known as Salisbury Plain. Sparsely populated even before the Millennium Bug due to huge tracts being given over to the Ministry of Defence, the Plain remained an expanse of largely unspoiled grassland covering gently rolling undulations.

The bulldozers had gone into Amesbury and cleared the narrow main roads of all vehicles. The side streets were now choked with dented cars and vans, but the main roads through town provided easy passage for buses and coaches, even those steered by inexperienced drivers.

The lead bus, expertly driven by Rodney Wilson, lately of London Transport, came down High Street in what would have been the wrong direction of the one-way system in the pre-Bug days and into Church Street, passing shops and hostelries. Near the Church of Saint Mary and Saint Melor, before Church Street crossed the River Avon, Wilson brought the bus to a halt. Behind him, the snaking line of vehicles also came to a halt, the rearmost coach barely having made it into the beginning of town. When they were ready to make for Stonehenge, they would all be facing in the correct direction and could be driven along Church Street until it became Stonehenge Road, back to the A303 and then the short distance to the ancient monument itself.

The drivers turned off the engines and peace descended once more upon the town. The vehicles discharged their passengers. Those from the coaches stretched their legs and seemed glad to be in the fresh air, however chilly. Most of those who stepped down from the red double-deckers shuffled aimlessly to one side. They were herded towards the town centre and immediately put to work.

Like the sports centre in Tom's home town, the Amesbury Sports & Community Centre had been commandeered by the military during the height of the outbreak and converted into an emergency medical centre-cum-mortuary. Unlike the centre in Tom's home town, this one did not appear to have been the scene of civilian slaughter when sick people tried to escape the charnel house the interior had become and were shot down by soldiers who were probably themselves coughing and sighting down carbines through streaming eyes. The main Amesbury sports hall had been turned into a sick ward with a hodgepodge of fold-up beds, thin mattresses and sleeping mats. Most of their occupants had died where they lay.

Wearing plastic aprons, gloves and masks brought from London to minimise the risks of infection, the drones began to clear the sports hall of corpses and contaminated bedding. The drivers of the bulldozers and crane had done their job well. In addition to clearing the main thoroughfares of stalled vehicles, they had rooted out a small fleet of transits and flat-bed vans, which stood ready, petrol and diesel in tanks, keys in ignitions.

Since the work was familiar to the drones, they required little instruction. Without complaint, they bent to the task and soon a steady stream of vans was making its way across town, trailing the stench of stale death behind.

Holders Field at the edge of town, normally the site of the annual Amesbury Carnival and Show, had been designated as the local version of the Burning Fields. The bulldozers had paid a visit here, too, and removed the fences and gates that prevented ready access to the fields. Instead of processions, displays and stalls selling local crafts and cake, the field would play host to pyres of rotting bodies and stinking mattresses. Summer laughter and gaiety would be replaced by roaring flames and noisome smoke.

The sports centre would house the drones for their stay in Amesbury. The main sports hall would not hold a thousand, so they would overspill into the squash courts, gymnasiums, changing rooms, offices, wherever there was space for an exhausted body to lie.

Nearby houses and hotels and offices were also decontaminated to provide shelter for the people and for the hundred drones excused clearance duties.

Work went on late into the evening. Darkness hid the pall of black smoke hanging in the sky to the east of town, but could not mask the acrid smell wafting and eddying in the winter breezes.

When the tasks were completed, drones were led through the night, stumbling with exhaustion, to the River Avon. There they were made to strip and sluice themselves clean of the filth that caked them, despite the protective clothing. Not even the shock of near-freezing waters could stir them from their lethargy.

The storage compartments beneath the coaches had been stocked with food, spare clothes, sleeping bags and supplies of lighter fluid for use in the Burning Fields. Clean drones were dressed in fresh clothes and fed. Handed a sleeping bag each, they were led back to the sports centre where they found a space to lie down. Only perfunctory watch was maintained over them; they were too weary to cause problems, even had they the wit to do so.

In the hotel suite, Milandra smiled at her Deputies.

"Well," she said, "so far so good. That's base camp established for our stay here. In the morning, we go to the site and get started."

"With the crane shouldering the heavy lifting duties, we should be ready within two or three days," said Grant. "Four tops."

"Remember the first time?" said Wallace. "Took frigging months to lift everything into place with tree trunks for levers and ropes that kept snapping."

Simone scowled. "You have to keep going on about the first time. Like it was fucking special or something."

"Okay, Simone," said Milandra hurriedly. She didn't want another squabble on her hands. "We sometimes forget you were born on Earth Haven after the original Beacon was activated. George didn't mean anything by it." She continued quickly before Wallace had chance to say otherwise. "Within four nights from now, we'll activate the Beacon."

Simone clapped her hands. "Yay! I want to be in charge of one of the stones." She shot Wallace a dark look. "Since I wasn't there the first time."

"And then?" said Lavinia. "Back to London?"

"I've been thinking about that," said Milandra. "How about we spend what remains of winter and the spring in Cornwall? It has a milder climate than the rest of this island. And it will be the best place to witness the Great Coming."

Grant frowned. "Much remains to be done in London. The Grid is to come back online, the water supply to be restored. Wembley Stadium needs to be decontaminated, if necessary, and the approaches cleared. Vermin and dogs to control or eradicate. Ongoing decontamination of houses. Food collection. Don't forget, we'll have seventy thousand extra bodies to accommodate and feed. It might take weeks or even months for them to assimilate with us and us with them before we can even think about holding a Commune."

"If a Commune is what's decided," said Milandra. She held up her hand to stall Wallace's protests. "Yes, George, I agree that a Commune to eradicate the surviving humans is the most likely outcome, but I don't want us to assume it's the *only* possible outcome."

"The only one that makes any sense," muttered Wallace.

Milandra turned back to Grant. "Everything you say, Jason, is of course correct. All those things and more need to be done over the next few months. But they are already in hand. It isn't necessary you be there in person to oversee them. I propose we place that charge on another."

"Who?"

"Tess Granville."

Wallace snorted. "The Bossy Aussie."

Milandra smiled. "I prefer the term 'assertive'. She can keep an eye on things just as well as you, Jason. You can provide her with a full briefing, if it will make you feel better. And we can receive regular reports in Cornwall."

Grant sighed. "I suppose…"

"Good. Anyone else have any objections to spending a few months in Cornwall?"

Lavinia shook her head.

"If it's likely to be warmer than London then I'm all for it," said Wallace.

"I was looking forward to hunting more rats," said Simone, her expression surly.

"Cornwall has rats," said Milandra. "You can be in charge of keeping them under control, if you like."

Simone's face lit up like a child being offered ice cream. "I like."

"Okay. I was thinking we take one of the London buses. One of the Red Ladies, as Rod calls them. Ever since watching that movie *Summer Holiday*, I've wanted to ride in one."

"Shit movie," muttered Wallace.

"Oh, it possesses a certain innocent charm," said Milandra. "We'll need a driver, of course. I thought Rod might like to come. It seems to be doing him good to be away from the big city."

"Hmm," said Grant. "He'll want to lead the convoy back to London. He feels it's his responsibility as the most experienced driver."

"The other drivers will manage perfectly well without him," said Milandra firmly. "We can send those salt trucks back the night before so there won't be any problem with icy roads."

"What about drones?" said Grant. "We'll need to take some to clear corpses wherever we end up in Cornwall."

"And to burn the rats," said Simone.

"Let's see…" said Milandra. "What if we take twenty drones? The five of us and Rod will be able to manage them easily. We won't even need to keep them with us. Once they've done all we need them to do, we can send them back to London."

"They'll have to walk," said Lavinia.

"There'll be no hurry. We can instruct them to stop regularly to eat and to rest so they arrive back in London fit to work."

"Or we can instruct them to step off a cliff," said Wallace. "Twenty drones less won't make a difference."

Simone grinned. "Yes! Let's make them step off a cliff. Or walk into a bonfire. See if they pop like rats."

Milandra repressed the urge to shudder.

"We can decide at the appropriate time," she said. "All we need to decide now is whether we go to Cornwall after the Beacon's been activated."

Grant shrugged. Nobody demurred.

"Right," said Milandra. "That's settled then. Now we need to eat and rest. There's work to be done."

Peter and Diane did not return to the room in which the others waited. Once darkness had fallen, and Will and Dusty were safely inside, Tom went looking. He found them in the kitchen, stuffing their faces with food as though they hadn't eaten for weeks.

"We've been waiting for you," Tom said. "Bri's desperate to hear what you discovered."

"Sorry," said Peter, speaking around a mouthful of food. "We had to eat."

Tom narrowed his eyes. "Why? What have you been up to?"

Peter swallowed. "We contacted Milandra. The girl needs a

doctor. Milandra's located one."

"A doctor? Where?"

"Ireland. He should be on his way to Britain. We need to meet him in Holyhead."

"Holyhead? In Anglesey? That's miles out of our way."

It was Peter's turn to narrow his eyes. "What are you talking about? I didn't know we had a 'way'."

Tom took a deep breath. "Ceri and I are going to Stonehenge." He held up a hand. "Don't say anything. I know I'm not Rambo. I know we're likely to get ourselves killed. But we're agreed: we'd rather die trying to save ourselves than wait around for it to happen anyway."

"Tom, listen to me for a moment. Milandra specifically warned us from trying to interfere with the Beacon. A thousand of our people are travelling there. What chance do you think you'll stand? It's suicide, man."

"Maybe. But we have to try. I'd like you to take me and Ceri back to Wick tomorrow, please. We need to find a car."

"What about Bri and Will? Going to get them killed, too?"

"No!" Tom thought for a moment. "You two can take Bri and Will and go meet this doctor in Holyhead. We don't want the kids coming with us whatever happens."

Peter stared at him for a long moment. Tom held his gaze. Letting out his breath in a long sigh, Peter looked away.

"What exactly is wrong with Bri?" Tom asked.

Peter glanced at Diane, who chewed the rest of her mouthful and swallowed before replying.

"Subdural haematoma is my best guess," she said.

Tom raised his eyebrows.

"The girl has clearly suffered a blunt trauma injury to her forehead," said Diane. "It's likely that blood vessels have been ruptured and are bleeding into the subdural space. That's the gap between the brain and the skull."

"How do you know this?"

"I was a nurse in the Second World War. Later, I worked in a private hospital in Los Angeles." She glanced at Peter. "To relieve the boredom." Diane looked back at Tom. "That hospital was very exclusive and we mainly treated the after-effects of botched plastic surgery or the sort of illnesses that beset old wealthy people. But occasionally we'd get a millionaire producer who'd been out on his yacht and forgot to duck at the right moment, so I've seen this type of injury before."

"Can Bri be cured?"

"Only with surgery to remove blood clots and relieve the pressure on her brain."

"Oh, Christ. And if she doesn't get the surgery?"

"Depends whether it's acute or chronic."

"What's the difference?"

"The speed and inevitability of the outcome if left untreated."

"Which type do you think it is?"

"Well, when we looked into her mind, I could only see she's been suffering from headaches. She hasn't experienced any other symptoms that might indicate an acute condition. Dizziness, nausea, slurred speech, that sort of thing. There *is* a gap in her memory—it resembles a patch of fog—that's concerning." Diane shrugged. "I'm no doctor."

"But your best guess is that her condition is chronic?"

Diane nodded.

Tom sighed. "That's good, right?"

"Better than an acute subdural haematoma, but still not good."

"What will happen to her?"

"It might take weeks. Months even."

"What will? Speak plainly."

"Without surgery, it's likely the girl will die."

Chapter Eighteen

Colleen awoke three or four times during the night with the feeling she was being watched. Each time, she glanced over the softly-snoring form of Howard, certain that Clint was awake, but he was hidden in deeper shadows. Being unable to see him at all, not even the whites of his eyes, somehow made it worse.

She came out of a fitful doze as the interior of the pub was lightening with the dawn. The shadowy figure of Clint gradually came into view. He lay on his side on the bench, facing her. This was the first time she had seen him without the ridiculous Stetson; his hair was a sandy colour and matted with grease. His eyes were closed and he breathed steadily, but she suspected he was faking sleep. She suspected everything he said and did was fake. Never before had she taken such an immediate and intense dislike to another person.

Yes, she would gladly sail with Howard across the Irish Sea to get away from the man. She would attempt the Atlantic Ocean in a bath tub rather than spend another night in his vicinity.

The duvet she slept under was thick and cosy, but Colleen kept her leggings and tee-shirt on. The Pope himself couldn't have persuaded her to undress with Clint in the room.

Pulling back the duvet, she swung her legs to the floor. Immediately, her skin began to crawl when the sensation of being observed returned. She glanced at Clint, but his eyes remained closed. She picked up the golf club; she always felt more secure with that in her hands.

"Off to play a round again, my beaut?"

Clint's eyes were fully open and the smirk sat on his puffy lips as if it belonged there.

"Going for a pee," she muttered, sitting back on the mattress to pull on her boots. "I don't go outside without it. And I'm not your beaut."

"Well, ma'am, you might want to start treating me a bit sweeter.

We could be the last two people left alive of child-producing age. I think Howard is past it." He sniggered.

Colleen stood and tugged on her pullover. Then she shrugged on her coat. Gripping the club tightly, she stepped over the slumbering form of Howard and made for the door. As she passed Clint's bench, she leaned a little closer and whispered, "If we *are* the last two child-producing humans left alive, the human race is fucked."

"Don't know 'bout that," Clint drawled, "but you might soon be."

Colleen glanced back before opening the pub door. For a heart-stopping moment, she'd thought he was going to lunge for her there and then, but he hadn't moved from the bench. Cursing herself for a fool to risk riling him, she stepped out into the morning air.

A light drizzle fell from a low, leaden sky. A dog lapped at one of the containers of water lining the pavement outside the pub across the road. It looked up when Colleen approached and bared its teeth.

She brought the club down to clatter onto the surface of the road. The dog jumped and skittered away from her. She brought the club down again and the dog took to its heels.

Colleen strode forward, grabbed a sloshing pan and went inside to perform her ablutions.

When she re-entered *The Quays*, five minutes or so later, Howard was awake.

"Morning," he said. "I was just asking Clint if he'd like to rustle up some breakfast while we pay a visit to the supermarket. I noticed cartons of long-life fruit juice last time we were there. Some O.J. will go nicely with beans and ham."

Colleen didn't like long-life juice, but rubbed her stomach and forced an enthusiastic smile to her face.

"Mm. Sounds good," she said.

Clint was sitting up. The cowboy boots and Stetson were back on. A fresh cheroot had appeared in the corner of his mouth. He scowled. "I ain't much of a cook," he said.

"That's okay," said Howard cheerily, "because we don't have much in the way of cooking equipment. Just a couple of basic camping stoves. All you'll need to do is open the tins, chop the ham and heat the food up. You can chuck it all in the same pan. It goes down the same way."

Howard had already donned his shoes. He looked at Colleen. "I'll take my case. I need to check out the pharmacy section to see if they have any powdered antibiotics."

"Why d'you need your case to do that?" Clint's eyes narrowed.

"If they stock antibiotics in powder form, I need to collect as much as I can. Infection is one of the greatest dangers we face in this new world."

Clint considered for a moment. "I can see that. But you didn't answer my question. Why d'you need to take your case? You can bring back whatever you find in anything."

"Ah, but I can't. Not without risking spoiling them. You see, my case has special storage compartments for powdered drugs to ensure they are kept airtight and bone dry. To prevent contaminating them."

Clint considered again. "All right," he said. He smiled. It was difficult to tell in the gloomy interior, but Colleen didn't think the smile reached his eyes. "I'll follow you two out. I have morning business to take care of." He winked at them. "I'm a regular twice-a-day guy." He lifted the leather jacket from where it hung on the end of the bench. Puffing his cheeks a little with effort, he zipped it over his sagging stomach.

Still clutching the golf club, Colleen turned and stepped back out of the front door. The two men followed her, Howard carrying his suitcase-sized doctor's bag. The drizzle had become a little heavier and Colleen pulled her jacket closer as she and Howard set off in the direction of the supermarket. Before they disappeared around the corner, she glanced back. Clint was standing in the middle of the street, watching them.

"Is there a multi-storey car park near the university?" Howard asked in a low voice.

"Er, yeah. On Drury Street. Why?"

"Do you know the way?"

"Yes. *Why*?"

Howard led her in a half-run across the road and up a side street.

"This isn't the way to the supermarket," said Colleen.

"I know. And keep your voice down. Take us to Drury Street, but we need to circle around and avoid Temple Bar. I'll explain as we go, but we need to hurry."

Colleen felt a rush of excitement.

"We're leaving now?" she said in a stage whisper.

Howard nodded. "Still too loud." They had reached the end of the side street and he glanced back. "We must be quiet. He's probably already looking for us."

Colleen thought of the switchblade and her stomach gave a lurch.

"Drury Street's over there," she said, nodding to their left. Then she pointed ahead. "But we could go past the castle, then double back on the other side. If he is following us, maybe he'll think we've gone into the castle."

"Okay. He *will* come after us."

"How do you know? He might be back in *The Quays* making breakfast as we speak."

"He had no intention of making breakfast. He didn't ask where we keep the food. Not even where the tin opener is. I think he only had one thing on his mind."

Colleen drew in a sharp breath and grimaced.

"Let's be away from him, then," said Howard. "Lead on."

They set off once more. Colleen was aware that her strides, with her long legs, were greater than Howard's, but he kept pace without apparent difficulty. While they ducked down side streets, walking briskly but stepping as quietly as they could, Howard started to explain in a low voice.

"While you were across the road, I talked to Clint, or whatever his real name is—"

"Dermot. Dermot Ward." Colleen reached into her pocket and extracted a battered leather wallet. "I saw him patting his jacket last night. Checking something was still there."

"And you took it?"

"I spoke to him as I went out this morning and the jacket was hanging there. I could see the pocket and…" She shrugged. "Couldn't resist. I meant to replace it as soon as I got back, but we came straight out again."

"So his name's Dermot?"

"Yep. There's a staff ID photocard. It's him, all right. He's a night watchman at an electrical goods depot."

"Ah. He'll have noticed it's missing."

"He must have known we were onto him. All that bullshit about being a personal bodyguard in Wyoming." Colleen sighed. "Only three people alive in the whole of Dublin so far as we know, and one of them's a feckin nutjob."

"He was obsessed with you. You were only gone a few minutes and he must have mentioned you half a dozen times. Full of innuendo. And each time with a look that gave me the willies. I knew we had to get away from him without delay."

"What was all that about the antibiotics and your case?"

"I needed to bring my case." Howard frowned. "I don't know why. I mean, every doctor's attached to his case, but there's nothing in here that can't be replaced. Yet I *needed* to bring it… That was a load of crap about the special compartments for powder."

"He seemed to buy it."

"Hmm. I'm not so sure."

Colleen came to a halt to get her bearings. She glanced behind. The rain was heavy enough to limit visibility, but there was no sign of pursuit from Clint. She began to cross the road.

"If we turn off a little farther on, we can skirt around the castle."

A large rat scurried across the road in front of them. Colleen tightened her grip on the club, but the rodent ignored them.

"Why the car park?" she said.

"To be sure of escaping Clint, we need transport. I assume you have no idea how to hotwire a car?"

"Nope."

"Me, neither. So we'd have to find one with keys. Time consuming, but not our biggest problem."

"And that is?"

"Dead batteries. The cars in this city haven't been used in weeks. The odds of finding one with keys *and* a battery juiced enough to start it are, I'm afraid, slim to none."

"So why are we making for a car park?"

"We'll need to bump start the vehicle, which means it needs to be on a hill."

"Dublin's a fairly flat city," said Colleen, at last seeing where this was going. "But a multi-storey car park has lots of ramps."

"Exactly. And as soon as I thought of a multi-storey, I remembered Brian's car."

"Who's Brian?"

"My next-door neighbour. Retired bachelor. Nice chap. He came to my house in a right state. Eyes streaming. Coughing. Could barely stand. Said he'd parked in a multi-storey near the University, but had come over so ill he'd left it there and caught the bus home. He said the light was hurting his eyes so badly, he just needed to lie down in a darkened room."

"The light did hurt," murmured Colleen. "Sinead couldn't stand it."

"Like someone practising acupuncture, badly, on your eyeballs."

They walked the next few yards in silence. Colleen turned to the left and they began to walk behind the western end of the castle grounds.

"Brian only stood at my doorstep," said Howard. "He wouldn't come in. I offered to examine him, but he refused. He handed me his car keys and asked if I'd fetch his car when I had chance. He had a haunted look in those streaming eyes. As though he knew he was a goner, but felt he had to go through the pretence of acting like he'd recover. I put the keys into my coat pocket, but never came to fetch the car. I was a little distracted. My own family had fallen ill by then."

Colleen shifted the golf club to her other hand so she could reach out with the one nearest Howard and give his arm a squeeze. He glanced at her and offered a wan smile. His cheeks glistened, but with rain or tears she could not tell.

"Brian's car," she said. "It's still there?"

Howard pulled a hand out of his coat pocket and held up a set of keys. "Been carrying them around with me for weeks. I'd completely forgotten about them until last night. Yes, the car should still be there. Between us, we should be able to wheel it to one of the down ramps and I can gain enough momentum to bump start it."

"Better hope he didn't park on the ground floor."

"That thought had occurred to me. And another. Let's hope the exits aren't blocked by a wreck of some sort."

"We'll find out soon enough." Colleen looked to their left. They were now passing in front of the castle. "Drury Street's not far."

They fell silent. A pang of anxiety twisted deep in Colleen's stomach. She cast the occasional glance behind, but there was still no sight or sound of Clint. If he was following, she hoped he would think they had sought refuge in the castle. If he could find a way inside, it might take him hours to discover they weren't in there.

At last, they turned a corner and entered Drury Street.

"Thank the Virgin Mary," muttered Colleen.

The road was empty. No abandoned vehicles or wreckage or rotting bodies. Not even any rubbish. Apart from the silence and complete absence of people, this might be what Drury Street had looked like when everyone was up in Croke Park for the Gaelic football final, or watching Ireland play New Zealand over at

Lansdowne Road.

They hurried forward and reached the entrance to the car park. It was clear. Colleen breathed a fresh sigh of relief. The breath caught in her throat when she heard the sound.

Not as crisp as the last time she'd heard it, probably due to the muffling effect of the wet streets, but instantly recognisable nonetheless.

Click-clop… click-clop…

Tom opened his eyes when something warm and damp pressed against his cheek. Dusty was nuzzling him.

"Gerroff," Tom muttered, pushing him away. "Daft bugger."

He didn't mean it. In pensive moments, he looked at Dusty and wondered whether he would still be alive if he hadn't found the dog. Nursing the animal back to health had given Tom a focus at a time when his mood was black and was likely to have ended with him swallowing the sleeping pills he had collected from neighbours' medicine cabinets. Man and dog had grown stronger together, and the yawning pit from which Tom's dead mother beckoned him in the dark had receded.

Tom glanced over at Ceri in one of the single beds across the huge room. She was fast asleep. He decided to let her sleep on.

He started to slide out of bed and Dusty jumped to the floor with a soft thud. He looked back at Tom expectantly.

"Okay, okay, keep your fur on. I'm coming."

Tom paused with his feet on the floor and raised a hand to his head. He uttered a soft groan. After Bri and Will had gone to bed, he'd told Ceri about Diane's prognosis for Bri and between them they'd emptied a bottle of vodka. More a beer or wine man, he wasn't used to spirits. He rose gingerly and dressed.

Downstairs, Tom found Diane in the dining room, a huge pot of coffee on the table before her.

"Peter's gone up to his room," she said, "but he's made your breakfast. And the dog's."

Tom grunted and went into the kitchen. A tin of ham had

been chopped up into a bowl on the floor. Another bowl, filled with water, stood next to it. Dusty bounded forward and got stuck in.

A pan of beans bubbled softly on the barbecue, next to another of chicken soup.

"Yum, yum," muttered Tom. "More beans."

He took half of the contents of each pan and left the remainder to simmer for Ceri.

Once he had eaten, and his headache had subsided, Tom called to Dusty.

"C'mon, boy. Let's go outside so you can make room for the ham you just wolfed down."

Licking his lips, Dusty trotted to Tom's side and they walked back through the dining room where Diane was still sitting.

"Good coffee?" said Tom, more to say something than out of genuine interest.

"Mmm," she murmured. "I find coffee very soothing."

"It must be the alien in you," said Tom. He wasn't feeling particularly charitable this morning. "That much caffeine and us humans would be climbing walls."

Diane said nothing. She sipped from her mug and did indeed look soothed.

Although the wind had not picked back up, the outdoor temperature had dropped a few degrees from the day before. Tom thrust his hands deep into his jacket pockets and hunched his shoulders.

Dusty looked up at him, ears pricked. He wouldn't leave Tom's side without his say-so.

"Off you go, then," said Tom.

With a gruff bark, Dusty bounded away, pausing on the lawn to make room for the ham, before racing across the pebbles and down to the beach. Tom followed at a more leisurely pace.

Judging from the narrow strip of sand that was visible and the lethargic nature of the waves, the tide was high and preparing to go back out. At the edge of the waves, his back to Tom, crouched

Peter.

Dusty had avoided him and was running along the tideline, sniffing at whatever took his interest. Tom approached Peter without speaking, curious about what he was up to.

Peter was bending forward, dipping something into the waves. Tom walked to his side and looked down at what he was holding. A silvery container, a little like a vacuum flask; the lid hung down by its side, attached by a strip of black plastic. Tom had seen this container before, but not open.

Withdrawing it from the sea, Peter gave the flask a shake to swirl the water around the inside, then tipped it up. The water that ran out was cloudy, like freshly dissolved aspirin, but off-white. Creamy.

"What are you doing?" Tom asked.

Peter glanced up and Tom was startled to see his cheeks were damp with tears.

"I would have done it," Peter said. "If I'd had the chance, I'd have taken it."

He dipped the flask back into the water and repeated the process. This time, the water that poured out was less cloudy.

"What are you talking about?"

"I would have done it," Peter repeated. "Killed them all."

"Killed…? Who, Peter?"

"The sailors. That sub." He shivered. "It makes me no better than the rest. Worse, if anything. My reasons are entirely selfish."

"I have no idea what you're talking about. Why on earth would you want to kill those sailors?"

Peter shook his head and continued to dip the flask, swirl the water around and pour it back out.

"That powder…" said Tom. "Is it the Millennium Bug?"

"Yep. The last of it."

The water ran out clear. Peter nodded and stood.

"Can I…?" asked Tom.

Peter handed him the flask. The metal was ice-cold in Tom's hands. He peered inside; no trace of powder remained. He lowered his nose to the opening and inhaled.

"Smells a little like toffee."

Peter was already walking away. He reached the pebbles and sat down, facing the bay.

Tom walked over and sat next to him. Peter's cheeks had dried in the cold breeze, but he wore an expression of dejection. Tom handed the flask back to him.

"The sea," said Tom. "It's contagious now?"

"Doubt it," said Peter. "The powder will disperse and degrade more quickly in the water."

"Why did you get rid of it?"

"The better question would be why was I keeping it."

"Okay. Why were you keeping it?"

"In case I ever needed it. I nearly found a use for it."

"The men in the sub. You were going to use it on them. But why?"

"To stop them interfering with the Beacon. If they'd agreed to fire missiles at Stonehenge, I'd have made sure the powder in this canister found its way onto their sub."

"I thought…" began Tom.

"That I was on your side?" Peter looked at Tom for the first time since they'd sat. "I am."

"Then I don't understand…"

"I want the Beacon to be reactivated. I want the rest of my civilisation to reach Earth Haven. I don't care whether they land safely on the planet's surface and I don't want them to eradicate the surviving humans."

"You're making no sense."

Peter sighed. "Tom, it's about longing and knowledge and selfishness." He looked back out to sea and for a few moments was silent. His right hand crept inside his coat and fiddled with something around his neck. "I can't remember whether I've ever told you, but I held Megan in my arms while she lay dying."

"Did she know about… um, your true nature?"

"When I found myself falling in love with her and coming to

realise what love actually is, I showed her what I am. I was terrified she would reject me, but I couldn't abide having a secret from her."

"She obviously accepted you."

"She accepted that I would not age. I accepted I would one day lose her. Those fifty years with her… When the pain of her going threatens to overwhelm me, as it still does sometimes, I remind myself to be thankful we had that time together. Then I welcome the pain for if it didn't exist, neither would those fifty years with her. It becomes bearable."

"There's a quote by someone: 'Don't cry because it's over, smile because it happened.'"

"Exactly," said Peter. "I hadn't heard that before. It's a very fine quote."

"Megan must have been a special lady."

"Oh, yes. She taught me how to love; how to give and not expect to receive; how to surrender yourself entirely to another. It turned me away from what I was, a tiny component of a much larger whole. I became an individual."

"Peter, you don't have to answer this, but I'm curious: *could* you have had children together?"

"She wanted to try. I refused. Even if I was able to successfully impregnate Megan, which is a matter of some doubt, I did not know how the pregnancy would affect her. Although our fertilisation process is mechanically similar to humans', our birthing process is vastly different. You see, our females discharge the foetus complete with placenta after only a few weeks and it continues to develop independently of the mother. Megan's body would have wanted to retain the foetus for the normal gestation period for humans, around thirty-six weeks. The metabolism rate for our young is quicker, much quicker, than humans'. If her body's urge to retain the developing foetus had won out, but our metabolism rate had prevailed…"

"I see," said Tom. "Ugh."

"Quite. It wasn't a chance I was prepared to take."

"What about the thing you can do with your minds? The telepathy? How was she with that?"

Peter glanced at Tom and raised his eyebrows. "I thought you didn't believe in all that stuff. Don't you refer to it as 'mind tricks'?"

Tom shifted a little, making the pebbles clink. "I'm not sure what I believe. It's obvious you can do things with your minds that we can't, but it could be an advanced form of hypnotism."

"Doubting Thomas, eh? But to answer your question, Megan was fascinated by my ability to speak to her without talking. She could have kept me out permanently, like you can, but chose to let me in. I tried to teach her how to do it, but the areas of her brain she needed to tap into lay dormant. Brianne is the first human I have seen who has opened pathways to those areas." Peter picked up a pebble and tossed it towards the sea. "Megan once placed her hands to my cheeks, looked deep into my eyes and asked me if I was God. She immediately looked shocked, as if she had voiced something sacrilegious. A strong chapel upbringing Megan had. She never spoke of it again, but the notion remained with her, right up to the end."

"You don't think you're God, do you, Peter?"

Peter gave a thin smile. "Of course not. I used to find the idea of a supreme being completely ridiculous."

"Only 'used to'?"

"Now I'm not so sure."

"Really?" Tom felt perplexed. "You say you can travel at far in excess of light speed by harnessing the expansion of the universe and that you've travelled almost five hundred light years across it. You say you can create complex life forms and program them as you wish by tweaking their DNA. And yet you believe there may be a god?"

"We know a lot," said Peter softly, "but we don't know everything. When I fell in love with Megan, I began to see things differently, to question what I'd always accepted without question. The concept of the soul intrigued me. In my culture, we have no need for such fancies. When one of our number dies, their knowledge and experience pass to the Keeper. If that is what constitutes the soul, it is subsumed into the whole. But what about a human's knowledge and experience, their personalities? People can be similar to each other, but each is unique. What happens to their souls when they die?"

Tom grunted. "That's a question which has vexed the greatest minds to have ever existed. Wars have been fought over it."

"I wouldn't let Megan go. At the end, I held her more than just physically. I could feel her intellect tugging to be free. Her intellect... her soul? Megan was exhausted with living. She was ready to leave. I was stopping her." Peter's voice hitched a little and he took a deep breath to steady it. "I could not have held on indefinitely. Her will to leave was stronger than my ability to hold on. I was merely delaying the inevitable. But I hoped to cling on to at least a portion of her... to retain a part of her within me." He sighed. "With her last breath, she whispered to me, 'Peter, you have to let go. God is calling me. I will always love you, but let go...' And I did. When the light faded in her eyes, I tried to follow with my mind. But I could no longer find her. She had gone to a place I can never follow." He bowed his head.

Tom tentatively reached out a hand and placed it on Peter's back. He left it there, feeling awkward but wanting to offer some sort of comfort. He was unclear what all that Peter had told him had to do with the silvery flask and the sailors. He began to wonder how long he should leave it before raising the issue again, without appearing insensitive to Peter's feelings, when his musings were interrupted by a shout from behind them.

"Tom! *Tom*! Where are you?"

It was Ceri. Tom sprang to his feet and scrambled up the bank of pebbles.

"Here I am," he called. "What's wrong?"

"Oh, Tom, come quickly." She was standing outside the front door of the hotel. Even from this distance, she looked pale and scared. Diane appeared behind her in the doorway, wearing a puzzled expression.

Tom descended the storm bank. He could hear Peter following. Away to his right, he saw Dusty approaching from the beach, attracted by Ceri's voice. As Tom began to cross the lawn, he called again. "What's wrong?"

"It's the children. Bri and Will." Ceri's face crumpled. "They've gone."

"Huh?" Tom felt as though someone had thumped him in the stomach. "What d'you mean they've gone?"

"Gone. Disappeared. I went into their room to call them down to breakfast. Their clothes and backpacks aren't there. Their beds haven't been slept in."

Zach eschewed Interstate 95, preferring to follow Route 1 for no other reason than it more closely hugged the coastline than the interstate. He was in no hurry, content to head south in leisurely fashion, stopping whenever and wherever he felt like. If they encountered an obstacle he could not drive around, such as burnt-out wreckage spanning all three lanes of the highway, he'd calmly turn and drive in the opposite direction until he came to a place where he could cross to the opposite lanes and continue on their way. There was no rush.

Amy seemed content with whatever he decided. She didn't speak much, which was okay with Zach. He was still becoming accustomed to the sound of another person breathing alongside him.

On their first night on the road, she offered herself to him during their stopover at a cheap-looking motel Zach pulled into simply because it was the first place they came to after darkness began to fall.

Zach considered her for a moment.

"How many men you been with?"

Amy bit her lower lip. "Oh, a few."

"How many really?"

She shrugged. "You'd be the first."

"You're a rare woman, Amy. In your twenties and still a virgin. That's a rare thing indeed."

A tear squeezed from the corner of one eye. "My momma never let me near boys. She said they's all evil. All after one thing."

"I'm going to thank you, but decline. I ain't laid with a woman for nigh on fifteen years." Zach might have achieved isolation, but the urge to satisfy a primal need had driven him from his cabin once or twice a year to the ladies of the night plying their trade in Augusta. As long as he laid down his cash, he wasn't required to converse with them, which suited him—and them—just fine. The urge had stopped making itself felt as strongly as he passed into his fifties, and the trips to the state capital ended.

Another tear squeezed from her other eye. Her bottom lip quivered.

"Don't take on so," said Zach. "You don't want to be deflowered by an old fart like me."

"I… I…" She let out a deep sigh and Zach swayed back a little as sour breath washed over him. "I don't want…" The rest dissolved into a mumble.

"Didn't catch that," said Zach.

She looked up and jutted out her chin. "I said I don't want to die a virgin."

"Doubt there's much chance of that. I suspect that women of child-bearing age gonna be in high demand. Assuming there's young men still around."

"Are there? Young men?"

"Dunno. But if there's us, chances are there's more."

Zach insisted they sleep in separate bedrooms, not because he was afraid he would succumb to her limited charms, but because he remained a little wary of her.

"Don't take it personal," he told her as he left her room to head for his own. "I ain't trusting of anyone."

Zach locked his door and placed the back of a chair under the handle. He slept with the Beretta within easy reach. The pistol was one thing he *did* trust.

Chapter Nineteen

Bri attempted to leave without Will. She sat in a chair, trying to look like she was reading a book by candlelight, waiting for him to fall asleep.

The boy was acting weirdly. He had refused to undress or get under the bedclothes. He lay on top of the bed, fully clothed down to his swanky training shoes. Bri pretended to ignore him, while all the time watching him surreptitiously through her eyelashes.

At last his eyes closed, his breathing slowed and deepened. Moving carefully so as not to make the slightest noise, Bri put down the book and stood.

"I'm coming with you." Will was sitting up, wide-eyed, his mouth set in a firm line.

She shook her head. "Not this time. You have to stay with the grown-ups. They'll keep you safe."

"I don't *have* to do anything any more."

"Well, you can't come with me. It's going to be dangerous where I'm going."

"Don't care. I'm coming. If you try to stop me, I'll wake the others."

"What? Don't you dare. They'll never let me go."

Will shrugged.

Bri stared at him, her mind a mixture of indignation and affection for this annoying, lovable boy. She puffed her cheeks and blew out in exasperation.

"Okay, buster," she said. "You can come, but on one condition: when we get to where we're going and I tell you to stay back or stay hidden or whatever, you bloody well do as I say."

"All right."

"Promise?"

"Cross my heart and hope to die."

"Come on, then."

They crept down the dark corridors and stairs of the hotel, freezing every time a floorboard creaked. When they passed the room in which Tom and Ceri slept, Bri felt sure she heard a faint whine from within. They tiptoed past, Bri's heart in her mouth while she anticipated a volley of barks that never came.

The bolts on the front door sounded shockingly loud in the silence. They hurried away from the hotel, expecting to hear a shout from Tom or Peter. That, too, never came.

The night air was bitterly cold, giving them cause once more to be thankful for their 'shopping' spree in Harrods. A finger-nail paring moon hung in the clear sky before them.

Will gasped. "I never knew there were so many stars."

The surface of the road shone like buffed ebony in the starlight; they could see well enough without having to use torches, with the added benefit of being able to keep hands buried snugly in pockets.

A horse approached them, snickering a soft greeting before going on its way. Bri sensed only curiosity in the beast, but made sure the protective aura held good. Better to have it and not need it, she reasoned, than the other way around.

It took them the best part of two hours to reach Wick. If Will's leg had still been sore, he might have struggled, but he assured Bri it had healed completely and he was no longer even aware of it. She felt quite pleased with herself.

"The cycle shop's up a side street," said Will.

"Ceri told you?"

"Yes. She said she noticed it when they were looking for tools."

"She's very fond of you. I think you remind her of her son."

Will glanced up. "I don't want another mum. Just a big sister."

It took them a while to find something with which they could smash the plate glass in the front of the cycle shop. The choice of bicycles wasn't as varied as the shop in Lambeth, but they each found a machine that would do the job.

As they rode the bikes slowly towards the sea front, Bri glanced across at Will.

"Missing your other bike?"

He nodded.

"Me, too," said Bri. "Hmm. We could call at Nottingham on the way south. Our other bikes should be where we left them inside the pub."

Will grinned. "Yeah!"

They found the hotel near the harbour where the others had been staying, and helped themselves to the stockpiled food and water. Bri added one of the tiny paraffin camping stoves.

"Only a few tins and bottles each," she said. "We can't afford to be unstable while we ride."

"Will they mind us thieving their stuff?"

"No. They'll be glad we've got food with us." A shadow passed across Bri's heart. "I wish we didn't have to sneak off like this. They'll be worried, particularly Ceri. But they didn't leave me much choice."

Will gave a huge yawn.

"I'm tired, too," said Bri, "but we can't stay here. If they notice we're gone during the night, this might be the first place they come looking for us. We'll ride out until we find somewhere we can sleep away from the town."

The sky remained clear and the road continued to glow faintly while they rode south. They could see sufficiently to ride in relative safety, although they proceeded with caution.

Once they had left Wick behind, they turned onto back roads and lanes until they found a deserted crofter's cottage. With the smell of sheep's wool and stale wood smoke in their nostrils, they both fell into an exhausted sleep.

Bri stirred not long after first light with a full bladder. She felt stiff and in need of more sleep, but she knew they needed to keep moving. She awoke a reluctant Will and, after a hurried breakfast, they were back on the road.

Most of the U.K. stretched before them to the south. They would need to traverse the largest chunk of it to reach their destination. Even if they rode like the wind, they still might not make it in time.

Looking out of place alongside such prehistoric majesty, like scaffolding on the Parthenon, the bulldozers stood on grass beyond the path encircling Stonehenge. Beside them stood the crane, unloaded from the flatbed lorry. The bulldozers had torn down and removed the metal fences that kept out non-paying members of the public. Once more the ancient stones could be approached from any direction without obstruction, as had been the case for millennia.

Milandra stepped down from the coach onto the parking area adjoining the highway. She strolled across the silent road and along the path until she stood before the monument, remembering this place when last she had been here, almost five thousand years previously. Not a great deal had changed. There hadn't, of course, been roads, fences, hedges and far-off buildings back then. Dark swathes of distant forest had been replaced by farmland. There had been more hills, but since the entire plateau was composed of chalk, they had eroded to bumps and dips and undulations.

Stonehenge itself had altered from what Milandra recalled. She was familiar with the current layout—it was one of the world's most iconic images—but could remember the site before a single stone had been erected. Even then it had been a sacred place to the natives: a worn chalk path led across the plain, marking the route of pilgrimage, and wooden posts staked out the monument in an eerie foreshadowing of the Beacon.

The Commune had taken place between the wooden posts, in and around the space now occupied by stones. The survivors of the Atlantic splashdown, almost ten thousand strong, joined intellects and the incumbent Keeper called the tribes of Britain to them. The Britons had laid aside their crude weapons and petty grudges, and come. Then, over many months, they had brought in the bluestones.

This was the first time she had viewed the site since the addition of the larger sarsen stones. Although Milandra could appreciate the aesthetic value they added to the monument, they would have to be removed.

Jason Grant came and stood by her side.

"Takes you back, doesn't it?" he murmured. "You weren't the Keeper. Not even the Chosen. Not then."

"Nope." Milandra uttered a mirthless chuckle. "I was around one-forty pounds lighter, too."

"Who'd have thought all those centuries ago that so much time would go by before the Great Coming?"

"Over half of those who stood here and took part in the Commune have passed."

"And only a handful replaced. Our numbers on Earth Haven have grown thin. Soon too few of us might have remained to carry out the Cleansing."

"Or mankind would have completed Earth Haven's destruction." Milandra shivered in the fresh breeze. "Come. Let us assess the task at hand."

Together they walked towards the stones. In front of the outer circle lay a bundle of material. They drew nearer and could make out that the bundle was made up of clothes. At the same time, a familiar odour reached them on the breeze.

Inside the circle of sarsen stones, lying among the bluestones, were around thirty corpses of men and women. Each one was naked. The cold weather had slowed decomposition, but crows and foxes and rats had made ragged holes in the flesh.

She and Grant stared at the bodies, neither speaking. Near them the remains of an elderly couple lay face to face, arms encircling, as though they had decided at the end to go wrapped in each other's embrace. Milandra's gaze wandered around the circle; many of the bodies were lying in pairs in a similar pose.

She sighed. "It's one thing to know that we've caused so many deaths. Quite another to see the evidence laid out before us like this."

She glanced sideways at Grant, aware she may have spoken a little recklessly, but he was nodding as if he agreed with her.

Others were arriving and Milandra shook herself to dispel the feeling of melancholy that had settled into her old bones.

"Okay," she said in a businesslike tone. "First thing is to set the drones to removing and burning these corpses."

"I recommend they are taken to the Burning Fields," said Grant, "or else the stench of singeing hair and flesh will be in our nostrils for the three or four days we're going to be here."

"Agreed. We're going to have to endure that stench at the end, but no point in prolonging it unnecessarily. They can begin by taking the bodies out of the circle. Then the crane can make a start on moving the sarsen stones."

"I suggest that then the bluestones are all moved outside the circle so we can establish where the original pits are situated."

"Some have already been excavated. Locating the others shouldn't be difficult. The pits will have to be redug, along with the holes for the stones to sit in behind them." Milandra glanced at the skies. "No sign of rain at present. The ground is hard, but the bulldozers may be able to help with digging the pits."

"No," said Grant. "There's no finesse with those things. The pits will have to be dug by hand to ensure the energy is properly channelled."

"I'll leave that to your expertise, Jason." She looked around at the stones. "This place was a fortuitous find indeed. You can feel the power beneath our feet." She nodded towards the corpses. "I wonder if those poor souls could feel it, too, and that's why they decided to spend their last hours here."

Grant turned away to start issuing orders.

Milandra strolled around the edge of the circle, feeling the energy in the ground reinvigorating her. Three or four nights from now and their work here would be done. There would be nothing more they could do to prepare for the Great Coming. The success or otherwise of that venture lay in the hands of her people travelling from Earth Home.

The outside walls of the car park were clad in slatted slabs of concrete that allowed little natural light to enter, making the interior dim and shadowy. Trying to step as quietly as burglars, Colleen and Howard hurried to the back of the car park to where the first ramp bent around to the right to reach the next level.

Colleen paused, hugging the shadow of a concrete pillar, and peered back at the entrance.

Above the bass line of her heart, she could hear the *click-clop* of Clint's cowboy boots. She held her breath while the sound grew louder.

Unmistakable due to the Stetson, Clint's silhouette appeared at the opening and began to cross the gap. Colleen started to breathe out… then inhaled sharply. He had stopped. Slowly, he turned to face into the car park.

Colleen stepped fully behind the pillar and peeped around it. A squeak of alarm tried to escape her lips and she thrust her knuckles into her mouth to stop it. Clint was striding towards her.

She glanced behind to the ramp to warn Howard, but he wasn't there. Forcing a lid on the panic rising in her throat like bile, Colleen began up the ramp. She didn't need to glance around the pillar to see if Clint was still advancing. The steady *click-clop* told her everything she needed to know.

At the top of the ramp, she started along the next level between the rows of parked cars. Not every space was occupied; clearly some drivers had felt well enough to collect their cars before going home to climb into their death beds.

Grey daylight slanted in from the side and end walls, but pillars and cars cast deep shadows. Colleen peered apprehensively into each dark place she passed in case Howard had decided to hide, though why he should do that her thoughts were not clear enough to consider.

She reached the end of the level and faced a choice. Another ramp led upwards to the next storey; a horizontal driveway led across to the other half of the car park that contained the down ramps to the exit. A quick glance behind her confirmed what her ears had already told her: Clint had not followed her up to this level. She could no longer hear the clomp of his boots, not even faintly. She listened harder, straining for a sound that might give her a clue to where Howard had gone, but the car park was as hushed as a cathedral.

Mentally flipping a coin, Colleen crossed to the other half of the structure. She looked to her right. Shadows and silence. Unlikely to be concealing Howard, but she needed to be sure before continuing upwards. Taking a deep breath and a tighter grip on the golf club, she crept forward on the balls and toes of her feet, senses alert for any sound or movement. Silence and stillness reigned. Reaching the end of the building, where a shadowy ramp led back to the ground floor, she stopped to listen again. If Clint was moving, she'd be able to hear him. He was either standing stock still or had left the car park.

Daring to relax a little—just a little—Colleen turned and began to retrace her steps to find a ramp leading to the upper level. She wasn't sure how many storeys the car park contained, but she must surely find Howard on the next one.

The hand came from behind and clamped around her mouth before she could so much as gasp. A smell of damp leather enveloped her. Another hand gripped her right forearm, squeezing so tightly that she cried out against the fleshy palm pressing against her lips. The muffled sound of her cry was drowned by the clatter of the golf club hitting the floor.

"Hello, my beaut," drawled a voice in her ear; a voice she despised. A waft of curdled-milk breath caressed her face and she almost gagged. Something pressed into the small of her back. The hand clutching her arm let go and withdrew. Before she could react, it reappeared holding a metallic object. A click and the thin blade slid out. It glittered darkly, despite the lack of light.

"I think you might have something belonging to me," said Clint.

The switchblade moved towards her face and paused, less than an inch from the skin of her right cheek. She tried to pull back, but she had nowhere to go. The back of her head hit something hard and unyielding. A shoulder.

Another waft of foul breath. "Move your right hand *slowly* to wherever you've got it. Take it out and hand it to me."

Her eyes never leaving the blade, Colleen moved her hand to her jacket pocket and extracted the wallet. She held it up.

"I'm going to take away the hand over your mouth. If you scream or call out to gramps, I'll slit your cheek so you can clean your teeth without parting your lips."

Colleen drew in a shuddering breath when the hand let go. Her tongue darted out and she tasted the salty sourness of his sweat. She almost gagged again. Leather-clad arms still encircling her, the knife was passed from right hand to left; the right relieved her of the wallet.

"Now…" said Clint.

The object in her back moved down a little until it pressed against her buttocks. It passed along one cheek, pausing to push tighter in the middle, before passing over the other cheek. The blade swayed in front of her face, mesmerising her like a serpent being charmed.

Clint's voice sounded a little breathless, as though he had run up a flight of stairs.

"My beaut, you have one hell of a rump. I'm gonna ride it like a rodeo mustang. Oh yes siree. We'll find a car, I think. One that's unlocked. Or we'll smash a window. You won't scrape your knees as much on the back seat of a car. But first…"

Colleen tensed when the right hand reappeared, without the wallet, and moved to her jacket. It pulled the zip down to her navel. She spoke the first words that came into her head that might give him pause.

"Howard has a gun."

The blade moved towards her face and she gasped at how cold it felt against her cheek. She was helpless to prevent the whimper escaping; she sounded like a puppy.

"Like hell he has. Where is the old fart anyhow?"

"Gone to fetch it. He's meeting me here."

The flat of the blade pressed harder against her cheek so that she became acutely aware of how sharp the edges were. She feared her skin was already parting under their touch.

"Liar, liar, pants on fire. Ha! Your arse will feel like it's on fire by the time I've finished riding it."

The pressure of the blade decreased a little, but it remained pressed to her cheek. His right hand moved inside her jacket. It pulled up her jumper and the tee-shirt she wore beneath. She did not wear a bra; her breasts retained much of the pertness of youth and, now liberated from social mores, she enjoyed the freedom of going without. When the hand settled, hot and clammy, against the skin of her midriff and began to slide upwards, Colleen moaned.

Whether her assailant deliberately chose to misinterpret the sound of disgust as one of pleasure, she didn't know, but an answering moan came from behind her and the grinding against her backside resumed. Faster and harder. Feverish.

From somewhere above her came a noise; a once familiar, but now rare, noise. It was too loud to miss, but it barely registered, so focused were Colleen's senses on the knife against her cheek and the hand moving towards her breasts.

Clint, too, must have heard the noise; it was growing louder by the second. He, too, chose to ignore it; or was so caught up in the heat of desire that he paid it no heed.

While the hand circled her left breast and her flesh recoiled, a glimmer of an idea popped into Colleen's mind. She moaned again, a low, sensuous sound that portrayed the opposite sensations to those she was actually feeling.

Faster and harder came the movements against Colleen's buttocks. Louder and shorter came the hot breaths against the side of her head. Tighter and more urgent came the kneading of her breast. She bit her lip to prevent uttering a cry of pain and breaking Clint's concentration.

The noise from above drew closer. A dark shape moved into sight, emerging from the down ramp. Bright, white light shone forth, banishing shadows to the farthest corners. Colleen scrunched up her eyes against the glare.

She heard a gasp and the pressure of the blade against her cheek lifted. The grinding motion against her backside ceased and the hateful hand's grip on her breast eased.

Still with eyes closed, Colleen stepped smartly forward, using her hands to shove away Clint's arms, unknowing and uncaring of where the switchblade was being waved. If it was still near her face, she evaded it.

Pivoting on the ball of her left foot, Colleen about-turned and opened her eyes. Mustering all the force of which she was capable, she kicked out her right leg. At the same time, she yelled, "Up yours, *Dermot*!"

Her knee jolted with the impact and a bolt of pain shot up her leg to her thigh. She couldn't remember pain so satisfying.

With a shriek, Clint brought both hands down to clutch at his groin. The knife clattered to the floor. Colleen had time to notice his stockinged feet, before he collapsed in slow motion to his knees. His face, all the more pasty in the harsh light, contorted in anguish. He bowed his head, lank locks of hair falling forward like strands of a greasy mop.

"Colleen! Are you okay?" came Howard's voice from behind her, raised to be heard over the rumbling engine.

She turned, shielding her eyes against the glare of the headlights, and walked to the side of the car. Howard's anxious face peered through the open window.

"Took your time," she said.

"I couldn't find the car. By the time I did, I could hear voices from below so I guessed he'd found you. I struggled to push the car and steer it on my own. I'm sorry…"

Howard looked so wretched that any anger Colleen felt towards him for deserting her melted away.

"No harm done. Greasy bastard had his hands all over me and was about to get his rocks off when you rudely interrupted him."

Howard glanced past her. His eyes widened.

"Get in," he said. "Quickly."

Colleen looked back. Clint had raised his head and was glaring at them with hate-filled eyes. He looked in no condition to do anything quite yet, but he was clearly beginning to recover.

She wasted no time. Scooting around the back of the car, she opened the passenger door and climbed in.

"Let's go," she said.

As they passed the kneeling figure, Clint turned his head and watched them. Colleen craned around to see what she hoped would be her last ever view of him. In the reflection of the car's rear lights, his eyes glinted red, like a demon's.

Howard drove down the ramp to ground level and Colleen breathed a sigh of relief.

"Good old Brian!" she exclaimed, patting the dashboard.

At the foot of the down ramp lay a small bundle. Howard drove over it and they both felt the Stetson hat and cowboy boots crumple beneath the tyres. They glanced at each other and smiled.

An hour or so later, they were pulling up at Dun Laoghaire marina.

"Next stop, Great Britain," said Howard.

"One thing," said Colleen. "I'll risk my life by crossing the sea with you, but I must have a shower."

"There's one on board. Basic, but it will do the job."

"Good. I have to wash all trace of *him* off me."

They paused long enough to collect a few essentials and load them into the Range Rover. These included Dusty's basket, the two shotguns and boxes of shells.

Diane climbed into the front passenger seat. Ceri and Dusty jumped into the back. Before Tom joined them he looked at Peter, who was about to step into the vehicle.

"Tell me, Peter," he said in a low voice that would not carry inside the car. "If you were prepared to wipe out those sailors with the Millennium Bug if they'd tried to stop the Beacon being activated, what are you planning on doing to me and Ceri?"

Peter shook his head. "You're missing the point, Tom. The sub possesses the means to destroy the Beacon before it's activated. You and Ceri do not. You're perfectly safe. At least from me."

Peter ducked into the vehicle. Tom stared after him for a moment before following.

He smiled at Ceri. Her smile in return was forced and she quickly looked away. She spent much of the journey to Wick scanning the coastline and countryside, straining for any glimpse of Bri and Will.

Peter drove towards the southern coastal road and Tom leaned forward.

"Tell us how this Beacon works."

Peter sighed. "It won't do you any good."

"Nevertheless."

In the rear-view mirror, Tom could see Peter's brow wrinkle into a frown. It was Diane who spoke.

"Sixty-three bluestones arranged in a circle," she said in a monotone. "Sixty-two people standing in the gaps between them. By holding both arms outstretched, they touch the stones to either side, thus completing the circle. The Keeper stands in the centre of the circle and directs the pulse of energy towards Earth Home. There will be a short window of twenty minutes at around five o'clock in the morning when Earth Haven and Earth Home are sufficiently aligned to be sure our people will detect the signal."

"Does it need to be a clear night?"

"No. If it is, the Keeper can confirm alignment by checking the positions of the stars. If not, she will trust that the calculations are accurate."

"These bluestones were transported almost two hundred miles from West Wales. What's so special about them?"

This time Peter answered. "They possess certain properties, like magnetism and acoustics. They are thought to have magical healing powers." Peter shrugged. "That might be a rumour put about by that rogue Myrddin." Diane grunted and Peter glanced at her. "You knew him?"

"Yes. But on Earth Home."

"I knew him here," said Peter.

"Hold on," said Tom. "Myrddin? Do you mean Merlin? As in the wizard?"

"Yep," said Peter. "One of us. He was already old when we came to Earth Haven. A couple of millennia here drove him quite mad. He started using our influence over humans to convince them he possessed magical powers."

"Jesus Christ! Are you being serious?"

"He's another. And, yes, I am being perfectly serious."

Tom breathed out heavily. "Well, you certainly don't *seem* crazy…"

Peter gave a short laugh. "Ever the Doubting Thomas."

"The stones," said Tom. "Why drag them all that way?"

"We used them because they are natural conductors of earth power."

"What's that?"

"Energy that runs in lines through the ground around the world. About fourteen of these lines converge at the site of Stonehenge; it was already a revered place when we arrived."

Ceri broke off her scrutiny of the scenery. "Pah! You're talking about ley lines. They're so much New Age bullshit."

Peter glanced at her in the rear-view mirror. "It's true that man has not found any scientific evidence to support their existence and we all know that mankind's scientific knowledge is complete, right? Ergo, they can't exist." He gave a shrug. "Nevertheless…"

"Now's not the time to debate whether they exist," said Tom. "Can we just assume they do, Cer?"

Ceri grunted and resumed staring out of the window.

Tom addressed Peter. "Okay. There's this energy converging on the site of Stonehenge. What about it?"

"The stones conduct that energy. We divert it to the Keeper by touching the stones to complete the circle."

"And that's it? You touch the stones and they're activated?"

Peter cleared his throat, but did not speak. He shifted a little in his seat. Tom looked at his reflection in the rear-view mirror, but

Peter did not meet his gaze.

"Tell me, Diane," said Tom. "How is the signal activated?"

Diane turned to look at him. She stared intently into his eyes.

"Are you certain you want to know?"

Tom suddenly wasn't sure that he did, but nodded.

Diane shrugged and turned back to face the front.

"Sixty-three drones will be lined up, one in front of each stone," she said. "If they are repeating the process that was employed the first time, each drone will stand in a shallow pit in front of the stones. They will kneel at the edge of the pits so that their chests rest against the stones' surface. A length of rope will be tied around them to keep them in contact with the stone."

Tom swallowed and glanced at Ceri. She had again momentarily broken off her inspection of the passing scenery to listen. She grimaced at him.

"Then?" Tom prompted.

Diane's voice remained low and passionless. "Behind each drone will stand a person, holding a sharpened blade. At a signal from the Keeper, each person will cut the throat of the drone in front of them."

Ceri groaned and Tom felt his stomach twist.

"This will activate the Beacon," continued Diane. "The Keeper will direct the main pulse of energy at Earth Home. When the blood has stopped pumping from their throats, the drones' bodies will be untied and dropped into the pits in which they kneel. They will be set alight. The energy from their burning will keep the Beacon active for a few more hours. The Keeper and the people touching the stones won't need to maintain their positions once the initial pulse has been sent. The stone circle will do the rest of the job on its own."

"I feel sick," muttered Ceri.

Tom glanced at her. She had grown pale.

"Get some air," he said. "I could do with some, too."

Ceri pressed the button that lowered the window and took great gulps of cold air. Tom breathed in deeply.

"Human blood…" he mused. "Full of energy, right?" He glanced again at Peter in the mirror and at last Peter returned the look. He nodded grimly.

"Why do you burn the bodies?" asked Tom. "If the pulse has already been sent?"

Peter answered. "The pulse is a powerful, concentrated beam of energy. Think of it like a laser beam. If by some miscalculation the pulse isn't picked up by our people… There are many variables, not least being space curvature and the rate of universal expansion. If we have misjudged either, the pulse could miss. In contrast, the signal powered by the burning bodies will be less concentrated, less powerful, but will spread over a wider area and so should be detected even if the pulse is not. It will be more difficult to plot the source of the weaker signal, but it should nevertheless work."

"Hmm," said Tom, his mind churning with another thought. "Let me ask you this: according to your tale about the ancients and their flight from Earth Home, they were being hunted by a deadly enemy?"

"Ye-es," said Peter slowly. The frown had returned to his brow. "That is what the markings on the black tablets they left behind told us."

"Then, according to your tale, there's at least one other sentient species out there in space. A fearsome species at that. Scary enough to force an entire civilisation to up sticks and hotfoot it away across half of the universe."

"What's your point?"

"My point is this: how do you know your signals won't be picked by that other species? Your people might arrive with warships hot on their heels. Earth could become the setting for a real-life *Star Wars*."

"Ah. That possibility was considered when we first constructed the Beacon. But it was firmly discounted. You see, the ancients existed many millions of years ago. We have existed for as long, or maybe *nearly* as long. Our collective memory begins within a century or two of the ancients leaving Earth Home when we arrived to a deserted planet."

"You *arrived*? Where from?"

"We don't know. As I have told you, we don't keep written records. Our collective memory makes them obsolete. But why our memory begins when it does and where we lived until then, or whether we even existed, is not known."

"Maybe the Keeper knows," said Diane.

"Maybe," agreed Peter. "She would need to search through many millions of years of memories and experiences to find the answers, which perhaps explains why no one has ever thought to ask her. It would be a monumental task."

"Um," said Tom, "about the scary aliens…"

"They don't concern us," said Peter, "because throughout those millions of years of known existence, not once have we encountered this species or come across any evidence to suggest it even exists."

"Apart from the black tablets," said Tom.

"Yes. Apart from the tablets left behind by the ancients. If what they hinted at in those tablets is true, that there is a fierce, warlike species that hunted them, we have seen nothing of it. Perhaps, if it did exist, it has died out."

The Range Rover had reached Wick. Tom fell silent while Peter drove through the town and back to the hotel where they had stayed.

When they got out, Dusty barked excitedly, as though he recognised his previous home. He sniffed around the front door, tail wagging like a turbocharged metronome.

"The children!" gasped Ceri. She ran forward and burst into the hotel, the others close behind.

"Are they here?" asked Tom, while his eyes tried to adjust to the interior gloom.

"No," said Ceri. Her shoulders sagged.

Peter strode to the kitchen that lay beyond the bar. The others followed.

"They've been here," he said. "Some food has gone. And one of the spare camping stoves."

"Thank goodness," said Tom. "At least we know they're safe and have some provisions." He walked over to Peter so he could look him squarely in the eye. "Promise me, Peter, that you'll search for them. At least for the rest of today."

"I will," said Peter. He glanced at Diane. "*We* will."

Diane nodded.

"Find them, please," said Ceri. "Take them with you to Anglesey. Keep them safe."

It was lighter in the kitchen than the bar; Tom could see tears welling in Ceri's eyes like blown glass.

"You two could come to Anglesey," said Peter. "You can still have your own car—we'll stand more chance of finding them that way—but I urge you one last time: please, *please*, turn from the path you seem so set on. I repeat that there is absolutely nothing the two of you can do to prevent the Beacon being activated."

Tom looked at Ceri. She looked back at him, tears running freely down her cheeks. For a second, he thought she was going to cave and his stomach flipped at the thought of continuing alone, but then her lips thinned. She nodded grimly.

He turned back to Peter.

"We have to try."

Part 3: He Who Would Valiant Be

Chapter Twenty

Repositioning of the bluestones had not proceeded without difficulty, but by mid-afternoon of the fourth day, the Beacon was ready to be activated.

Around eighty stones had been quarried and transported to the site all those centuries past. Of those eighty, only forty-three had remained visible. Some of the missing stones had been broken up to create healing amulets and the like, or as building materials in nearby settlements. The rest had gradually become grown over and disappeared beneath the ground like sinking ships. Many of the submerged stones had formed part of the original Beacon and still thrummed with power to those who could sense it. Locating them had been a fairly simple task; removing them from the icy clutches of the earth proved trickier. The bulldozers once more demonstrated their worth.

Digging out the pits had also been arduous. Drones worked in shifts with picks and shovels. When their shoulders began to droop with exhaustion and broken blisters on their hands dripped with blood, fresh drones took their place. Each of the original sixty-three pits not already excavated by archaeologists still contained the charred skeletons of the drones who had powered the first beacon. Milandra felt a strange sensation while she gazed down at the huddled remains.

"History repeating itself," she murmured to herself, a phrase often bandied about in support of the operation that would become known as the Cleansing in the days when the question of whether such an operation was necessary had still been a debatable point.

Thanks to the crane, raising the bluestones had been relatively easy. When the sixty-third stone thudded into place, the work was accomplished. In truth, it could have been finished sooner if they had worked through the nights. Grant had located a council depot with floodlights and diesel-powered generators.

"Use those and we could be done in two days," he told Milandra.

"Hmm. Saving a couple of days is neither here nor there now," she said. "A council depot, you say? Do they have equipment for highway maintenance?"

Grant was ahead of her. "Plenty of bitumen," he said. "I think they call it 'tar' over here. We can fashion pitch torches like we used the first time."

Milandra smiled. "It has a certain symmetry."

"I'll get people right onto it."

They had greatly overestimated the number of drones required. Half of them had already been sent back to London. The other five hundred were making ready to return that afternoon, which would only leave the hundred. Around one hundred and fifty people would stay; enough to control the hundred and perform the activation. Afterwards, twenty of the surviving drones would remain behind with Milandra, the Deputies and Rodney Wilson. The remaining seventeen would accompany the rest of the people back to London, while Milandra's party would make for Cornwall.

Sixty-three bluestones had been used in construction of the original Beacon because sixty-three proved to be enough to garner earth power in sufficient concentration. Now sixty-three bluestones once more stood in a circle, pointing to the sky like accusing fingers. Some of the stones were huge monoliths, similar in size to the sarsen stones now lying off to one side where they had been dumped by the crane. Many more were not a great deal larger than a man. Big or small, the gaps between the stones were uniform: wide enough for a person to stretch out their arms and touch the stones to either side.

In front of each stone was a pit about half the size of a grave. A coil of rope lay on the ground next to each pit. The *scratch-whizz-scrape* of steel on stone punctured the calm as sixty-three knives were sharpened in readiness.

Milandra nodded, satisfied all was as it should be.

"Might as well send the crane and 'dozers back, too," she said.

"Is there any point?" said Grant. "There'll be plenty more in London if we need them."

"True. But at least have them removed off site. All that metal and paint doesn't belong in this place."

"Feeling a tad sentimental?"

"A tad, maybe. When we return in the morning, will it be too cold to walk here?"

Grant glanced at the sky. "It's clear at the moment. If it remains so, it will be extremely chilly."

"Well, send word that we and the hundred are to be dropped off, but the buses and coaches are to return to Amesbury. It might be sentimental, but this place is so... *elemental*, I don't want the ambience spoiled by reminders that we live in the age of the space shuttle and microchip. Oh, and the same goes for guns. Concealed handguns are fine. Anything else remains in town."

Grant shrugged. "Can't see why not," he said. "It's not like we're going to be attacked. All the same, I'd feel happier if we post a couple of guards overnight. Don't want all our hard work spoiled by unexpected guests."

"Okay then." The noise of sharpening steel had stopped. "It sounds as though everything is ready. Let's get back to the hotel. We'll rest and feast. Tomorrow's the big day."

The postcard-pretty village of Shrewton lies a little over two miles to the west, and a touch to the north, of Stonehenge. Tom did not dare take the car any closer to the ancient monument. The roar of car engines had become so out of place in this silent new world that even the faint sound of a distant engine was bound to be noticed.

Ceri had grown as silent as the countryside. They had spent two days driving around Scotland and the north of England, searching in vain for Bri and Will. On the third morning, Tom insisted they head south. As it was, he was afraid they might be too late; that the Beacon had already been activated. Ceri protested, had wanted to continue their fruitless hunt, and withdrew into herself when Tom refused. For the last day and a half, she had barely spoken two words.

In the coldness of Ceri's silence, Tom missed Dusty all the more. He had held the dog's head between his hands and told him he must go with Peter and Diane. The dog licked his cheek as if to signify that he understood and jumped into the Range Rover at Tom's command. When only the people he didn't much like, Peter and Diane, had joined him inside, he hadn't protested. He gazed out of the window at Tom while the vehicle pulled away. Although Tom knew it was for the best, part of him felt like it was tearing in two.

Before they parted company, Peter handed to Tom two familiar items: a coiled length of plastic garden hose and a screwdriver. Tom's throat muscles spasmed when he recalled the fiery taste of petrol.

"My syphoning kit," he said with a nod of thanks and a wry smile.

"Don't forget," said Peter, "choose older models. Less likely to have anti-syphoning devices."

Ignoring the urge to go looking for a Ferrari on the grounds that it would be impracticable if they did find the children, and remembering how he'd found the light blue Jaguar in pristine condition in the garage of a neighbour's house, Tom concentrated on the residential areas of Wick in his search for a vehicle. He soon found one: a black Nissan saloon around nine years old but with only thirty thousand miles on the clock. Tom's nose told him that the previous owner lay upstairs quietly decomposing. He found the car keys hanging from a hook by the back door. Although it couldn't have been used in weeks, the engine thrummed into life at the first attempt. Tom gunned it. Aside from a little hesitancy that would soon be blown away on the open road, the engine sounded in good nick.

So it proved. Although the car would not have won awards for speed or style, it carried them reliably on their search around the north and then on their long trek south.

Tom parked the Nissan at the edge of Shrewton and killed the engine. It was a couple of hours after noon and they had been on the road since first light. He was looking forward to stretching his legs and relieving his bladder. Beyond that, he was trying not to think too far ahead.

He turned towards Ceri. "This is close enough," he said. "We walk from here."

She grunted.

"Look, Cer," he began. "I know you're upset because we couldn't find Bri and Will, but it's not my fault. We need to stick together if…"

Ceri was shaking her head. She turned a grim face to Tom.

"It's not only that," she said. "It's that they didn't feel safe with us. They felt they needed to sneak away in the middle of the night. If we can't look after our young, maybe we don't deserve to survive." She sighed and laid a hand on Tom's arm. "I know it's not your fault. I'm sorry."

"Well, I haven't given up on finding them yet. It's obvious when you think about it."

"What is?"

"Where they've gone. Bri was adamant she wanted to try to do something about stopping the Beacon. They left that same night after we'd refused to allow her to help."

Ceri's eyes grew wide. "You think they've come here?"

Tom nodded.

"No," said Ceri. "That's impossible. They can't drive. It's too far to cycle."

"Hmm, I'm not so sure. They're young and fit—"

"Bri's got a brain injury that's slowly killing her!"

"But she's otherwise as fit as a fiddle. And Will was telling me how strong his leg muscles have become after cycling to Nottingham from London. With empty roads, dry weather and a little luck…" Tom shrugged.

"In a way, I hope you're wrong," said Ceri. "I hope they're

hundreds of miles from here. And yet… something tells me you're right. Damn it!"

They dressed warmly and carried the shotguns tucked under their right armpits, the broken barrels resting at an angle on their forearms. Loose shells filled the pockets of their outer garments. Otherwise, they travelled light with only food, water, a road map and a pair of binoculars in the small backpack slung over Tom's shoulder.

The main road out of the village bent sharply to the south after about a mile.

"This is where we head across country," said Tom, stopping to consult the map. He glanced at the fields rolling away to the distance. "There's a lot of military land around here that's likely impassable. I was a little worried we might have to approach Stonehenge by road. But this looks like farmland."

They clambered over a metal gate and followed a dirt track eastwards for a few hundred yards. When it petered out, they crossed fields that might never again be ploughed and seeded, not speaking much. Now they were so close to danger, they each became preoccupied with their own thoughts.

"What's that?" said Ceri, peering ahead.

Tom shrugged off his backpack and extracted the binoculars they had picked up in an outdoor pursuits shop in Leeds. According to the packaging, the lenses were coated with an anti-glare substance that would prevent the sun glinting off them and revealing the presence of the observers to the observed. Marketed for bird watchers, Ceri had remarked they would be useful for stalkers and perverts.

"Let's hope these are truly anti-glare," Tom commented. He glanced up. The sun hung low and wintry-weak in the sky, but behind them. He raised the glasses to his eyes and adjusted the focus until the distant object Ceri had noticed came into view.

"Well?" said Ceri impatiently. "What is it?"

"Not sure… If it is Stonehenge, it looks nothing like the photos."

"Well, it wouldn't, would it? Let me see."

Tom handed her the binoculars.

"Hmm," she said. "Last time I was here, there were tall fences all around to keep people out who hadn't paid." She swung the binoculars slowly to the right. "I should be able to tell… Yes! That looks like the car park the other side of the main road. There are coaches and… they look like London buses. London buses?" She lowered the binoculars and shrugged. "It's the site of Stonehenge, all right. It looks like they're all set to go. It must be happening tonight."

"Or has already happened."

"If so, why are they still here? These binoculars aren't powerful enough to make out people, but all those buses and coaches…"

The roar of engines revving sounded in the distance. She raised the glasses.

"They're leaving," she said.

Ceri provided a running commentary on the number of coaches and double-decker buses pulling away in the opposite direction. She also mentioned a couple of yellow bulldozers and a crane leaving on the back of a flatbed lorry.

When the sound of the last engine had faded to nothing, she lowered the glasses again.

"They've all gone," she said, rubbing her eyes. "We need to get closer to see if they've left anybody guarding it."

Instinctively crouching, they moved across the fields towards the circle of stones Tom had seen through the binoculars. They both wore drab-coloured clothes, but Tom was painfully aware they were drawing near enough to be visible to the naked eye of anyone looking in their direction.

"I think this is close enough," he said in a low voice.

Ceri nodded. Her face looked pale and drawn.

They lowered themselves to grass that was starting to stiffen in the cold air as the sun prepared to sink for the night. Tom placed the backpack down and they rested the shotguns on it to keep them off the ground. For the first time that day, Tom noticed his breath condensing in the late afternoon chill.

He took the binoculars off Ceri and trained them on the stone circle.

"It looks deserted," he muttered. He moved the glasses away from the circle towards an area littered with gigantic stones, which looked as though they had been unceremoniously flung to one side. "No... wait!"

A movement had caught his eye. He adjusted the dial and two figures came into focus. They were sitting on one of the stones that lay on its side. Between them, spread out on the surface, were objects that Tom could not make out clearly at this distance. The two figures were lowering their hands to the objects and then bringing their hands to their mouths.

"Two guards," he said. "They're eating. A man and a woman, I think. They're wrapped up well against the cold so difficult to tell."

Tom passed the glasses to Ceri so she could see for herself. When she lowered them again, she looked even more drawn, as though nearing the end of her fortitude.

"What now?" she said.

"Well, I can't see any guns..."

"Doesn't mean they don't have them." Ceri bit her lower lip. "Suppose they don't have guns. There's only two of them so they shouldn't, according to Peter, be able to control us with their minds..."

The last thing Peter and Diane had done before leaving Wick was to cast what Peter called a 'protective pall' over Tom's and Ceri's intellects.

"It will prevent them from sensing you from afar," Peter told them. "It will also offer some protection against mental domination, at least against only a few of them. Any more than three acting in concert, if nearby, will probably be able to control you."

Now Tom regarded Ceri closely. "What are you saying?" he asked. "You think we should take the guards out?"

"No!" She lowered her voice. "What I was going to say... even if we can overcome them, what then? Push the stones over like dominoes? They're sunk into the ground. And look at the *size* of them. Peter was right. There's nothing we can do."

"Please don't give up on me now." Tom thought furiously. "There probably isn't much we can do right this minute. If only we could have persuaded that pompous pillock Irving…" He sighed. "No use crying over spilt milk. Look. I'm going to stay. Watch them perform their ceremony or whatever they call it. Maybe during that…" He tailed off when an image of him charging into the circle waving a shotgun about popped into his mind. His imaginary self looked ineffectual. Ridiculous.

He reached into the pocket of his jeans and extracted the car keys. He held them out to Ceri. "You leave if you want. Really, it's fine. Go find Peter and Diane. Maybe they've picked up the doctor. Maybe they have the kids with them."

Ceri stared at the keys and reached out her hand. Tom's heart plummeted. Her hand closed over his.

"If you're staying, I'm staying," she said softly.

Tom's vision blurred. He looked away, wiping briefly at his eyes.

"Thanks," he said, his voice thick.

"So what do we do? Sit here and wait?"

"I guess so. That's about all we *can* do."

They cycled in from the north, skirting around fenced-off military areas. They arrived late into the evening—the fourth evening since they had left the crofter's cottage outside Wick—in the garrison town of Larkhill. The town lay about a mile north of Stonehenge, according to the Wiltshire guidebook they had found in an echoing library the previous night.

Beyond the point of exhaustion, they entered the first building they came to that wasn't locked, leaned their bikes against the wall and removed their helmets. They dumped their backpacks and sank to the floor next to them in the dark.

"Ouch," said Will. "This floor is too hard."

"I know," said Bri. "My bum feels as though I've been tobogganing without the toboggan." She let out a deep sigh. "I think we've made it in time."

Will glanced in her direction, but said nothing. She had been saying weird things for the past four days, as though she knew stuff she had no right knowing. It made Will feel a little scared.

The four days seemed a kaleidoscope of endless roads, tortuous hills, snatches of corpse-like sleep and aches so deep that Will's body had become numb, inured to constant pain. Bri had driven him on as though possessed of an all-consuming hunger that only continuous pedalling could come close to satisfying. Will had responded to her coaxing, her encouragement and her lambasting until his lungs felt they would burst from his chest and his legs into flame. There had been many times he'd wished she had left him behind in Scotland lying on the soft bed.

If still possessed of any energy when the sun went down, they had ridden through the night thanks to powerful lamps they had picked up along the way and attached to the handlebars, until sheer fatigue drove them to seek shelter for a few hours' sleep.

"Wow," murmured Bri. "Just wow."

"What?"

"That was some ride. I honestly didn't think we'd make it. You were awesome."

She reached out and ruffled his hair.

"The motorways were the best," said Will.

The wide, well-surfaced roads were only sparsely littered with abandoned vehicles and wreckage-strewn accident sites, as if people had realised early on in the crisis that they could not outrun the virus and had taken to minor roads in hope of avoiding it. Some of the hills they cycled up had been so long Will thought they might never end. But the down inclines had been *fun*. Bri reckoned they had reached speeds of thirty miles per hour.

"I was a right cow at times," she said. "Wasn't I?"

"Yes."

She laughed.

"Bri?"

"Yes?"

"Why are we here?"

"You know Stonehenge?"

Will shrugged. "Seen it on telly."

"Well, it's some sort of beacon."

"What's a beacon?"

"It sends out a signal. A bit like a radio. The people who did bad things to you... there's more of them coming. A lot more. Like Peter showed us."

For a moment Will forgot his aches and pains. "Spacemen. Oh boy, oh boy—"

"No, Will. It's not good. If they get here safely, they'll kill everyone who survived the Millennium Bug."

"Why? I don't want to hurt anyone."

"I think..." Bri let out a long yawn. "Yes, I think they're afraid of us."

Will let out a longer yawn. His eyes kept closing of their own accord. He scooted closer to Bri and laid his head against her arm. She started to say something else, but Will had stopped listening.

In a suite of offices in Amesbury that had once been home to a firm of solicitors, Joe Lowden stretched out on a row of padded seats in the reception area. He had been for a late evening walk after consuming a large dinner, and had been ordered to bed down for the night. Around him, snores and grunts indicated that those sharing these offices had already succumbed to slumber.

Sleep eluded Joe. Something was bothering him. If it was possible to experience an itching sensation in your mind, that is what Joe was experiencing. A maddening itch that can't be scratched, like skin beneath the plaster holding together knitting bones.

Images of a small boy and a filthy man and a red-lipped woman still played across his mind, but something else was trying to intrude on those images, to break through them. Causing the itching sensation.

Joe turned onto his back and stared at shadows on the stippled ceiling. He whispered a word.

"Grimsby."

His brow furrowed. He had no idea what the word meant. And yet...

He wasn't aware of it, but Joe had recently turned eighteen. He had been taking every recreational drug he could lay his hands upon with mad abandon for the past three years or more. The brain through which the electric shock was passed in Hillingdon Hospital was already a little addled, neural pathways already scrambled. Consequently and perversely, the damage caused to his brain when they attached the electrodes to his brow and flicked the switch was less than had been caused to the other people standing in line beside him.

Freed from the effects of drugs, his body still in the latter stages of development, some of the damaged pathways in his brain were mending. Only a little, and gradually, new concepts—at least, old ones that seemed new—were trying to make themselves felt.

He whispered again.

"Joe. My name is Joe."

Almost three hundred miles from Amesbury by road, at the north-westernmost tip of Wales, lies the small island of Anglesey. Four people—two men and two women—were making their way through the night on foot across the Britannia Bridge. Both this and the other bridge spanning the Menai Strait, connecting the island to the mainland, were blocked to anything larger than foot traffic by knots of crashed and abandoned vehicles.

The people picked their way between debris, stepping around corpses, making startled rats break off from their meals and scurry away beneath cars. One of the men carried a black valise, handling it carefully as if it contained all his worldly wealth.

At the mainland end of the bridge, a bronze Range Rover

stood waiting.

When at last the party reached this vehicle, one of the women paused as though reluctant to get in. One of the men—the smaller one, carrying the valise—spoke to her and eventually she relented. She stepped into the back seat with the smaller man.

The other man walked to the back of the vehicle and opened the tailgate. A black dog jumped out, barking excitedly. Although the dog's tail wagged, it did not jump up at the man or seem to pay him the slightest attention.

The man waited patiently while the animal attended to its business, then motioned with his head for the dog to get back into the car. It obeyed and the man shut the tailgate.

He stepped around to the right-hand side of the vehicle and got in.

Peter turned and looked behind him. The doctor, Howard, offered him an uncertain smile. The young woman, Colleen, sat stiffly, casting nervous glances into the rear compartment where Dusty sat impassively.

"*Really*," Peter said, "he won't hurt you."

"I don't like dogs," said Colleen in her Irish accent. "But I'll be fine so long as he doesn't jump up at me."

"And how is your sense of balance now?"

Colleen gave a strained smile. "It still feels like we're tilting from side to side. But it isn't as bad as it was."

Howard placed his hand on her arm and gave it an affectionate squeeze. "You did great. Not many first-time sailors can cross the Irish Sea without throwing up."

Peter faced forward and started the vehicle.

"Remind me," said Diane in the seat next to him, "why are we going south? Shouldn't we hole up here and wait for them to find us?"

Peter sighed. "You know why. We have to find the youngsters. Get Bri examined by Howard." He shrugged. "They're not here, so it's likely they'll be down there. And maybe while we're there, we can save that idiot Tom from getting himself and Ceri killed."

"Or perhaps get ourselves killed," said Diane.

Peter glanced at her. "If you want to stay, I can't make you come. But decide now. We don't have time to debate it."

Diane was silent for a moment. Then she shrugged. "Ah, what the hell. I seem to have become a sucker for a good cause."

The Range Rover's headlights pierced the darkness. Peter drove in the direction of Liverpool. From there, they would head southwards. If the way was clear, they should arrive at Stonehenge in time for activation of the Beacon.

Chapter Twenty-One

The low *thrum* of engines roused Ceri from a fitful doze. She winced a little when the cold stiffness that had settled into her bones made her joints creak with protest. She scrabbled for the binoculars and nudged Tom.

"Huh?"

"Wake up. They're coming."

Through the binoculars, Ceri could see a glow on the horizon while headlights approached. After a minute or two, the glow resolved into two beams of light.

"One coach," she said. "Two coaches… three. And a double-decker. No, two double-deckers."

She lowered the glasses. The headlights were clearly visible without them, drawing nearer away to their right.

"What's the time?" asked Tom.

Ceri glanced down at her wristwatch. Faint starlight was sufficient to let her make out the luminous dial.

"Ten past four, but I don't know how accurate this is."

Tom grunted. He climbed to his feet and began to move away in the direction they'd come from yesterday.

"Where are you going?" she hissed.

"Loo," muttered Tom.

Ceri rubbed her hands together and breathed on them to try to coax some feeling back into her fingers. When she raised the binoculars, the small procession had come to a halt. In the gleam of the headlights, she watched passengers step down from the vehicles.

After a few minutes, she became aware of Tom returning.

"Better?" she asked, without lowering the binoculars.

"I feel sick," he said. "What's happening?"

"A lot of milling around. They're lighting torches, the old-fashioned type with flames. Those two guards have walked over to join them. There must be almost three hundred people in total.

But, Tom, they're two separate groups. Most of those who were on the London buses just sort of shuffle about. Vague, unfocused. I think they're… well, human, but not normal."

"They're the sacrifices," said Tom. "If Peter hadn't been with us when they were called to London, that's how we would have ended up."

Ceri grimaced and felt a knot form in her stomach. Taking deep breaths of frigid air, she continued watching through the binoculars. It felt less real to view what was happening through lenses, as though being once removed from the event placed her apart from it. Protected her.

"They're crossing the road… walking towards the stone circle. The buses and coaches are leaving."

She was aware that Tom kept shifting about like a fidgeting four-year-old.

"Are you all right?"

"Need the loo again. Won't be long."

By the time he returned, the milling mass had started to form into something more organised. The humans—Ceri could not think of them as drones—shuffled into a line that began at the edge of the stone circle and snaked back towards the road. Torches had been thrust into the ground at regular intervals, casting the scene in a flickering, sepia glow. A trestle table had been set up next to the line of humans; on it stood two boxes. Another line was forming of what Ceri assumed were non-humans, starting at the table.

A clunking sound caused her to tear her eyes away from the glasses. Tom was fiddling with his shotgun.

"What are you doing?"

He looked at her. The starlight did nothing to make him appear less ashen. He wore an expression of such hopelessness, Ceri's stomach tightened further.

"I need to get closer," he said, his tone flat.

"No, Tom! There are too many of them. Peter was right: it's suicide."

"I have to try." His eyes looked a deep grey. Dead eyes. "Well, here goes nothing…"

He tensed himself to begin moving forward. To not have to look into those dead eyes again, Ceri raised the binoculars. She drew her breath in sharply.

"Tom! Wait!"

"No, I have to—"

"Wait! I think… Yes! It's Bri!"

"Huh?"

"Tom, Bri's there. I can tell by the way she moves. It has to be her."

"What's she doing?"

"She's joining one of the lines of people. *Their* line." She swung the glasses from side to side, sweeping the scene. "Can't see Will, but he must be here somewhere. C'mon. Let's both get closer."

Ceri dropped the binoculars to the grass and grabbed the other shotgun. Together, in a crouch, they started to work their way forwards.

Sleep stubbornly eluded Joe Lowden for the rest of the long night. He didn't mind, except it would have enabled him to escape the infernal itching sensation deep within his head. The fact he was once more capable of minding or not minding had not yet registered as one of the old-new concepts leaking into his consciousness.

What did register, when they were roused in the early hours of the morning, was that his chin no longer wanted to dangle slackly to his chest, allowing spittle to fall in a stringy stream. That it might be a good idea to disguise this fact also registered. Joe allowed his chin to loll, like the others', and resisted the impulse to wipe spit away.

He knew who he was: Joe Lowden, a northern lad. He did not yet recognise every image playing in his mind. Some of the people, some of the places he could not yet put a name to. But more than anything, he knew he was in a heap of trouble.

When they were ordered to leave the building and make for the bus, Joe shuffled along with the rest, careful to keep his expression blank. He sat on the bus, staring slackly ahead, expressing no interest in his surroundings.

He slouched off the bus when ordered and joined the aimless milling about. Torches were lit and, by their sputtering light, Joe and the others were marched across a road then crunching grass towards a stone circle. The bad feeling that had been growing in Joe's gut intensified. He wanted to lean to one side and throw up the lavish dinner from the evening before, but forced himself to keep moving. He allowed his pace to slow a little, not sufficiently to be noticed, but enough that he began to drop towards the rear of the shuffling mass.

The order came to form a line and a new memory surfaced. A white hospital room; the smell of ozone and sour milk; people with guns; people without guns staring at him. He was standing in a line, one he didn't want to be in. One that would end badly when he reached the front and it was his turn to step behind the plastic curtains…

Joe was buffeted while people walked past him. His legs wanted to turn and move him quickly in the opposite direction. He stumbled deliberately, as though confused, and more people pressed by. Before attention turned on him, he shuffled forwards, but slowly, allowing more people to overtake him. In this way, by the time he came to a halt at the end of the line, there were only a few people behind him.

Making sure to keep his expression vacuous, Joe waited.

Bri opened her eyes to pitch darkness and groaned. Her legs, back and backside—*especially* her backside—felt like they had been tenderised with a steak hammer. Fresh pain coursed through her temples; bright white spots danced in front of the darkness.

Grimacing and muttering curses, Bri fumbled at her pockets and dry-swallowed two painkillers.

"Will." She shrugged her right shoulder against which his head rested. "Will!"

"Mm…"

"Wake up. Time to get moving."

"Wanna sleep…"

"I know. Stay and sleep if you want, but you'll have to lie down or lean against something else."

When his voice came again, all trace of sleepiness had disappeared.

"Where are we going?"

"Stonehenge. Dress warmly."

Bri rooted around in her backpack until she felt the Harrods hat. She pulled it low over her ears.

While they walked through the bitter night air, Bri's stiffness eased and the trek became easier. Her headache began to fade to the dull background pain to which she had grown accustomed. The only debilitating factor that remained was utter weariness.

They had left their torches behind and proceeded cautiously. The low wire fences they came across gleamed in the starlight and they were able to clamber over them with minimal difficulty.

Tension grew in Bri with every step southwards they took. It must have rubbed off on Will because he said very little.

When a flickering orange glow appeared ahead of them, Bri stopped. She lowered her mouth to Will's ear.

"Remember I said you could come so long as you stayed put when I told you to?"

Will nodded.

"Well, this is where you stay put."

"But—"

"But me no buts, mister," Bri hissed. "Cross your heart and hope to die. Remember?"

A pause. He nodded again.

"Good. Whatever you hear, don't come any closer. If I don't return, go back to our bikes and get the hell out of here."

Bri straightened. She avoided looking at Will's face; she could not stand to see the expression that she knew must be there.

Before she could step away, Will grabbed her and hugged her fiercely. After a moment's hesitation, she threw her arms around him and hugged him tightly back. She had to tear herself away.

She glanced back once. He stood watching her. It was too dark for her to make out his features, but his shoulders drooped. She raised her hand in a brief farewell and did not look back again.

Bri lowered herself into a crouch when she drew closer to the flickering light. By it, she could see a ring of tall stones. On impulse, she dropped to her knees on the freezing ground and tugged at the stiff grass. The muscles in her back complained, but she ignored them. After a few failures, she managed to tear away a small sod. She brought it to her mouth and breathed on it, trying to soften the frozen clump of earth. When she judged it as soft as she could make it, she raised the mud to her face and smeared it, working it well in below her eyes. She doubted it would stand up to close inspection, but she hoped the grime would mask her youthful complexion. She had overheard Ceri tell Tom, in aghast tones, that these people did not have children or teenagers, that they were born as adults. Bri couldn't see how *that* would work, but now wasn't the time to ponder.

She crept forward until she was just outside the wavering pool of light thrown by the torches. She could hear muffled voices, but could see no one. All the action seemed to be taking place at the far side of the stones.

Keeping outside the light, Bri moved to her left, describing a circle. People came into view, standing in lines or milling about as though waiting to take up more permanent positions.

From what Peter had told her, and from her own experiences since awaking in London with no memory of *before*, she knew she was safe from detection through her mind. The protection she had put in place could not be penetrated, even if three of them acted together. She suspected it would take a lot more of them than that to be able to exert the same control over her that she had witnessed them exerting over Will.

No, the danger lay in the possibility of *physical* detection. She tugged her hat lower so that it nestled almost on top of her eyes and covered the scab on her temple.

She continued to circle, having to weave between huge blocks of ancient-looking stone lying higgledy-piggledy in the grass.

Drawing level with the mass of people, Bri drew in a deep breath. Standing as erect as she could in the hope of giving the impression of being taller, she strode forward into the light.

She expected at any moment to hear a challenge, but continued on, trying to look as though she was part of proceedings. Maybe because she was managing to convey an aura of confidence, of belonging, or perhaps because nobody happened to be looking in her direction when she emerged from the darkness, no challenge came. She took in the scene while she approached.

Slack-jawed people formed a long queue from the edge of the stone ring. Another line was forming next to it, starting at a table upon which stood some boxes. The people in this second line wore normal, alert expressions. A blonde-haired woman near the front of the queue bounced up and down on the balls of her feet as though barely able to contain her excitement. Others in line also looked excited, but not all. Some looked grim or decidedly morose.

To one side of the queues, a clutch of three people stood near a short, black woman of enormous girth. All four of them seemed to be closely watching the lines forming. Now and then, one or other of the three would glance at the plump woman and Bri gained the impression she was in charge.

Bri focused her attention on a grey-haired man in the middle of the second line whose glance darted this way and that like someone seeking an escape route, and who took great gulps of air as if to ward off nausea. The queue of people behind him curved a little so that the watching cluster's view of him would be obscured. He would have to do.

Keeping her shoulders thrust back, but her head dipped slightly forward to cast her face in shadow, Bri strode up to the man.

He glanced at her without interest.

"I've been asked to take your place," Bri said in a low voice. She nodded in the direction where the woman in charge stood. "*She* asked me to."

"Huh?" said the man. He turned his head to see where Bri had indicated. When he turned back, relief flooded his features. "Milandra asked you to replace me?"

"Yep." Bri could sense hope pouring off the man. Whatever he was standing in line to do, it was clearly something for which he had no stomach.

Yet he didn't move away.

His brow furrowed and he peered at Bri more closely.

"Who are you?" he said.

"I'm Bri, of course," she replied in a tone that implied she was stating the perfectly obvious.

The man nodded as though it explained everything, and blinked as though he didn't quite follow the explanation.

"Off you toddle, then," said Bri, flapping her fingers at him. Adrenaline was making her cavalier. "Spit spot."

"Er, okay," said the man. "Um, thanks."

Bri turned her head, dismissing him. She daren't open her mouth again. She might have got away with the Mary Poppins impression, but she didn't trust herself to say anything more.

From the corner of her eye, Bri saw the man move away and breathed a silent sigh of relief. She watched him surreptitiously for a few moments, afraid he was going to approach the woman he had called Milandra to thank her for relieving him. But he walked in the opposite direction and soon was lost to view amidst milling bodies.

Bri risked a cautious glance at the person standing behind her in the queue. A middle-aged woman, staring off into the distance as if bored with the whole thing. The person in front of Bri was a small man who appeared to be paying her not the slightest heed.

So far, so good.

~ ~ ~

Snot ran onto Will's upper lip and pooled there. He wiped it away with the sleeve of his jacket. He used his other sleeve to wipe at his cheeks.

He had never felt so small and alone. He hadn't felt this abandoned even when waking alone in his mum's flat. At least she and Poppy hadn't *chosen* to leave him.

Yet he knew Bri wouldn't have chosen to leave him either, not if she felt there was a better alternative. She was trying to protect him and all he could do was stand there snivelling in the dark like some dipsy girl.

He took a deep breath and wiped the last of the tears and snot away. He had crossed his heart and hoped to die, but figured he was going to die anyway by the sound of it. He shrugged his thin shoulders. Might as well die from breaking a promise as from anything else.

Setting his face to the orange glow, Will set out after Bri.

Tom and Ceri reached the shifting edge of light. Tom gripped the shotgun tightly, both barrels loaded. For days he had imagined himself toting a gun, becoming a man to be feared, a man to be reckoned with; strange that now it came down to it all he felt was bowel-loosening terror.

He peered into the light. He could see Bri, standing in a slowly moving queue of people. When each person arrived at the table, a man standing behind it reached inside a box and passed over an object that glinted in the torchlight. Clutching the objects, the people stepped across to the line of humans. Each taking a human from the front of the queue by the arm, they led them inside the stone circle.

Tom tensed, readying himself to spring forward. Quite what he would do when he reached the circle, he had no clue. Die, most likely. He could feel the last of his resolve seeping away. If he didn't act now, he never would.

"Wait!"

Ceri grabbed his arm.

He tried to shake her off, but she held tight.

"Let's move around to our left," she whispered. "We can approach the stones unseen from behind."

"Then what?"

"I don't know. We can see what Bri does. She must have a plan."

If Bri had heard Ceri, she would have laughed; a high-pitched chortle edging towards hysteria.

"A plan?" she'd say. "I *wish*. I'm making this up as I go along."

Bri lowered her gaze when she approached the table, but the man standing behind it barely glanced at her. He held out a knife that she took from him. It felt heavy and cold. She briefly examined the blade while she walked away. It looked honed to a wickedly sharp edge.

What am I supposed to do with this?

Following the lead of the small man in front of her, Bri made for the queue of slack-jawed people. The small man gripped the woman standing at the front of the queue by the upper arm and led her between the nearest standing stones into the ring.

Next in line was a thick-set man, somewhere in his forties, she guessed. He stared vacantly ahead, a dribble of spit falling to his stained jumper.

Bri reached forward and gripped him lightly on his forearm. The man didn't even look around. Exerting the slightest of pressure, she nudged the man forwards and he began to shuffle towards the gap in the stones.

Then it happened.

The world wavered. Bri stumbled and tightened her grip on the man's arm to steady herself. A bright light went off like a flashbulb in her head, making her gasp.

The ring of stones, the lines of people, the thick-set man... They flickered like a malfunctioning film reel and blinked out. Bri was no longer there; she was inside the man's psyche, penetrating the cloud that enveloped it, delving into memories that he was no longer capable of reliving. When she saw herself in those memories, a fog lifted inside *her* psyche.

Bri's mind jumped again. To *before*…

Her eyes open on a shadowed room. She is lying, fully clothed, under the duvet in a double bed. A man, thick-set, somewhere in his forties, she guesses, is standing at the end of the bed, gazing down at her. His lips are parted in a sneer and his breath comes in short gasps.

"So you ducked in here to escape the snow, too, my dear," he says.

His voice is oily and the hairs on her neck crackle as though electrically charged. Her lower lip quivers and she clenches it between her teeth. This seems to make him breathe more rapidly.

Bri flings the duvet back and darts from the bed. He is slow to react. She is past him and out of the door. But she hears the heavy clomp of his boots on the stairs as he pursues her down them.

She runs past her bike and reaches the front door. The worn brass handle turns in her grasp, but the door is stiff; she'd found it difficult to force it open, and close it behind her, when seeking refuge from the driving snow. A sharp pain pierces the back of her head when he grabs a handful of her hair. He swings her around, flings her into the living room and she cries out.

She is on her back on a sagging settee. He crouches over her, hot breath flooding her face in sour waves.

While Bri struggles and whimpers, he holds her tight by leaning across her with his left arm. With his right hand, he reaches for something on the floor. It comes up holding a solid glass paperweight. He brandishes it above her face and she freezes, her eyes fixed on the heavy object.

"That's better," he croons. "No need to make such a fuss, my dear. It's not as if I have time now to enjoy you. I have to be getting to the hospital…" His brow beetles as though he isn't sure why he must go.

Bri says nothing. Terror and revulsion mute her.

The man's face smoothes out and he smiles. "Will you wait here for me, my dear, while I attend to business?" He chuckles and doesn't wait for an answer that she is incapable of uttering. "Of course you won't. So I'll just make sure you're still here when I return…"

At last released from paralysis, Bri starts to scream, but the sound barely begins to escape her lips when the paperweight crashes down in a vicious arc towards her forehead and everything turns black.

Chapter Twenty-Two

Milandra had started forward to enter the stone circle as soon as the sixty-third drone had been led in, when she heard the commotion. Possessing the well-hidden ability to cover ground quickly when she needed to, she was the first one there, squeezing through the stalled lines.

One of their number, a woman in a woollen hat pulled low to her eyes, had yanked her drone out of line and had him pinned against the back of a bluestone, holding the knife to his throat.

"Keep moving, people!" Milandra ordered. She saw Grant pushing through, an anxious look on his face, followed closely by Wallace and Lavinia. "Stay back, Jason. I've got this. Get those lines moving."

She turned her attention back to the woman. Whatever had caused her to react like this, it looked to have passed. The woman's shoulders sagged and she lowered her arm. The knife tumbled from her grasp. She let go of the drone and turned aside, stumbling to her knees and letting loose a thin stream of vomit.

"Hey, you!" Milandra called to a bystander.

The man raised his eyebrows.

"Yes, you!" Milandra searched for his name. "Larsson, isn't it? Come here. Grab that knife and take her place. She's sick."

"Okay," said Larsson. He sauntered over and picked up the knife.

The drone who had nearly had his throat cut prematurely seemed unperturbed by the experience. He stood leaning against the bluestone, staring at nothing. Larsson took him by the arm and led him into the stone circle. The lines of people and drones were moving again. In a few moments, they would all have taken their places.

Milandra stooped to where the woman knelt on the grass, head bowed. She reached out a hand to touch her shoulder, then withdrew it as though scalded.

Keeping her voice low so no one could overhear, Milandra hissed into the woman's ear, "Brianne! You should not be here. There are people who will kill you as soon as look at you. Get out of here, girl. Live to fight another day."

She straightened and glanced about. The last of the people in line was walking a drone into the circle. With no one to lead them, the remaining twenty-seven drones came to a halt. They could stay there for now.

Grant was watching her, a strange look on his face she could not read.

"Inside, Jason," she said. "Take your place. It is nearly time."

Milandra followed him into the circle.

Bri rose unsteadily to her feet, the taste of vomit thick in her mouth. Now she knew what had happened to her *before*. He must have removed her upper clothing while she was unconscious. What else he had done to her before leaving on her bike she hadn't seen because the resurgence of her own memory had dragged her out of his. Perhaps it was as well.

Even so, she had come close to slicing the knife's sharp edge across the man's throat. It was the vacant expression in his eyes that stayed her hand. He no longer knew what he had done or what he had intended to come back and do later. Killing the pitiful creature would not wreak vengeance on the man who had defiled her. That man was out of her reach.

She looked around. The queue she had been part of had gone. The line of slack-jawed people had shrunk to a handful; they stood in place as if unable to move until instructed to.

Only a few other people were about, clearing away the table and boxes. They paid her not the slightest attention. In the gap between the stones in front of her, blocking it, stood a man. He had his back to her.

Bri felt deflated. Beaten. What had she been thinking, that she could somehow prevent these people doing whatever they wanted? She was little more than a kid.

Will. He would be standing in that dark field, wondering if she was coming back. He would be scared and cold and lonely.

If she could do nothing else with whatever time remained to her, she could at least be a friend, or a big sister, to a little boy who had nobody else.

Bri began to walk around the circle, making for the back of it where she would strike across the fields in the direction from which she had come.

Tom and Ceri crouched behind a particularly wide bluestone. A length of coarse rope had been passed around it at waist height. Ceri tried to move it with her fingers, but it was tied fast somewhere out of sight.

The beating of her heart must, she thought, be heard by those standing within the circle. Despite the cold, the shotgun felt slick in her grasp from the sweat pouring from the palms of her hands.

She risked a peek around the edge of the stone. A woman had stood in the gap between it and the next stone. She had her back turned, facing into the circle.

"It's happening," she whispered to Tom.

He nodded and his lips drew into a tight line. He leaned back against the stone and took deep breaths. With a grimace, he slowly closed the barrels of his shotgun. Needing to pee, needing to run far, far away, Ceri fumbled two shells from her pocket. Barely able to hold them with shaking hands, she managed to insert them into the barrels of her gun. Then, with deliberate, exaggerated movements, she closed the barrels.

She held her breath, sure the clicks must have been heard. A voice *did* start to speak, but from inside the circle and it wasn't addressing them.

Ceri could not have made out the words the voice was saying even had she wanted to. A rushing sound like a raging waterfall had begun in her ears.

This is what the moment before death feels like.

She glanced at Tom and he nodded. She began to turn, to

stand and step through the gap between the stones, shoving the woman out of the way, when a movement the other side of Tom caught her eye. He had seen it, too. He had started to rise, but sank back to his heels.

Looking like she was enjoying a Sunday afternoon stroll, Bri came sauntering around the circle.

She saw them and stopped in her tracks. In any other circumstances, Ceri might have found the sight of her jaw dropping comical.

Bri rushed forward.

"What are you guys doing?"

The girl's voice sounded so loud that Ceri almost wet herself. She raised her hand to her lips and made a frantic shushing gesture. Bri dropped to her knees.

"It's okay," she said in a lower voice. "They're all busy. They don't care about us." She glanced down at their hands. "What are you doing with *guns*?"

"Are you all right?" hissed Tom. "We've been worried sick about you."

"I'm fine."

"Where's Will?" whispered Ceri.

Bri waved her hand vaguely towards the dark fields behind them. "I'm going to him now. We need to get out of here. All of us."

"No," said Tom. "You go to Will and the two of you clear out. Head for North Wales. Anglesey. Peter and Diane have gone there to fetch a doctor who can make you better."

"What about you two?"

Tom glanced at Ceri. "You go with them. I have to put a stop to this."

Ceri shook her head.

Tom turned to Bri. "Get going. I want you out of harm's way before the shooting starts."

Ceri tried to swallow, but found she had no spit left. Bri's eyes widened at mention of shooting. She grabbed Tom's jacket with one hand. With the other, she grabbed Ceri's.

That was when the stone behind them began to shake.

Milandra strode into the centre of the circle. The last drones were being lashed to the stones against which they knelt. The last of her people took their places. Sixty-two of them stood in the gaps between the stones, facing into the circle. Sixty-three drones knelt face-first to the stones, lengths of rope holding them in place, feet dangling over pits. At their sides stood sixty-three people, knives in hands. All eyes of her people turned to her.

Already she could feel earth power thrumming through the soles of her boots, longing to be unleashed.

Raising her head, Milandra peered at the stars. Earth Home's sun gave out weak light barely visible to the naked eye, even on such a clear night as this. It shone amidst a cluster of similarly faint stars, but Milandra had learned long ago which one it was. She identified it now and sighed with satisfaction. Earth Haven and Earth Home were in precise alignment to ensure the surge of power she was about to unleash found its mark.

She glanced at her wrist watch. It confirmed what she already knew.

Milandra raised her hands.

"My friends," she said in a clear voice, "we have toiled long to arrive at this juncture. From the moment I received the message telling me our people are coming until now, our labours have been exacting and many. You have performed them admirably. You have paved the way for our people's arrival to be a safe one.

"This last task will ensure they are guided to Earth Haven. As many of you will recall doing almost five millennia ago, we must activate the Beacon that will call our people home. Unlike the first time, some of you will, I know, find this task distasteful. I, too, find it so, but *it is nonetheless a necessary one*. Perform it with the same fortitude as you performed the Cleansing.

"It is time."

Milandra brought her hands sweeping downwards. Sixty-two

pairs of arms stretched to either side, touching bluestones to complete the circle. Sixty-three hands clutching knives reached out and sliced. Sixty-three drones slumped forward, held in place by the ropes. Their life blood, so full and rich and energising, gushed onto the stones.

The thrumming beneath Milandra's feet stopped. The earth drew breath. She mentally prepared herself for when it exhaled.

The people standing between the stones gasped and stiffened as if turned to steel. The bluestones began to tremble, sending droplets of blood into the air. A high-pitched humming sounded, growing louder and higher, becoming a moan, a wail, a shriek that threatened to burst Milandra's eardrums. The stones shook ever more violently until it seemed they must topple, then abruptly fell still; the shrieking cut off like a switch had been thrown.

Milandra steadied herself. Nevertheless, the blast of energy almost lifted her off her feet. She was barely aware of the people who stood between the stones slumping while she in turn grew ramrod stiff. Her entire being zinged with the force of the power she wielded.

For a moment, Milandra revelled in the sensation that she could do anything she wanted. For a moment, she was a goddess, terrible and almighty and filled with majesty.

Then she raised her arms and once more directed her gaze at Earth Home's sun. With a twinge of regret, she let the energy fly.

Bereft, she sank to her knees.

From the corner of her eye, she saw Grant step forward from his place between two stones. With an effort, she raised her head and glanced about her. The last of the drones' twitching death throes had stilled. People with knives were coming forward to cut the ropes and topple the bodies into the pits.

"Bring forth the lighter fluid," Grant called to those who remained outside the circle. "Douse the bodies and burn them. Our work here is then done."

He hurried over to Milandra.

"Okay?" he asked.

She nodded. "Give me a moment and I'll be fine."

The circle filled as people between the stones left their places, and immediately thinned out when they and those wielding knives made their way to the parking lot. Milandra happened to be looking at the clear space in front of the two stones between which the small boy entered.

She grasped Grant's hand and he stared down at her in surprise.

"Jason," she said, urgency lending her voice potency. "Get Wallace out of here. Don't let him near. He's only a boy."

Grant's brow furrowed in confusion. Milandra inclined her head and Grant looked to where she indicated.

The boy was standing just inside the circle, gazing wide-eyed at the bodies of the drones while the first flames licked over them, his top lip quivering. His voice was tiny, croaking with fear, but Milandra heard him clearly.

"Please. Has anyone seen Bri?"

When the flickering orange light appeared ahead of them, Peter switched the engine off and let the car coast to a standstill.

"So nobody'll hear us," he said. He turned to Diane. "I'm not sure if we're in time. That bloody wreckage."

They had lost an hour having to retrace their steps upon encountering a pile-up blocking all three lanes of the motorway.

"We're too late," said Diane quietly. "It's happening right now. Can't you feel it?"

And Peter could. A sense of being close to a source of immense power. He unbuckled his seat belt. "I'm going to see if there's anyone left alive to rescue," he said grimly.

"I'm coming too," said Diane, opening her door.

Colleen uttered a shriek from the back.

"What the…?" began Peter.

A black shape hurtled past him, across Diane's lap and out through the door before he could do anything.

"Dusty!" he called, but the dog was gone. "Damn!"

He turned around. Colleen was crouched into the corner of the back seat. Howard, too, looked a little startled.

"You okay?" he asked the woman.

Colleen nodded. "It was so sudden, he scared me."

"Both of you, stay here," Peter said. "You should be safe. Me and Diane are going to try to find the others."

"Mightn't you need our help?" asked Howard.

Peter shook his head. "I'm afraid of what we're going to find. I don't want to place you two in danger as well. Sit tight, okay?"

They nodded.

"Good. See you soon."

He stepped out of the car into the cold morning air. Diane joined him and they began to walk through the darkness towards the flickering glow.

"It's done," said Diane. "The Beacon's been activated. I can no longer feel the power."

"Neither can I. I only hope that bloody fool Tom hasn't managed to get himself killed yet."

No sooner were the words out of his mouth, than the first echoing shots rang out. Peter broke into a run.

Tom, Ceri and Bri clutched at each other while the stones shook. When the high-pitched humming rose to a shriek, they clenched their fists against their ears.

The stillness and silence took them by surprise. For a long moment, they continued to press their fists tightly to their ears. Eventually, like waking from a deep sleep, they blinked and tentatively lowered their hands.

"Is it over?" whispered Ceri.

Tom was about to reply, when something slithered over his head. Ceri ducked and thrust her hand to her mouth to stifle a scream.

Tom looked up. His breath escaped in a rush.

"It's okay," he hissed to Ceri. "It's only the rope. It's gone slack. Looks like it's been cut."

Ceri glanced up, wide-eyed. Her face broke into a grimace.

"They're dead," she whispered. "The people who powered the Beacon."

Tom slumped back against the cold stone.

What do we do now? Now that we've failed so miserably at this.

Before he could voice the thought, Ceri let out a shriek. Not the muffled squeak she'd uttered when the rope touched her, but a full-on, blood-curdling screech that drilled into his skull.

She had leaned across to peer around the stone and was pointing through the vacant gap with an unsteady arm.

"Will!" she cried.

Bri leapt up and dashed through the gap into the circle. Ceri scrambled to her feet, clutching her shotgun, and followed. Still holding his gun, Tom stood and tried to go after them, but his legs refused to carry him.

"No!" he muttered. "You will *not* let me down, not now, you bastards."

With an effort of will he didn't know he possessed, Tom got his legs moving and half-ran into the circle.

That's when things became a little confused.

A couple of people were walking slowly around the edge of the circle, dousing in some sort of liquid bodies lying crumpled in holes in the ground. They continued in their work, apparently unconcerned by the drama unfolding around them. The corpses they had already visited had flames licking from them and the stench of searing flesh began to make Tom's eyes water.

Bri had reached the opposite side of the circle. She was kneeling, hugging Will close to her. He had his arms tightly about her neck as if he never meant to let go, eyes squeezed shut. Ceri stood in the centre of the circle, holding the shotgun ready, waving it between knots of onlookers.

It was the onlookers who demanded Tom's attention.

A group of five or six people, led by a blonde-haired woman with a scornful grin on her face, was looking intently at Ceri. While he watched, Ceri froze as though turned to stone, her shotgun pointing at no one in particular. Tom's head jerked and he felt a familiar tingling inside his skull. Another group of people was staring at him. The protection put in place by Peter and Diane was rapidly being breached.

Before the last of his free will was torn away, Tom swung the shotgun around and pulled the trigger twice in quick succession. He hadn't aimed and the shots went wide and high, but they sounded shockingly loud in the enclosed space. Most of the people in the two groups flinched and ducked. The recoil made Tom stumble, but his head cleared and his will was once more his own.

Ceri swung into action. She brought the gun around and pointed it at the group who had been looking at her. The blonde woman continued to stare, her expression of scorn unwavering.

"Run, you mothers!" Ceri yelled.

She raised the gun, aiming above their heads, and let rip. She had broken the barrels to reload by the time Tom realised he ought to do the same.

The two groups broke up in confusion when some of their number turned and fled from the circle. The blonde shouted after them in a high-pitched voice, like a little girl's. One or two people paused, but most continued in their flight.

Ceri snapped the barrels back into place and pointed them at the woman.

"Begone, bitch!" Ceri screamed.

The woman's mouth twitched into a sneer. Then she tittered. Ceri uttered such a roar of rage that Tom thought she was going to shoot the woman. The woman must have thought the same for the sneer disappeared to be replaced by an expression of unhappy uncertainty. Without making another sound, the woman turned and ran.

No sooner had she gone than two new people rushed into the circle. A man and a woman, both armed with handguns, both looking as if they knew how to use them.

The woman was dark-haired and dusky. Beautiful, not that

Tom had time to appreciate it. She was pointing her pistol at his chest. He had barely fumbled two more shells from his jacket pocket. Tom had rarely seen a gun before the Millennium Bug. Now, for the fourth or fifth time since the outbreak, he looked down the business end of one. The woman's finger tightened on the trigger…

Tom twitched violently at the report, but it was the woman who ducked. Ceri had let loose with another barrel and was pointing the shotgun at the woman, one barrel still loaded.

"Next time I aim to kill, bitch!" hissed Ceri.

The woman took a step back, looking less sure of herself.

Tom finished reloading and closed the barrels. His jaw dropped when he saw what the man who had entered the circle was doing.

He was staring at Bri, a smirk curling his lips. Bri had extricated herself from Will's embrace and risen to her feet, standing in front of him. Will's pale, wide-eyed face peered from behind her back. The man's arm was held straight out before him, the pistol aimed unwaveringly at Bri.

"You led us a merry dance," the man drawled in an American accent. "Time you paid."

Tom saw the man's knuckle whiten. He brought the shotgun up, but he was too late. The man fired.

Will was quicker. He darted around Bri, giving her a shove that sent her sprawling to one side. The bullet caught Will high on the left side of his chest. With a startled yelp, he crumpled to the grass.

"Nooo!" Tom yelled. He yanked at the shotgun's trigger and was almost thrown down by the recoil. The shots again went wide.

Ceri swung her gun from the woman and discharged it at the man. The grass near his feet exploded and he leapt back in surprise.

Before Tom could rush to the boy's side, he became aware that the dusky woman was once more training her gun at his chest. She smiled and Tom closed his eyes.

He heard the shot, but didn't feel a thing. He opened his eyes.

The woman was lying on her back, shrieking while a snarling black dog tore at her wrist.

"Dusty?" said Tom. "How…?"

The woman dropped the gun and Dusty gave a last shake of her wrist before unclamping his jaws. The woman began to scrabble backwards along the ground, her face contorted in fear and pain.

Dusty turned towards the man. He was pointing his pistol directly at the dog.

Tom didn't waste time shouting or trying to reload the shotgun. He ran at the man, swinging the gun like a club. The stock struck the man on the cheek and his shot pinged harmlessly away.

Ceri had reloaded and stalked forward, determination stamped across her features. Dusty approached from the side, a low growl rumbling deep in his chest. Tom wielded the shotgun like a baseball bat, ready to land another blow.

"Wallace! The dog!" Tom glanced towards the dark-haired woman. She called to the man between pain-clenched teeth. "Set it on them!"

"Don't even think about it." Ceri's voice was low and so full of menace that Tom wanted to take a step back from her. She tugged the stock of the shotgun tighter to her shoulder. "If the dog so much as growls at me, I'll blow your fucking head clean from your shoulders."

The man stared at her, a vivid bruise already colouring his cheek. He glanced across at the dark-haired woman, who was disappearing through a gap in the stones, still crawling backwards.

He shrugged and dropped the pistol.

"Didn't intend to hurt the boy," he said. "Sorry."

Ceri's voice was little more than a snarl.

"Scram."

The man turned and walked away.

Tom looked quickly around. No non-humans remained within the circle. The stench and smoke from burning bodies were growing thicker.

He sank to his knees and held his hands out to Dusty.

"Come here, boy."

Tom buried his face in the dog's fur and, for once, allowed Dusty to lick his face.

Then he turned towards Will.

Bri had his head cradled in her lap. Ceri looked on, her face drained of colour. Will gazed up at Bri, his features calm.

"Don't you dare leave me," Bri was saying. "Do you hear me, William Harry Clarkson? You're not going anywhere without me again."

Will raised a hand and brushed at a tear on Bri's cheek.

"Bri," he murmured. "Like the cheese but without the e."

His hand dropped to his chest and he smiled. His eyes fluttered closed.

Chapter Twenty-Three

Milandra stepped gingerly out of the circle. It wasn't that her strength had been sapped by the ordeal; more a case of lethargy brought on by possessing such great power and letting it go.

She could see Grant remonstrating with Wallace and Lavinia. Throwing his hands into the air in disgust, Wallace stomped away towards the road where the buses and coaches were pulling up. Lavinia trailed behind him like a little girl.

Milandra glanced around. The remaining drones were being shepherded towards the buses. While she watched, one of the drones, a young man, sidled to one side and slipped away. Nobody else noticed. Milandra grinned to herself and said nothing.

She beckoned to Grant.

"Wallace left willingly, then?"

"I've a feeling he'll try to double back. Full of hatred for that girl."

"Well, never mind him—" Milandra jumped when a couple of shots, close together, boomed out. She laid a hand on Grant's arm. "Never mind that either. I need your help."

Grant raised his eyebrows.

"Ronstadt can't be far away. I want you to help me locate him."

"And then?"

Milandra drew in a long breath. This was it: the point of no return.

"Jason, you're probably aware I feel more than a little sympathy for humanity…" She broke off. "Why are you grinning like that?"

"I've been waiting for you to say it. Took your sweet time about it."

They both jumped when the next series of shots exploded in the circle. People began to run out from between the stones. Milandra pointed them towards the parking lot.

The Chosen appeared, looking uncharacteristically flustered.

"To the coach, Simone," Milandra said in a tone that brooked no argument.

To her surprise, the Chosen merely nodded and hurried away.

Milandra shook her head. "Wonders will never cease," she said.

"Goddamn it!" muttered Grant, looking to the far side of the circle. "I'm sure Wallace and Lavinia just went back in."

"Leave them," said Milandra. "They're liable to get themselves killed, but it's their call." She turned back to face him. "So, you're willing to help?"

"Try stopping me. But let's get away from this war zone."

Peter approached the stone circle from the adjoining field, Diane hard on his heels. The last shot had been fired a minute or more ago and a knot of dread curled tight in Peter's stomach at what he might find.

The torches still burned, but he could see no one outside the circle. Apart from one man. Peter slowed when he neared him. Barely a man, more a boy.

"Who are you?" Peter asked, coming to a stop. He probed. Definitely human.

The boy's eyes widened. "You're one of them. Just met another of your lot. He had a lump on his cheek. Gave him another one to match." The boy's hands curled into fists.

Peter nodded. "I am one of them, but I'm on your side. What's your name?"

"Joe. Joe Lowden."

"Come with me, Joe."

Peter started for the circle. He heard the boy gasp when Diane ran up, but he carried on. He reached the stones and stepped cautiously inside.

Bitter smoke immediately stung his eyes and he had to squint to make anything out.

"Oh no," he muttered.

He strode forward.

"Ceri," he said. "Take Brianne down to the road across this

field. When you hit the road, turn right and follow it. You'll find the Range Rover. Wait for us there."

Ceri turned her tear- and smoke-stained face to him.

"He's only a boy…"

"Come on, Ceri. I need you to be strong. Take Brianne to the car."

Ceri nodded. She reached down and tugged at Brianne's arm. The girl tried to shake her off, but Ceri was insistent. Brianne gently lowered Will's head to the ground. Reluctance pouring from her like sweat, she stood and allowed Ceri to lead her sobbing from the circle.

Peter stooped to Will. He placed his head to his chest and listened. Faint, but it was there. The flutter of a pulse. He probed. The boy's mind had faded, but…

"He's still alive," he said to Tom, who was standing with his hand resting on Dusty's head. "But maybe not for much longer." He gave a deep sigh. "Shouldn't move him, but it will be quicker to take him to the doc than fetch the doc here. And we need to get him away from this smoke and stench."

Diane arrived in the circle, panting. With her was the boy, Joe.

Peter pulled Tom down to him. "Listen closely. You need to get your arms under his shoulders and his knees. Above all, make sure you support his shoulders. If the bullet's still in there, we need to keep movement to a minimum. Joe here will help you."

Tom nodded. His face looked grey; the man was in shock.

Peter clutched Tom's arm tightly, hating himself for doing it but wanting to make sure Tom understood.

"Tom, there's a doctor in the Range Rover. His name is Howard. Take Will to him as quickly as you can."

Tom grimaced at the tightness of Peter's grip, but nodded again. Peter was relieved to see his gaze appeared a little clearer.

"Where's your car?" said Peter.

"Huh?"

"The car you came in. Where is it?"

Tom pointed vaguely over his shoulder. "Shrewton. It's a mile or two to the west."

"Okay. Once you've taken Will to the doc, go and fetch your car. There's too many of us to fit into the Range Rover and we'll need to find a hospital. Take Ceri and Brianne with you. It'll keep them out of the way while Howard works on the boy. Colleen can help him."

"Colleen…?"

"I'll explain later. Go to your car and drive it back to the Range Rover. Don't use any lights. I think most of them have gone, but it won't hurt to exercise caution."

"Bit late for caution." Tom turned haunted eyes towards him. "Will's been shot and the Beacon's been activated."

"But nobody's dead yet. Right, come on. You need to get going."

"What are you going to do? You and Diane?"

"Oh, we're going to meet up with Milandra. I've a feeling she's going to help us."

Peter let go of his arm and watched Tom carefully pick Will up, carrying him as Peter had instructed. Dusty and Joe walked alongside, the boy watchful. Peter sensed that Joe was not quite right in the head, as though recovering from some sort of brain injury, but he was comforted to see him walking with Tom, apparently ready and willing to help bear the burden if necessary.

A few minutes later, in a field beneath a clear sky in which the first weak rays of sun were beginning to make themselves known, Peter and Diane met with Milandra and Jason Grant. They stood in a rough circle and the other three lent their intellects to Milandra. With a smidgeon of the power she had received while activating the Beacon and retained for this very purpose to boost their effort, they held their own version of a Commune.

Their combined psyches stretched upwards and outwards, covering a great deal of western Europe, soaring over the Atlantic to the eastern seaboard, reaching partway to the Rockies before running out of steam.

The message was simple:

Come to the United Kingdom. Here the final reckoning for mankind will take place. Come now.

Afterwards, energy spent, they parted with barely a word.

In a small coastal town in Connecticut, Zacharias Trent opened one eye. He now trusted the woman enough to share a room with her. She had not repeated her offer for him to share her bed, for which he was thankful. It was hard enough becoming accustomed to everyday interaction with another human being without having to deal with that sort of shit, too.

Amy was also awake. Her eyes gleamed faintly in the darkness while she looked at him.

"Just had the strangest dream…" Zach began.

"About the U.K. and final reckonings?"

Zach sat up, wide awake.

"Ever been to the U.K., missy?"

"Nope, but I reckon I got a hankering to go there now."

"D'you know, I have a similar hankering…"

Across much of the eastern third of the United States and most of western Europe, survivors of the Cleansing awoke with a new compulsion.

Nearly all would try to answer the call.

They didn't know what it was, didn't much like the sound of it, but they wanted to be there—*had* to be there—when the Reckoning took place.

About the Author

Sam Kates lives in South Wales, UK, with a family, a computer and *way* too many books. To connect on social media:

Website: samkates.co.uk
Facebook: www.facebook.com/writersamkates
Twitter: @_Sam_Kates_
E-mail: samkates@samkates.co.uk

Note

Please consider leaving a review—reviews can be of immeasurable help to authors in gaining visibility and running promotions.

Thank you for purchasing and reading this book.

To sign up for news of releases and special offers, most of which are only available to subscribers (no spam, promise):

http://www.samkates.co.uk/stay-in-touch/

– Sam Kates
January 2015

Printed in Great Britain
by Amazon